The Great Swabian Migration

Translated from:
Der Grosse Schwabenzug by Adam Müller-Guttenbrunn

Published by Pannonia Press in conjunction with
the Danube Swabian Foundation of the USA, Inc.

With grateful thanks to our translator, Linda Byrom, and editing team, Eddy Palffy, Mike Walter, and Annerose Goerge.

We would also like to express our gratitude to all of the individuals who helped with this endeavor by proofreading and offering suggestions and words of encouragement.

Note from the Publishers:
We had this novel translated because we thought it would be an interesting way to tell our young people about their roots, about how the Danube Swabians floated down the Danube River to find a new homeland hundreds of years ago. Not all of the author's personal views are shared by the publishers and translators of this book.

Cover picture by Stefan Jäger, 1906.

This book was originally published in German as
Der Grosse Schwabenzug by L. Staackmann Verlag, Leipzig, 1913.

Pannonia Press
P.O. Box 1062
Palatine, Illinois 60078-1062

© Copyright 2012, All rights reserved
Printed by UniqueActive, Cicero, Illinois 60804

Library of Congress 20122944165
ISBN 978-0-9657793-4-0
Printed in U.S.A.

Table of Contents

Maps	iv
Foreword by Jacob Steigerwald, PhD	vi
The Message from the *Konstabler*	1
The Marriage Arrangement	9
In the Vienna Council Office	15
The Bridal Ship	24
Count Mercy's Homecoming	37
The Governor's Audience Day	50
The Kurucs	60
The Great Migration Begins	80
The Swabians in Vienna	97
Fronleichnam in Old Vienna	106
Two Special Cases	113
A Guest from the Banat	120
Baroness Helene	134
In The Meadows of Mohács	139
A New Homeland?	144
At the *Sieben Kurfürsten* Inn	155
Father and Son at their Great Work	165
The Governor's Excursion	173
An Unusual Wedding Feast	187
The Missing Settlers	191
Delibáb	202
All Kinds of Conflicts	206
A Solemn Conclusion	222
Epilogue	231
Appendix	234
Glossary and Pronunciation Guide	240
About the Author	243

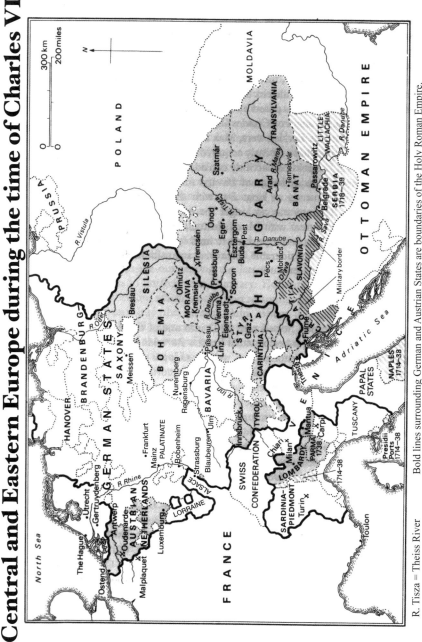

Danube-Swabian Settlement Areas until 1944

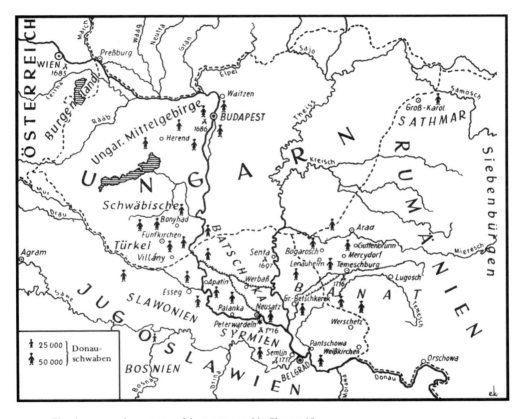

The above map shows many of the towns noted in Chapter 18.

Temeschburg - German name for Temesvar
Gr. Betschkerek - was Neu-Barcelona in its original settlement
Mieresch = Marosch River
Donau = Danube River

The political divisions are from after World War I, when the area was divided into Hungary *(Ungarn)*, Romania *(Rumänien)*, and Yugoslavia *(Jugoslawien)*.

Foreword

In 1683, when 13 Quaker families from Krefeld were crossing the Atlantic as the first cohesive group of German immigrants to America, Duke Karl V of Lorraine (1643-1690) and King Jan III Sobieski (1624-1696) of Poland achieved the decisive victory over the Ottoman Turks at Vienna that led to the gradual liberation of Hungary, including regions where German colonists subsequently initiated what became the Danube Swabian ethnic group.

After heirless Louis II (1506-1526), King of Hungary and Bohemia, had died fighting Ottomans at Mohács in 1526, his crown passed into possession of the Habsburg dynasty. Hungary was under Ottoman domination for over a century and a half by the time Christian forces managed to free the country in the early 18th Century. Amid wide-ranging subsequent imperial reconstruction initiatives following the Treaty of Passarowitz in 1718, implementation of plans to populate fallow and marshy local terrains in uninhabited isolated areas with settlers from Habsburg domains began to be realized between 1722-1726 under Emperor Karl VI (1685-1740), father of Maria Theresa (1717-1780), the eventual Queen of Hungary, Bohemia, and Croatia and wife (1736) of Emperor Franz I Stephan (1708-1765).

The resourceful writer, editor, and stage director Adam Müller-Guttenbrunn (1852-1923) was a descendant of Banat settlers. While working and living in Austria, he kept in touch with his 'Swabian' heritage by writing about it interpretively. In his prized novel, *Der Große Schwabenzug*, the author provided readers with plausibly imagined contextual scenarios concerning the first of three migration episodes of German-speaking Hungary-bound settlers that occurred under imperial sponsorships.

During ensuing decades, folks of various nationalities from the Holy Roman Empire of the German Nation, along with earlier immigrants to Hungary, continued to respond to calls for new colonists in regions like the Banat, the Bacska, and the Baranya. A sizeable part of the latter became known as "Swabian Turkey." Since Hungarian noblemen had established settlements on their private estates in the Sathmar region during 1711/12 involving families from Schwaben (Swabia), diverse subsequent German-speaking immigrants to other regions were called "Swabians" as well, regardless of their actual Germanic homeland derivation.

Queen Maria Theresa sponsored the most wide-ranging succession of immigrants to Southern Hungary between 1763 and 1772 – including colonists of various nationalities - not just speakers of German. The third (and last) sizable official immigration phase took place under Emperor Joseph II (1741-1790) in the mid-1780s. Unlike his mother Maria Theresa, who only endorsed colonizers of Catholic faith, Joseph II admitted Protestants as well.

As far as different ethnic groups in multi-national surroundings of liberated Hungary were concerned, being able to perpetuate their respective cultural and linguistic identities was a given right; however, when Joseph II initiated his plan to have German replace Latin as the administrative language, non-German nationality groups in multi-ethnic Hungary perceived it as devious meddling and contested the action until the former format was re-adopted.

Rising self-consciousness within nationality groups was among factors that led to the crushed Hungarian revolution of 1848/49. By means of the equalization treaty of 1867, Austria duly granted the government in Budapest more rights. Incongruous allegiance among local Germans had already manifested itself in 1848, when more than a few sided with Hungary rather than Austria. Some even changed their German names to Hungarian versions. Others were prompted to do so under bureaucratic or public pressure until WWI. Germans desirous of pursuing formal education in their native language beyond an elementary level either had to have parental financial means of support to study in Austria, or accept being magyarized while getting educated in Hungary.

Confounding entries in ship records, regarding the nationality of immigrants from Hungary to Canada or the U.S.A. for example, were sometimes attributable to limited understanding by clerks entering applicable data, but quite often passengers' own mismatched input was to blame, especially if a particular ancestor came from a post-WWI successor state of Hungary, such as Romania or the Kingdom of Serbs, Croats, and Slovenes (called Yugoslavia after 1929). Family name changes that occurred under stress, or out of deference toward the host country, did not routinely amount to abandonment of one's nationality. This was evident during the early 1940s for instance, when quite a few families chose to re-adopt German surnames.

In formal discourse, Hungary's 'Swabians' have been referred to as German-Hungarians or Hungarian Germans, along with other local German groups; however, these terms were no longer entirely applicable after more than half of the minority wound up in the countries named, when imposed territorial transfers decimated vanquished Hungary by two-thirds of its former size at the end of WWI. In the early 1920s, the name "Donauschwaben" was coined regarding the resultant tripartite Danube Swabian minority, as a way to tell them apart from other resident German-speaking indigenous groups.

Over time, Hungary's mix of Germans commonly called "Schwaben" evolved into a particular ethnic group of its own. With due recognition of the minority's tough beginnings under unaccustomed climate conditions in harsh, malaria-infested wasteland settings, successive generations distinguished themselves through impressive agricultural achievements, which amplified the general living standard. Factors that resulted in the post-WWII undoing of the three branches in their historic pioneering habitats are quite complex and require further synchronized research.

Among ruthless upshots was the reality that more than half of the Danube Swabians of Hungary were expelled to different zones of occupied Germany after WWII, based on agreements between the victorious powers. Without any known equivalent external authorization, Marshall Tito and his communist followers decided to get rid of Yugoslavia's German minority altogether. As of autumn 1944, partisans resorted to ever more open vendettas against residual Germans of Yugoslavia. Civilians of non-German nationality who spoke up in behalf of any ostracized group member were always silenced at gunpoint by means of vicious threats and intimidation. Communists had collectively labeled all of the ethnic-German group members as culpable fascists.

Tito and associates knew very well that their furtively adopted AVNOJ decrees engendered grave human rights violations; thus, they carried out their most dreadful offenses covertly and/or at night, for fear of eliciting universal protests and risking exposure of brazen wrongdoers. Talking openly about actions taken by partisans to achieve their reprehensible goals remained strictly prohibited for decades—way beyond Tito's lifetime (1892-1980). Inquiries concerning the whereabouts of the country's former Germans tended to be only partially answered, by indicating that they had fled, or were evacuated to Germany.

What vindictive Yugoslav communist partisans never figured on having to own up to was the incriminating fact that roughly one-third of nearly two-fifths of the country's Danube Swabians who came under Tito's rule perished as a result of genocide and ethnic cleansing, including categorical refusal of medical care to targeted minority members. Coverage of attendant harm and injustice, in media other than German-language conduits, remained harder to encounter than the proverbial needle in a haystack. Consequently, having had the truth kept from them for so long, young majority-group generations in successor states of former Yugoslavia have experienced great difficulties in coming up with crucial overdue restitution plans as a condition for European Union membership.

Since Romanians regarded the Danube Swabians as a valued manpower resource, the country's diverse German minority was not subjected to mass expulsion; however, tens of thousands of ethnic-Germans from Romania, Hungary, and Yugoslavia were deported to the Soviet Union as forced laborers for up to five years, after Christmas 1944. Six years later, more than 10,000 Danube Swabians of Western Romania were forcibly relocated to the country's Baragan Steppe as compulsory participants in a rash agricultural experiment that lasted from 1951 until 1956. Rather than exercising the option to return to their former homes afterwards, many of the heedlessly uprooted and hideously displaced minority group members wished to emigrate to Germany instead; however, permission to leave the country was hard to get, until special arrangements involving hefty payments in hard currency to the communist regime (1965-1989) of Nicolae Ceausescu enabled tens of thousands to leave. Funding involved came from the West German government and from private sources. The number of Danube Swabians left in Romania has continued to drop further.

Countries, in which 'down-and-out' Danube Swabians found new beginnings since the post-WWII-era include Australia, Austria, Brazil, Canada, France, Germany, the U.S.A., and others. Group member descendants of earliest and ultimate newcomers to English-speaking lands have long wished for translations of significant works about the Danube Swabian ethnic minority, because they could also facilitate family research through better understanding of historic and social contexts. May this and other translated works provide additional impetus toward constructive steps forward!

Following is a sampling of how kindred ethnic groups, or organizations, may be reached over the Internet:

Danube Swabian clubs in Canada can be located via the web site
http://www.dvhh.org/dta/canada/index.htm

Links to Danube Swabian clubs in the U.S.A. are found at the site
http://www.dsfoundationusa.org/links.html

Danube Swabians in Australia seem to congregate in social establishments for Germans, Austrians, and/or Swiss descendants, such as the following club in Adelaide, for example:
http://www.austrianclubsa.com/

Links to German clubs in various Australian cities are accessible via:
http://www.teachers.ash.org.au/dnutting/germanaustralia/e/vereine-heute.htm

Web pages for exchanging information, views, and data include the following:
http://archiver.rootsweb.ancestry.com/th/index/DONAUSCHWABEN-VILLAGES/
http://archiver.rootsweb.com/th/index/BANAT/
http://www.dvhh.org/
http://donauschwaben-usa.org/
http://www.genealogienetz.de/vereine/AKdFF/

The capitalized acronym refers to a genealogy work group that also has members in North America, for example. Some AKdFF-sites are available in Dutch, English, French, German, and Hungarian.

Though shattered and driven to scatter as a result of persecutions under former communist regimes, descendants of Danube Swabians continue to carry on laudably as cherished contributors amid societies on four continents: Europe, the Americas, and Australia.

Jacob Steigerwald, Ph. D.
U.S.A. 2012

The Great Swabian Migration

This novel is historical fiction and was not written as an objective history. It tells the story in a subjective manner using a combination of fictional and historic characters.

Chapter 1

The Message from the *Konstabler*

The messenger from Ulm brought a letter to the *Schwarzen Adler* Inn. "It's for the honorable widow Therese Scheiffele," he exclaimed to the young maid who took it. "And I deserve a glass of Söflinger wine for bringing it today. The letter wouldn't have come until Sunday if brought by overland mail. It came from far away."

"I'll pass that along," said Gretel and nodded with a smile.

He continued under his heavy burden, dispensing packages throughout the whole town of Blaubeuren. He had brought many items from Ulm, the free imperial city of the German Realm[1], where trade and commerce flourished and everything imaginable was available, even coffee. The young Prelate's wife had secretly ordered this from him, and he had been able to obtain half a pound. The Ulm skippers had brought it back from Vienna. It had cost an entire crown *Taler*. What if his Reverence found out? ... Of course, as soon as the Augsburg newspaper had publicized the new fashion of drinking Turkish coffee in Vienna, the women of Ulm felt the need to follow the fashion as well. And before all the influential people of Ulm had even so much as seen a coffee bean, the prelate's wife of Blaubeuren just had to get herself some coffee. Serves him right, the spiritual Father, thought Peter. Why did he get himself a wife from so far away? He had to have a woman from Mainz, of all places, and one with such extravagant tastes! Weren't there any minister's daughters in Württemberg?

That is how Peter Fischer, the Ulm messenger, discussed things with

---

1 German Realm: (*Deutsches Reich*) At this time Germany was not yet a federation; it was a conglomeration of independent principalities (states) with no leading monarch. These states were part of the Holy Roman Empire of the German Nation. See map, page iv

himself as he went from house to house making his deliveries. Peter was no simple beast of burden; he drew his own conclusions about every order he took. After he did his rounds through the crooked streets, he returned to the *Schwarzen Adler*, where he had delivered the first letter.

Laughing, Gretel brought him the well-earned glass of Söflinger wine. "Frau Therese says you can have two, if you like," she said.

"Lord God of Frankfurt, since when is Frau Therese a big spender?" Peter cried.

"Shhhh," said Gretel. "They're all sitting over there."

The proprietor's entire family was sitting in a corner of the busy inn, gathered around the *Schwarzen Adler's* owner, who held the letter which Peter had brought. He painstakingly read the contents aloud, as most women could not read and write at the time. It was not yet the custom for girls to receive an education. They had plenty of other things to do in the house, yard and kitchen.

Peter saw how difficult it was for the innkeeper to read the letter. He finished his wine and slowly made his way toward the family. Not just because he was curious, but he was a better reader, more used to written material than most people. As he approached, ready to help out, the fat proprietor waved him away. "Stay away from us," he arrogantly told Peter and continued reading. Therese, his sister, tried to soften this rejection. "Have yourself another Söflinger, Peter," she said and winked at him. He understood that she would later ask him to read the letter to her a few more times.

This was the third letter in two years. Was it another letter from the *Konstabler*[2] Pless, that good-for-nothing from Ulm who had joined the Kaiser's[3] army after he blew through the inheritance from his grandmother? Pless had fallen for the beautiful Therese of the *Adler* Inn years ago, but she had already been promised to the son of the *Blauen Hechten* Inn in Ulm. Heaven knows how he had found out that Therese was a widow now and lived in her father's house. After all, Pless had moved to Hungary to fight the Turks with Prince Eugene and had even made it as far east as Belgrade. He had described this in full detail to Therese in his two previous letters, which the whole town had read. What might be in this latest letter?

Peter retreated. He sat down with a few men, some farmers from the Alb

---

2 *Konstabler*: Artillery Officer
3 *Kaiser*: Emperor. The Kaiser being spoken of here is Emperor Charles VI (Karl VI) of the Habsburg family. The Habsburgs were located in Vienna, and Charles VI was not only Holy Roman Emporer of the German Nation, he was also Archduke of Austria, which was part of the Holy Roman Empire.

Chapter 1 — The Message from the *Konstabler*

region, some from the Blautal valley, and others from even farther away. They were his good friends from the road; he saw them about a hundred times a year. The Ulm messenger was well liked by all. He brought them news, and they joked around with him a lot.

However, today they were having a serious conversation, talking about their problems. One of them had five sons, another had four, and yet another actually had six. Where should a farmer get enough land for all of them?[4] The monastery would not give up even one acre. The Count, who owned much of the land, had not yet decided what to charge a farmer who wanted to lease part of his property. The boys would have to become craftsmen or soldiers, and all of them would have to go to foreign lands. One man's oldest son served in Switzerland, another had two sons working as craftsmen in Vienna, a third man's son was a soldier in Paris. Nikolaus Eimann had two sons who had joined the Kaiser's troops in Vienna[5] and another had joined the army in Holland. They would have to be soldiers for life because the taxes were too high and the country was too small. God only knows when a bullet would strike one of them.

Peter Fischer listened intently. He smiled and said, "How often have I told you that you have too many children? But don't worry, the Swabians[6] who have no more land here can go to America. The New World belongs to us if your wives remain so fruitful. Nothing to worry about!"

They laughed and wanted to know more about the New World, and Peter had plenty to say. He had read much on the subject in the local paper. The entire *Rheinpfalz* was said to be emigrating to America. The emigration fever struck more people every day.

Eimann paid for Peter's third drink in order to learn from him the easiest and least dangerous way to get to that highly acclaimed land, America. He claimed to have the courage to go take a look. Was it true that you could buy ten acres of land there for just one Ulm guilder? Peter confirmed this and quietly added, "And no nobility! No priests or counts can lord it over you there!"

The innkeeper came out of the corner by the courtyard window, where his family had gathered. His sister would have gladly withdrawn to the ad-

---

[4] This was a problem because the German custom was that the eldest son inherited all of his father's land, so the other sons needed to somehow get their own property.
[5] At this time, the Kaiser was fighting the Ottoman Empire in Hungary, to expand the territory that his family, the Habsburgs, ruled.
[6] *Swabian*: in this case refers to a person from Swabia, which is a region in Germany. Blaubeuren and Ulm are in Swabia.

jacent room, the more elegant *Herrenstube*, but he stuck to the old tradition: the host and his family were in the *Wirtstube*, among the regular guests. They should all feel like they had been invited by him, as his father used to say, and his father had been a good host.

The innkeeper greeted each guest individually and inquired about market prices, about their families and their communities. In one area sat a few quintessential *Erzbauern* from the Alb, farmers who lived like kings on their land and who always came back from the market with full wallets. They liked to separate themselves from small farmers who lived in little cottages. But they still half listened to the loud conversation at Eimann's table. Now the host shook hands with Herr Eimann from Gershausen, who took the opportunity to ask him what he thought of America.

"The English have been there for a long time," the proprietor said. "They will not wish anything good for any Swabian looking for his fortune. Many from the *Pfalz*[7] return from America as beggars."

He knew of a better land; one could get there from Ulm by way of the Danube River.

"Hungary!" Peter cried out. "You must be talking about Hungary!"

"The messenger knows all about it already," the innkeeper said laughingly. "He checks everything out!" He sat down with the people at the table and told them about the letter his sister Therese had just received. Jakob Pless —the one from Ulm—had explained that all of Hungary had been cleared of the Turks and there was peace. Prince Eugene had discharged many soldiers and given them the freedom to settle in the Banat region of Hungary, around the Fortress of Temesvar.[8] Settling there didn't even cost a *Kreuzer*. Each settler was awarded as much land as he could cultivate. If Jakob were a farmer, he could obtain fifty *Joch* (seventy five acres) of land with a house and yard —that is, if he understood agriculture. The Kaiser had given Prince Eugene and his generals large ownerless parcels of land as a gift for their services. Some got so much land that it included twenty to thirty villages, most of which were deserted. Farmers and craftsmen were needed everywhere. Jakob thought that any landless Swabians should migrate, if they had the courage.

"This land is available at no cost?" "75 acres?" "No cost including the house and garden?" The guests of the inn were full of questions. Even the

---

7 *Pfalz* (Palatinate), also called *Rheinpfalz* (Rhenisch Palatinate): A region on the western border of the Holy Roman Empire of the German Nation.
8 The country of Hungary in 1718 covered the regions which are now Hungary, Croatia, Slavonia, Bosnia-Herzegovina and Serbia. The Banat was a region of Hungary. The Banat is currently divided between Romania, Hungary and Serbia.

Chapter 1 — The Message from the *Konstabler*

Erzbauern perked up their ears.

"That's what Jakob writes." The innkeeper shrugged his shoulders. "So it is probably true."

"Something is fishy," declared one of the listeners. "There must be some kind of trick," another insisted.

"Well," Peter interjected, "sometimes they have the plague to contend with, but otherwise the region is healthy."

"Pless did not even mention the plague," the innkeeper said reprovingly. "He will become rich there."

Eimann grew flushed with excitement. He thought of being able to care for his six boys through this opportunity and eagerly suggested that they immediately find a boat that would go down the Danube.

"Better to wait a little," advised the host of the Adler. "Jakob thinks that the time will come when the Kaiser will call for people to go," and he went on to other guests.

Therese Scheifele, the blonde young widow, sat quietly in the corner with her needlework and pondered the contents of the letter she had received from Jakob Pless. Her sister-in-law was working in the kitchen and the others had left, so she sat alone. Who would have thought that Jakob would remain so loyal? She had already been a bride many years ago when she had floated down the Danube to Regensburg on a barge owned by the Pless family. Jakob had seen her there. She had immediately liked him in his sailor's uniform. What a strapping young man Jakob was, and so in love with her. Two weeks later he was in Blaubeuren and wanted to ask for her hand in marriage. He couldn't believe it was too late! And then when she got married and became the landlady of the *Blauen Hechten* in Ulm, Jakob had gone away. Of course they said there were other reasons that drove him into the arms of the Army recruiters, but she knew better. And now it seemed he was interested in her again. Why else would he write so often? And tell her he was now discharged and knew how to obtain wealth and respect? Why did he even include soldiers' songs in his letters? Next time the *Kantor*, the church organist and choir master, came by for a drink, she would have to ask him to read her the song. Her brother had not been able to read it properly. Of course there had been notes written underneath the words, only the *Herr Kantor* could read those—then he could sing the song to her. But first, she wanted to find out exactly what was actually written in this last letter. She needed someone else to read it to her because she did not completely trust her brother. Towards the end it seemed that he had not read every sentence in its entirety. He had his own plans for her. But she would keep her eyes open and would not be talked into an arranged marriage a second time. She had had enough with the first one who was a heavy drinker, may he rest in peace. If Jakob, the fool, had only remained in Ulm, things would now be different. She would probably not be sitting here in the Blaubeuren Inn again; she would perhaps be a shipbuilder's wife.

Jakob had been promoted to *Konstabler* in the Kaiser's Army and had been wounded twice. What if he was a cripple? He did not write anything about that, but she would like to know. Being twenty eight, she was too good for half a man. How old must he be now, she asked herself. Thirty, no more than that, she surmised.

When her brother stopped near her corner, she asked him to read the letter to her again. He grumbled: "Tomorrow is a better day. Today is market day and we are very busy. The business comes first." Although he did not require her to help out, it wouldn't hurt if she and Gretel helped her brother. Being the daughter of an innkeeper, she knew how valuable two extra hands could be. Therese got the hint.

"A *Stein* of Ulm beer for the pastor? And a couple of sausages?" Therese greeted the pastor of Kirchheim with a smile, showing him and his female companion into the adjoining little guest room. She moved from table to table, serving the guests. The noon hour had arrived and the market had closed down. Some of the customers had another drink just to be served by her. When Therese got to Peter Fischer, she secretly slid her letter to him. He was to look at it first in order to read it to her later in her room.

The old fox ran his hand across his grey head and smoothed his braids in anticipation. He was looking forward to getting a tip from her, and was also brimming with curiosity. Leaving the guest room, Peter went to look for a quiet corner where he could read the long letter in peace. It might not please the innkeeper if he realized that Peter had the letter. The crafty messenger knew that the information in it would be valuable to more than one person. Eimann, for example, might make it worth Peter's while to share this information. Peter had never met anyone who craved property as Eimann did. He'd walk to Hungary on foot if someone would give him even an acre of barren land.

So let's see, what does the *Ulmer Spatz*[9] write about Temesvar?

Peter Fischer had gone out to the barn where his cart stood to read Jakob Pless's letter. He read it aloud and added his own comments.

"Hmm, hmm, hmmm ... '*not a soldier anymore. The Peace Treaty of*

---

9 *Ulmer Spatz*: a nickname for someone who is from Ulm.

Chapter 1—The Message from the *Konstabler*

Passarowitz[10] *has been signed. Prince Eugene went back to Vienna, the regiments are now at peace. Count Mercy is now Governor of the Banat, a hot-headed Lorrainer who wants to out-do Prince Eugene.'* ... now let's see... *'He would like to keep all discharged soldiers in Hungary.'* Hmm... not much of a discharge if you have to stay in Hungary! ... *'He gives us what we want.'* Aha, it seems he likes the Swabians... That's good... *'He is looking for skilled craftsmen. He wants to build a city out of this wretched Turkish nest - like Ulm.'* Hmm, why not like Paris?

" *'I am learning quite a bit about construction while we are building the forti- fortif-* damn this word - *fortifications and houses. But I can think of something much, much better to do when we are done. For this I need a woman who understands the business of an inn with lodging.'* Ah ha!

" *'A new city, a new fortress where many great men often have to stay, but there is no decent inn. Many of the German victors went home with Prince Eugene: Markgraf Ludwig von Baden, Kurfürst Max Emanuel von Bayern and many a hero from Swabia; but thousands of former soldiers remained here as free men, here where there are no German girls.'* Ah ha, ah ha!! *'When Markgraf von Baden left a year ago they humbly submitted a petition before his departure asking him to send some German girls. The Markgraf had laughed and said he would correct that need; he said he would make an announcement in Stuttgart.'* "

At this point Peter laughed out loud.

" *'But that was long ago and no Swabian girls have arrived. I'm supposed to ask if you can find out if Markgraf Ludwig will keep his promise of sending German girls to the Banat—or whether he is dead.*

" *'There is much talk here that General Mercy sent a referendum to Vienna wherein he asks the Hofkammer to populate the barren land of Hungary with all the nations of Europe. He wants farmers. There is room for hundreds of thousands of them. I'm a city person and do not understand much about farming. But when the Kaiser calls, many of my countrymen should come, they will get land at no cost.*

" *'My dear Therese, if you want to make an Ulmer happy, consider making a trip on the Danube from Ulm to Peterwardein. Take along as many marriageable girls as you like. Here they can marry men who already have*

---

10 This peace treaty was signed in Passarowitz (Požarevac), which is now located in Serbia, in 1718. The Ottoman Empire had already lost much of Hungary to the Habsburgs; now the Kaiser, Emperor Charles VI, received the Banat of Temesvar, a part of Serbia which included Belgrade, and, to the south of Transylvania, the region of Little Wallachia. This became a part of the Austrian Habsburg possessions, not of the Holy Roman Empire.

a house, courtyard and seventy-five acres of land. My father will give you his best barge and in three weeks you will be here, where the forever true Jakob awaits you with love. I have already ordered a priest. Do not say no when someone comes to arrange the marriage. I have been an honorable person all my life. Trust me, dearest Therese.'

"Ah, the time has come, Jakob is looking for a wife!" Peter cried.

Finally he had discovered the point of the letter, which had been very difficult to read. He read it again to himself so he could read more smoothly to Therese. He succeeded in this. She was stunned by the conclusion, which her wily brother had purposely mixed up when he read it so that she would not comprehend its meaning. Her mind was in a whirl. Of course, as soon as she had received the letter, she should have guessed that a Swabian who wrote three letters in two years must have serious intentions. Therese gave the messenger six coins for reading the letter to her and made him repeat it two more times, until she had committed it to memory. She wanted to read it out loud to her brother so he would be astonished that she could read it to him.

Chapter 2

The Marriage Arrangement

Soon everyone was talking about *Konstabler* Pless's letter, not only in the *Adler* Inn, but in the entire town of Blaubeuren.

News of the opportunity in Hungary was spreading. Similar letters from soldiers arrived not only in Swabia but also in Württemberg and Baden. One could also read about it in the Frankfurt, Augsburg and Stuttgart newspapers. Because of this, there was more talk of emigration to Hungary rather than America. It took three months to get to America as opposed to only three weeks for the Banat. The trip on the Danube River seemed to be much safer than the treacherous ocean. Of course, the Danube was also perilous in some places: it was said that the little whirlpool at Aschau and the big one near Grein could be life threatening. As of yet, no one had taken a ship past Vienna on the Danube, since Ulm ships only went as far as the Kaiser's city. On the other hand, many German regiments were stationed in Hungary, so conditions couldn't be too bad there. Also, Germans were supposed to have lived there since ancient times. No one knew much about them, and it was not known whether they had survived the Turkish occupation. The *Kantor* was discussing these matters with Frau Therese. "But why shouldn't those Germans have survived? The Swabians can endure twice as much as other people."

What a miracle the reconquest of Hungary had been! The area, which had been taken over by the Turks for one hundred and sixty years, now belonged to the Kaiser who had conquered it over a period of thirty years, one battle at a time.¹ Duke Charles of Lorraine, Margrave Ludwig of Baden, Karl Alexander of Württemberg, *Kurfürst* Max Emanuel of Bavaria²—all of them had led the Kaiser's troops, and the troops of the German states, from Vienna to Belgrade. Their great student, Prince Eugene, had now completed their campaign. He had dictated the terms of the peace treaty after this long war of liberation.

"Do not believe," stated the *Kantor*, "that the Peace Treaty of Passarowitz³ should not matter to us in the old Roman Empire. After all, the French took advantage of the Kaiser's weakness when the Turks were at Vienna's doorstep. They robbed us of Strassburg⁴ and all of Alsace. Now our army is available to fight again, and who knows? Maybe Prince Eugene will retake Strassburg, which has been occupied by the French for almost forty years."

With great enthusiasm, the *Herr Kantor* read the soldiers' song about Prince Eugene. He sang the melody, following the musical notes which Pless had included with the text.

Prinz Eugenius, der edle Ritter,	Prince Eugene, the noble Knight
Wollt dem Kaiser wied'rum kriegen	Wanted to get the city and fortress of
Stadt und Festung Belgerad.	Belgrade back for the Kaiser.
Er ließ schlagen einen Brucken	He had a bridge built
Daß man kunnt hinüberrucken	That the army crossed
Mit der Armee wohl vor die Stadt.	To win back the city.

"The song is heavenly," the *Kantor* exclaimed. "It's like a beautiful hymn. It's like the *Tedeum laudamus* of Saint Ambrosius."

The *Kantor* sang as well as he could to Therese and the regular customers in the main room of the inn. He was adamant: "Prince Eugene will bring Strassburg back to us! We all have to learn this song."

Wörndle, the assistant to the schoolmaster in Blaubeuren, agreed whole-

---

1 The Habsburgs began to battle the Turks in 1683. By 1699, they had acquired most of the old Hungarian kingdom, and by 1718, all of it.
2 These leaders were all from German principalities. Lorraine (near Alsace) was then a German State but is now in France.
3 The Treaty of Passarowitz (1718) was significant because not only did the Ottomans lose substantial territories in the Balkans to the Habsburg Austrians, it also ended the westward expansion of the Ottoman Empire. Without having to worry about the Ottomans, the Kaiser could focus on other matters.
4 Strassburg: the capital of Alsace. Alsace was originally a German State and most people living there were of German ethnicity.

Chapter 2—The Marriage Arrangement

heartedly. He was an Alsatian and liked to talk about his homeland. Today he went on and on, lamenting that what the French had done with Alsace was absolutely shameful. Their regiments had been greatly reduced by Prince Eugene's army at the Battle of Malplaquet,[5] and the French had built them up again with German men. They had dragged German boys from the fields and forced them into the French army. 'Emigration!' had been the catchphrase in Alsace for quite some time already. They all wanted to live under the Kaiser's rule again. Hadn't they always been good Austrians? After all, Alsace had been part of the Holy Roman Empire, which the Kaiser ruled. Also, the inflation rate was rising every year in Alsace, he continued. It was a difficult life there; it was worse there than here in Blaubeuren. The nobility and clergy continued to expand their power, but the peasants had less and less land because they needed to divide it between their children. In addition, the French now wanted everyone to convert back to Catholicism. The Alsatians, who were Lutheran, had resented this under the Kaiser's rule, and now the French demanded the same.

The gentlemen present suggested that Wörndle write to his friends in Alsace and let them know about this new region of the Kaiser's territories, the Banat.

Yes, that's what Wörndle would do. He told Therese that he would be much obliged if she would loan him the letter, so that he could put part of it in the Strassburg newspaper. We could in this way also remind Ludwig von Baden, affectionately called *Türkenlouis*,[6] of the promise which he gave to his soldiers in the Banat to send them German girls to marry.

They laughed. "Yes, it would be great to give him a reminder!"

At this point, Gretel burst into the room, "Therese, someone is here to see you."

"Who is it?"

"Two gentlemen from Ulm," Gretel replied. Therese stood up and Gretel's eyes widened when she noticed how attractively she had dressed for the day. So she must be serious…

The guests started talking as soon as Therese had blushingly left the room. Everyone had an opinion or comment.

"It looks like she does want to go."

"She's not afraid?"

---

5 In the Battle of Malplaquet (1709), part of the War of Spanish Succession, Prince Eugene of Savoy led the Austrian Habsburg troops against the Bourbons of France and Spain.
6 *Türkenlouis* was Margrave Ludwig (Louis) von Baden's nickname because he scored a resounding victory against the Ottoman Turks at Slankamen in 1691.

"For awhile she denied that she was going."

"Her brother is firmly against it."

"That might make her want to go even more."

There was much speculation, but everyone agreed that the two men were there to arrange the marriage between Jakob Pless and Therese.

Would Gretel go with her to Hungary? *Herr Kantor* wondered.

Gretel affirmed that if Therese wanted to take her along, she was ready. "Where there is a lack of girls, a woman can select the man she wants!" she declared.

"But are you not already promised?" said Wörndle, shaking his finger at her.

"What's the use? The monastery where Josef works will not allow him to marry," Gretel responded defiantly.

"You're tired of waiting, are you?" asked Wörndle. One look at the voluptuous girl and he understood completely. She said nothing and went to get some fresh Ulmer beer. She shook her hips as she walked, stamping her feet so that the floor shook.

The *Kantor* bemoaned women's obsession with getting married. It was good that the church hierarchy forbade marriages of those without means. There were already too many people in this world. Whoever did not have a house should not take a wife. Why should we have marriages between gardener boys and servant girls?

Wörndle disagreed. Oppression of the common people should finally come to an end. The stewards of the monastery and the counts had better watch it before all the peasants leave. Right now, a rabbit is of more value to them than a human being. They ought to give up some of their land and allow more marriages to take place, rather than forcing virginity on the people. That could end badly. Everyone might leave.

"Nobody can leave without a permit," said the *Kantor*. "How would he cross the borders? You can't get through the Ulm city gates without papers and people say it is even worse in Bavaria. There, those without papers immediately have to put on a soldier's uniform."

"That is my point," said Wörndle. "There is too much power in the world and too little justice!"

Meanwhile, Therese went upstairs to the living quarters, where her brother was conversing with the two gentlemen. Her sister-in-law greeted her as she was going upstairs: "Hurry up, one of the men has a huge bouquet of flowers!"

When Therese entered, the older gentleman with the flowers spoke first.

Chapter 2 — The Marriage Arrangement

He bowed rather gracefully and introduced his friend, Ulm master ship builder Ludwig Pless, the father of *Konstabler* Jakob Pless.

"I am Jakob's godfather, Anton Specht. I witnessed his baptism thirty years ago, and today it is my duty to bring this beautiful bouquet to the bride whom my godson has chosen. I can see that the beauty of the red roses is surpassed by the roses on your cheeks. I come in the name of Jakob Pless to ask the honorable and virtuous Therese Scheifele for her hand in marriage on behalf of my honest and upstanding godson. My godson is now established enough that he can afford a wife and establish a household."

The little man was almost out of breath when he finished his speech. Without giving her reply, Therese invited the gentlemen to sit down. She accepted the flowers with a curtsy and seated herself with them and her brother.

Now Ludwig Pless began to speak. The shipmaster was a stately man in his fifties. Therese knew him, as he had often had his morning drink in the *Blauen Hechten* Inn with other craftsmen. Jakob's blue eyes came from his good-natured, amiable father. The only time that Therese had seen Ludwig Pless upset was when his oldest son had become a soldier. He had stayed away from the *Blauen Hechten* Inn for a year, and it seemed to her that he thought… well, he had given her peculiar looks when he saw her. But she had nothing to feel guilty about. She had liked Jakob since her trip to Regensburg, but she had never told him that. With honor and dignity, she had been true to the man whom her father had chosen for her. Scheiffele had not been a bad man. His only downfall had been the drinking, which had killed him in the end. Now she had been a widow for three years. Why should she not receive these men who had come to arrange a new marriage? She was ready to speak freely and without guile. Their message was not unwelcome in her view, even if she had to say goodbye to her German homeland.

Ludwig Pless had much to say. His son seemed to have become an upstanding man, but he did not want to come back to Ulm. It pleased the father that he still respected the old homeland and wanted to have a wife from here. What Jakob wrote showed his good will. Jakob would get some money from home, three hundred crown *Taler* now, and the rest after his father's death. With that he could begin to build the inn he had planned. He needed nothing more than a willing wife who knew about the business.

"I will be his wife," said Therese. "Extend my acceptance to him and tell him to prepare for the wedding. I have the courage to travel and I'm ready. But I want to bring my aunt from Regensburg and one or two girls to help run the business."

The innkeeper of the *Adler* entered the conversation. "I can tell you what my sister brings to this marriage. She, too, has three hundred crown *Taler* and I will pay another two hundred *Taler* from our father's estate. They are in my account and will collect interest. If Jakob needs this money he should let me know half a year in advance."

"This is a good dowry and if you are willing, we will now sign the wedding contract," affirmed the satisfied Ludwig Pless. "I will build a barge with two cabins. I will provide eight strong oarsmen and a helmsman who are familiar with the Danube River from here to Vienna. I have a few workers who are eager to go beyond Vienna to settle in Hungary and become independent. So the bride will be in good hands. God willing they will make it all the way to Hungary."

The godfather replied, "Amen."

The *Adler* innkeeper went to get a bottle of Rüdesheimer wine and to invite his wife to come into the room, as she had been bursting with curiosity as to the outcome of the visit.

He did not like to let his only sister go to a foreign country, but since it appeared to be what she wanted, he could no longer stand in her way.

Chapter 3

In the Vienna Council Office

The Hungarian records were kept in the Austrian Council Office (*Hofkanzlei*) of Vienna, in the splendid new government building designed by Fischer von Erlach. This office was busier than the Bohemian, Hungarian and Transylvania council offices combined. It was flooded with requests for property in reconquered Hungary. Every colonel believed to have earned the same rewards as the leading officers, whom the Kaiser had so richly awarded with land.

Hofkammerrat[1] *Stephany* was pressured by many. He encountered difficulties whenever he tried to operate in the best interests of the country rather than give in to the court favorites and fortune seekers who surrounded him. Spaniards, Italians, Flemings and Scots, who possessed nothing but their swords, worked their way up through the Kaiser's army and wanted to acquire land in the new territory. Just as the mercenaries of the Kaiser's army had acquired wealth by taking for themselves what was seized from the old Protestant German nobility in Austria a century ago, so many wanted to use the expulsion of the Turks in order to entrench themselves in Hungary. Land was no longer available in the hereditary lands, the predominantly German-speaking possessions of the Habsburgs, but acquisition should be possible in this newly conquered province.

Many beautiful women were behind this; they patronized and schemed as hard as they could. But Stephany stood firm, and he had the authority of his patron, Generalissimo Prince Eugene, supporting him. Stephany's opinion was that they had not captured Hungary from the Turks only to give it all away to the officers of the army. Even when the powerful Countess Maria

---

1 *Hofkammerrat*: Imperial Councillor

Althan tried to use her influence to award some of the newly acquired land to the applying officers, he put her off by saying that they had to wait for the Hungarian Council Office to sort through the records and determine which properties still had rightful owners, and which were available to give away. If he could buy some time, then perhaps these mercenaries would go looking for fortune elsewhere before the land was available.

The *Hofkammerrat* was not always entirely successful in preventing these give aways. Sometimes the president of the council was informed from above that this or that applicant had been granted some property. In that case, he could not dissent. But for the most part, Stephany had been able to impede these requests for property. Stephany was idealistic and had a strong sense of justice. In addition, he was backed by Prince Eugene's authority. Between the two of them, they had in effect set up a dam to stop the flow of land being given away.

This allowed the commissions set up in Pressburg, Kaschau, Fünfkirchen, Arzo and Agram[2] to continue their work without interference. They needed to clearly define the ownership, which was in a state of confusion after the long occupation by the Turks. It was difficult, sometimes impossible, to know who the rightful owners of the land were. Who could remember? The Turks had occupied the southern region for one hundred and sixty four years; they had dominated the central region, where the Magyars[3] resided, for almost as long.

The families who had not been killed or died out had emigrated during the long Turkish reign; thousands of public records had been lost or destroyed. Since the reconquest of Hungary, many of the Hungarian nobility had used cunning or force to stake their claim to large sections of property, whatever they took a liking to. They now had to prove their right to the property. Because if the property didn't rightfully belong to anyone, then it belonged to the Kaiser, who had liberated it. Even those who could prove legal ownership of the property would have to pay a liberation tax to the war fund, since the cost of this long Turkish war was immense. Sorting all this out would be a bureaucratic nightmare and would take many years.

Joseph von Stephany's business and legal acumen had been proven. Only he could have filled this difficult office, and only he was trusted by everyone. He had requested ten years to sort everything out and clarify to whom each parcel belonged. Only then could he carry out suggestions and review the

---

2 These were all cities in what was Hungary at the time. Pressburg is the German name for Bratislava, now the capital of Slovakia. Fünfkirchen is the German name for Pécs, a city in Hungary west of the Danube River.
3 Magyar: Hungarian

petitions for the settlement of the wastelands by new subjects. At this time the size of the population could not be determined because it was impossible to conduct a census. The Hungarian nobility did not want to take part in a census in fear of being taxed; the common folk had a fear of being drafted into the army. It was estimated that at this point there were barely two million Magyars in Hungary and three million of other nationalities. Stephany was convinced that there was room for hundreds of thousands more in the vast countryside.

He would not allow himself to be pushed around. There was no hurry to implement the "Impopulation Decree", which some members of the royal court held to be unfeasible and some simply found uninteresting. The only impatient people were those who hoped to get a piece of land for themselves. After all, elevation to the nobility was dependent on the possession of noble estates. However, it was Stephany's mission to convert these many ownerless properties to public land owned by the government and then give them to industrious subjects, and he was looking for German settlers because they were the most productive.

Actuary Franz Hildebrandt approached *Hofkammerrat* Stephany. He maintained the ever-growing list of properties that had been granted. It was also his responsibility to record how the men who received the Kaiser's generosity were managing their property. Stephany always wanted to be informed of these details. Already some of the recipients had sold their properties at ridiculously low prices. In his opinion, many recipients of property should have been given cash rather than land. But the royal court gave what it had—money was scarce, but there was plenty of land.

Hildebrandt had only good things to report today. Counts Veterani, Caprara, Bathyányi and Breuner had begun to colonize with zeal. Three hundred German families had been brought to their private properties. The Generalissimo had been the first to colonize; he had settled Germans on his property at Bellye in the county of Baranya and in Promontor near Pest. Count Schönborn had imitated him at Munkács. And now Counts Bathyányi and Károlyi were following suit in Szatmár, and Bishops Nesselrode and Csáky in Fünfkirchen and Mohács. This was also being done by the Prince's favorite, Count Mercy. Quietly he had also founded a Swabian[4] settlement on his property surrounding Tevel.

---

4 The German people who settled Hungary were all referred to as Swabians, whether they came from Swabia or a different region. This is likely because most emigrants first went to Ulm in Swabia and began their trip down the Danube River from there. The term 'Danube Swabians', which is currently used, was not coined until after World War I.

"Mercy! He seems to be involved in every part of the Banat!"

"Yes, he is everywhere, *Herr Hofkammerrat*, on both this and the other side of the Danube. He is building the Fortress of Temesvar in the Banat and is building a castle for himself on this side of the Danube."

"If only the man was not so high strung. He has had two heart attacks. The Generalissimo is very worried about him because this Lorrainer is one of his best Generals."

The actuary was surprised at this sharing of confidential information. The *Hofkammerrat* was seldom so open. Hildebrandt ventured to say a word on behalf of Count Mercy: "We should not aggravate him any further by giving him problems here in Vienna; perhaps we should give him what he asks for."

"What, agree to everything he wants? The building of the Fortress of Temesvar was estimated to cost ten million, and it will probably cost twenty million. It is sinful! But wait, you wanted to report something else. You have not finished telling me everything."

"Yes, *Herr Hofkammerrat*. It is my solemn duty to report that among the newly immigrated Swabians there are a few Augsburg Protestants."

Stephany rose quickly. He buttoned up his coat, and paced back and forth two times in his spacious office. Then he stood before Hildebrandt: "Does that matter to us? It's none of our business. Hungary is big. Why do you bring this up? It is not forbidden for the counts to bring in Protestants. That may still come, when the domains that belong to the state start being settled. For the time being, the generals and Hungarian counts, some of whom are Calvinists, can do what they like. What business is it of ours? We need hard-working hands. Christians! Are not the Germans all Christians?"

Hildebrandt shook his head. "Protestants!" he growled. "I do not want to be the one held accountable for this. Remember, when Temesvar was conquered, the Generalissimo ordered that only German Catholics were allowed to settle in the inner city, because only they could be trusted."

"That's something else. A newly conquered fortress is another matter. He sought to quickly establish a unified prosperous German community in what had been a neglected Turkish city. That is something completely different."

"Prince Eugene settled only German Catholics on his property in the Baranya and at Ofen (Buda)," Hildebrandt said stubbornly.

"That was his personal business," answered Stephany.

Hildebrandt was silent for a moment. Then he said, "Will *Herr Hofkammerrat* verify that I dutifully reported the matter, if asked?"

"Yes, but the hell with it! Don't be so afraid. Austria has much to make amends for along these lines. Very much!"

Chapter 3 — In the Vienna Council Office

Stephany continued to pace in his office long after the slightly offended Actuary had departed. This did not fit his plan. The work of resettlement could never be properly completed if such narrow restrictions were put on its development. He was convinced of that. Were not some of the Magyars Calvinists? Were not the Siebenbürger and Zipser Saxons[5] Protestants? What was the harm in a few thousand more coming? Just don't bring it up! Don't ask questions about it. Oh, this actuary, with his clumsy ways! Now he had burdened him, the *Hofkammerrat*, with even more problems. But he could bear them.

Kaiser Karl was a devout Catholic, but he looked the other way when there were religious differences. He was the Regent, the ruler of this territory, with the power to decide this question, and Joseph von Stephany looked up to him with respect. Because of the Peace of Westphalia, each Regent had the right to determine the religion of his own state and its people. At that treaty, the German *Fürsten* had brought back the principle *Cuius regio, eius religio* "whose realm, his religion", which had been present in the middle ages.[6]

The question of religion could be raised directly with the Kaiser, but it would be best to avoid that. And above all else, let's not let the Jesuits have any input in this matter! He, the *Hofkammerrat*, had his own plans for the settlement of the new territory. As his plans were not fully developed, he did not want to reveal them just yet. Maybe it would be better to just act on his basic principles instead of presenting them explicitly. The *Hofkammerrat* was clever in that he worked quietly and successfully avoided clashes. The president of the *Hofkammer* was always a count, but he was leader in name only—in reality the leading hand was Joseph von Stephany. The president needed to appear to be in charge to outsiders, but behind the scenes it was Stephany who had the wide view of what was needed. The more he stayed in the background, the broader his influence was.

Another official came in to report that a document had arrived from the Hungarian Council Office, and nobody knew where it belonged.

"The Magistrate sent me," Gottmann, the young secretary, reported.

"What's it about?" von Stephany asked the secretary.

"It is about two conflicts they are having, Herr Councillor. Firstly, it is a

---

5 *Siebenbürger* and *Zipser* Saxons were Germans who had settled in *Siebenbürgen* (Transylvania) and in the Spiš area, from the 12th to 15th centuries. Both Transylvania and Spiš were in Hungary at the time of this narrative; they are currently in Romania and Slovakia.
6 *The Peace of Westphalia*, 1648: At the time of this treaty, each individual state had its own ruler, such as a Grand Duke, Duke, Margrave, Count, Landgrave, Prince of the Church, etc. (These rulers were called *Fürsten* in the German States.) The treaty stated that for Central Europe, the individual leaders *(Fürsten)* would determine the religion of their state.

complaint against the *Stadtkommandant*[7] of Temesvar. He forced a Roman Catholic priest to marry a Protestant couple. If the priest did not comply he would be forced to leave the Fortress Temesvar."

"Ah! And why did he do that?"

"Because there is no Protestant minister there."

"So they asked us for one?"

"On the contrary, *Herr Hofkammerrat*! To prevent this from happening again and to ensure that the inhabitants in the city will convert to the true Catholic faith, twenty Catholics have petitioned that the three mosques in Temesvar be immediately given to three Catholic orders. They ask for Jesuits, Franciscans and Piarists. It cannot be tolerated that Protestant soldiers become citizens of Temesvar unless they convert. It is against the orders of the Generalissimo."

"Who lodged the complaints?" the *Hofkammerrat* asked.

"The priest who was commanded to perform the marriage and nineteen members of the parish, supported by the Notary Erling."

"That does not concern us at the moment," said Stephany thoughtfully. "This should be forwarded to Count Mercy in Temesvar. He is the Governor of the Banat. The *Stadtkommandant* is his subordinate. Send the petition to the count but make a copy and file it. It may be important some day."

The official bowed and turned to depart. The *Hofkammerrat* called after him, "By the way, Herr Secretary, and let all of them know, especially the laudable Hungarian Magistrate in Vienna, that matters concerning the Banat, the Batschka and the military border do not belong to the Hungarian *Hofkanzlei* but to the Austrian Council Office. These are provinces of the Kaiser and are ruled from Vienna.[8] When will they finally understand that?"

With a smile, the secretary bowed and withdrew.

The *Hofkammerrat*, however, became very thoughtful. Questions were being raised that he would rather have kept quiet.

A ray of sunshine, in the form of Stephany's blond young daughter, lit up the office. "Mademoiselle Charlotte," a servant announced as the girl entered. Lottel had come to invite her papa to go for a walk before lunch. She carried a bouquet of flowers and let her father smell them. It was heavenly on the *Schottenbastei*, she said. Everything was blooming already. Spring had come overnight. The Councillor was glad to be taken away by his darling daughter. It was the hour in which the fewest noblemen were to be found on the

---

7 *Stadtkommandant*: Military ruler; city commander
8 When the Kaiser's army conquered Hungary, this extended the territory that his family, the Austrian Habsburgs, ruled. This is why the Austrian *Hofkanzlei* had the final say on these matters.

Chapter 3 — In the Vienna Council Office

promenade in the *Stadtgraben* or on the bastions, and he gladly took this time to rejuvenate himself.

Joseph von Stephany was Viennese, a middle-class citizen of Vienna who had earned his *Beamtenadel*, his nobility as an official of the Habsburg court. He felt as proud of his native city as anyone of the aristocracy. How magnificently the battered city had been rebuilt after the last Turkish siege: row after row of palaces, wide boulevards that had replaced the bastions and moats, and the beautiful paradise of gardens outside the city gates, behind which the new suburbs appeared.

Trade and commerce flourished, and from all over the empire the aristocracy flocked to the city of Kaiser Karl VI to bask in the radiance of his court. The influx of foreigners from around the world was almost too much for the cramped old city; even the *Hofburg*, the Imperial Palace, was deemed to be too small ever since the Turkish threat had disappeared. The Imperial family built summer palaces outside of the city gates, and the nobility followed suit. Soon a circle of villas belonging to *Fürsten* surrounded the inner city beyond the six hundred foot wide ring, the glacis,[9] on which construction was forbidden. Like a diorama created from an artist's hand, the many-towered city rose out of this scenic frame up to the sky, and the graceful steeple of St. Stephen's Cathedral dominated the new cityscape.

Joseph von Stephany had only been three years old at the time of the Turkish siege but he still remembered his father in the uniform of the Citizen's Militia. He had seen the new city rise up from the old and saw with astonishment how everything grew and prospered.

He lived in his parental home on Renn Street, next to the *Schotten* cemetery where his parents and his wife, who had died so young, were buried. He and Lottel visited the grave almost daily. Every path to the *Schottenbastei* went past her grave. And they were so used to stopping by, that both of them talked about her all the time as if she was still living.

"Were you at mother's?" the *Hofkammerrat* asked every evening.

Today, as usual, they stopped at the cemetery when they walked past and the daughter laid the spring bouquet which she'd been carrying onto her beloved mother's grave. Lottel made the sign of the cross and quietly placed her arm in her father's. He lifted his hat silently to greet his wife. She had left this world when their daughter was barely eight years old, and now the two of them had been walking past for seven years already and still felt

---

9 Glacis: a slope in front of a fortification designed to make it easier to defend against attacking forces.

close to her. They repeated her favorite sayings; Lottel had learned to cook her favorite meals from her aunt, who ran their household; and her mother's favorite flowers adorned her grave throughout the year. "She is better off than we are," the aunt once said, "and we should not cry for her." Lottel believed that. She never cried for her mother but did everything for her sake. The Councillor had taken the loss very badly. He still held a secret of which Lottel was unaware. She had never been told that her mother died of the plague. Stephany didn't want her to know. He never wanted to be reminded of his wife's terrible suffering.

Inside the *Schotten* gate, father and daughter climbed the stairs up to the wall. The day was bright and warm; the April sun was already vigorous. A light breeze blew from the west, from the Vienna Woods, and the air smelled like fresh violets and newly plowed fields.

They strolled to the *Burgbastei* and further to the Kärntner Gate, where the first stone Viennese Theater stood, which the mayor had built years ago for Italian operas. But now Stranitzy leased it. He and his wife used to watch the comedian as a street performer from their window when he performed at the *Freyung*, a public square near their house, and his wife had laughed so much at his antics. Now he was a celebrated performer, but the *Hofkammerrat* did not like him. He found him to be too crude. Stephany had once accompanied Prince Eugene to France and Italy and had seen the best that theater offered. It pained him that in the German Imperial City of Vienna, rough improvised comedy thrived and was even more popular than the Italian artists that the royal court preferred. The Councillor did not know that sophisticated fine arts would eventually triumph over the more dubious tastes of the Viennese. He merely felt that it was inappropriate for this gauche street comedy to be performed in a theater which had been built for opera.

The *Hofkammerrat* and his daughter stood above the Kärntner Gate, taking in the wonderful double view: in one direction, the heart of the inner city; in the other, the imperial summer palace Favorita and the many mansions of the nobles. A splendid four-horse carriage came along Kärntner Street. People came running from the shops and doorways, waving their hats and shouting "*Vivat, Vivat!*"

Everyone knew the white Isabelle horses of the Generalissimo, and the cry of "*Vivat Eugenius!*"—"Long live Prince Eugene!" was taken up by those strolling on the *Bastei*. They, too, waved their hats. The City Guard presented their arms as the carriage raced by. The Councillor's gaze followed it with great interest.

"Look, Papa, he is going to the Palace Favorita," said Lottel.

Chapter 3 — In the Vienna Council Office

"Yes, to the royal court," the *Hofkammerrat* said thoughtfully, and turned to go back. "Prince Eugene likely has much to discuss with His Majesty. Such a hero! Such a statesman! But he also has enemies."

"Those who are jealous, Papa! But the Kaiser won't listen to them, will he?"

"The Prince's enemies are always close to the Kaiser, my child; they are all around him and the Prince is often away," said the *Hofkammerrat* ambiguously.

"Papa, do you believe that they will manage to denigrate the Prince?"

"Well, some things have changed. The greater his glory, the cooler they have been to him in the court."

"I don't understand that. He is definitely not good looking, but whenever I see him I'd like to give him a kiss."

"Well, I'll tell him that next time I see him!"

Lottel laughed and blushed. "But, Papa, don't misunderstand me. I only meant..."

"Yes, yes, I know what you meant."

He teased her all the way home to keep her from asking him questions that he couldn't answer. She didn't need to know that the Kaiser's mistress was one of the most dangerous enemies in the court. She admired the Kaiser. Why should he make her think ill of him? After all, who doubted that the Prince would also win the battle against the courtiers. Not him, so why talk about it?

Tante Mathilde had long been looking out of the window for the latecomers; their dinner would spoil if they did not arrive soon. Everyone in the city had already eaten. Soon the bell would toll the blessing at the *Schotten* monastery, and she would not be ready to attend.

Songs drifted up to her as a procession, complete with flags and pictures of the saints, passed by on its way to St. Stephen's Cathedral. Tante Mathilde crossed herself and folded her hands until the procession had passed.

Lottel saw her aunt's white bonnet from far away, and she waved to her. When the old lady finally saw her, she raised her finger as if to say, "hurry up!" and disappeared into the house. *Hofkammerrat* Stephany pulled out his Swiss watch and looked at the time. Yes, it was late. A large group coming home from a pilgrimage to *Maria Zell* had cut them off at Schotten Street, which meant that he'd had to remove his hat until hundreds of the faithful had passed by.

Once the good aunt heard this, she immediately forgave the two and gave them their dinner without reproach.

Chapter 4

The Bridal Ship

It was no small task for Therese to get ready for this adventurous journey to a strange, wild country and for her marriage to Jakob Pless. The entire little town took part in her worries, and many advised her, for God's sake, don't go on that trip. The groom must come and fetch you. Dear God, what a misguided idea that was! Frau Therese laughed at them. They probably thought that he could take a yellow mail coach from Temesvar, and travel just like one did from Stuttgart to Ulm. They did not understand that it would take weeks and months, not to mention a small fortune, to undertake such a journey of two hundred German miles. The trip down the Danube River, that was not all that difficult. With God's help, anyone could manage it. But coming up! For that, the Danube was useless. Only Satan could build a barge that went upriver. The honest Shippers' Guilds of Ulm, Regensburg and Passau could not do such devil's work. To be sure, horses could be used to pull flatboats from Günzburg to Ulm, but from Peterwardein in Hungary—that would take two years!

Therese had to take many trips to put her dowry together. She was in Ulm more often than at home in Blaubeuren. She travelled to Regensburg three times on an *Ordinari-schiff*[1] to convince her fearful aunt to go with her. While she was there, they went to Nuremberg to make the most important purchases. Trade flourished in that city and it had the best selection of everything. If Jakob wanted to build an inn in the German style in Temesvar, which had been Turkish for so long, she had to plan carefully and make sure

---

[1] *Ordinari-schiff* was the name of the type of ship that took passengers to Vienna every week. This had begun in 1696; before then the Danube had not been used to transport people on a regular basis.

Chapter 4 — The Bridal Ship

she brought everything she needed to be a good innkeeper's wife. The finest pewter dishes, plates, bowls, pitchers and jars were to be obtained at the foundries of Nuremberg. Copper pans and kettles could be purchased only there. The Nuremberg master craftsmen took only boys from Nuremburg as apprentices. The copper craft had been perfected in Nuremberg and was not taught to outsiders; the finished product could only be sold in that city. And it was like that for many other goods. Her father had explained this to her years ago; he had purchased much of his equipment in Nuremberg. Now she went to the same sources.

She brought a mountain of rare items to Regensburg and left them with her aunt, where they should be ready for her bridal ship when it came down the Danube. And she also took orders from her friends. The *Kantor* needed a trumpet to accompany the Prince Eugene song, and trumpets were made only in Nuremberg. He would gladly have also purchased a clarinet, which had been invented in Nuremberg, but he did not have quite enough money for that.

These trips were also a source of encouragement for Therese. She learned more about Hungary than Jakob had written her, much more than was known in Blaubeuren. Many Germans had already emigrated there, settling on the west side of the Danube, where the Turks had first been driven out. The German Magistrate of Fünfkirchen had already ordered items from Nuremberg as early as 1697. Only the Banat area on the east side of the Danube, where she was now going, was new territory, they told her. Upon hearing this, her courage grew even more.

Ludwig Pless custom built a ship for his son's bride. Not an *Ulmer Schachtel* [2], as they were known on the Danube, but a new type of barge. He built two rooms in the center for Therese and her companions, as well as a tiny kitchen in the back. In the front was a covered deck that served as a shelter for the shipmaster and the eight oarsmen, who could not be left completely exposed to the elements on such a long trip. The barge was constructed of pine timbers that were 90 feet long. On this specially made barge only shorter timbers would be used; on an open barge they were 146 feet long, and on a flatboat they were 125 feet long. His custom-built vessel was a hybrid of the famous Kehlheim Flatboats which went to Vienna every Wednesday and the Ulm *Ordinari-schiff* which left for Vienna every Sunday. This ship cost three hundred Ulm Guilders to build, and when it was brought to Peterwardein it

---

2 *Ulmer Schachtel* (literally: crate from Ulm) is the name given the wooden boats that were typically taken on the Danube from Ulm to Vienna or Hungary. These ships were very crowded and unsanitary, and passengers did not have cabins but were exposed to the elements.

would be worth four times as much for the *Bojaren* and Turkish *Spahis*[3] who had likely never traveled on such a ship to the Black Sea. The profit was to be his gift to the courageous bride.

    At first Pless only planned to equip the ship with eight oarsmen and a helmsman, all of whom wanted to emigrate. Was that wise? It seemed risky! The Danube was dangerous in Hungary. But where could he get a captain for the whole trip? To become a captain, the Shippers Guild required men to be at least thirty years old and married. They did not trust an unmarried man with the money, because there was no incentive to return. However, a wife and child would ensure a married man's return. A captain had to be an honest man. He could not be a drinker, player, or skirt chaser—in short, he needed to be an established citizen. The captains of the Shippers Guild were honest and trustworthy. But since they were established here, they only went as far as Vienna and no further.

    Every time they arrived in Vienna, the captain would have to sell the ship he had just taken down the river. Since this was to be done as quickly as possible, the ships were often taken apart and the wood was sold. As soon as this business was taken care of, captain and crew would head back. If the stay in Vienna was too long, the crew would eat and drink the profits away. So as soon as the ships from Ulm and Regensburg arrived in Vienna, the dealers were already waiting. Deals were rapidly closed so that the captain and crew could quickly board the wagons for the return trip through St. Pölten and Linz to Ulm. Captains could have traveled farther downriver to Hungary, but the Ulmer captains did not want to do that. They had been allowed to become captains because they were settled in Ulm. This was Pless's dilemma.

    Then one of Pless's men, Anton Oberle from Swabia, volunteered to make the trip to Peterwardein. He had made his five trial trips to Vienna and was qualified to become a captain as soon as he got married. Pless thought he would be an excellent captain, but it seemed that Oberle was reluctant to marry. He could have chosen any of the ship masters' daughters and any would have gladly taken him, but he was not interested in settling down. Pless had a talk with him before the spring trips began and Anton confessed that he wanted to go out into the wide world. He had a *Wanderlust* which he could not overcome. Pless made him an offer: If Oberle would pilot Pless's ship to Peterwardein, he would be released from his duty. Pless would even give him a couple of crown *Taler* on top. With joy, Anton agreed to the pro-

---

3 *Bojaren*: the ruling class (nobility) or large landowners in what is now Romania.
   Spahi: a cavalryman of the Turkish army

Chapter 4—The Bridal Ship

posal. His eyes shone with the desire to see foreign lands and to brave all the dangers such a trip would entail. This was the perfect assignment for him!

One morning when the melted snow had run off from the rugged mountains and the spring wind blew into the valley of the Blautal, the host of the *Adler* Inn harnessed his horse and drove his sister to Ulm. It annoyed him that Gretel was going with Therese, but he could not prevent it. Two farm girls from Gerhausen came along, bringing their meager possessions with them. They, too, wanted to seek their fortunes in a foreign land. As they had looked for positions as domestic servants in Ulm or Regensburg, these lively Swabian girls had heard of the scarcity of women in Hungary, and were more than willing to help increase the number of marriages in the Banat. Therese gladly brought them with her.

As they drove past the Söflingen monastery, Gretel wistfully kept her eye out for her Josef. Would she see him, she asked herself. Would he escape the monastery to join her, now that she was going out into the wide world? She had relayed a message to him three times through friends, to let him know that she was leaving. If he did not come it was not worth it for her to wait for him.

In Ulm, most stayed the night in the Plough Inn, but Therese slept at the home of her future in-laws. A wedding feast was celebrated the next day at the Pless home. Friends and relatives from both sides of the family brought gifts. The happy father had to take the place of the bridegroom. He charmed the beautiful young bride and gave her the first kiss. The guests spoke a lot about the missing groom and reminisced about his silly youthful pranks. His mother made some good suggestions about what Jakob liked best and what he liked to eat. She was a full-figured woman with red cheeks and a warm heart. When she uttered Jakob's name, her voice choked with emotion.

At four in the afternoon the party broke up, and they wandered out past the *Gäns* Gate to the landing. There the Ulm flag was waving cheerfully over the brand new ship. Everything on board was immaculate and the wedding guests stared in awe. The deck was enclosed by a railing; on it stood a few benches and chests and baskets full of Therese's household belongings. The two cabins were full. The bride would sleep in her own bed on this trip. No one had ever traveled downriver on the Danube in such style, said the Ulmers, not even the Kaiser when he had traveled to the Orient, or the English Ambassador Montague and his Lady, who were now in Turkey. It would be a pleasure to travel on this ship.

After a while the mood became serious. The thought hung in the air: would the young women, the captain, the helmsman and the eight oarsmen never be seen again in their homeland? There were plenty of onlookers on shore and quite a few clandestine tears. Many a young beauty had fallen for young Captain Anton Oberle, who had scorned them and was now going out into the wide world.

Pless now gave the Captain the signal to leave. It was time to put an end to the long farewell. He whistled for the oarsmen to take their places. He wanted to make sure that they would reach Regensburg that day to pick up the aunt and there was no time to lose. Tomorrow morning the trip would begin in earnest.

At last they were underway. Everyone on the shore waved farewell. Mother Pless called out, "God bless you, God bless you. Be sure to give my Jakob lots of love!" as she wiped the tears from her eyes.

Therese stood in the middle of the boat for a long time. Gretel cried; she would have liked to jump into the water and swim to the shore. But Therese was strong. She folded her hands and looked toward the Ulm *Münster*. The cathedral had never looked as big and beautiful to her as on this day of departure. A seriousness came over her and she uttered a prayer which she had not said since her First Communion. This parting from her homeland was beautiful. She was overcome with a soft nostalgia. Would Jakob ever thank her for her decision? Would she find a happiness with him, which had been denied her in the past?

The steady thrust of the oars woke Therese from her reverie. Suddenly, as she turned to go to her room, she heard a cry of joy.

"Josef! My Josef is here!" Gretel shouted over and over.

From behind the crates and baskets crawled a young man who had been hiding beneath a pile of rough horseblankets the oarsmen were to use as beds. Josef, a tall, dark young man with bright dark eyes, stood up and stretched his limbs. Gretel ran to him and kissed him tenderly. "You are here, you are here!" she shouted and laughed and cried.

Then the Captain of the ship came over and sternly asked, "Who is this? What does he want? Does he have his papers?"

"No," said Gretel. "He has nothing; he is my sweetheart."

"That's all I need at the Bavarian and Austrian borders," declared the captain, "a stowaway! He will have to go ashore at Günsburg."

Hearing this, Josef Anderl was dumbfounded. What? How could this be? Had he escaped from the monastery only to be put in the army? He thought you didn't need any papers to go to Hungary.

Therese interceded. The Captain must figure out how Josef could be smuggled past the border. Could he sit with the oarsmen, or perhaps hide

Chapter 4 — The Bridal Ship

under the horse blankets?

"This is not a good start to the trip," the master grumbled. "I've never before traveled to Vienna with contraband."

Josef thanked Therese for her kind intervention and declared that he would be of service to her, as long as she needed him. He was not only a gardener; at the monastery, he had learned many trades and had even learned to play the French horn. So there were many ways for him to be helpful.

The ship glided past Günzburg and floated into the dusk of the May evening. Josef and Gretel sat on a bench in front of Therese's cabin and began to sing folk songs, some happy and some sad. They were overjoyed that they were now free and would soon belong to each other. No priest, no count or other official could keep them apart.

Exuberantly they sang:

Morgen will mein Schatz abreisen,	Tomorrow my sweetheart departs,
Sum, sum;	la, la;
Abschied nehmen mit Gewalt,	Takes leave with vigor,
Sum, sum;	la, la;
Draußen singen schon die Vöglein,	Outside the birds are already singing,
Singen schon die Vöglein	Birds are already singing
In dem dunklen grünen Wald,	In the green, dark forest,
Sum, sum;	la, la;

But the next song was sung in a minor key:

Und es fällt mir so schwer,	And it would be so difficult
Aus der Heimat zu gehn,	To leave my homeland
Wenn die Hoffnung nicht wär	If the hope were not there
Auf ein Wieder- Wiedersehn.	To see it once again.
Lebe wohl, lebe wohl, lebe wohl,	Farewell, farewell, farewell,
Lebe wohl, lebe wohl aufs Wiedersehn!	Farewell, farewell until we meet again!

The simple melodies touched everyone. The captain, the helmsman, oarsmen, Frau Therese and the two girls from Gershausen all sang along. They felt a peculiar pain in their hearts; none of them believed they would ever see their homeland again.

Base[4] Gutwein, Therese's widowed aunt, boarded the ship at Regensburg. When they reached Nuremberg the next morning, all the items which Therese had purchased for the inn were loaded onto the ship. Therese sent Josef out

---

4 *Base* (pronounced Bah-se) in this case means aunt. The term *Base* could also be used to refer to any older woman.

to buy a French horn, whatever the cost. He was to play it for them on the long journey. He soon came back with the instrument. Everything was now in order, and the Captain cast off. They drifted below the bridge, and off they went on their long journey.

They stopped at Straubing and in Passau they stayed overnight. All the men left the ship, except for Josef who stayed to keep watch. He had rowed for a few hours and otherwise made himself useful, but he did not feel tired. He stood guard until the oarsmen returned at dawn. Then he lay down in front of Frau Therese's cabin and slept. In the cabin next to hers were the three other women. Did they need his protection? Josef did not ask, he simply felt the need to do this. This became his custom every night during the entire trip.

At the border at Engelhardtszell, nobody asked Josef for any papers and the bridal ship was not inspected. The Austrian border guards, who usually thoroughly inspected every *Ordinari-schiff* that navigated the Danube, simply took the toll money. After noting that besides the crew there were only women aboard, they did not inspect the barge further. Nonetheless, the ship had to stay overnight at the border.

The trip was not without dangers. Even before Passau, the ship had to be wary of boulders and crags in the bed of the Danube. At Aschau the sandbars were in a different place every day. This required the watchful eye of the Captain in order to get through without any trouble. By and by, the Danube narrowed because the mountains were closer together, and the water rose. The rushing current took them quickly past the romantic scenery toward Linz.

At first, *Base* Gutwein, who had not traveled since the death of her husband, was very nervous about the dangers they might encounter. She sat next to Therese every day, helped her with her needlework, told her stories about the glorious Holy Roman Empire, admired every castle and cloister they passed and dutifully prayed her rosary. After she had finally relaxed, she admitted to being pleased that she had been persuaded to accompany her niece. She could see a good bit of the world and still remain a subject of the Kaiser. She had lived in Regensburg since she was a child, had witnessed many glorious assemblies of the Imperial Diet[5] and had known all seven *Kurfürsten*[6]

---

5 Imperial Diet (*Reichstag*): General assembly of the various principalities of the Holy Roman Empire of the German Nation, which after 1663 met at the Regensburg City Hall.
6 *Kurfürsten* (English: Electors) were the ruling monarchs who had the power to elect the Kaiser, the Holy Roman Emporer. They and the Kaiser assembled at the Imperial Diet. Every principality had a *Fürst* or *Kurfürst* in charge of it, but only the *Kurfürsten* could elect the Kaiser. However, though the office of Emperor was elective, from 1453 to 1740 a Habsburg was always emporer.

Chapter 4—The Bridal Ship

in her time. She had seen three Kaisers in person: Leopold, Josef and the current ruling Kaiser, Karl. The aunt declared that she was not easily impressed, but truth be told, she now was enjoying the trip, and Linz was a beautiful city. Her dearly departed husband had driven the postal coach belonging to the Count of Thurn and Taxis.[7] He had traveled through the Rhineland but had never been on a romantic trip like this through Austria. Nor had he ever seen Vienna. Oh, how she looked forward to seeing Vienna!

Therese let her talk and talk, but was occupied with her own thoughts. She was wary of Anton Oberle, the ship's captain. She had noticed him hanging around her door and that of the girls. He had a hatred for Josef. Today he had made the young man row for ten hours straight, while giving breaks to each of the oarsmen in turn. Then she heard him state that Josef and Gretel should be put off the boat in Vienna, that Josef would not be able to get a job "down there". She disagreed and informed him that Gretel belonged with her, and she was promised to Josef. Both would go with her to the end of the journey. This did not please Anton, and the rest of the day he rolled his eyes whenever he looked at her.

At Linz, the whole group left the ship for the first time and stayed at the *Bayrischer Hof* Inn. They wanted to prepare for the three day trip to Vienna, and needed their strength for the dangerous whirlpool at Grein. It was not really necessary for Therese to go ashore at Linz, since her room was well-stocked with everything. However, she was uneasy about the captain. So she decided to disembark in Linz with all the girls to keep her eye on him. She rented two rooms at the *Bayrischer Hof* for the night, one for herself and her aunt, one for the other three girls. She was determined to make her own decisions without worrying about others' opinions.

The aunt did not notice any discord. Whether on the river or on land, she kept up an inexhaustible stream of stories her late husband had told of the places he had traveled. "We have it so easy with this wonderful trip we are taking," she sighed. "But the people of the *Pfalz* have had such hardships, they have suffered so much in the past ten years!" In the *Pfalz*, farmers never knew to whom their next harvest would go, the French soldiers or their own, or to the Swedes or the Kaiser. The wild game around the area was more important to the great lords than the people. Punishment was cruel for those who killed deer for food, and the common people had no rights. And the problems with religion were sacrilegious. The Lutheran and Reformed churches con-

---

[7] The noble House of Thurn and Taxis is a German family that was a key player in the postal services.

stantly quarrelled, and those who wanted to convert back to Catholicism were despised. Her blessed late husband had long seen it coming and suddenly, his predictions were right. People began to emigrate from the *Pfalz*. They bought their freedom from the count, baron or *Fürst* to whom they were indentured and left. Many were in dire poverty. Others left defiantly and proudly, with their own horses, wagons and servants. Although they appeared to be happy, it broke their hearts to depart from their homeland.

"Where did they go?" asked Therese.

"To America, to Russia, to Hungary, what do I know," responded *Base* Gutwein. "After a while, it was forbidden to leave. But that did not matter. What was once openly allowed is now simply done in secret. I think we will meet many people from the *Pfalz* when we get to the Banat, and they can tell us about their journey."

She talked on and on until she finally nodded off. The windows to the street were open and from below, one could hear the noise and loud singing of the ships's workers. Snatches of songs were heard every time the door was opened or closed.

The night watchman came by and announced the eleventh hour. Then he banged his *Hellebarde*[8] on the doors and all was still.

"Quiet in the hostel!" he called out and moved on. They all laughed after he left, but slowly it became quiet and the singing ended. Nobody wanted to be thrown in jail and have to stay here.

Everyone was ready to go at the break of day. The glorious May morning sun shone into the narrow streets of the historic city when Josef Anderl came to let everyone know the ship was ready. He limped a little and had a black eye. Gretel was shocked at the way he looked. What happened to him, she wanted to know. Oh, nothing. He had fallen over a wooden beam during the night. He told her she should be happy that he did not fall in the water, which would have been quite a predicament.

Gretel was satisfied with that explanation, but Therese gave him a sharp look, and he would not look her in the eye.

Onboard, everything was in perfect order. Master Oberle greeted everyone courteously and cheerfully. "Today is an important day," he said. It was customary that they all pray the "Our Father" together before this stage of the trip began. But he would let each individual decide if they would join in. When *Base* Gutwein heard this she clasped her hands together. She had to disembark and hurriedly go to confession, or at least go to mass. She did not

---

8 *Hellebarde*: halberd, a long-handled medieval weapon

Chapter 4—The Bridal Ship

want to die so unprepared.

Anton Oberle grinned scornfully and whistled to the oarsmen. This was the signal to take off.

Base Gutwein went into Therese's room, knelt down and prayed. But Therese brought out her needlework and sat on the bench. She was quite tranquil. After a while she called to her aunt to come out of the room. They would not reach the whirlpool until late in the afternoon, and she should come look at the beautiful ever-changing scenery.

The aunt, now composed, came out of the cabin. But she still had her hymn- and prayer book with her.

The Danube was broad and mighty here. They had traveled through a narrow passage yesterday, but as they had approached Linz, the river had become much wider, with islands in the middle. It flowed around the city in a big, wide curve. The left bank was mountainous, and the right was flat. Linz, with its mountainous background and the high old *Kaiserburg* castle, slowly faded from view behind the dark forests which surrounded the city.

Gretel helped Frau Therese organize her dowry, the two Swabian girls from Gershausen cooked and *Base* Gutwein read to Therese from her holy books. Cities and markets, pilgrimage churches, castles and cloisters floated past. There was less talking, and the mood was more serious than it had been in the past few days.

In the afternoon when Grein was near, the women retreated to their cabins one by one. Only Therese came back out. She left Gretel with her aunt; now Gretel had to pray with her to all the Catholic saints, even though she was an Augsburg Protestant.

There was Grein… the island Wörth and the whirlpool came into view.

The water was high and the ship was hard to control. The water foamed and swirled around the crags and only a trained eye could determine how the ship should be steered to avoid being shattered against the rocks. Usually there were three routes in which the ship could be steered: along the forest on the left, through the wild water in the middle or in the high water on the right. But the snow melt from the mountains had swollen the Danube so much that only a broad gurgling flood could be seen, foaming over the deadly crags.

This was Anton Oberle's moment of triumph. With all hands at his disposal he steered the ship over the high water and only a small bump was felt when the end of the ship scraped on an invisible rock. Pots and pans rattled in the kitchen, and Frau Therese, who was standing up, staggered a bit.

"We made it!" the captain called out, and Therese gave him a grateful look. He had been waiting for that look. He gazed at her admiringly with sparkling eyes. She lowered her eyes, not wanting to return his gaze, and went back to her room to join her aunt.

"We made it!" she repeated.

Then all of them came out and looked back at the dangerous rapids, the gurgling, turbulent whirlpool which they had safely passed. Everyone praised the captain and the rudderman. They were now free of the danger of the whirlpool. Even the two Swabian girls, Susi and Bärbl, who had seemed fearless, now admitted to *Base* Gutwein that they had been very anxious.

The crew laughed at them. Some of them had made the trip ten times, and even if many tales of the dangerous whirlpool had made the rounds, none had ever been on a disastrous trip. So they said now. The sailors had been quiet and serious all day, but now all were happy and talkative and even sang a song. It was a melody which they accompanied with the rhythm of their oars. The song was about the whirlpool, its dangers, and a noblewoman who decided not to cross it because of her fears. The words and melody seemed as well known to them as the "Our Father".

Als wir jüngst in Regensburg waren,	When we were in Regensburg of late
Ha, ha!	Ha, ha!
Sind wir über den Strudel gefahren,	Our ship rode over the whirlpool
Ha, ha!	Ha, ha!
Ei da waren Holden,	There were a few girls
Die mitfahren wollten.	Who wanted to ride along
Schwäbische, bayrische Dirndelein juchhe!	Swabian, Bavarian maidens, hurray!
Muß der Schiffmann fahren.	The shipmaster was to take them along.
Und ein Mädel von zwölf Jahren,	And a girl twelve years of age
Ha, ha!	Ha, ha!
Ist mit über den Strudel gefahren,	Rode along over the whirlpool
Ha, ha!	Ha, ha!
Weil sie noch nit lieben kunnt'	Because she had not yet loved
Fuhr sie sicher übern Strudelsgrund,	She rode safely over the whirlpool's depths
Scheute nicht Gefahren.	With no fear of danger.
Ha, ha!	Ha, ha!
Und vom hohen Bergesschlosse	And from the high mountain castle
Ha, ha!	Ha, ha!
Kam auf stolzem schwarzem Rosse	Rode proudly on her black horse
Ha, ha!	Ha, ha!
Adlig Fräulein Kunigund,	The noble maiden Kunigundel
Wollt' mitfahr'n über Strudels Grund,	Wanted to ride along over the whirlpool
Und kein' Taler sparen.	Was ready to spend many *Taler*
Ha, ha!	Ha, ha!

Chapter 4 — The Bridal Ship

Schiffmann, lieber Schiffmann mein,	Shipmaster, oh dear shipmaster,
Ha, ha!	Ha, ha!
Sollt's denn so gefährlich sein?	Would it be so dangerous?
Ha, ha!	Ha, ha!
Schiffmann, sag mir's ehrlich,	Shipmaster, tell me truly,
Ist's denn so gefährlich?	Is it such a dangerous thing?
Bin noch jung an Jahren.	I am still a young maiden.
Ha, ha!	Ha, ha!
"Wem der Myrtenkranz geblieben,	"One who still wears the myrtle wreath
Ha, ha!	Ha, ha!
Landet froh und sicher drüben,	Will land safely and happily across
Ha, ha!	Ha, ha!
Die ihn hat verloren	The maiden who has lost it
Ist der Tod erkoren."	Will surely die instead."
Gundel, Gundel, Kunigundel juchhe!	And so the maiden Kunigundel
ist nit mitgefahren.	Turned back and did not ride along.

The jovial whirlpool song brought all the women out on deck with *Base* Gutwein in the lead. She convinced the oarsmen to repeat the song, which she had never heard before.

All their fears were now forgotten; the mood lightened and everyone was in high spirits. The oarsmen were exhausted as they approached Maria Taferl in the evening. Up in the heights was a twin-towered church, the *Gnadenkirche*, a pilgrimage site which was visited by hundreds of thousands of the faithful every year. The sinking sun surrounded the church with an unearthly glory. *Base* Gutwein was overcome by this sight and said a prayer of thanks.

After they landed, Therese called Josef Anderl over and asked him to find lodgings for the night for everybody as he had done in Linz. In this place of pilgrimage that should be no problem. The aunt wondered why go ashore, and Gretel said she wanted to stay on board. Therese hesitated.

The captain said contemptuously as he touched his cap, "I am going ashore. I have a girlfriend here who has already been waiting for two weeks for my kisses. Good night to all of you!" Then he turned to the oarsmen. "We continue to Tulln tomorrow at three."

"At three in the morning?" the aunt exclaimed.

"Then we'll stay on board," Therese decided.

The three girls sat together outside and chatted; the May evening was too beautiful to go inside. The oarsmen, all strong young men, lay on their horse-blankets at the back of the ship, ate their bread and talked about their future. A few wanted to be farmers with their own land, and some wanted to pursue a trade. Only two were sailors at heart and wished to live on the water until they died. They wanted to travel until they reached the Black Sea and then they could work for a pasha.[9] Josef Anderl, who was on the back of the ship with them, said he wouldn't mind building a beautiful garden for a pasha near the Golden Horn.[10]

When the girls softly began to sing, Josef limped over to them. He brought his blanket with him, and had the French horn from Nuremberg as well. He accompanied their songs every evening. Sometimes he played a three-step and the girls danced a bit.

The rudderman looked at him derisively, and had his own thoughts about Josef and the captain.

After a while, Gretel signaled to Josef to stop playing, because the aunt was fast asleep.

Softly, softly the girls hummed their songs so as not to disturb the sleepers in the cabin. As the water rushed beneath them, the moon rose over the dark mountains of the Danube.

The girls shivered; the May evening on the water was quite cool.

Susi and Bärbl rose. Gretel told them she would be going in soon.

First she asked Josef why he had been fighting with the captain the night before. Josef shrugged his shoulders, but she persisted with her questioning.

"Well, think of it this way," he finally said. "Imagine the cabin over there is a goose stall, and I am the guardian. No fox is going to get in there under my watch!"

Gretel laughed and gave him a kiss. Then she scurried after the girls. Once in the cabin, they giggled and snickered about Josef, the geese protector. But he laid his rough blanket down and stretched himself full length in front of both doors, his Nuremberg jack knife at his side.

---

9   Pasha: a titled official in the Ottoman empire
10 The Golden Horn is an estuary that goes through Istanbul.

Chapter 5

Count Mercy's Homecoming

A sturdy horse-drawn travel coach accompanied by two mounted Hàjduks[1] rumbled through the new Vienna Gate of the fortress of Temesvar. Each Hàjduk had a shotgun over his shoulder and a pistol in his belt. Horses and riders were covered in dirt and dust. A layer of dried clay made it impossible to see the color of the coach, and one could only surmise that the four horses pulling the coach might be black. The coach wheels had apparently been axle-deep in mud on the way to Temesvar.

It was already growing dark as the stately coach neared the inner city, which looked rather desolate during its reconstruction. Next to half-built brick Western-style buildings, Armenians and dark Greeks in wooden shacks sold cheap merchandise and haggled with their buyers; waste water from the houses ran through the streets; a few goats grazed in the town square and geese swam in a large puddle. They all scattered, honking and bleating loudly, as the stage coach approached. The shirtless sun-browned boys who had evidently been watching over the goats stretched out their hands in hopes of a gift. One of the Hàjduks struck at them with a short-handled whip, which extended in a flash over heads of the intrusive boys. At this, the boys drew back; they knew from experience that there were knots in the whip which really hurt.

The Kaiser's black and yellow flag waved over a bullet-ridden Turkish minaret on the southern edge of the square. Atop a half-destroyed mosque, a cross sparkled in the setting sun.

The streets through which the coach drove were enlivened by a crowd of

---

1 Hàjduk: a mercenary foot soldier in Hungary

people whose colorful clothing reflected their ethnicity. Serbs, Wallachians,[2] Bulgarians, Greeks, Armenians, Germans in long colorful coats, in red and white and yellow stockings with buckled shoes and three-cornered hats with a braid in the back, went busily on their way. A few Germans stood in front of their houses, chatting. Here and there, a turban was to be seen among the groups of people.

Tall Grenadier Guards in bearskin hats, armed with swords and clubs, stood here and there on street corners and sharply observed where everyone was going. They pointed their clubs to direct the people; it seemed to be their duty to gradually clear the fortress of all who did not belong before evening came. Apparently many were just workers here during the day. The throng slowly made its way to the city gates, and it was noticeable that no one in German garb was among them.

No one had paid much attention to the coach, but now it drove past the guards on the Parade Square, and the officer on duty recognized the grey head of the passenger. He saluted and gave the head guard a signal, whereupon the guard loudly shouted, "Present arms, present arms!"

By the time the guards had rushed to formation and the drummer had given a drum roll, the four span of horses had already passed them. It stopped on the far side of the Parade Square in front of the most stylish new home in the entire city. The servants rushed out and a crowd gathered in no time, since word had spread quickly after the guard had recognized the coach's inhabitant.

"General Mercy is back!" they called out one to another. As a sign of respect all removed their hats as Mercy stepped out of the coach. He was supported by his nephew, Anton von Mercy, who had come out of the coach first. The general had a healthy color on his cheeks, and his eyes were bright. He had been gone for a year and a half; he'd commanded the army in Italy and Sicily, was wounded and then went to Vienna to heal. The Kaiser had called him away from the Banat, where he had begun a great cultural revolution, because he had needed him in the Spanish-Italian campaign. But now he sent him back to the Banat, to those who loved and respected him like a father despite his severe manner and strictness. They knew that he wanted what was best for them. He willingly returned to this miserable barren swamp land, which sorely needed his strong hand and superior spirit. Prince Eugene had named him Governor of the Banat after the land was recovered from the Turks. Mercy saw it as his life's work to fulfill this task in a worthy manner.

---

2 Wallachia is a region of what is now Romania

Chapter 5 — Count Mercy's Homecoming

And everyone knew this.

Count Mercy had a stately appearance; his bearing was that of a true soldier. He stood a head taller than his nephew and his face was the kind that was not easily forgotten. Two large brown eyes shone beneath a powerful forehead. Their gaze was penetrating and created the feeling that no secrets could be hidden from them. A strong nose, firm resolute chin and a full mouth completed this manly face, which was subdued only slightly by the crimped powdered wig. The General's voice was consistent with his overall appearance; it sounded like a trumpet and its tone induced fear.

He gave the crowd a grateful look for their respectful greetings and walked slowly toward the gate. One could see that he was tired and stiff from the long journey, and he favored his left leg. That was likely where he had been wounded.

After the baggage was removed from the sturdy coach, it was driven to the new barracks, led by the Hàjduks. The crowd dispersed. Soon the whole city knew of Mercy's homecoming. That same evening, word spread that the General had become a Count. They had known he had been awarded sizeable properties by the Kaiser, under Prince Eugene's recommendation, immediately after the Battles of Peterwardein and Tesmesvar.[3] Now it appeared that the Kaiser had seen fit to award him the title of Count.

Everyone was pleased with this news, for it was a well-deserved honor for the great leader and friend. The new citizens of this city had felt like orphans in his absence; there had been no one here whom they could depend upon. His representatives did not appear equal to the job. Much had been neglected. The strict orders of the Governor seemed to have been forgotten. His plans had not been completed, ostensibly because no money was available. This would now change. Mercy would be able to get the funds from Vienna.

The fortress was still open on two sides; only the Vienna and Peterwardein Gates could be considered finished. How could one be sure that peace would prevail? Didn't hordes of Tatars[4] still swarm the countryside causing trouble? Again and again one heard stories of travelers who disappeared without a trace. Robber bands dared to come into the outskirts of the new cities. If they were pursued, they would disappear into the thickets of the swamps where they were safe. The German mayor, Herr Balthasar Tobias Hold, breathed a sigh of relief at the news that the Governor was back in

---

3 The battles of Peterwardein and Temesvar, led by Prince Eugene and General Mercy, were instrumental in helping the Austrian forces capture what was then Ottoman-occupied Hungary.
4 Tatar: a member of any of the Mongolian peoples of central Asia who invaded eastern Europe in the 13th century.

town. He would now be able to get a good night's sleep.

Mercy's arrival had taken his people by surprise; no one suspected that he would be back so soon. They had believed that he still lay in the hospital in Vienna! But he was here again, and they would soon see how healthy he was.

"Open the window!" he barked at his Italian servant. "One could suffocate in here! It hasn't been aired out for a year!"

He ordered an evening meal for himself and his nephew. In the meantime he showed Anton his home. It was the former palace of the Turkish Pasha, Mehemed Aga, who had held onto Temesvar for so long that the Banat had been liberated by the Kaiser's troops twenty full years after the lands on the other side of the Danube had been recovered. He had been a courageous heathen. Mercy had had this palace renovated by a Viennese master. The harem's quarters had been converted to a series of guestrooms. The nephew could take two of these rooms for himself—but he might have to watch out for bad dreams. One should be wary in a place where a harem has once been, said the General, but his nephew laughed irreverently.

Jakob Pless stood in the courtyard of his spacious inn as the workers finished and left for the day. He did not yet know who had just driven over the city square. All the workers respectfully greeted the tall man whose bearing was that of a former soldier. He was known to be a strict taskmaster, as he knew something about every trade and exhorted the builders to complete their work without delay. The front wing had been completed first, so that the inn could be opened for business. Now they were working on the stables, the carriage house and the adjoining buildings which were not quite as critical. The landlord had made the plans himself and the foreman in charge of the construction was a soldier from his regiment, a man originally from Pforzheim.

Many compatriots questioned the wisdom of the *Konstabler*, who risked his own and his wife's money on such a great undertaking. His plans for the inn were worthy of Frankfurt or Strassburg, or of an inn on a main postal road of Germany. Jakob Pless did not think he was making a mistake. He firmly believed that this new city had a great future and he was preparing for it. His bright clear eyes lit up with joy, showing that he was satisfied with the work, which had to be finished before the onset of winter. He saw it progress every day, and Therese shared his happiness. Before their first child was born, everything would likely be complete.

Chapter 5 — Count Mercy's Homecoming

Evening came and Pless locked the outer gates to the building site. Then he went into the *Gaststube*,[5] which already had been in business for two months, to light the lamps. "Jakob, Jakob, have you heard?" Therese called out as she came out of the kitchen, her cheeks flushed. "Your General has returned!"

"Governor Mercy?" Jakob exclaimed excitedly as he put a match to the oil lamp which was a new style from Vienna.

"Yes, yes, Josef brought the news."

"Most beautiful hostess, I'd like to kiss you right now," he said, looking at her with eyes full of love and taking her in his arms. She raised her full lips to be kissed.

"Oh, you, you!"

She and Jakob had already been married for two years. She had survived the dangerous trip to Hungary and still loved him as much as the first day they had met. She called him the "Never Satisfied" because he never got enough loving, yet she was thirsty for his kisses too. "Jakob, people are coming!" she said, and pulled away from him.

The evening guests, mostly citizens of Temesvar, arrived and each brought the news: "Mercy is here again!" "The Governor has returned!" Their happiness showed in their faces. Even the officer's table was filled earlier today than at other times. Every table drank a toast to Mercy, and the guests talked about his recent adventures in Italy. New hope seemed to have found its way into discouraged hearts. Life was not easy in the budding city of Temesvar, where their guardian angel had been missing since Mercy had left. The fact that he was now back, a victor and a Count, his good health restored, made the German citizens of Temesvar very happy. The officers were proud of him. They began to sing the Prince Eugene song and all the guests chimed in.

Gretel served beer, just as she had in Blaubeuren where she had first heard that beautiful song. Were they in a foreign land here? Some people might say so, but it did not feel that way to her.

Jakob Pless's new inn had quickly become a favorite among the people, civilians and military officials alike. The *Konstabler* was overjoyed that his benefactor was here again. Mercy had sold the house and land to Jakob at a reasonable price. The twenty eight rooms on the second floor were not yet fully furnished, as the furniture had to be ordered from Vienna. Still, it was presentable and fit to be seen by the Governor. The inn still needed a

---

5 *Gaststube*: the area of the inn where people came to eat and drink.

name. Jakob had a special plan in this regard and wanted the Governor's permission.

This evening, the name of the inn was once again the topic of discussion at the city councillors' table. That the finest guest house far and wide had to have a special name—that, everyone could agree to. City Councillor Andreas Pfann suggested the same name, '*Zum Konstabler*', every time. Peter Mayer was against this, he was for 'The Beautiful Lady'. But Therese was too modest for that. Who would look at her when she was a wrinkled old lady, she asked jokingly. She would have to hide from the guests. Jakob was very annoyed whenever that name was suggested. That was the last thing he needed, he declared. There were already too many men who came to ogle the beautiful hostess. The diners laughed and predicted that it would probably just end up being yet another 'Red Rooster' or 'Brown Deer', but Pless kept silent about his plans.

Herr Peter Solderer, the second Councillor who had joined the reserved table, had called his large store in the Wiener Gasse 'To the Roman Emperor'. He felt that the name had to be something historic. There were already enough Red Oxes, Golden Lions and Black Bears in the world. He felt that if one was lucky enough to found a new business in a new German city, one must put up a sign that would easily convey that this was a new German venture. "Centuries from now, the spirit with which the first German citizens of Temesvar rebuilt the city should be obvious," Solderer said with feeling. He thought 'To the Roman Emperor' was a name which showed the loyalty these citizens had to their homeland.

That notion pleased Jakob Pless. He had attended three years of high school and knew something about history. Many of the ideals that his teachers had preached still lived within him. They had not left him, even during the hard times when he was a soldier. He had never lost his connection with his homeland, and the children he might have, God willing, should also have that connection. Someday, when they were running the inn, they should know that the inn's sign was a shield of honor. He would call his guest house 'To the Seven *Kurfürsten*', if the Governor would allow it. Therese wondered about the name and he explained it to her. "You know," he said to her, "The four lay Electors (*Kurfürsten*) of the Holy Roman Empire have all been here. They fought with us against the Turks and they took part in the liberation of the country. And the first colonists to the Banat came from the lands of the three religious Electors: the Archbishops of Mainz, Cologne and Trier. You know that these Seven Electors have always elected the German Kaiser. May they, we pray, always elect a Kaiser who will save and protect this German

Chapter 5—Count Mercy's Homecoming

settlement so that it will never become Turkish again."

Therese had smiled. She understood. *Base* Gutwein from Regensburg would be happy about that. She was on a first name basis with most of the Electors, if you could believe what she said. Therese felt that these *Kurfürsten* could be like patrons, guardians of this first large German guest house here in the Banat. Jakob told her that he wanted to paint a picture of the Electors on the gable of their inn. However, she was not to talk about this until it was all set. Therese knew how to keep a secret.

Peter Solderer's speech pleased Jakob so much because he had this secret. Even if Solderer had taken 'The Roman Emperor', Pless still could take the '*Sieben Kurfürsten*', those who elected the emperor. Ha ha, Peter had not thought of that, Jakob laughed to himself.

Outside, festive music began to play in honor of the returned Governor. All the guests got up and went to the window. Here and there, little tallow lights were being lit behind windows, as a voluntary lighting of the city in honor of the returned Governor. The public followed a parade of soldiers through the streets to the palace. The pipers played a new march written by one of the trumpeters in honor of the General, and the people called out "*Vivat! Vivat Mercy!*"

When the crowd reached the palace, the Governor stepped onto the balcony and saluted the passing soldiers. The public waved to him and he waved back gratefully. "*Vivat! Vivat Mercy!*" sounded from every street, and more and more windows were lit up in the city.

When the Governor and his companion finally entered the dining room adjacent to the river, a pitcher of red wine and some refreshments awaited them. "Close the window! Close the window!" the Count called out, and his nephew held his nose with his finger in order to avoid the fever-bearing air. "Beastly, what? That comes from the swamps that surround the city. But I will drain and dry them, I swear it," declared Mercy. "The worthy citizens deserve it."

A servant came and cleared the air with a smoking bundle of dried plants. He smiled. Had his Excellency forgotten that in this miserable land one can only open the windows when the sun is shining? Why had he previously asked to have them opened?

The young Captain, Anton Mercy, did not talk much at the table. He was lost in thought. He had followed the advice of his famous uncle and had left the Bavarian army to join the Imperial Forces without misgivings. But why did he have to come here? It was so nice in Vienna. An indescribable longing pulled him toward Vienna. What was it that drew him there? He didn't even know…

The long trip to the Banat had been awful. The boat trip from Vienna to Ofen had been pleasant enough. However, in the last four days, they had driven on land with unimproved roads, through mud and swamps, surrounded by the croaking of millions of frogs, and the horses had been bothered by swarms of flies until they became furious. This he would never forget. Was it worth the trouble to conquer and develop this land?

The uncle sensed his nephew's uncertainty but laughed about it. The young man may have his weaknesses, but the uncle, Klaus Florimund Mercy, was made of stronger stuff than his Bavarian relatives. As a seventeen year old cadet he had fought beside his father in the battle to save Vienna. He had taken part in the storming of Ofen (Buda) and all the battles that followed. He had been in the field for thirty years. Now it was time to partake in another type of battle: the fight to reconstruct the country. It had been neglected for one hundred and fifty years of Turkish occupation and he needed to secure a good future for the German settlers. May God grant him another thirty years so he could devote them to this particular struggle. Then he would have completed his legacy.

The General had come from Vienna, having been given great authority from the Kaiser. This evening he felt more contented than he had in a long time. His officers would not have recognized him in this happy state. The handsome young man beside him, Anton von Mercy, would become his heir and carry on his noble name. It had been easy for him to give his nephew Anton the rank of Captain in Vienna and arrange that he be at his side. He would educate him and familiarize him with his plans. Then, if the General should be called away again, another Mercy would be there to finish his work. He still had not adopted him, but the papers were already prepared in Vienna and were to be a surprise for his nephew. How often he had wished for a son. But he'd never had time to court a bride. Just like his Generalissimo and many other military heros, he remained single. Now he would have an adopted son, an heir. He already had a bride in mind for his nephew.

Anton von Mercy asked his uncle if he was thinking about something pleasant, or if it was the return to his homeland which made him so contented. He pronounced the word homecoming with a derisive tone. The Count disregarded this tone as he sipped the black Turkish coffee with satisfaction. They still did not know how to prepare it in most of Europe; you had to come

Chapter 5—Count Mercy's Homecoming

here if you wanted to taste this precious brew. The nephew had no taste for this thick, hearty liquid.

"Why do I feel so good?" asked Mercy. "Nephew, there are many reasons. One has his memories and dreams. Our family could easily have stayed in Lorraine and planted cabbages. Was it a good spirit that drove us, the owners of huge estates, out of the country to take part in the wars of Europe? My grandfather fell in the battle against the Swedes, his brother against the French, and my father's head was split open by a Turkish sword in Ofen (Buda). Where will the bullet for me be cast? I've always been ready for it to hit me one day. We followed our Duke to Vienna, to the Habsburg Court and pledged ourselves to the Kaiser. But, I often ask myself why we Mercys do not seek a stable life, but are doggedly attracted to the soldiers' profession. Isn't there something more worthwhile to do in this world?" said Mercy.

"For instance, dear uncle?"

"Ah, you too cannot think of anything more important," laughed the Count. "You are a true Mercy." He sipped his coffee until only the dregs were left, and had his cup filled again. Then he crossed his injured left leg over the right one and leaned back. The servant gave each man a *chibuk*, lit the Turkish pipes, and silently disappeared.

"However, I want the name Mercy to be remembered for something different from what my ancestors were known for. I want to become a different Mercy than I have been in the past," said the Governor, puffing with pleasure on his pipe. "I hatched this plan as we lay before this city for six weeks, while the Turks refused to give up, safeguarded by the swamps which helped to protect it. On the 5th of August we had our great battle, the battle of Peterwardein,[6] where they christened me "Crazy Mercy" because I forced my squadron through Turkish regiments and then attacked them again from the rear. It was a crazy move. But it was successful. The Turks had finally received their death blow, even in this province, and were in full retreat. But the city center was still held by the Turks. In Temesvar, Mehemed Aga commanded a good twelve thousand Turkish troops and a regiment of Kurucs."

"Kurucs? Who are they?" the nephew asked.

"You don't know who the Kurucs are?" The Count laughed. "I can tell that you are from Bavaria and still very young. So you didn't know that some of the Magyars joined the Turks and fought against us as we battled to liberate their land? For two hundred years they sided with the Turks against

---

6 In the Battle of Peterwardein (August 5, 1716) at Petrovaradin, (now part of Serbia), 40,000 Austrian troops of Prince Eugene of Savoy defeated 150,000 Ottoman Turks under Pasha Darnad Ali.

the Kaiser. Zapolya, one of their leaders, led Sultan Suleyman toward Vienna in 1529, Tököly did the same with Pasha Kara Mustafa in 1683, and finally their friend Rakoczy with his Kuruc army made it all the way to Vienna a few years ago. The French did not want the House of Habsburg to become too strong after the Kaiser had defeated the Turks, so they gave the Magyar princes the means to wage war against Vienna. The Habsburgs had barely liberated Hungary when the Hungarians sent them their thanks. Hungarian nobles turned against us along with their leader, Rakoczy, when they had to pay liberation taxes." Mercy was in thoughtful silence for a minute, then he continued. "Rakoczy has now fled Hungary and is in exile at the mercy of the Sultan. His troops, my son, are called Kurucs, just like Tököly's troops were. They have been fighting against us as we have liberated their fatherland from the Turks, from Vienna to Belgrade. Here, too."

"Is that how the Magyars are?" asked the young Captain, astonished.

"Not the people! They are not like that! Just the nobility—they never wanted a strong hand to come and create peace and order for their unhappy repressed people. However, we can talk about that another time… what is it that I was talking about?" He puffed again on his *chibuk* so it would not go out.

"You were talking about your plans…"

"Ah yes … I decided to become a different kind of person, a different Mercy than my ancestors. It was when Generalissimo Prince Eugene sent us here: Count von Württemberg with the infantry, Johann Palffy with the cavalry, and I with my light and heavy artillery, which we used at Peterwardein.[7] That is how I became familiar with the land between the three rivers, from Orsova to Arad and up to the borders of Transylvania. The Banat, this land between the Danube, Theiss and Marosch rivers has always been a natural fortification for the Romans, the Goths, the Avars, the Huns, as well as the Turks. But there was never peace in this region.

"So if someone were to convert it to a land of culture, of peaceful civilization, this piece of land would have to be eternally grateful. This is what I told myself as we carried our artillery from the new fortress in Arad and from Lippa on our way to capture Temesvar. Such wild, amazing plant life in the virgin forests of this mild southern climate. This ground has not seen a plow since Roman times. The miserable villages have died out. Wolves live in

---

7 After Prince Eugene and General Mercy's victory at the Battle of Peterwardein, they led their troops to Temesvar, which is in the Banat region of what is now western Romania, and captured that city.

the *Erdhütten*[8] where people used to live. Not one songbird was to be found in the whole country—only vultures circled the air and millions of crows searched for corpses. While our guns spewed fire against the fortress, I confessed my secret wish to the Generalissimo, who had taken over command: I want to be like the roman emporer Trajan[9] to this rundown land after we have conquered it. I will plant the civilization of western and southern Europe here. The army would have to begin this work of peace, and a hundred thousand farmers should complete the work.

"The magnificent Prince smiled at this idea. He did not like to listen to visionaries. But he did listen to me. The first thing he said was, '*O vanita, o vanita!* (Oh vanity!)' The Generalissimo did not think it would be possible to tame this land. He only wanted to conquer it in order to establish militarily safe borders. But the next day he had come around to my way of thinking and stated that my vision was indeed '*una cosa grande*' (a great cause). After all, he was attempting something similar on his own Hungarian properties. He would give further thought to my proposal when he was back in Vienna.

"On September 23, we defeated a troop of Turkish reinforcements who were rushing to Mehemed Aga's aid, and let him know that all his hopes were now dashed. But he would not surrender. Even though he knew that Prince Eugene had conquered stronger fortresses, he proclaimed that it was his duty to defend Temesvar to the last man. He was protected on three sides by swamps. He had only one side to defend and his cannons answered ours very well. The Turks did not seem to lack provisions. If an early winter came, we would be powerless. Our best hope to conquer the city was to set it ablaze with nonstop cannonfire. So we got all our heavy guns together. We bombarded the city for three days and three nights and took the suburb of Palanka. We blasted holes into the city walls. On the fourth day Mehemed Aga raised the white flag. He realized that his defense was useless. Since the entire land surrounding the city had fallen, he must also give up its center. But honorably, not otherwise. The Prince said he would allow the defeated troops to leave in honor. That was not good enough, Aga replied. The Kurucs who fought with him must be allowed to accompany his army to Belgrade. At this, the Prince laughed aloud, because we had not even known that

---

8 *Erdhütte*: a house that was underground for the most part with very short stamped earth walls protruding, and a roof atop. South Slavic peoples lived in these types of houses during the Ottoman occupation. They were inexpensive and adapted to their lifestyle, which was often nomadic since they mostly raised animals.

9 Trajan was a roman emporer from 98 to 117 AD. He is best known for his extensive public building program which reshaped the city of Rome.

Rakoczy's people were here, too, fighting against us. The Prince asked for a pen to sign the surrender agreement."

"He signed it?" the nephew cried.

"More than that, my son. He wrote in the margin with a firm hand '*La Canaglia puo andare dove vuole: Eugenio von Savoy.*' (The rogues may go wherever they want.) These words made the rounds throughout the army and were also repeated in Vienna by the messenger who delivered the news of the fall of Temesvar."

The Captain laughed. "*La Canaglia!*"

"After the signing of the treaty, gifts were exchanged. The Pasha sent the Prince two snow white stallions and other gifts. He gave me a sword with a golden handle which I will show you tomorrow. In return, the Prince gave the Pasha a golden watch that announced the hour, which the Pasha thought was a wonder. The Turk had never seen anything like it. Our officers joked around that when it strikes it will remind him that the time has come for them to leave."

"And the country was free?"

The count nodded. "These last Turks went through Pantschowa to Belgrade, and the Kurucs with them. A year later we beat them once more in Belgrade."

"And in Temesvar? What happened here?"

"We entered the City of Temesvar on October 18, 1716. It was in a dreadful state. We celebrated the fifty-third birthday of our Generalissimo beside a smoking pile of rubble. He soon went to his winter quarters in Vienna and turned its command over to me. When he departed, he promised to tell the Kaiser of my *cosa grande* (great cause). He offered me his full support, and he kept his word. Now I am Governor with discretionary powers and have a free hand to do with this land whatever I wish. I want to transform it to look like Lorraine, Alsace, Champagne, or the *Rheinpfalz*."

The Captain looked at him, stunned. "Where will you get the people from?"

"From there, from precisely the regions I just referred to! There are already a few hundred families here. Thousands more will come, tens of thousands!"

"Now I understand. From the lost or half lost territories of the Kaiser, the people still loyal to the Kaiser will be brought here?"

"Yes, yes! Do you now understand that I am a new Mercy, with a new vision?" he called out cheerfully. "That 'Crazy Mercy' has now been destroyed and like a phoenix from his ashes, a new Angel of Peace will arise. The

Angel of Peace with the lame leg!"

"Dear uncle," the Captain said warmly, "It is not for nothing that I studied civil engineering in Bavaria. My technical knowledge will help in the rebuilding of this region. If I do not die in this climate, I want to become your assistant!"

"Bravo, my nephew! Those are the first intelligent words which you have spoken since we left Vienna. I thought you had not only left your heart behind in Vienna, but also your head."

And he leaned over to his nephew, who was blushing like a girl at this last sentence, and sealed their agreement with a firm handshake.

Chapter 6

The Governor's Audience Day

A gray autumn morning lay over the city; the sun could not break through the fog that came from the swamps. But the front of the Governor's mansion was bustling with activity as the delegates stood in line for an audience with the Governor. The military was given first priority. Then came the Catholic clergy. The servants knew exactly in which order they were to be presented, and they explained it to Mercy's nephew, the Captain, since as adjutant he would need to know this. First came the Jesuits, next the Franciscans and then the local pastor. Only after the City Council and mayor had been seen would the Serbian Eastern Orthodox priests be admitted. Then came the *Knes*, the Serbian mayor of Palanka, which was the Serbian suburb of Temesvar. Next came the Rabbi, head of the Sephardic Spanish Jews. And so on.

The military dignitaries courteously greeted the Count. They gave reports about the security and problems of the city and its surroundings, the terrible health of the troops, the progress of the construction of the fortress and of the new barracks in which Mercy wanted enough room to house three regiments.

"No money, no money," they reported. The Governor had good news for them. The construction could continue with a renewed tempo. Mercy had received funds, even enough to build an armory to house their artillery. He had hired a French master builder for the construction of the fortress who would begin his work in the spring. Mercy announced all this in his loud trumpet-like voice. Also, two hundred kilograms of quinine were on the way to relieve the fever among the troops. Tell the doctors not to be stingy with the medicines, Mercy ordered.

The Provincial Superior of the Jesuits, Lorenz Pez, came with another priest. Count Mercy saw them for the first time, they were new. He asked them to be seated and was eager to hear what they had to say. He had arranged for them to be called to the Banat because the Jesuits were considered to be the best teachers and the most eager promoters of the school system.

"Respectable Lord, we have come to ask for your Grace's protection in this city," the Superior, a dark, lean monk, said humbly. "We were asked to take over the large mosque with its neighboring premises. With God's help, we would like to turn it into a seminary for our order, but we will need a new roof and a church tower. In this neglected, uncultured city where so many different people and religions have come together, we have a difficult task ahead of us. In order for religious principles to take hold in the city, the full rigor of ecclesiastical authority will be required, and even the military force will need to bow before this authority."

"Hmm…" Count Mercy was noncommittal.

The Provincial Superior continued, "It will be necessary, Respectable Lord, that you choose a personal confessor in order to set a good example. We would be honored if your Grace would choose one of the Jesuits as your spiritual guide."

"Excuse me," the Count said. "The parish priest has taken my confessions quite satisfactorily up to now, and we also have an army chaplain. I feel closer to them."

The Superior bowed and smiled humbly, although his expression showed his disappointment. He went on, "In this city there is still no sacred statue. We are very bewildered by that and ask for the money to erect two statues. We want to dedicate our seminary with a statue of the Virgin Mary. The first statue must be for her, we need a pilgrimage destination for Roman Catholic believers. Also, we need bells for the church; beautiful chimes would be an ornament for the city."

"Most esteemed Fathers, for that I regrettably have no money. Be patient and wait until your community is bigger and more prosperous, then you can collect the money from the believers. But if you would like to erect a school where the skills of reading, writing and arithmetic are taught, I will do my best to support you."

"Oh, that will be coming soon!" exclaimed the Provincial Superior's companion, but the Superior amended his words with the observation, "First we must lay the religious groundwork in the city, Your Excellency."

"Yes, yes, this must be established." Mercy stood up. "Well, go ahead and work on that, my esteemed Fathers, and I will do what I can."

The Provincial Superior saw that it was time to go; after all, many others were waiting to see the Governor, but he still had something on his mind. He remained standing before the Governor and looked into his big brown eyes.

"Respectable Lord, I have another question to ask you and must report the answer to Rome."

"So ask, Father," replied Mercy earnestly.

"What will happen to this land between the three rivers?"[1] the Superior asked. "Does it belong to Hungary and will St. Stephen[2] be its patron here as well? Or is this another province? If it is not part of the Kingdom of Hungary, then this God-forsaken land shouldn't be without a patron saint for even one more day. We cannot be without an advocate in heaven. The Holy Father in Rome can assign us a patron."

"This land," said Mercy, emphasizing every word, "belongs to the Kaiser. Even before it fell to the Turks, it belonged to Peter Petrovich[3] and not to the King of Hungary. Now it is a liberated land, a land where not one Magyar lives. In any case, there is room for a new patron in this region. If the Holy Father will give us a saint, we will immediately erect a statue in his honor."

"We thank you," said the Provincial, and both Jesuits bowed deeply before the Governor. They went away satisfied.

Count Mercy smiled after them. After all, they were working for the Lord. He thought, 'May they bring the grace of a new saint to this land. It certainly could use the intercession of its own patron. St. Stephen has enough to accomplish on the other side of the Marosch River.'

A poor bent old man with a flowing white beard stood on the threshold, a barefoot mendicant wearing a hair shirt, a rope tied at his waist.

The Governor walked toward him. "Herr Quardian, you are welcome here," he said, shook his hand and led him to a chair. The monk nodded his bald head thankfully and sat down.

"Excellency," the old man whispered with an Italian accent, "I just want to show you that I am still living, but not for long, oh no! Very happy, Excellency is in good health. Excellency will help make this land Christian again. *Gratia! Gratia!* Happiness great."

Count Mercy nodded his thanks. He had known Francesco Quardian, a Franciscan monk, for a long time. Amazingly, his Order had survived the one hundred and sixty four year Turkish occupation in this city. The Pashas had

---

1 He is referring to the Banat, which is bordered by the Danube, Theiss and Marosch Rivers.
2 Saint Stephen (975–1038) was the first king of Hungary. He successfully Christianized the majority of Magyars (Hungarians) and is the patron saint of Hungary.
3 Count Peter Petrovich of Temesvar, thought to be of Serb descent, was appointed commander of the Banat in the 16th century by Sultan Suleyman after the Turks took over.

Chapter 6—The Governor's Audience Day

tolerated this cloister in their midst, since it was so small that it never housed more than three or four monks at a time. Their church had been changed into a mosque and the monks were only allowed one prayer room to practice their religion. This had been enough, since the Christian community had slowly died out. At the end there were not even two dozen Christians left in this fortress city, and the cloister, which had not received new monks from outside the city for over a century, was on the verge of extinction. A lay brother, an old monk and the almost one hundred year old Quardian were the last of their flock.

"I am grateful that you made the effort to come see me," said Mercy. "How are you? Are you doing well?"

"No, no," the old man sighed.

"You look healthy—better than you did four years ago."

"Thank you, thank you… this is because I am happy… no more crescent moon … crosses everywhere. Jesuits do good work … I am old, Pater Vitus is old. No one comes to us. Forgotten! Forgotten!" Quardian said wistfully in his broken German.

"Haven't you written to Rome, Herr Quardian? To remind them of your existence here?"

"No, no…I cannot write, Pater Vitus cannot. Poor, forgotten, turkish Franciscans…"

"I will have someone write a letter for you," suggested Mercy.

"No, no! Then have to go away to the poor house. No, no… want to die here. *Prego*, do not write… when we dead, Excellency start a new monastery. Bring young monks in… Please, let us stay," whimpered the old man as he stood up to leave.

"I will be happy to, Herr Quardian. May you live in peace," said the Governor as he escorted the old man to the door. He went to his desk and wrote: 'Let the Piarist Order know that the old Franciscan monastery and church will be available for them soon. Request German monks.'

In the meantime, the new assistant announced the *Stadtpfarrer* (parish priest).

Johann Wunderer, a portly man with a cheerful demeanor, entered.

"My highest compliments, your Grace," he said. "My sincerest congratulations, Count Mercy!"

"Thank you, thank you, *Herr Stadtpfarrer*," said Mercy. "You are thriving here, I see."

"Yes," the other laughed. "One performs his duty."

"How is the church community doing?" asked the Count as he offered his guest a seat.

"It is growing, it is growing! We will need a new church soon, your Excellency."

"*Herr Stadtpfarrer*, you will be happy to hear that I thought of you when I was in Vienna. There the great architect, Fischer von Erlach, is building a new church which will be dedicated to Saint Karl Borromäus. It will be a masterpiece. I was with him when he explained his plans to the Kaiser. And I thought to myself, if we could only have a church in Temesvar built by this man! I could not dismiss this thought. Before I departed Vienna, I went to see him again, accompanied by *Hofkammerrat* von Stephany. *Herr Stadtpfarrer*, he promised me that he would draw plans for a cathedral here in Temesvar! This will be for you, for your parish. The cathedral will be built in the town square."

"A thousand thanks, gracious Count, I am most moved. I only hope to live to see it!"

"I am not too worried about that," the Count laughed. "But now tell me, Reverend, are people marrying diligently, are children being born, is your congregation growing from the inside?"

At this, the jovial priest became serious. "Your Excellency," he responded, "I have nothing good to report in this regard. Last year, I baptized only sixty children, but buried five hundred people."

"What!" cried Mercy in amazement. "Did we have the plague here?"

"Absolutely not. Just the swamp fever, which we've always had."

"That is appalling! ... but didn't you just tell me that your congregation is growing?"

"Yes, because of more people immigrating here. But there are not enough women arriving, not enough German girls."

The Count quickly walked to his desk and made a note of this information. He said to the priest, "From now on we will only accept married couples. Every man must bring a wife with him."

He walked back from his desk, but did not sit down again. The *Stadtpfarrer* stood up as well.

"Has the *Stadtkommandant* ordered you to perform any more marriages?"

"No, no." The priest smiled. "And the Jesuits already converted the couple that I married. They are now Catholic."

"So everything is in order? Not a single lost sheep in the entire city?"

"Not quite! We still have one Protestant couple. But the army chaplain married them, not me."

Chapter 6 — The Governor's Audience Day

"Oh? I suppose now we'll have to wait for the Jesuits to do their work!"

"Yes, indeed!" the *Stadtpfarrer* heartily agreed. As he was leaving, he commented, "Your Excellency, I am very much looking forward to the new cathedral. Many, many thanks!"

In the meantime, the governor's nephew had entered a lively discussion with the town council representatives. Just the sight of these German men did Captain Anton Mercy some good. Hearing their Swabian, Bavarian and Frankfurt dialects, all mingled together, really lifted his spirits. Their clothes were a sampling of southern German traditional dress from various areas, and each had his hair done differently, but they shared the same blue eyes and open countenances. How good it was to see German people in this remote wilderness!

The Captain announced the following visitors to his uncle: "Mayor Tobias Balthasar Hold, his deputy Peter Solderer, City Councilors Andreas Pfann and Peter Mayer, and Herr Notary Erling."

Hold, who as *Stadtrichter* was the mayor and municipal judge, carried a long staff made of dark ebony, with a silver knob and a gold silk tassel, as a sign of his honorable office. He held his three-cornered hat in his right hand, the staff in the left, and strode forward. He bowed deeply in front of the Governor, and the others, who were standing in a row one step behind him, bowed as well.

"Respectable Lord," said Tobias Hold, "the German City Council of Temesvar brings you reverent greetings. We would like to profess our great joy over your Grace's safe homecoming and remain always at your Grace's service. We have come to express our congratulations and to receive your Grace's orders."

"I thank you, *Herr Stadtrichter*, and all of you, gentlemen of the Council, that you have come," was the Count's simple and heartfelt reply. "We all know each other already, and we will be working together to bring the city out of the unfortunate disastrous condition which it is still in." Turning to Hold, he said, "I am pleased that you have been called upon to head this community again. You were the first German mayor of this city and performed your duty in the most difficult of times. This has not been forgotten in Vienna. May you carry on the work, *Herr Stadtrichter*, as you have in past years."

"Oh, Excellency!" Tobias Hold responded deprecatingly. "My fellow citizens have once again put their trust in me and I am eager to earn it. My young deputy, the valiant Peter Solderer, is a great support."

"Does the Council have any requests or grievances?" asked the governor.

"Please inform me of everything."

"Excellency, we do not want to take up the first few hours that you are back with our hardships. Our list of requests has grown rather long in His Excellency's absence," said Hold.

"For example, *Herr Stadtrichter*?"

"All right, then. Hm." The mayor cleared his throat and said firmly, "Are we a German municipality, Excellency?"

"Yes, that you are," responded the Governor. "The Generalissimo ordered that this Fortress be populated with German Catholics. All other peoples were to move to the outlying areas. Has this changed? I would hope not."

"Excellency, the Serbs are demanding the same rights as the Germans. It is a constant conflict. Their *Knes* in Palanka and the Serbian clergy are stirring up trouble against the Germans. We fear for our lives in this fortress city."

"You must be exaggerating, *Herr Stadtrichter!*"

"No, no," some of the men mumbled quietly.

"He's telling the truth!" Andreas Pfann called out in his Swabian dialect.

"I will look into the matter," responded Count Mercy earnestly. "So, that was a grievance. What are your requests?"

"We need help in a hundred small areas, Excellency. To help us build a city hall, laborers from the army and bricks from Vienna. A place near the city wall to build a juvenile detention house; there are too many rascals here. And drinking water, Excellency, clean drinking water! A spring has been discovered in the outskirts of the city, near the factories. Our bridge builders are so skilled, we want them to fashion pipes out of tree trunks and construct a water main that leads to the town square. If we don't get fresh water, we will all die here."

"I can appreciate your eagerness in this regard," Mercy replied. "That will be done. Gentlemen, that's a promise to you. My new assistant, my nephew, has some training as an engineer. He will build your water main." They all thanked him wholeheartedly.

But he continued to ask them, "What else?" and they set forth their requests, point by point. One of them was this: people could not have money sent from the homeland since it wasn't secure and was so far away. The Notary Erling had an idea. Up to now, nobody had wanted to pursue his plan but with the backing of the Governor, it would be as good as done.

"So, explain your idea to me!" said Mercy.

Erling cleared his throat. "Excellency, I submissively make this sugges-

Chapter 6—The Governor's Audience Day

tion: There are many offices spread throughout the German Reich and in Vienna, and even here, where the Kaiser's soldiers go to get their pay. The money could be brought to one paymaster's office and paid out at another."

"What, would it be that simple?" asked the Count thoughtfully. The attorney attested to this. And yet it couldn't be that straightforward, Mercy mused. "I can't approve of simple transfers without some kind of safeguard in place, otherwise all kinds of things could happen. I will look into it." He wrote himself a note. Certainly, this was a good possibility. Why shouldn't the soldier's pay offices be used to transfer money? There must be a way to do this securely.

Then the Governor wanted to know if business and commerce had increased.

"No," replied Peter Solderer. "The amount of business we had in the first few years was misleading due to the large army stationed here. Now that there are less military people, we can tell how isolated this city really is. No one comes to market; both sellers and buyers are lacking. Sometimes it seems like we are living at the end of the earth."

"That will change in the next ten years!" the Count exclaimed. "And in twenty years it will be like Augsburg or Nürnberg here. Big things will happen here. Every one of you should write to your homeland and exhort your friends to come here! We need German people! Married couples with children! Because I fear that too many others will come when the Kaiser calls. After all, the Kaiser has Italian and Spanish subjects, too. German people should come to the area surrounding this city and settle all the way up to the border of Transylvania and also on over to Belgrade—farmers and merchants should hasten over here. Then this city will have what it is missing! We need German plows and German mothers! Ask your friends to come!"

"Your Excellency! We respectfully request your leave, so that we can impart this wonderful message to the entire city council," Tobias Hold said with deep feeling.

"Adieu, good sirs. God be with you in your work!"

The Governor shook everyone's hand. None had ever seen this fearsome soldier exhibit such open humanity and generosity. It truly seemed to be the beginning of a new age for this much-tried city. The governor stood at his desk and wrote himself notes about everything that had been discussed, point by point, just key words in writing that was barely legible to someone else. His nephew alerted him that the Serbian priests would like to be admitted. Should he put their audience off for another day?

No, no, he felt ready to meet them now. But they should bring their *Knes* from Palanka with them, as well. Why so many individual audiences?

The black-bearded Serbians entered. They looked a bit coarse for priests, but were dignified and manly. The stout *Knes*, the mayor of the suburb Palanka, stood behind them. They greeted the Governor in Serbian. But then the senior priest continued in Latin, which was much better. Mercy had learned that language thoroughly in the Jesuit school in Vienna.

They aired their grievances against the administration of the city. The Serbs had been here before the Germans. This land had belonged to their voivode,[4] Peter Petrovich; Zapolya had sold it to him. The Serbs had lived within the city walls during the Turkish occupation, no Pasha had banished them. That hadn't happened until Prince Eugene, the highly praised conquerer, had come.

The Count was greatly incensed by this speech, and he gave an order for silence in a voice like none had ever heard. "Because these Serbs became so degenerate in the hundred sixty years of Turkish occupation and slavery, the Generalissimo could not build up this community with them and could not entrust any imperial fortress to their stewardship. Become civilized human beings, and we can talk about your rights!" he thundered at them. "For now, the suburb of Palanka will have to be good enough for you. I will impose martial law on the city of Temesvar and in Palanka, and woe to any who cause unrest or disturbs the peace! You fought against us, just like the Kurucs, and your earlier rights have been nullified by that. There was no mention of you in the agreement with Mehemed Aga! So what do you want?"

As his forceful voice resounded in the hall, the group of Spanish Jews who were waiting outside took flight. Their rabbi said that they would come another time.

But the Serbian priest did not allow himself to be intimidated. He bent his shaggy head and let the tirade just go over him. He knew that temperamental people who made such outbursts tended to calm down and were ready to talk rationally after a while.

"Mighty Lord," he said, "my unhappy people do not deserve your condemnation. Age-old rights do not just go away. The Turks were harsh to our people, we were their slaves. They lived in our fathers' houses. Now that the Turks are gone, to whom do those houses belong?"

"Not houses, barracks!"

"All right, then. To whom do the barracks belong? We request and

---

4 Voivode: a military commander or governor of a town or province in various Slavic countries.

Chapter 6—The Governor's Audience Day

demand to be allowed back into the inner city. We ask that we can at least live within the city walls as a minority. The Swabians, who of course are like half Gods compared to us, can be the majority; we want to learn from them and not be subservient like we were under the Turks. We too believe in Jesus Christ."

Count Mercy looked into the speaker's glittering eyes and was silent. Then he asked the priest his name.

"Father Joannes."

Mercy wrote the name down and added the words 'set up another meeting later.' Then he turned back to the group and declared: "I have listened to your opinion, Father Joannes, and you have heard mine. Perhaps in the future these might converge. Your people should learn the German language, and prove your rights to your possessions here in the city. I am here to assure that every subject of the Kaiser gets what is rightfully his. But woe to anyone who causes trouble in this city!"

The Serbians left, satisfied with this statement. Not all hope had been taken from them; on the contrary, there was the possibility of a new beginning.

"Is anyone else in the waiting room?" asked the Governor.

The Captain declared that one more was waiting for an audience: Herr Jakob Pless, the owner of the new Guest House in the main square.

"My *Konstabler*? Good Jakob Pless from Ulm? Let him in! He shot well and accurately for me at Peterwardein and here. Every shot met its mark. He is more than welcome to see me!" cried the Governor.

Chapter 7

The Kurucs[1]

"What's this mandate from Vienna about?" Baron Parkoczy shouted at the portly gray haired man who had just entered the room. "Notary, what am I supposed to verify? Translate this for me!"

The Notary from Mohács, Julius Martonffy, wished the stern Baron so many good mornings that they would last for many days, but even this extravagant greeting did not placate Parkoczy. "What does this say?" the Baron ranted. He pressed the document, which was the cause of his rage, into the Notary's hands. Then he ripped open the window and yelled into the courtyard to the dog, "Quiet, Caraffa, quiet!" so forcefully that the dog immediately stopped barking.

Martonffy had guessed that the document contained something important, since he had been brought to the castle in Dobok not by an ox-cart as usual, but by the Baron's horse-drawn carriage. He took a deep breath before he answered. His response to the Baron, who tended to be loud and forceful, was to calmly look around for a place to sit. Taking a seat at a bulky table, he spread the papers before him.

"Respectable Lord," he replied. "This is a decree from the Hungarian Council in Vienna. What part of it should I translate?"

The Baron looked at him menacingly. "Do you know Latin or don't you? Don't you see that this document is not written in Latin, but in a language which we speak but cannot read? What is going on at the *Hofkanzlei*? Do they want to make the language our farmers use into a written language? Such a patchwork of new words which no one in my house understands, not my sons, nor my wife. On the other hand, she claims to understand enough of

---

1 Kurucs were Magyars (Hungarians) who fought with the Turks against the Habsburgs.

this drivel to know that I have to verify something. Damn it, what is it? Why didn't they write to me in Latin?"

In the meantime the Notary had begun to work. As the Baron lit up his *chibuk*, his Turkish pipe, and paced back and forth in the hall, the little man from Mohács tried his best to translate the document to Latin from the national language. This was new to him as well, that the Hungarian *Hofkammer* in Vienna wrote documents in the Hungarian language. 'There must be some kind of nut in charge of that office,' he thought to himself.

The Baron's step became quicker and quicker and his face grew redder and redder as he paced the narrow room. From time to time he drank from a pewter mug that stood on the table. He seemed to be overcome with a great restlessness.

"Come on, haven't you gotten to the important part yet?"

Keeping his mind on the pages before him, Martonffy waved him off. He did not allow the Baron to distract him. There were multiple pages of text and he, too, was not familiar with the written Hungarian language. He understood Turkish better.

The Baron had an inkling as to the contents of the document. He knew that some property owners in the Baranya and Tolnau Counties had been called to account. They had to prove their ownership of their property. Two had been chased away. Their properties had been surveyed by those foreign devils, the Kaiser's engineers who seemed to be all over the place and were accompanied by the Kaiser's foot soldiers.

Had the Turks been chased away so that Bohemian or German tracking dogs could sniff out the properties that had belonged to the Hungarian nobility for ages? Shouldn't they be happy that the properties have masters again? What do those foreigners know about our national customs? What do they know about who is a lord here? Here, the masters are not those who possess the most acres of land, but those who possess the most serfs. There is plenty of land here, but not enough people. The Kaiser's men better not come to him, the Baron! He'll chase the imperial usurpers away. They talk of a liberation tax! Ha, ha, ha! Who should pay such a tax? He would knock the heads off those who demanded anything from him. He picked up the mug once again, to drink to that thought.

Martonffy the Notary now raised his voice. "Your Grace, please sit down. I will read the document in Latin." He ceremonially began to read. *"In nomine Patris et Filii et Spiritus Sancti. Amen.* I, Karl III, the King of Hungary by God's grace…"

"Go to hell!" shouted Baron Parkoczy. "You can read this introduction to a peasant but not to a Colonel of Tököly's army.[2] But go on, go on."

Martonffy did not allow himself to be hurried or frightened. He continued to read,

" 'The Kaiser and King demands that Stephan von Parkoczy, in the name of Holy Trinity, prove his right to the property in Dobok, Apar and St. Marton which he currently occupies, since there is no record of the Parkoczy family ever owning these properties. For over150 years they were incorporated under the jurisdiction of the Turkish pashalic of Mohács. Only the castle Parkoczy with five uninhabited villages are on record as having belonged to this family. The three great properties, measuring twelve square miles, which Parkoczy claims as his, are to be vacated in three months if no title naming Parkoczy as owner can be found.' " The letter continued, asserting that the three castles, Dobok, Apar and St. Marton had been taken from the Turks by the Kaiser's troops led by Margrave von Baden. The Parkoczys certainly had not helped to liberate this property, as no Parkoczy had been in the Imperial Army. That noble name had been regarded as having died out. Parkoczy was to report to the Hungarian Council in Vienna without delay and give evidence of his claim to the property. Otherwise, by default, it would be handed to the Imperial Commission as public property and settled by colonists.

Parkoczy sat, speechless and red-faced, as Martonffy read to him with great pleasure.

"Read it again!" the Baron demanded and Martonffy read it again while Parkoczy paced back and forth, stamping the floor.

"Just let them come," Parkoczy shouted. "They will have to reconquer Dobok. We have an arsenal of weapons: Thirty swords, one hundred shotguns and two Turkish cannons. Let them come, these robbers," he stormed. "Let them try to take what belongs to us. There will be bloody heads! I reconquered these properties with Tököly. Understand?"

The Notary let the Baron have his tantrum and listened calmly to his tirade. Then he remarked dryly, "With that statement you have proven nothing. Quite the opposite, actually."

"How, what?"

"Your Excellency will have the grace to show me all your pertinent family papers."

"Not now! Do they believe that I am a false claimant like some others? It is for them to prove that I am in the wrong. How can I prove anything?

---

2 The Kurucs did not recognize the Habsburgs as King of Hungary. Our fictional Baron fought with Imre Tököly, who led a kuruc rebellion against the Habsburgs from 1678-83, and in a second kuruc rebellion under Ferenc II Rakoczy, which was 1703-1711. (See Appendix.)

Chapter 7—The Kurucs

Can I resurrect my ancestors who were killed by the Turks? Hm? Can I do that? They can look for my papers over there, in the burnt-out castle of the Parkoczys."

"So you do not have any proof, Your Excellency?" asked Martonffy.

"Who says that?!" the Baron roared. "I will get the documentation if I must. Some papers may be with my cousin Banffy in Transylvania. That's where my family stayed when we fled during the Turkish occupation. Didn't they realize that people had to leave during the occupation? It's not like Margrave von Baden called us here to help him. We were in Transylvania, where the Hungarians belonged. At first we were with Tököly and then with Rakoczy. Now that the Turks are gone, we are back again and no Imperial Council will drive us away. Isn't this supposed to be peacetime? You can't call this peace! We were safer during Turkish times. But wait, I will be back." Parkoczy then went to the inside of the castle, opening the dilapidated door through which the wind blew even when it was closed.

Martonffy, the old Notary, looked after him contemptuously. He, too, was descended from the landed gentry, from a family of landowners who had lost everything during Turkish times. But nobody knew about that anymore. He didn't even know where his family's property had been. He was childless and had accepted his lot in life. He made a good living as a notary, but he was not indifferent to the suffering of his fatherland. In his lifetime, he and his family always felt as if they lived in Turkey, not Hungary. His grandfather and father had lived in Mohács as craftsmen, and they had practically become Turks. He himself spoke better Turkish than Hungarian. If Duke Karl von Lothringen had not come in 1687 and reconquered Mohács and all the counties on this side of the Danube, Martonffy would have become a Turkish Janisary instead of a Hungarian Notary. The Bishop of Pécs (Fünfkirchen) had taken him under his wing and had him educated as a lawyer. The Bishop was an early sponsor of German settlement and had promoted the education of priests, teachers and officials because he knew that the Swabians[3] would need them. That's how the young Martonffy obtained a position working for the diocese. Unfortunately, he never got possession of his family's former property. Nobody knew about it anymore. What could he do?

In these confusing times, people with a good knowledge of the law were needed and he was one of them. Some individuals' level of affluence grew wildly; former Pandurs[4] became big-time landowners. They just took the

---

3 Recall that Swabian refers to any settlers who came from Germany.
4 Pandurs: armed and liveried servants of Hungarian noblemen.

land. No one could hinder them; strength is what ruled. But now law and order were being restored. Prince Eugene had called Notary Martonffy to Bellye after the Kaiser awarded the Generalissimo a princely estate. Viennese officials needed someone who was knowledgeable about the land and its people and who was familiar with Hungarian laws, before they started to re-settle the land.

What a large tract of land had been given to Prince Eugene—a fifteen square mile area! However, all the serfs had been taken away as slaves to Turkey and there was no one left to plant or bring in a harvest. Virgin forests, ridges and hills ready to be planted with grapes, vast fields for crops—scattered among these were abandoned, burnt out villages, where the *Erdhütten* used to be occupied by Turks and Tatars. Few of the indigenous peoples remained; here and there one found Cumans[5] living in animal-like conditions, Serbian refugees, and Gypsies. To record and certify all this as Notary was the job assigned to Martonffy. It had been an unhappy task ... This is what his fatherland had become? What a tragedy!

But then he observed German immigrants who came down the Danube year after year and passed through Mohács to Bellye where thirty-five villages had been laid out for settlement. Martonffy, the Notary of the Prince, certified their settlement passes, helped them find lodging and showed them the way to their new homesteads. He made good money at it. These were splendid men, red-cheeked blond women, families with many children—and most did not come empty handed. Some farmers brought agricultural equipment with them, and craftsmen brought tools. The women and girls carried huge packages, but they were light because they were comforters stuffed with feathers. A few families came by land, bringing their own horses and wagons.

And only two years later, Martonffy already saw many of them with their products in the markets of Mohács, Fünfkirchen and Szekszard. People were surprised by the Swabians' products, by what they could grow in what was once called "The *Hinterland*." Prince Eugene had known what this earth was worth. Others had known it too. But did Baron Parkoczy even think of doing the same thing? He and his sons lived like wild men on these immeasurably large properties, worse than the Turks, and oppressed whomever they could. It could be that they had never owned this property and didn't belong here. That could very well be.

The Baron finally came back. "Here is your proof, so that you didn't

---

5 Cuman: a Turkic people who occupied parts of southern Russia and the Moldavian and Wallachian steppes during the 9th, 10th and 11th centuries and were driven out by the Tatar and Mongol invasions and some of whom passed into Hungary where they were absorbed.

come all the way over here for nothing. This is for Dobok, this for Apar and this is for St. Marton!" He laid out three Latin documents in front of the Notary.

Martonffy curiously picked them up. Parkoczy noted how quickly he paged through the document and how his face gradually showed his disappointment. "Your Excellency, these papers are useless. All they say is that ten years ago you applied for possession for these properties. Nothing else."

"Well, what else do you want? When the order was published requesting that families report the loss of their property, I put in my application. The county acknowledged this. An ancestor of mine was a top official here, for heaven's sake!"

"Respectable Lord, you will have to travel to Transylvania to get the other documents," said Martonffy and shrugged his shoulders.

"You pen pushers! Go hack each other's eyes out!" the Baron shouted angrily. "What do the people in Vienna think that I am, a robber?"

Martonffy looked smartly into the angry face of the Baron and said, "Perhaps they noticed that the Baron's family is in possession of three very large properties, all of which border one another, which is something that doesn't happen very often."

"Ever since Árpád,[6] Grand Prince of the Magyars, settled the Magyar people in this region 800 years ago, our family has possessed property here. Three Parkoczy brothers lived on these three properties, side by side."

"Respectable Lord, I am convinced of that," the Notary said flatteringly, "but that should be provable somewhere."

"Who knows, who knows."

"What about Castle Parkocz?" asked the Notary.

"The burnt out little castle Parkocz? Do you want me to move back there? That was our ancestral home. Later it became a home for the widows."

"Very convincing, your Honor. But is this documented?"

"That is the unwritten tradition of our house. No one in our family ever bothered with writing. They relied on the sword."

A pale, tall lady entered the room. Her appearance was almost youthful; but her earnest face, which looked rather careworn, betrayed her age. "Here you are, my dear wife," said Parkoczy and went toward her.

The Notary stood up and bowed in reverence.

"*Bonjour, bonjour*, Martonffy," said the Baroness, but her dark eyes lin-

---

6 Árpád led the Hungarians in crossing the Carpathian mountains to settle the Pannonian, or Hungarian, Plain in 896 and was Grand Prince of the Magyars c. 895–907.

gered on the heated face of her spouse. She appeared to be deeply concerned because her husband looked so agitated.

"You had guessed correctly as to the contents of this dogged paper, my dear Helene. Should the Notary read it to you?"

"*O merci*," she said in a dismayed tone. "When I look at your face, I know everything. Well, this has also happened to other families. What can we do about it, Herr Notary?"

"We need written evidence of ownership, gracious Baroness."

"We will defend ourselves with our weapons," Parkoczy cried out in a loud voice. "Let them come! I can fight! I remember how I fought before."

The Baroness looked at him scathingly. "What?! You need to let go of that notion. This problem will not be solved by force!"

"I will travel to my brother-in-law in Banffy to search for documents. He often said that we had claims on this property."

The Baroness stood there thoughtfully. A ray of sunshine came through the window, lighting up the worry lines on her face. She came from a proud family. She was born as Countess Erdödy and still was an Erdödy, despite her married name. She had many influential relatives and it must be possible to resolve this.

"How much time will they give us?" she asked softly.

"Three months, gracious Baroness, but that time will be extended if you are looking for the documents."

"Well, then there is time enough to travel to Vienna."

"To Vienna!?" Parkoczy shouted. "Not I, never!"

"Dear Stephan, then you will allow me to go right away," the Baroness said pointedly.

Astonished, the Baron asked, "Are you serious?"

"I see no other way. I have to get involved once more," was her sharp reply.

Martonffy understood none of this but applauded the Baroness for her effort. "That is very good, Your Grace, very good. Vienna is a good place to go to take care of these matters. They love the new Hungarian territory."

The enraged look on the Baron's face silenced the Notary. However, the Baron swallowed the retort that was on the tip of his tongue because his wife gave him a peculiar look. Finally he spoke: "We will not need your services for this matter, Herr Notary. We will not send written evidence back with you, we will not use force, instead we are going to petition Vienna directly."

The Baroness smiled at his statement but said nothing.

Suddenly, an unruly looking young man ran into the hall, his rifle on his

Chapter 7—The Kurucs

back.

"Papa, Papa," he called out, "two wolves and a boar!" He set the gun behind the door and hurriedly dragged the two wolves into the room.

"Andor, Andor," his mother cried. "Slow down!"

A tall young man who had the beginnings of a mustache on his upper lip appeared behind Andor, carrying a gun over his shoulder. He laughed heartily over his brother's impetuousness and then dragged another animal into the room. It was the wild boar.

The Baron was proud of his sons' hunting skills. He congratulated them and began a boisterous discussion, wanting to know where and how they had killed these animals.

"Three more of these and we'll have our winter coats," said the Baron, tapping the wolves gently with his right foot.

In the meantime, the Baroness turned to the Notary. She wanted to know exactly what kind of papers were needed to prove their rights to the Viennese. In addition, she asked him if he thought it would make a good impression in Vienna if the Baron would ask for colonists like other nobles had, even before getting all of his papers together. Why wait until the Kaiser colonizes this land? She had always advised her spouse to do what the other nobles were doing.

The Notary replied that this definitely would not hurt. Whoever colonizes today will be favored in Vienna. The Baron will prove that he is a great nobleman and is thinking about the state, which needs farmers and tax payers.

The Baron who had caught the tail end of this conversation, looked angrily at his wife. "Do not bring that up again! It will not happen! A great landowner needs serfs. Are the Swabians around Fünfkirchen, Bellye and Mohács serfs? Hmm? They come as free men into this country and they want to be upper class like us. But not here, not on my land!"

After this irate outburst he turned back to his sons. But the older son, Pista, had begun to listen to this conversation. He walked over to his mother and the Notary. Like his brother, he looked rough and unkempt in his hunting clothes. His *guba*[7] was torn, his hair had not been combed for a long time, and his hands were red with blood like those of a butcher. He looked more like a robber than a nobleman, but beneath his crude appearance one could detect his mother's elegance and superior spirit. He immediately understood what the discussion was about; he, too, had guessed at the contents of the mandate from Vienna in advance.

---

7 *Guba* (Hungarian): a short Hungarian coat made from pelts of animals

Pista listened earnestly to Martonffy's claims about the advantages of having Swabians settle on their property. They were independent settlers but belonged to the lower class of taxpayers. If they were left alone for a few years, they would become the best cash cows in the country. They would conjure up a new prosperity by coaxing the best harvest from the soil. They would pay the war tax for all their masters.

"From where does one get these Swabians?" asked Pista. "Papa does not want them, but I do. If not here in Dobok, then over there in Apar and St. Marton."

"That is not so simple for private landowners," answered the Notary. "Swabians do not trust everybody. It depends on who calls them. But if the Gracious Lady Baroness travels to Vienna and can prove possession of her property, she could ask for colonists. Who knows, the Imperial Council might even send some."

The Baroness nodded. "God willing, I will be successful. In the meantime, perhaps you can convince my husband of the wisdom of this plan. Will you come over to see my three wild men when I'm gone?" she said with a smile. "Pista is a quick learner."

The Baron had called for a couple of serfs to drag the two dead wolves out of the hall. Pista asked them to leave the boar, he felt that dinner would taste better if he had the odor of the boar in his nose. Since they spoke of dinner, Martonffy excused himself, but that was only to be polite. He knew very well that they would not let him go before evening. After the noon meal, they always drove out to the meadow to the great *Szallas*[8] to witness the shearing of the sheep. Then they visited the herds of pigs grazing in the pasture. These were the only two sources of income for the Baron, who was proud of his two thousand sheep and one thousand swine. Afterward, when the group came from the *Puszta*,[9] he always had a great thirst. Martonffy always had to give the Baron the satisfaction of being drunk under the table by him. Even though prices for wool were down and the sows didn't sell for much either, the Baron's sheep and pigs still brought in a couple of barrels of wine. The sons, too, liked to out-drink their guests. The Parkoczys of Dobok would not be outdone in this regard.

A kettle of pork goulash was placed on the oak table. They all received a big wooden spoon and a pewter plate, with a slice of sheep cheese next to each plate. The wine jugs were steadily refilled. The *chibuks*, Turkish pipes,

---
8 *Szallas* (Hungarian): stock enclosure
9 *Puszta* (Hungarian): a treeless plain in Hungary

were refilled by old Jancsi, the Hàjduk servant of the Baron. He struck up a fire and laid the glowing ember on the tobacco. Later, when it began to get dark, he would bring a container of lard with three wicks. They burned quite well and gave off a pleasant odor.

Her Grace, the Baroness, always faded into the background at mealtimes. She stayed at her mother's side. Countess Erdödy, a very proud old lady, did not sit with everyone else during meals and would only be served by her daughter. She had lived in Vienna and Paris for half of her life and hated the Asiatic behaviour of her son-in-law and grandsons. But she still chose to live here. Helene was her favorite child and she herself was already eighty. Now that her homeland was free of Turks, she had returned and intended to die here.

Martonffy understood completely that the hopes of the Baroness rested on the influential Viennese friends of her mother. Helene was very silent during dinner, because thoughts of her mission occupied her. Since the men were going to drive out to the *Puszta*, she said good-bye to Martonffy. She told him that she would see him again in the fall. He courteously wished Her Grace good luck and gave his humblest regards to her mother.

The trip to the *Puszta* showed off all the things which Parkoczy was proud of, as usual. The wool grew in abundance on the sheep, the cheese made by the shepherds' wives tasted all right, and the herders reported that they had not had such a good year in a long time—at least five hundred piglets were expected this spring.

At this the Baron laughed, and twisting his long brown mustache, commented, "What do we need Swabians for? At Apar and St. Marton, God has let sheep and pigs thrive, just like here. God has amply blessed Hungary with bacon."

"Respectable Lord," the Notary responded with a smile, "the notables in Vienna do not want bacon, they demand taxes! But these pigs are free and independent! They do not pay taxes."

"To hell with the officials in Vienna! We don't want anything from them."

"But who will pay the war debts? In the end they shall even have to tax the nobility."

"Then the world will collapse," exclaimed Parkoczy. "The Turks might as well come back again. We will all go with Rakoczy again if he calls."

"*Vizony!*" the boys chimed in, "certainly!" and their eyes sparkled. They were real Kurucs and their father was proud of them.

Martonffy was silent. For the first time he found this ride through deserted villages and bleak over-grazed meadows to be depressing. Swamps and acacia forests were the only variation to this desolate plain. He thought of Bellye. How different it looked there, like a paradise in comparison to this deserted land. The Swabians had even brought vines from the Rhine to make Vilyaner wine, which everyone liked to drink so much here. Must it remain so barren here? Does this God's plain only belong to the pigs and sheep? Here they grew only as much wheat as they needed for their own bread. Why not a thousand times more? Because the people are missing. In upper Hungary there was a famine again. People died like flies. Did that have to be? What use is bacon when the bread is missing and the state has no income?

The old Notary spoke about these serious things on the return trip. Parkoczy was irritated and silent, but his sons were listening. Later, when all were drinking wine, they continued to talk. Andor asked endless questions.

Parkoczy's thirst was greater than ever. His mood lifted rapidly when they all sat down to take part in a goulash meal. In his heart he was comforted that his wife was going to undertake the trip to Vienna. He told himself, 'She will clear things up there.' The Erdödys had always been true to the Kaiser. They had always belonged to the *Fideles*.[10] 'Yes, she will be able to clear things up.' He poured himself a good amount of Vilanyer wine.

The young Kurucs were in good spirits. The wine loosened their tongues, as well as their father's. They made fun of old Martonffy who always spoke so earnestly, although at this point his tongue was heavy and he could not say much. Andor played the cymbals and Pista sang Kuruc songs, soldier's songs which their father's comrades from the Rakoczy revolt had taught them, songs full of hatred towards the Germans in the Kaiser's army.

"Hoi, hoi, hoi!" the father called out encouragingly. Pista knew which song he liked to hear and sang:

Dieses Land ist ohnegleichen	This land is like no other.
Willst du auch die Welt durchmessen;	You can look all over the world.
Weizen wächst hier, Gold und Silber,	Wheat grows here, as well as gold and silver
Das des Kaisers Schweine fressen,	Which the Kaiser's pigs will eat.
Hoih! Hoih!	Hoi, hoi!

---

10 *Fideles:* a derisive name for Hungarians loyal to the Kaiser/King.

Chapter 7—The Kurucs

Früher waren die Madjaren	In the past the Magyars
Nicht so große Mamelucken	Were not such great Mamelukes[11]
Heute aber herrscht der Deutsche	Today the Germans rule
Und wir sollen feig uns ducken	And want us to cower to them.
Hoih! Hoih!	Hoi, hoi!
Früher hatten wir noch Kleider	In the past we had clothes
Reich verschnürte, ganz famose,	Which were richly embroidered, splendid
Heute trägt man deutsche Jacke,	Today we wear German coats
Deutsch ist Hut und Frack und Hose	German hats, jackets and pants
Hoih! Hoih!	Hoi, hoi!
Hundgeborene Germanen	Dog born Germans
Hergelaufenes Gesindel,	Riffraff who came here
Bald erscheint der Held Rakoczy,	Soon our hero Rakoczy will come
Und er schnürt euch dann das Bündel.	And he will catch you all in his snare.
Hoih! Hoih!	Hoi, hoi!

Baron Parkoczy laughed boisterously and drank to his sons.

The Notary had known about this terrible song for a long time. It angered him that it was sung today, just when the Baroness had decided to seek grace from the Kaiser; but he could feel that he had already drank too much. He could no longer make his tongue say the words which he wanted to speak.

"Young man," he slurred, "You should…you ought to…be ashamed of yourself."

"Hoi, hoi, hoi, why?" Pista asked brightly.

"You wi-wi-will un-understand why…"

Pista was quiet. He thought back to what had been discussed earlier. Hadn't he, too, thought it might be a good idea to get German settlers?

It had already been dark for quite a while when the servants took the Notary, who was thoroughly drunk, outside and laid him on an ox-wagon to take him home. Andor lay on a bench and slept. Pista sat beside his jug of wine and did not want to give in to sleep. Parkoczy himself went out to the wagon and ordered that Martonffy be wrapped in a *Bunda*, a full length sheepskin coat, because the night was cool. Two sheared sheep were laid at Martonffy's feet in payment for today's consultation. Now the Notary would have company when he awoke, the Baron thought drily.

Swaying, the Baron returned to the house, then he collapsed on the floor. After a while he called out "Pista, it seems to me that you are drunk."

"Yes, yes," answered Pista with a heavy tongue. With great effort, he

---

11 Mameluke: a member of the military caste that ruled Egypt and Syria in the middle ages until it was taken over by the Ottoman dynasty.

drank another glass to his father's health, but his father was already snoring.

    Baroness Helene had been gone for weeks. Her graciousness and good spirit were sorely missed. Everywhere they went, her husband and sons felt her absence. But the grandmother, the Countess Erdödy, simply secluded herself and withdrew into the southern wing of the castle. She lived there with only a French chambermaid for company. They had to have special meals cooked for the old lady and her servant. She ate at different times and lived completely separate from the others. It was as if a ghost from former times was in that section of the castle. She missed her favorite daughter, to whom she had fled after a stormy and fateful time. She approved of her daughter's trip, supported her and wanted what was best for her. Of course, she did not have such good wishes for her son-in-law, whom she called *Contre Coeur*,[12] but because he was a part of Helene and the boys' family, she felt that she must include him in her prayers.

    Her aged bright eyes looked back into the past. Eugenie Erdödy, "the beautiful Erdödy," was a patriot; she loved her fatherland, which bled from a thousand wounds and had been butchered and torn apart with wolfish passions. She was just a child when her father had once said that it was a misfortune that Hungary did not join the world power of the Habsburgs when it lost its own dynasty. Her husband, a Protector of the Crown, was of the same opinion. The constant quarrels between small groups of power-hungry usurpers, none of whom had enough power or even the knowledge of how to unite Hungary, was like poison to the Hungarian people and had paved the way for the Turks to totally subjugate the country. These usurpers would rather be vassals of the Sultan, half-asiatic pseudo-Kings in their little kingdoms, than *Fürsten* under the protection of the Christian West. Twice they had led the Turks toward Vienna in order to assure themselves the grace of the Sultan. They had wanted to give the Turks the Capital of Christianity in order to safeguard their own portions of Hungary.

    As if it was yesterday, she saw before her the scene in 1683. Zichy Pista called on them in Pressburg and said, "Brothers, Tököly has betrayed us."

    "To whom?" Christoph Erdödy asked. "To the Turks or to the Kaiser?"

    "You are right to ask," Zichy replied bitterly. "Tököly goes with whoever offers him more. He speaks of religious freedom, but he really wants to

---

12 *Contre Coeur:* a French phrase meaning "against the heart." Most likely she called him this because she felt he went against his homeland and his Christianity when he sided with the Turks.

Chapter 7—The Kurucs

become king. Now he wants to seize the Holy Crown of Hungary for himself—St. Stephen's crown,[13] which we are sworn to protect. He is coming with Kara Mustapha and is leading him to Vienna."

"Like Zapolya before him!" Erdödy exclaimed, greatly distressed. "It's always the same … Yes, Brother, we have been betrayed. To use the help of the Turks to try to protect the pure Protestant faith from the Roman Catholic faith is foolish. Whoever uses the force of Kara Mustapha to get St. Stephen's Crown of Hungary for himself is a traitor. Better the pope than the Turkish Pasha!" He concluded by proposing, "The Crown must be moved to Vienna."

Zichy was against this idea. Perhaps there was still a safe place in Hungary where the Crown could be hidden. They discussed this at length. No, there was no such place. Then the Kaiser's emissary, General Capliers, entered the room. He strongly advised that the Crown immediately be brought to safety in Austria. Zichy demanded a document from the Kaiser guaranteeing the Crown's security, and Capliers assured him he would have the Kaiser's signature on it.

So Erdödy took the Holy Crown of St. Stephen to Vienna. When, along with the Kaiser's court, the crown was moved to Linz during the Siege of Vienna, Erdödy stayed there as its protector as well. For months, the anxious question remained: would Vienna fall to the Turks? All of Christianity held its breath. Then came the relief troops[14] from Poland and from the German *Fürsten*.

Erdödy had always favored the Habsburgs. He was proud of the fact that the Holy Crown of Hungary never sat on the head of Tököly, the Turkish vassal. He declared that only the head of a free, proud King would be worthy of the Crown of St. Stephen.

When Countess Erdödy had followed her husband to Vienna and then Linz, they had left a great deal of turmoil behind them. The Hungarian nobility sided with Tököly and the Turks. They turned away from the Kaiser because he could not pay them. The Turks also paid nothing, but said they would after they conquered and plundered Vienna. In these terrible times the Countess had entrusted her children to a cloister.

If only she had not done that! Helene, her favorite daughter, disappeared

---
13 St. Stephen's crown, sent to him by Pope Sylvester II, has remained through the centuries the sacred symbol of Hungarian national existence. It goes back to when Stephen asked the Pope to baptize him and crown him, which helped Hungary to be accepted by other countries in Europe and reduced the chance of it being taken over.
14 In 1683, after Vienna had been besieged by Turkish forces for 2 months, troops from Poland, Saxony, Bavaria, Baden, Franconia and Swabia arrived to help the Kaiser. These relief troops allowed the Habsburgs to win the Battle of Vienna.

during that time. No one could tell her where her child had gone. Countess Erdödy had been inconsolable. She had searched for the child for years. Once her husband was freed from his duty as protector of the crown, she went with him to Paris and then to London. She was seen as a great beauty there, but she never forgot Helene. All her children went on to live ordinary lives, but Helene was still missing. She was presumed dead, but she was not.

Baron Parkoczy, a follower of Tököly, had secretly won her heart. He had kidnapped her from the cloister and she did not dare contact her mother. She did this only after she had found out that her strict father, the protector of the Crown and enemy of Tököly, had died. Her mother did not disown her. She sent for her to come to Vienna and graciously welcomed the daughter whom she had given up for lost. In the end her mother came to Hungary, her fatherland, which had been liberated by the Kaiser's troops. The powerful Habsburg German Kaiser Leopold had also been elected King of Hungary; he now wore the Holy Crown of Hungary which her husband had loyally saved from Tököly and the Turks. Those were the Countess's proudest days.

Countess Erdödy was old now and perhaps forgotten in Vienna. Now it was a different Habsburg Kaiser who carried the Crown of Hungary on his head, already the third Habsburg who was King. But there were still men in Vienna who had once revered the beautiful Countess and who would remember the great service that her spouse had given. Helene would not knock on their door in vain.

That she, the Countess Erdödy, was now helping Baron Parkoczy annoyed her immensely. She doubted his legal claims. She had never heard of him owning this property and was sure that he belonged to the minor nobility of the country. But as mother and grandmother, she had to close her eyes and help her son-in-law, the Tököly sympathizer, as much as she could. It would not be easy. Even if the Kurucs had once had the right to these properties, they had been forfeited. Only the leniency of the government could award them back to him.

Of her grandchildren she only saw Andor from time to time, and rarely Pista. A warm relationship never developed between her and her grandsons. They were born Kurucs and laughed at what their grandmother said. Her pride would not tolerate this, so she became a recluse. She sunned herself on the balcony of the south side of the castle and never stepped into the courtyard. Her memories and a couple of French books were enough for her in this world. She hoped to soon depart into the other world.

Stephan Parkoczy, her *contre coeur* son-in-law, was enjoying life now that her ladyship was not here. He had borrowed the young Cuman wife of

Chapter 7—The Kurucs

Béres, his main servant in St. Marton, to be his housekeeper and she did anything he wanted in fawning submissiveness. He promised her two pigs, a nice sheepskin coat for the winter and a golden ducat. For that, she said she would sleep with him as long as he needed her, as well as the sons, if he would like. For these last words, the Baron immediately slapped her on the mouth. She had to promise that she, Katicza, would be there for him alone, and for nobody else. If she broke her promise she would get the *Bastonade*, a whip across the soles of the feet—a Turkish torture.

The first time she sat beside his father at the table, Andor looked at the buxom woman with wide-open eyes. When the Cuman woman drank with them in the evening and became affectionate with his father, he suddenly stood up and spat in her face. Then he stormed outside. Only with great effort could Pista hold their father back, who wanted to beat Andor to death. "I'll kill him!" shouted the drunken Baron.

Next morning Andor was gone, having taken the best horse in the stable. The Baron thought he would come back that evening, but he did not, and that did not bother Parkoczy. One less person to spy on me, he thought.

A few days later, the Baron sent for a Jewish merchant from Mohács, to whom he sold all the wool from his sheep. He also sent ten serfs to various cities like Fünfkirchen and Szekszard to sell his pigs and make some money. Before they were sent, Parkoczy made them swear on a crucifix that they would bring back every cent they received for the merchandise.

He needed money. His concubine, the beautiful Katicza, needed nicer clothes and jewelry. When the annual harvest festival came, she should be queen. He promised her that one evening when they were drinking wine. Katicza was mortified at the thought. Queens were always virgins, but she already had two children at home in St. Marton. The Baron agreed and said she would be a noble lady and would receive the harvest wreath.

Pista became very angry at this. "That she will not be!" he choked with fury, "or I will go and join Andor! By the time harvest arrives, Mama will be back—and that is for her to do at harvest festival!"

The Baron looked at him with vacant inebriated eyes. "By the time harvest comes, we will be long gone from here," he said and let his heavy head sink to his chest.

Pista got up from his seat.

So this was the situation. That was his father's secret worry, because their mother had stayed away so long. The Baron had such little faith in his rights to own this property.

The proud young man, on whose brown cheeks the first sign of a beard was just appearing, suddenly became sober. He pushed away the pewter jug, of wine which Janczi had just brought in. He did not want to drink another drop until he had seen everything with clarity, until he fully understood the situation. But he knew that this would not be possible today. And just like Andor he went out into the night full of revulsion and disgust over what happened. But he would not run away like his crazy younger brother. He would stay and be vigilant. He would entrust himself to his grandmother. She had to know more about what threatened them.

Pista stormed out of the house to cool his hot head. Far to the west was the crescent moon. A frosty wind blew over the plain. It felt good. He dropped onto the dewy grass and looked up at the stars. Which one was the Parkoczy star? Was it even still up there? With his young fists he wanted to secure it, fasten it back up there way at the top. But how? He had to laugh at himself for his boyish thoughts.

The earth beneath him reverberated. Pista pressed his right ear to the grass and clearly heard the sound of horses' hooves. It seemed far away in the meadow. Who would be coming this time of the night? The rider did not seem to be in a hurry. It must be a serf coming home from another farm.

In the soft light of the moon the castle looked almost ghostly. The four round corner towers with their pointed roofs had guarded the Parkoczy clan for centuries. The Parkoczys? Pista had never heard otherwise, and did not want to believe otherwise. It could not be anything else. His father was drunk again. It was dreadful that his father was always so drunk that he hardly knew what he was doing. Pista vowed never to drink with him again. When his mother left he had promised her not to drink with his father, but he had broken his promise. He was too weak. But now he wanted to be strong. He had a plan to save his father, and himself, from the wine. He could not even state this plan aloud, but he would carry it out; he would get rid of his temptation.

The hoof beats grew closer. Who could it be? Was it Andor?

It was he! His youthful silhouette was clearly visible in the light of the moon. Pista stood up. Where could his younger brother have been for three weeks? His horse was lame and could hardly carry him.

The rider saw a dark shape get up. He stopped and peered into the night.

"It's me, Andor—it's Pista!"

"*Servus, servus* (greetings)," said the young man. He swung himself off the unsaddled horse and embraced his brother.

"Where are you coming from and how did it go?"

"Good, good. Let me first take care of Gyuri, then I can talk. The poor horse is completely exhausted." He went to a nearby well, let the horse drink, and then woke up the stable boy and asked him to give Gyuri a double ration of oats. At first the stable boy thought he was seeing a ghost. He made the sign of the cross, then he kissed Andor's hands and dusty feet and went to take care of the tired horse. The dogs barked; they came running and wagged their tails when they saw it was Andor. They, too, licked his hands.

Only now did he go back to Pista, who was leaning against the trough beside the well and waiting. Only Caraffa accompanied him, the mighty wolfhound that his father had named after the Kaiser's bloodthirsty general. In a few big leaps, the animal was with Pista, then he went back to Andor and did not leave his side.

"Well, where were you?" Pista repeated his question.

"You will never guess in your whole life," said Andor and sat beside him at the edge of the trough. "At first I wanted to ride to Mama. But I didn't even know where Vienna was located. Then I said to myself, this horse would not make it that far. I had taken two sides of bacon, a block of cheese and a loaf of bread, which I put in my saddle bag, but no money. Can you ride to Vienna without money? I did not even have one *Kreuzer*. During the first week I looked at the Parkoczy properties. Have you ever seen all of our property? I don't believe so."

"I've been in Apar and St. Marton quite often, stupid. I know everything there is to know about our property," said Pista.

"Ha, ha, that's what you think! I have seen so many things you know nothing about. Mostly I slept in the ruins of castles. I know every meadow, every farm and every horse thief. I drank with them to our brotherhood."

"Even though you had no money?"

"The *Betyaren*[15] paid for me. They believed that I was a young beginner and was one of them. I also found a girlfriend," Andor said.

Pista laughed.

"Oh, the stories I could tell you about her. She is the daughter of the hostess at the Apar Inn. She grew up among the *Betyaren*, but she is an angel. Don't laugh! Pista, my brother, let me tell you how big and beautiful our property is. I rode for days without seeing a human being. There were no roads, no plowed fields, only forests, swamps and dry meadows. Here and there were groups of dilapidated huts. I don't think we have even five hundred serfs in our twelve square miles of land, and there is room enough for twenty villages! It is all empty—where will the King get his soldiers if

---

15 *Betyaren:* 1. outlaws or highwaymen 2. Scoundrels, rogues, rascals

everything is empty?"

"Hm. Where there is nothing, nothing can be taken from us," Pista shrugged his shoulders. "At first the Turks murdered and plundered here, then came Tököly, then the Kaiser's representatives, then Rakoczy; they all took soldiers from everywhere and now there is peace, but only until a new generation has grown up to create more soldiers."

"No soldiers are growing up among our people," said Andor. "I never saw children anywhere. But I was also in areas where everything is growing: wheat, corn, oats, barley and grapes, where villages are full of children and there are cows in every stable, where there are even schools and people are learning to read and write."

"Where is that, where?" asked Pista.

"Not too far away, over in Bellye by *Jenö Herceg* (Prince Eugene), by the damned Swabians. The area is jokingly referred to as Swabian Turkey. This 'Swabian Turkey' is in Högyész and Tevel and its surrounding area. You will not believe how much I saw in three weeks. You can see a good part of the world in that amount of time. Just think: there are priests, teachers and schools in Fünfkirchen. They have a bishop by the name of Nesselrode and now the Swabians are building churches of stone in the German villages."

"The farmers are doing that? You're crazy!"

"I'm not crazy. You won't believe all the things they can do! I tell you, these farmers have people among them who can build a wagon which is better than those made in Mohács. Others make chests like those the Countess brought from Vienna. There is a tailor and shoemaker in every other village so you don't have to go to Ofen (Buda) when you need a new pair of *csisma* (boots) or father needs a new suit. So you can imagine what kind of people these are. And the farmers and their fields, Pista, go and look at them! Now I know what paradise might look like!"

"Pshaw, paradise is not only inhabited by Swabians," answered Pista derisively. But the stories his young brother told impressed him. In the three weeks he had been away, the boy had become a man. He had indeed experienced more than Pista ever had.

Andor had laughed over Pista's remarks about paradise, but suddenly he became very earnest. His mind had been so full about his experiences that he had forgotten what he was going to ask Pista. Had their mother come home yet? What was new in the house? Did Katicza still rule the old man?

"She rules him even more than before. You have come at the right time if you want to spit on her again," Pista replied. "But let's go to sleep. The moon has already set. You can tell me more tomorrow."

Chapter 7—The Kurucs

They started to walk toward the castle. But when they reached the dark slumbering building, Andor said he would go see Gyuri for a little while. The stallion was half lame and he wanted the stable boy to give him a rubdown, or do it himself. Caraffa accompanied him to the stable.

Pista was pleased to be left alone. There was something he needed to do. A small shed which contained scythes and other agricultural tools stood in the courtyard. He went in, took a hatchet and disappeared into the dark building. A heavy door creaked in the distance.

Then after some time Andor appeared and looked for Pista. Quietly he called, "Pista?" No answer. He whistled. Only after his third whistle was there an answering signal from the inner hall of the castle.

Pista came out and walked to the shed in the darkness. There he flung the hatchet on the stone floor so that sparks flew.

"What are you doing?" asked Andor.

"Let's go to bed," said Pista. "You must be dead tired."

"What did you do?" asked Andor again.

"Oh, don't ask so much," said Pista.

And in silence they went to sleep.

Chapter 8

The Great Migration Begins

The gates of the free imperial city of Regensburg were not opened until the bell ringer of St. Peter's rang the sixth hour. This mild May night, many visitors had spent the night outside the gates, either on the banks of the Danube, near one of the wharves, or in the meadows of lower Wörth, because the lower priced inns within the city walls were full to overflowing. The shipmen were all staying at *The Green Duck*. The Kaiser's officials who were on government business stayed in *The Golden Angel*. But no emigrant dared to even go near *The Golden Cross*, where the Kaiser stayed when the Imperial Diet was in session in Regensburg. They all looked reverently at the tower of this famous inn, which had housed many Kaisers, and listened to stories about what had taken place in that building. A thousand or so farmers and craftsmen came to Regensburg every week to take a ship to Hungary. Barely half of them could find overnight accommodations within the city gates. The others had to spend the night outside the city walls. Loitering in the city after dark was not allowed. The Obermünster Convent took in some of the women and children; St. Emeran's church and the brothers of the Schotten could house three dozen Catholic families. The others would have to rely on God's grace to find someplace to stay until their ships departed. After all, no one had asked them to leave their fatherland in such great numbers. They had been advised against this in vain.

People in their wagons coming to market anxiously waited at the gate until they could enter Regensburg. They came from *Stadt am Hof* across the Danube or from other cities on this side of the river, and were impatient because there was so much to take care of before Pentecost Sunday. They had already heard that the city was overrun by visitors and that all rooms were occupied. Some worried that with these great swells of people there might be a shortage of items they needed to purchase, and then they would have to go on to faraway Augsburg. But others came to try and get good deals. Rumor had it that many emigrants had brought along all their worldly possessions, but now had doubts about whether they could bring them all the way to Hungary. This attracted a lot of opportunists who came to the city to buy their goods.

After the bells were rung at St. Peter's Cathedral, the bellringer played a chorale on his trumpet. Those waiting at the gate listened attentively. The hymn called them to devotions, and quite a few murmured their morning prayers again.

Soon the drawbridge came down, its chains rattling, and the city awoke.

On the banks of the Danube everything came alive. Masses of emigrants poured into the city, and smoke rose from the Ulm ships which had docked overnight. The ships' kitchens clanked with the sound of breakfast being prepared for the oarsmen.

Emigrants from Baden and Württemberg had arrived on these ships yesterday. They had a head start on their trip to Hungary, having obtained their papers back in Günsburg, Swabia, where a commissioner of the Kaiser was seated. The commissioner could take care of the paperwork for anyone who could show that they had been authorized to leave by the public authorities of their homeland. Another of the Kaiser's commissioners was here in Regensburg, but the process took much longer because of all the people. People were here from all over the southern and western regions of Germany: from Hessen, Franconia, Nassau and Westphalia, as well as Luxembourg, Alsace and Lorraine. Even those who had obtained their papers in Frankfurt had to have them confirmed here before they could continue the trip to Vienna. There was a shortage of ships, so patience was needed.

The local people stood at the riverbank, their *Trachten*[1] looking bright and colorful in the sun. They looked on while the *Ulmer Schachteln*, as the ships were called, prepared for departure. The *Ordinari-schiff* was always first to leave. It took longer to go through customs stations at Passau and Engelhartszell because it carried the most wares, and many of the goods had to be taxed. The border guards were very thorough.

Now the captain of the *Ordinari-schiff* went to the steering wheel and raised the flag of Ulm.

---

1 *Trachten:* the clothing people wore. Every area in Germany had a different local costume which had developed over the years, and so the *Trachten* they wore could identify from which area they came.

"*Los!*" was the cry that signaled it was time to depart.

The oarsmen were at their posts and the *Ordinari-schiff* began to move away from the shore. People waved their hats and cheered loudly as the ship rushed under the middle of the fifteen arches in the Regensburg bridge, carried away in the best flow of the current.

It was a full two hours before the Ulm emigration ship was to leave, but the Swabians were already in their places. Some sat with wives and children on benches, others lay on colorful bedding amid farming equipment and household items. Several horses stood under a canopy, and parts of disassembled wagons leaned against it. Even two goats bleated on the ship. An onlooker on shore laughed at this. Why did these people make so much trouble for themselves? Couldn't they obtain goats and horses and plows in Hungary? He read the Kaiser's Proclamation aloud to the assembled spectators: "When you arrive, the Kaiser will give you a pair of horses for forty guilders, a pair of oxen for fifty guilders, a cow for eighteen guilders, a plow for only five guilders. Everything will be available, down to the last detail. This list even includes two lamps and lamp cleaner. You will not have to pay for anything until you have a good harvest. You have ten years before everything has to be paid off. What kind of idiot would lug all his household goods with him? Or feed his horses for many weeks, for nothing? I would not take even a nail along."

Michel Luckhaup from Zweibrücken in the *Pfalz* looked directly into the speaker's eyes. "You are from the city," he replied. "You don't know what it is worth to have your own horses, which you know you like, and your own wagon."

"And the goat provides milk for the children while we are underway," his wife put in.

"Pah!" the first speaker exclaimed. "I'll give you all some good advice. You should turn everything you have into money. Take nothing along but money!" He called out in a loud and clear voice, repeating himself over and over. Every one of these families had brought something along and the merchants were only too happy to relieve them of their goods.

As the crowd was watching the Ulmer ship which was to leave next, their attention was diverted by the sound of bagpipes and a wagon creaking along the country road. When they turned to look, a strange sight met their eyes.

A long covered wagon pulled by two horses, one brown and one black, turned from Nuremberg Street and headed toward the city center. A man with a brooding face drove the wagon and two strong young men with guns over their shoulders walked along its left and right sides. A young farmhand

Chapter 8—The Great Migration Begins

walked in front of the wagon, playing a merry folk song on his bagpipes. Children looked out from inside as their mother pointed out the Danube, the boats and the crowds of people on the shore. The back of the wagon contained a cage with colorful chickens, and every once in a while a rooster's crow mingled with the hens' cackling.

A group of onlookers who wore the same traditional *Trachten* as those in the wagon shouted their greetings when they saw this veritable "Noah's Ark" go by. "Hey, that's Trauttmann!" "It's Philipp Trauttmann!" they exclaimed, as they walked over to the wagon, smiling and laughing.

"Those are people from the *Pfalz*," others cried, having identified them by which *Trachten* they wore. "A cheerful folk!"

"*Grüss Gott*, my countryman!" greeted Michel Luckhaup. "You seem very festive, are you driving to a wedding?" he said jokingly.

The driver pulled the reins and the horses stood still. He turned to Luckhaup and his earnest tanned face lit up. "*Grüss Gott,* neighbor," he replied. "I have to go into the city. It's a great inconvenience, this requirement that we have to report to every city we go through." He called to the bagpiper, "Matz, stop playing already!"

"The best thing for you would be to leave the wagon here and walk into the city. There's no room to stay overnight. Everything is so busy, we've been waiting out here for three days. In there, they'll take your guns away."

"Just let them try!" said Philipp Trauttmann defiantly. "I'll have something to say about that! The pass which I got in Frankfurt states that I am emigrating to Hungary with my horse and wagon. I have permission to carry two rifles for our protection."

"Well, then, that's a different story," responded the men surrounding the wagon.

"Where can I get good lodging in the city?" asked Trauttmann.

"*Landsmann*, all the guest houses are full!"

"To the devil! My horses need a day of rest. It's quite far to Straubing."

"Then you better drive over to Hof. That is the more direct way."

Trauttmann leaned back toward the inside of the wagon and told his wife, "I have to go into the city."

To his sons he said, "Hannes, Peter, stay here and keep watch!" and to the bagpiper, "Matz, feed the horses!" Then he drove his "Noah's Ark" to the side of the road and stepped down from the wagon.

Everyone admired the sight of Trauttmann, who looked like a blond giant, and at thirty-eight years old, was clearly in the prime of his life. When they saw that such a man was leaving his homeland, they felt that their own flight was justified. They peppered him with questions, wanting to know which way he had come and why he had left the *Pfalz*.

He had driven for eight days through Mainz and Frankfurt for his official pass and came through Würzburg and Nuremberg to Regensburg. Here he must cross over the Danube, and in two weeks he should be in Vienna.

"Such a long trip!"

Upon hearing this, the others did not envy him as much, since it would only take them a week to get to Vienna. If only they could board the ship already! But tomorrow they should be leaving.

They asked him why he, an *Erzbauer*, one of the farmers who was better off than most, was leaving his homeland. Hmm, he responded. Why are so many others leaving as well? All had the same concerns. The German states did not protect the *Pfalz* against French invasions. You never knew to what country you belonged, who would get your taxes or to which *Fürst* some of the fruits of your hard labor would go. The district and local officials were bastards. Like bloodsuckers, they took from anyone who had something. The count's game ate the seed in the fields—that is, whatever was left after the soldiers had marched through and trampled the good earth—and you were not allowed to do anything about it. On top of that, now there was talk that the *Kurfürst* would make them become Catholics. Trauttmann declared emphatically, "My parents were good Lutherans and I'm supposed to dishonor them in front of my own children? That's just a disgrace!"

His wife reached down from the wagon to hand him his new hat. He put it on his head, double checked that he had his papers, and headed toward the city with his head held high.

People looked after him in amazement. Hadn't he read the Kaiser's proclamation? Didn't he know that the Kaiser only wanted Catholic colonists? Many of the men standing there had already converted to Catholicism either in Ulm or here in Regensburg, the bishop's city. Those who had not converted would likely be required to do so once they got to Vienna. It was said that some individuals had slipped through, but would that still be possible?

A drummer came out to the city's gate and made an announcement. The people ran over to listen. He announced that tomorrow, the next day, and the day after that, the biggest Kehlheim flatboats that had ever been seen on the Danube would be leaving for Vienna. The Shippers Guild needed two hundred oarsmen for these ships. Whoever wanted to go to Vienna free of charge should report to the Shippers Guild at the *Blauen Hechten* Inn. Payment also included food and lodging at the *Blauen Hechten* until the ships left. Also, four women were needed on each ship to cook in exchange for free transportation.

With another drumroll he departed and went farther down to the landing past the bridge, where the massive flatboats lay ready for the trip. Their construction had been completed in the water right past the bridge, because they wouldn't be able to pass under the bridge once they had already been built.

The drummer's declaration made quite an impact. Young craftsmen who had been sunning themselves on the riverbanks sprang up and strode into the city. They would save the four guilders which it cost to go to Vienna. A week's free food was worth something, too.

The farmers looked at each other. Rowing? Didn't one have to be trained to do that, just like any other trade? A few of the older boys wanted to try it, and their mothers approved. Any money that they could save would be a help. In Passau, the Austrian Government would pay three guilders per person as travel money to go to Vienna, and once in Vienna, they would get another three to take with them to Hungary. But they had to come up with anything else they would need on their own.

"Jörgl, you're going to row," Frau Luckhaup said to her son. Margret Staudt didn't stop her son either, even though he was only seventeen. But he was big, strong and bold, and immediately wanted to sign up. After some hesitation, some of the men volunteered to be oarsmen too. "Oh well, it's not a disgrace to do an honest day's work, we may as well try it," they said to each other. Some had been a bit hasty and sold their houses and fields for less than they were worth when they answered the Kaiser's call. Others were in such a hurry they had not even done that and had left their property with relatives, so they were short on cash.

The men from the Shippers Guild now walked among the farmers and encouraged those who had misgivings. Rowing a boat was easier than plowing a field. How would it be possible to get to Vienna so cheaply, if everyone didn't help out? "Just think how much it would cost to bring back two hundred oarsmen and twelve cooks back from Vienna to Regensburg by stagecoach! You would have to pay ten *Taler*, not just four guilders. Help us out, so that the boats can leave tomorrow!"

These words helped to alleviate the qualms people had about working on the ship. More and more young men proceeded through the city gates to the *Blauen Hechten* Inn. The wives talked among themselves; some volunteered as cooks while others would look after their children. A couple of cheerful Swabian girls joined the women. Why shouldn't they be cooks on this trip— it would be fun.

A tall young man who was clearly not a farmer stood beside the helmsman on the fully loaded *Ulmer Schachtel* that was to leave that day. He looked toward the lively activities on shore and was happy that this migration of people was finally taking place. It was Wörndle, the schoolmaster's assistant from Blaubeuren, the one originally from Alsace. He, too, had been seized by a great wanderlust. He had been moved by the beautiful letters Frau Therese had sent from Temesvar. It seemed that a new German world was being established there. And German schoolmasters would be needed anywhere that German people lived. He thought about the Alsatians he had met on the ship who bitterly complained about their overlords. 'It seems that everybody wants to leave Alsace—serves the tyrants right that their best workers are moving away,' Wörndle told himself. They would create a new free homeland and not be turned into Frenchmen. They had to pay ten percent of their possessions to release them of their responsibilities as subjects of their masters. But, they paid what they were asked for without hesitation. Now, many of those who had paid to be free of their homeland suffered a terrible homesickness. It was as if heaven had cursed them. They had voluntarily left their homeland, paid so that they could leave, and now their hearts were torn in two. Many left people behind who were dear to them, and now wondered how their loved ones would fare. When you looked around the ship you saw few old people. The strongest and most enterprising generation was emigrating. Did the masters know what they had lost? Did they know how much talent was leaving them to go to another land? There is no way they comprehended this. And they did not share any of the heartache felt by those who were leaving.

As Wörndle stood there lost in thought, he heard the command "*Los!*"

Upon hearing this word, his heart was greatly moved. Good-bye, you aged helpless German land, which destroyed itself in unholy religious wars, which let itself be robbed of Alsace without fighting for it. Which could not protect the *Rheinpfalz* against its French neighbors. Good-bye! It hurts us to leave and we cry for you. May you someday be great and strong and respected again. May the Alsatians be proud of you again, Stepmother Germania.

With these powerful thoughts, Leonhard Wörndle stood beside the steersman and waved his three-cornered hat at the many towers of the city of Regensburg, as it slowly went out of sight.

Philipp Trauttmann had gone into the city and asked his way to the famous *Rathaus*, the city hall where for centuries the Imperial Diet was held. It was a dark, unfriendly building. He had seen so many German cities and had

Chapter 8—The Great Migration Begins

spoken in so many offices that he was quite familiar dealing with officials. That would be useful to him today. The building was full of people who came from all over the German fatherland and wanted to get passes on the basis of the discharge papers they had brought with them. They gladly let Trauttmann go to the front of the line because he only needed his pass stamped. It was only a verification, he said. He soon stood in front of the *Kommissar* of the police commission.

"Where do you come from?" asked the surly old man.

"From Bobenheim in the *Pfalz, Herr Kommissar,*" answered Trauttmann.

"Oh, and why did you come to us? Why did you not report to Frankfurt?"

Trauttmann smiled at the feisty old man and lay his Frankfurt pass before him. It was a huge paper with the Imperial Double Headed Eagle in the middle and ornamental borders on the side. It carried the coat of arms of the Imperial Representative and read, "The carrier of this pass, Philipp Trauttmann of Bobenheim, has the highest approval of the *Kurfürsten* and Hessian authorization to emigrate and is requested to report to the Imperial and Royal Police Authority in Vienna to get final permission for eventual settlement in the Banat with wife and family. He is taking along a hired man and has permission to be armed with two rifles. Civil and military officials are furthermore instructed to give their full protection and support."

"Ah! You are coming to have your pass validated!" The official turned the large pass over. It was confirmed and stamped by the Bavarian Embassy in Frankfurt am Main. From the border customs office Dieburg to Engelhartszell a charge of 2 Fl. 52 *Kreuzer* had been levied for the wagon and horses (a black gelding and a brown mare) and then one stamp after another was crowded together, one city at a time up until Regensburg.

"How big is your family?" asked the official.

"My wife and four children."

"How old are the sons?"

"The boys are fifteen, fourteen and ten, the girl is four."

"Good. And how old is your hired man?"

"Matz? He will soon be nineteen."

"Oh? Then he has to get married."

"Who, Matz?" replied Trauttmann incredulously.

"Doesn't matter what his name is. He will have to get married. Either here or somewhere on your way to Hungary."

"A hired man has to get married? Someone who has nothing but the clothes on his back and a yearly allowance of thirty guilders?" Trauttmann laughed. "He's just a boy!"

"Don't laugh! You are in an office. If they did not know this in Frankfurt when you were there, they will know it soon. Every man must be married. Only married couples may settle in Hungary."

"Excuse me, *Herr Kommissar*," Trauttmann replied, "but my wife and family are to be settled, not my hired man. Matz is my nephew, and I will look after him, when the time comes."

"The law is the law!" said the official angrily. "Go ahead and bang your head against the wall! Go ahead and see what happens! They will marry Matz to a gypsy woman if he does not bring a wife along."

The official then forcefully stamped Trauttmann's pass, gave him the emigration number 16,734 and gave him the directions to Straubing.

Then suddenly he asked, "And what is your religion?"

"Augsburg Protestant," answered Trauttmann.

"Ha ha! Go ahead and try to make it to Vienna! I'll see you again soon or you will convert to Catholicism!"

"That will not happen," Trauttmann said firmly.

"So? And you likely have a Protestant Bible in your wagon? Yes? Well, better make sure to keep an eye on that! Ha ha ha!"

"Good-bye, *Herr Kommissar*," said Trauttmann and left.

"A high minded peasant," the commissioner grumbled to himself. "He has no respect for his homeland since Hungary is open to him."

Philipp Trauttmann quickly walked back to his family. The commissioner had given him something to think about. He laughed about having Matz married while underway, but he would tell the boy nothing about it. Matz might even go along with it. Too bad that his three sons had not yet passed their eighteenth birthday, he thought facetiously. Then instead of one married couple, there would have been five going to Hungary. They could have picked up wives all along the way, in Passau, in Linz, in Vienna. Actually, this decree was not stupid. If you wanted to populate a country it was a good idea, thought Trauttmann. But what was this about becoming Catholic? And about having a Bible? That must be something the Regensburgers made up. The Imperial Ambassador in Frankfurt had never asked about religion, there was nothing in his pass about it, and they were going to a free country. If one needed to convert to go there, he could just as well have stayed at home.

So he reasoned to himself as he walked back, trying to sort out the turbulent feelings that the official had brought up. He reflected that it was good that he had not sold his fields but had leased them to his brother in the *Pfalz*. His confidence had received a blow.

When he went to the bank of the Danube he found his wife and children

Chapter 8—The Great Migration Begins

sitting in the sun, and Matz making a fool of himself. His nephew was doing somersaults like the English he had seen in Kaiserslautern, and then he played a new song about Prince Eugene on his bagpipes, a song which he had heard in Frankfurt. Matz didn't know all the words and was hoping to learn them in Austria, but the melody was being hummed everywhere here.

The Ulm ships had gone and the Danube's banks were almost empty this side of the bridge. Everyone's curiosity seemed to have been transferred to the massive Kehlheim flatboats downriver. On them they would soon travel toward their future, their happiness.

"Husband," said Frau Eva, "are you all right?"

"Yes," answered Trauttmann shortly, without looking her in the eye. "Matz, harness the horses, we are driving over the bridge to Hof."

Frau Eva pushed her blond hair, which had become disheveled from her daughter playing with it, away from her face. She looked at her husband with concern. Something was not in order. She knew her husband even better than he did, and he did not know how to hide anything from her. She tried to catch his eye but he evaded her by giving the boys all kinds of instructions. Trauttmann hid the guns and went deep into the back section of the wagon where fodder for the horses and seeds to be sown in Hungary were located. When his wife asked what he was looking for, he did not answer.

When Trauttmann returned he smiled to himself and said nothing. Frau Eva knew when to remain silent. She was a faithful wife, the kind often found in the wine country. Her husband meant more to her than anything else, and she would have carried him on her back to save him from danger, no matter how heavy he was. If he did not freely tell her something, then she could wait. Eventually he would let her know.

They drove over the bridge to the city of Hof. Down in the water lay the three giant ships which were to leave in the next three days, and hundreds of people who were leaving their homeland set up camp at the banks of the river. They could hardly wait for the Danube to take them to the new foreign land.

"Will we see our countrymen in Hungary again?" asked Ferdinand, as he looked down the Danube from his peephole in the wagon.

"Who knows?" replied Trauttmann.

It was a big day in Regensburg when the first giant flatboat built by the Kehlheim ship builder cast off with its five hundred passengers. The Shippers Guild had sought the opinion of Meister Jakob Fuchs in Köln before they built such large ships. Master Fuchs wrote to them that they had made flatboats three times as big on the Rhine River, boats which floated to Holland and carried a thousand or more people on board, so the Guild could put their worries aside. The shipmaster had qualified his statement by adding that he did not know the hazards of the Danube, and his opinion was given without any guarantee. Only during high water could those ships travel safely on the Rhine and that would also be the case with the Danube.

The shipmasters decided to try it here in May when the flow of the Danube was the highest, and the Kehlheimers sent for a foreman from the Rhine who knew his business.

The Ulmers looked at this large undertaking with envy. Their shipbuilders had come today to look at the ships: Masters Ludwig Pless, Neubronner, Besserer, Molfenter, Schad and Kaßbohrer. Each of them had built between twenty and thirty Ulm ships, but what was that compared to the large undertaking of the Regensburgers, who wanted to transport one thousand five hundred people in three ships in three days?

That had never happened—not on the Danube. How they boasted, these new pioneers! Georg Seemeyer, to whom the first flatship belonged, which he himself would command, fancied himself to be another Christopher Columbus. He had leased whole forests to cut down the tallest trees for his ships. He planned for a great deal of commerce selling the timbers in Hungary and was taking the people along almost as an afterthought. When he showed his Ulm guests his workplace, he bragged: "To run a real shipping business you need three hundred thousand *Taler*. One hundred thousand are growing in the forest, one hundred thousand are in the water and you must have one hundred thousand in your pocket."

They laughed about him showing off when they saw that he worked exactly as they did. But even if he hired the majority of his oarsmen, just as they did, he would need his own Laborer's Guild for as many men as were needed to load his oversized raft. He had to bring cattle, a hundred barrels of beer, and mountains of provisions on board. He couldn't expect everything to just fall into place, it had to be planned. It seemed that the shipmasters of Regensburg thought that the entire German population would emigrate to the East, and business would be never-ending. The people in Ulm were more cautious. Their Ulm boats always had enough passengers, if not to Hungary, then at least to Vienna. The mass emigration would soon be stopped by the *Fürsten* of the German states. What then?

Early in the morning, the emigrants who were to leave on the first Kehlheim flatboats went to the churches, St. Jakob and St. Emeran, in droves.

Chapter 8—The Great Migration Begins

No one wanted to go on this trip without first going to confession. In addition, thirteen young couples were married at St. Peter's church. The Kaiser would not allow them to cross the border if they were single. One of these couples was extremely happy to comply with this rule. The parents, aunts and uncles had all been against a marriage between Michel Gerber, the cabinet-maker from Emmendingen and their Trudel, but Trudel had wanted only him. Since they wanted her to marry another man, she ran away with Michel. They boarded one of the Danube ships, where they had been asked: 'Who are you? Where are your parents? Where are your papers? Are you married? Get off the boat, you gypsies!' What they could not do at home, they were ordered to do here. Oh, how gladly they obeyed, and they fit together better than any of the other couples. A girl from Nassau and a farm boy from the Black Forest, a Luxembourg weaver and a Swabian girl from the Bodensee—these couples would probably never have gotten together in their whole life if they had not been ordered to marry in Regensburg! Many other unlikely couples such as these were paired together. In this wedding procession of thirteen couples, all the dialects and all the *Trachten* of the south and southwestern regions of the Holy Roman Empire of the German Nation were intermingled. Did all of these couples understand each other? That was not certain. But true love overcomes any dialect. They would not have to worry about a dowry; that was the responsibility of the Kaiser who ordered these marriages.

Before the thirteen-fold wedding, they had to endure a long sermon, a sermon against frivolous emigration!

An old priest stood in the pulpit and thundered to the churchgoers in a powerful voice, "What made you decide to become settlers? Do not trust the recruiters who pretend to be rich and act as if they became prosperous in Hungary to impress you. They may well show you their golden pocket watches and flash their golden rings. They are sellers of souls, who get money for each person who leaves. If you can, go back to your homelands and carry the cross that God has given you with patience. Do not believe that Hungary is like the Elysian Fields.[2] Do not believe that its rivers flow with milk and honey, do not believe that crops will grow on the land without it being plowed or that you will not have to work as hard there as in your homeland. If someone tells you that a farmhand can become a master, or a maid a gracious lady, that a farmer will turn into a nobleman, or a craftsman a baron, he is lying. Whoever tells you that you can elect your officials and also

---

2 The Elysian Fields in Greek mythology were the final resting place of the souls of the heroic, a blissful land something like paradise.

remove them from office is a fraud. I know that your taxes and *Frondienst*[3] are not easy to bear in your homeland and that everyone has a desire to better themselves. But be careful that you are on the right path. Who knows if the new land, which did not nourish the Turks very well, will be better for you when you are coming in such large numbers? Look out, you may come into the servitude of foreign masters and your children and grandchildren may never thank you for exchanging the German homeland for a Turkish one, squandering their inheritance for an unknown future. Whoever did not burn the bridges behind him should turn around and go back! I do not curse those who have been misled to migrate to a foreign land, I pray for their well-being. But I will bless and call those happy, who turn back and remain loyal to their homeland, those who remain loyal to their princes and counts, whom God has placed over them. For the enlightenment of us all, we will now pray three Our Fathers."

The women sobbed and the men grumbled when the prayers came to an end and the old priest left the pulpit. He had not convinced them to go back, but the hearts of many became heavier as they thought of what lay ahead of them. "These warnings came too late," Staudt said to his neighbor Luckhaup. "Why is he preaching to us? He should be preaching to our overlords. If they wanted us to remain loyal to them, they should have acted accordingly."

The unfortunate crowd was happy that the speech to the thirteen couples who were to be married was given by another, much younger priest. He gave sensible advice to the couples who were forming these quick marriages and promised them a long union.

"It is exactly the foreign land to which you are going that will solidify your union," he said. "The blessings of those of us still in your homeland will stay with you, and you will be able to withstand the tests of this new venture together, rather than alone. It was God's will that you found each other, so stay together until death do you part." Then he blessed the young couples.

At noon, the first Kehlheim flatboat was ready to depart.

This boat contained a cabin for the shipmaster, a row of rooms for the emigrants, special rooms for the shipmaster's hired workers who worked for him all year and were to return from Vienna by land, two kitchens, a covered stable for a few cows and five oxen to be slaughtered, a sheep stall and a canopy for the horses the migrants took along. Their wagons had been disassembled to make room for all the people. Five hundred paying passengers

---

3 *Frondienst:* the common people had to work for a certain number of days each year for their overlord, usually working on the portion of his land that he had not leased to commoners.

had to be taken on board to make the trip feasible.

Provisions had even been made for a jail: six stakes, with chains welded on, protruded from the bottom of the boat into a small room. Anyone on board who broke the rules or stole something would be chained until they reached their next stop, where they would be given over to the court. The worst punishment was to drop the chained thief off on one of the uninhabited islands of the Danube. Nobody asked if this procedure was legal or not. That is how criminals were threatened in the interest of everyone on board who entrusted their lives to the crew of the ship.

No one who looked into Georg Seemayer's hard, gray eyes doubted that he would carry out this threat. He was a man of steel, this master of the Regensburg Shippers Guild.

Master Ludwig Pless from Ulm lingered on board the longest before the ship departed. He wanted to know all about the new flatboats, down to the smallest detail. He also enjoyed talking to the emigrants. In each he saw a future countryman of his son Jakob in Temesvar, and he asked all of them to greet his son and daughter-in-law when they got there. Tell them they should write more often, he requested. Mother is sick and longs for her oldest son. He told this to Michel Luckhaup and Johann Staudt, who said that they wanted to go to the Banat. They promised to give his greetings and message to Jakob, as they were sure to make it to the city of Temesvar.

When the young master called out "Ready!" and the anchormen waited for the sign to lift the anchor, old Pless was the last to leave the ship. He shook hands with Seemayer and wished him a good trip.

The Guild Master had two trumpeters on board who were waiting for his sign. As he took his place at the rudder and the Regensburg youth on the riverbank called out *"Vivat!"* he looked toward the trumpeters and nodded. The trumpeters' signal to depart resounded in the air. It echoed back from the surrounding heights and drowned out the rattling of the anchor chain, the commands to the oarsmen and the first oar strokes. The ship was underway! It looked like a floating village from onshore. The trumpeters played a song of parting which deeply moved everyone. *Ade, ade...*

Seemayer proudly waved to his colleagues from the Guild who were gathered on shore, and they watched his Kehlheim flatboat until it was out of sight. Many experienced skippers shook their heads. Those from Ulm commented, "If nothing happens underway, then this was a brilliant undertaking. But what if something does happen?"

The next day the second ship left and the day after, the third one left, each as full as the first. The masses of emigrants, however, did not stop streaming in.

Pentecost Sunday brought a happy surprise. Towards evening, a barge from Ulm flying a Württemberg flag arrived with one hundred and fifty girls on board. All were Swabian girls from the Black Forest! Duke Karl Alexander had honored the words of *"Türkenlouis"* von Baden. He had sent, as promised, a shipload of brides to the brave noncommissioned officers of the German regiments who had settled in the uninhabited regions of Hungary as bachelors. This had not happened as quickly as the settlers had wished and hoped for, but in the end he had succeeded. He made public the names of his discharged soldiers who had stayed in Hungary and invited unwedded young girls to leave their hometowns. Any who were brave enough to take him up on it were promised a free trip to Hungary, a dowry of fifty crown *Taler* and a hundred suitors able to support a wife. Each girl would be able to freely choose by following her heart.

As the "ship of maidens" arrived in Regensburg, hundreds of people came to the riverbanks attracted by the singing of the girls. It did not seem to be a happy song that they presented in chorus, as if they were sitting in their spinning room.

Es war ein Markgraf über dem Rhein,	There once was a margrave of the Rhine,
Der hatte drei schöne Töchterlein;	Who had three beautiful young daughters;
Zwei Töchterlein früh heuerten weg,	Two of them left home to marry,
Die dritt' hat ihn ins Grab gelegt,	The third stayed until he died,
Dann ging sie singen vor Schwesters Tür,	Then she went singing at her sister's door,
"Ach braucht ihr keine Dienstmagd hier?"	"Do you need a servant girl here?"
"Ach Mädchen, du bist mir viel zu fein,	"Young girl, you look much too pretty,
Du gehst wohl gern mit Herrelein."	You probably go out with the gentlemen."
"Ach nein! Ach nein! Das tu ich nit,	"Oh no! Oh no! I don't do that,
Daß ich so mit den Herrlein geh'."	I don't go out with gentlemen."
Sie dingt das Mägdlein ein halbes Jahr,	She hired the girl for half a year,
Das Mägdlein dient ihr sieben Jahr.	The girl served her for seven years.
Und als die sieben Jahr um war'n,	And when the seven years were done,
Da wurd das Mägdlein täglich krank.	The girl was sick each day.
"Sag, Mägdlein, wann du krank willst sein,	"So tell me, girl, if you are sick
So sag mir, wer sind die Eltern dein?"	Tell me who your parents are?"
"Mein Vater war Markgraf über dem Rhein,	"My father was the margrave of the Rhine,
Und ich bin sein jüngstes Töchterlein."	And I am his youngest daughter."

Chapter 8—The Great Migration Begins

"Ach nein! ach nein! das glaub ich nit,	"Oh no! Oh no! I don't believe that you are
Daß du meine jüngste Schwester bist."	the youngest sister of mine."
"Ach, wenn du mir's nit glauben magst,	"If you don't believe a word I say,
So geh nur an meine Truhe hin,	Go see that little chest in my room,
Daran wird es geschrieben stehn."	There you will find it written down."
Und als sie an die Truhe kam	And when she looked at that chest
Da rannen ihr die Backen ab:	The tears ran down her cheeks:
"Ach bringt mir Weck, ach bringt mir Wein,	"Let's get a loaf, let's get some wine,
Das ist mein jüngstes Schwesterlein!"	This is the youngest sister of mine!"
"Ich will doch kein Weck, ich will kein Wein,	"I want no bread, I want no wine,
Will nur mein kleines Lädelein,	I just want my wooden chest,
Darin ich will begraben sein."	In which I will be buried."

The Swabian girls sang this song from their homeland while the ship's master landed the boat for an overnight stay. It was still quite early, but they would not be able to get to the next good landing site past Regensburg on this day, so they had to stop here.

As soon as the story spread through Regensburg that an emigrant ship full of girls was docked at lower Wörth, more and more people came out of the city gates to stare at this wonder. But none of the young girls got off the boat, only the oarsmen and their master left the ship to meet their fellow Guild members at the inn. The girls were soon besieged by jocular young men on the bank trying to engage them in teasing conversation and jokingly making marriage proposals. The boys offered to show the girls the beautiful city of Regensburg and to taste a bit of their famous beer, which made kisses taste so much better. But the girls only laughed at them. The old helmsman from Ulm watched over this lightheartedness.

"But you could at least sing a song for us, a happy song," the boys shouted from the riverbank. "Yes, a song!"

"Well, why not?" said the girls and discussed it amongst themselves. They were all working on board, some were cooking, others cleaned up, still others brought blankets out of the cabins and spread them out for the girls to sleep on that night. But then a large, well-built young woman standing near the steering wheel asked the girls to stop working. She carefully selected eight girls and gathered them around her.

"Aha, the mother hen got her chicks together!" the boys called from the shore. "Something is going to happen!" And something did happen.

"*Hüt du Dich!*" the blond woman said to the girls with a smile, and they all sang the song: 'Be on Guard'.

Ich weiß mir'n Mädel hübsch und fein.	I know a girl so pretty and fine.
Hüt du dich!	Be on guard!
Es kann wohl falsch und freundlich sein.	She can be both friendly and deceitful.
Hüt du dich! Hüt du dich!	Be on guard! Be on guard!
Vertrau ihr nit, sie narret dich.	Don't trust her, she'll make a fool of you.
Sie hat zwei Äuglein, die sind braun,	She has a pair of big brown eyes,
Hüt du dich!	Be on guard!
Sie wer'n dich überzwerch anschaun	She will give you the evil eye,
Hüt du dich! Hüt du dich!	Be on guard! Be on guard!
Vertrau ihr nit, sie narret dich.	Don't trust her, she'll make a fool of you.
Sie hat ein licht goldfarbens Haar,	She has light golden hair,
Hüt du dich!	Be on guard!
Und was sie red't, das ist nit wahr.	And what she says is untrue.
Hüt du dich! Hüt du dich!	Be on guard! Be on guard!
Vertrau ihr nit, sie narret dich.	Don't trust her, she'll make a fool of you.
Sie hat zwei Brüstlein, die sind weiß,	She has two little white breasts,
Hüt du dich!	Be on guard!
Sie zeigt sie halb und dir wird heiß.	She half-shows them and you get hot.
Hüt du dich! Hüt du dich!	Be on guard! Be on guard!
Vertrau ihr nit, sie narret dich.	Don't trust her, she'll make a fool of you.
Sie gibt dir'n Körblein fein gemacht,	She'll reject you in a flash,
Hüt du dich!	Be on guard!
Für einen Narren wirst du geacht.	You will be seen as a fool.
Hüt du dich! Hüt du dich!	Be on guard! Be on guard!
Vertrau ihr nit, sie narret dich.	Don't trust her, she'll make a fool of you.

This made for a lot of jokes and liveliness on the riverbank. But dusk came soon, and the fun had to come to an end. The city gates would soon be locked. The boys promised that they would be back in the morning to spray the Swabian girls with Pentecost water [4] and said, "Sleep well!"

But before Regensburg was out of bed on Pentecost Monday, the ship of girls was gliding down the Danube, with a cheerful choir-song in the air. And to those who had seen it landing, it seemed to have been a dream.

---

[4] It was a tradition for boys to spray the girls with water on Pentecost Monday and the next day, the girls threw water at the boys. Back then, girls and boys were not allowed to talk to one another unless it was in a big group. A boy would throw water at a girl to show he liked her.

Chapter 9

The Swabians in Vienna

Back when he had been recovering from his war wounds, Count Mercy had used his time in Vienna wisely. First of all, he had gotten the Imperial War Council to agree to his plans. This was not a difficult feat, because Prince Eugene was now President of that council. The Prince had only one concern: it was not in the interest of the royal court, he said, to colonize Hungary in such a grand manner without first gaining the approval of the Hungarian Diet. This could lead to problems later. He suggested that the General speak to *Hofkammerrat* Stephany. Stephany may know how to achieve the "miracle," as Prince Eugene put it, of getting a resolution of the Hungarian estates passed which would endorse this settlement. The Prince himself wanted nothing to do with that task.

And so two key people met and had a thorough discussion of matters which concerned them. They got to know each other and became friends. Stephany had been surprised when Mercy approached him for help, since the latter seemed to be the more influential of the two men. Mercy was a friend of the Generalissimo, the entire Court was grateful for his services, the women raved about him as hero and victor, and he was selfless and charismatic. As such, the now-healthy General stood before the *Hofkammerrat* and asked for his advice and assistance. The General wanted to convince him of the importance of his vision for Hungary—an issue which had Stephany's whole-hearted sympathy, although he did not think it wise in his official capacity to let on how near this was to his heart.

They found they had much in common. Of course, they did not agree about everything. The Count had set his sights too high and had made some financial miscalculations. But perhaps Stephany could help him out there.

He believed the City Bank of Vienna could be convinced to fund the Banat if they had enough property signed over as security. At this, Mercy laughed. The whole land registry of the Banat was an empty page; one could give the bank an entire Dukedom as security.

The *Hofkammerrat* did not share Prince Eugene's political misgivings. He believed that in the case of the Banat, the concerns were not justified. What did the Hungarian Diet have to do with it? Yet the Prince's concerns were astute and not ill advised. And since after many years the Hungarian Diet was to convene again in Pressburg (Bratislava), Stephany would see to it that the Hungarian Council would file the Proposal for new immigrants and so achieve the "miracle" that Prince Eugene wanted. That is why Mercy was to hasten the survey of the land to determine the placement of settlements.

And so Mercy returned to his work back in the Banat, satisfied with what he had accomplished, and left behind a new friend and ally in Stephany. The last evening in Vienna was spent with his nephew at the *Hofkammerat's* home, and Stephany's daughter, Fräulein Lottel, served the guests with quiet grace. Both uncle and nephew promised her their gracious remembrances, and they out-did one another in chivalry. As witness to this warm departure, the aunt would later repeatedly declare that Lottel could easily become the wife of the Governor of the Banat, who was still a desirable man.

The hoped for "miracle" actually took place one year later. The Hungarian Diet passed a resolution that free settlers were to be called to this largely depopulated country; as much land as they could cultivate and a six-year exemption from taxes would be given to them. They would own the land and it would be inherited by their children. Their authority to bring religious leaders and teachers of their own faith and nationality, to form communities, and appoint magistrates in free elections was self-evident. They were to establish a new homeland and could not be forced into serfdom. The Kaiser and king was asked to publicize this in the German states and in all his other provinces (Article 103, 1723).

Oh, how the eyes of the Generalissimo flashed when Stephany gave him this news. He immediately suggested to act quickly to call Germans, only Germans. For twenty years, he had only allowed German farmers and craftsmen to settle on his land, and he knew their value. The *Hofkammerrat*, together with Mercy, had worked out a draft of the law down to the smallest detail which had given preferencial treatment to German settlers. Their version only needed the approval of the Kaiser. But the declaration had been changed by some unknown person in the royal court. In his draft, Stephany had left the religious question open. In the final version, Catholicism was to

Chapter 9—The Swabians in Vienna

be preferred. Stephany only wanted Germans to be called, but immigrants were now also to be summoned from Spain, Italy and France and also from the southeastern neighbors of Hungary, the Serbs and Bulgarians, who still suffered under the Turkish yoke.

The latter change surprised the *Hofkammerrat* the most. Stephany had believed that the suggestion to call only Germans had the highest chance of being supported because of the precedent set in former decisions and secret agreements. After all, in 1689 a commission entrusted with establishing order in Hungary, chaired by Cardinal Kollonic, had asked for German settlers. "So that the Kingdom of Hungary, or at least a great part of it, would become Germanized in time to temper the Hungarian blood which has a tendency towards revolution and unrest with that of Germans, who hold a love and loyalty to their Kaiser and would be devoted to him as King of Hungary." That was the theory at the time, which was to be confidential.[1]

But these days a different Kaiser was at the head of the royal court. There was a reason that Spain was referred to first. Kaiser Karl had given up his short tenure as Spanish King and rushed home so as not to forfeit the crown of *Karl der Grosse* (Charlemagne), since he was the last Habsburg.[2] However, he still had many loyal followers in Catalonia who awaited his favors, since they were ostracized in their own country because of their loyalty to him. The Spanish noblemen who had followed their King to Austria could easily be rewarded: they could either make their fortune in his army or could receive an endowed church office or a manor which had become ownerless during the Counter-Reformation. But the people? Hundreds of Spanish families had settled in the Naples region and in Sicily, but they did not feel at home there. Now they wanted to resettle in the Banat. As for the Italian provinces, they were just as important to the Kaiser as the German ones. In Alsace and the small portion of Lorraine that belonged to France, there were still allies of the House of Habsburg. And the Serbs and Bulgarians? Well, they were called because of the belief that they would all want to flee from the Turks to settle in the neighboring country. And so it seemed that the Kaiser's Court was not counting on too many Germans.

The *Hofkammerrat* was not the man to grumble about orders from the

---

[1] This was back when Emporer Leopold, Charles VI's father, had taken back part of Hungary from the Turks, including Buda and Mohács. The area had been depopulated and reduced to extreme poverty and a plan was made for resettlement. This unfortunate sentence, which was supposed to be secret yet did leak out, was part of the reason that the Hungarian aristocracy regarded the intentions of the Habsburg monarchy as suspect.

[2] Emperor Charles VI (Kaiser Karl VI) took over after his brother, Emperor Josef I, died in 1711 of smallpox with no living male heirs.

highest authority. He followed the Kaiser's orders without complaint, even though the revisions made to the final law were against his better judgment. And so the Proclamation was taken by courier through many lands and published in newspapers everywhere. Count Mercy adjusted to the new situation better than Stephany. He decided to make this new development fit into his vision. He sent a letter, which he had his nephew write, to the *Hofkammerrat*. In this correspondence he stated that he welcomed people from the south. But they should not be sent to the Banat unless they had something to offer. He wanted to cultivate new crops. He needed rice farmers and breeders of silkworms—they would have a future in the Banat. Also, precious fruits like melons, figs and almonds should prosper in this climate and he awaited the southern peoples who understood something about growing them. But his main objective for the settlement did not change: German farmers! German craftsmen! Then, too, he could never have too many German schoolmasters.

In his own hand, the general added a postscript: "When the first almonds grow here on this land, I would like to invite your pretty daughter to share them with me."

The Councillor showed Lottel this unusual addendum to the correspondence. But she asked, "And the Captain did not write a postscript?"

"No, no, my child," answered the father laughingly. "The General can be permitted to make such a remark, but not his assistant!"

So now many peoples were on their way to Hungary, having been called by the Hungarian Parliament and the Kaiser. The Spaniards and Italians came from the south through Croatia, the Germans all came through Vienna. And they arrived in unforeseen numbers, descending on the Imperial City like a flash flood in recent weeks.

"Mary and Joseph, such a mass of people!" exclaimed the women selling fruit and fish at Schanzl on the Danube, as day after day the ships from Ulm, Günzburg and Regensburg landed. When the three giant Kehlheim flatboats docked, the entire city of Vienna came; everyone wanted to see the emigrating Swabians. And the many Swabians who lived in Vienna pushed through the crowds even more to go and talk to their countrymen. The Viennese did not know whether they should pity the people who left their homeland or envy them for their courage and initiative. They did not seem to be in need of sympathy, these Swabians; they all appeared to be quite valiant and well-nourished. When an old Swabian, who set forth with his children and grandchildren to find his fortune in a foreign land, was asked by a Viennese citizen how he could do such a thing in his advanced years, he answered in his easy dialect, "Oh, anywhere the good Lord lives, the Swabian will be able to find a home."

The officials of the Austrian and Hungarian Councils, of the Imperial War Council, and of the Magistrate were all frustrated by the unexpected blessing they received in the week after Pentecost Sunday. Where to put them until they received customs clearance? In the *Regensburger Hof* on Lugeck Square and in the *Stadt Nürnberg* Inn, the cheap rooms were jam-packed; the other rooms were too expensive for this crowd, since they were intended for merchants from the German states, not for farmers. *The Blue Duck* Inn and the *King of Hungary* Inn were too formal. This left only the large country inns on the outskirts of the city and the *Passauer Hof* in the Salzgries district. But even they were filled to capacity. If the cloisters and military barracks would not accommodate the overflow, it would be impossible to find lodging for all of these people. Then one of the skippers suggested they spend the night on the ships, and this seemed to be a good alternative. Georg Seemayer was willing to accommodate the people on his Kehlheim flatboat for three more days at the cost of one Kreuzer per person. After three days, though, the ships would have to be taken apart, because the wood from the Black Forest had already been sold.

"What, the boats are to be taken apart?" the officials exclaimed. "How can we bring the emigrants to Hungary?" The gentlemen were impressed with his large flatboats and looked at them with practiced eyes.

Seemayer shrugged his shoulders and went down to the Rotenturm gate to take up his quarters in the *Regensburger Hof*, where he always had a room waiting for him. He was extremely tired. If the Kaiser's ship building authority wanted to have his three Kehlheim flatboats, they knew where to find him. He was careful not to reveal that this ambush on Vienna had been intentional and that he had counted on selling more than just the wood from these boats.

Almost a week after the large Regensburg ships, Philipp Trauttmann and his wagon, the "Noah's Ark," arrived in Vienna. He had gone easy on his horses, which had brought him and his family from the *Rheinpfalz* to Austria and were to also bring him to Hungary. All along the way he had encountered people going the same way he was, poor devils who could not pay the fare on the ship, people without passes who had left their homes to find their fortune in Hungary. He had also seen courage in the face of misery but had not been able to help.

Near Passau, a strong young man had pushed his pale ailing wife in a wheelbarrow, while the children walked alongside. "Where to, *Landsmann*?"

Trauttmann had called to the man.

"To Hungary."

His wife Eva was so moved by the sight of the sick woman that she asked her husband to take the woman along on the wagon. Philipp shook his head. A sick woman? On his full wagon? That was not possible. The man should be able to find work on the way so that he could take a break. You cannot be in a hurry if you are walking and pushing a wheelbarrow. Our two boys already had to walk two hours each day in order to spare the horses. And Matz, too, had been walking. What would they do with one more on the wagon? She realized that he was right, but the loyalty of that man to his wife really touched her.

In Passau, where every ship had to dock for a day because its inhabitants were receiving the first part of their travel money, Trauttmann had to get his pass stamped once again. He did not receive any travel money and had not expected it. He traveled at his own expense and wanted to have a free hand in the choice of where he finally settled. In Engelhartszell, on the border, where the ships had to stop overnight for strict inspection, his pass had been thoroughly examined and Matz was once again called upon to get married. The border police were surprised that he had not converted to Catholicism, that the Kaiser's ambassador in Frankfurt had given him such a pass without stipulating that he would have to convert. "To send a brood of seven Protestants at one time!" exclaimed one of the financial officers. "Send them all back!"

Trauttmann came up with a response which he would remember with pride for the rest of his life. He said to the officer: "The best place to correct this mistake is in Vienna, where we will stay for eight days."

"Ah!" said the official. "The man can go," and stamped his pass. Then another official plainly asked Trauttmann whether he had a Protestant Bible with him. Trauttmann denied this.

"I'll see about that!" the official shouted and followed Trauttmann to his wagon.

"Everybody get off the wagon and take everything out of it!" ordered the official.

"What? You don't believe me?"

"It doesn't matter whether I believe you or not. Every ship that goes through the border is inspected. Look over there, farmer, do you see the smoke?"

Trauttmann looked in the direction in which the corporal was pointing and saw a smoldering woodpile. "Is that a funeral pyre for us?" he joked.

"You guessed it. It is a funeral pyre. It's a pile of Lutheran Bibles that are

Chapter 9—The Swabians in Vienna

being burned! Many on the ships denied carrying Bibles but we still found them. So, farmer, don't be stupid. Give me yours, it will save me the search."

Frau Eva and her children heard this rough exchange and they, too, looked toward the burning pile of Lutheran Bibles. So this was what her husband had kept secret from her in Regensburg? They were supposed to become Catholic. And her Philipp had wavered?

Glowering, Trauttmann stood next to his wagon.

"Go ahead and search!" he shouted. "We have time. But whoever clears out the wagon and finds nothing will have to put everything back. I am going to complain about this in Vienna. What is written in my pass? Does it not say that all officials should support me? Are you doing that?"

"Now, now, don't get all agitated. It is our responsibility that not one Lutheran Bible gets across the border. Understand?"

Then he climbed on the wagon and looked through everything, making a mess. He threw pillows, blankets and clothes around, grumbled and cursed and after a few minutes came into their view again without having found anything. "Go to the devil!" he called out and left.

"You too!" Trauttmann shouted after him with clenched fists. "Get the plague, you dog!" he added under his breath.

Frau Eva put her hand on his right arm and said, "Philipp, come to your senses. You don't want to be talking like that when we are about to go to a foreign land. That will not give us God's blessing on our trip."

He unclenched his fists and the tension left him. And as soon as his wife had restored order to the wagon, he urged the horses forward and drove hurriedly from that place. He did not want to rest there. But Eva and the children kept looking back at the smoking pile of burning Bibles at the Danube's banks. Since they had entered Bavaria, they had perceived that spirituality was expressed differently here, and it was doubly apparent in Austria. This country was undoubtedly Catholic. Statues of saints appeared on every road; people making pilgrimages cut across their way; they saw singing processions of believers here, outdoor May devotions and public prayers there. It seemed that everywhere they looked they saw signs of religious activity, which made the country seem romantic to them. The chapels high above, pilgrimage sites for thousands of the faithful, struck them as being poetic. But they asked themselves, are these German people? What they saw was foreign to them.

The day before *Fronleichnam*, the feast of Corpus Christi, Trauttmann drove his wagon into Vienna by the Mariahilf route. He had paid three *Kreuzer*, the charge for using the road, and set his horses in motion again when he saw something flash on the road ahead of him. It was a horseshoe! He quickly got off the wagon and picked it up. No common cart horse had lost this beautiful new horseshoe. He had never seen a finer one. Smiling, he handed his wife Eva the good luck charm for her to put into the wagon. Then he drove on. They arrived at their destination in good spirits without any other incidents. But the black horse must have hurt himself. He had favored his left front foot since yesterday. The stable master at their inn, the *Passauer Hof*, knew a good veterinarian next door who could help the horse. The hoof needed to be looked at. The vet wanted to know how long they were staying.

Trauttmann said that was uncertain. It depended on how things went in the city.

Even *Hofkammerrat* Joseph von Stephany was astounded at the wave of German immigrants that arrived in this month of May. Nobody had expected this. Naturally the Kaiser had sent Commissioners to all regions and they had worked hard all winter to recruit new settlers. Still, their work had resulted in these surprising swells of people, and not all Viennese officials could cope with this. The nobles in the Hungarian Council were the first to fail. They began to grumble because their lifestyle and pleasures had been disrupted. They let the emigrants wait in Vienna until they had used up every last penny of their savings. Many left for Hungary without a pass. Some were disgruntled and turned back, cursing those in Vienna. Such mismanagement, such a deception. The Imperial War Council, too, had other duties and responsibilities.

And so Stephany, as head of the Austrian Council, founded a seperate Settlement Commission, which was composed of representatives of each agency who would be dedicated to the matters in their jurisdiction. An army of clerks was given the task of clearing the backlog of applications. The *Hofkammerrat* assigned his old actuary, Franz Hildebrandt, to the commission, entrusting him with the details. He himself would set up the basic principles and make decisions in unusual circumstances. However, he kept an eye on all developments of the entire situation, constantly staying in touch with the commissioners in the German states, with Mercy in the Banat, and with all Bishops and Counts in Hungary who wished to have settlers on their property. He kept watch to make sure that the conditions which the state promised the colonists on public property were also honored on the private lands. Attempts to subjugate or to enslave the settlers were noted—at least those he knew about. These infractions were noted in a special book. He expected that the transfer of these settlers to another region would one day be possible. But in this vast land, hundreds of things could happen which he would never find out about. That is why he required anyone who came from Hungary with news or complaints to come before him. He also took the responsibility for another aspect of this process: the people who were waiting in Vienna were to be shown as many of the sights of the city as they could take in, so they would leave with a lasting impression of this great and beautiful Imperial City.

Chapter 10

Fronleichnam in Old Vienna

Even before sunrise, the Viennese were fighting to get good seats in the inner city. They all wanted to see and enjoy the *Fronleichnam*[1] procession, the greatest spectacle of the year, in which the Church and the Imperial Court joined forces. Guards had taken up positions before daybreak to help the police keep the streets free of horses and wagons and to keep people lined up in an orderly manner. Ever since the festivities in the suburbs had been changed to be held on the Sunday after Corpus Christi, the number of curious and faithful at the main festival rose from year to year. According to the *Stadtkommandant*, the crowds were getting to be so large that it would be impossible to control them, and he could not be held responsible unless he was allowed to close the city gates. His request was denied. After all, the rescheduling of the festivities in the suburbs had occurred to enhance the festival in the inner city, to allow total participation of all guilds and the population of the entire city. He was told to build platforms in side streets to accommodate the many observers, and that the police should closely monitor and fine the racketeers who charged excessive prices for renting window spots from which to watch. With these measures there would be room enough for all the spectators. Then, as if to further taunt the *Stadtkommandant* and his troubles, the Austrian Council demanded that an area be set aside annually on Graben Street, where everyone crammed together to watch, for a thousand or so Swabians and their families. The Viennese would have enough opportunity to see the *Fronleichnam* procession in their lifetime, but the Swabians would

---

1 *Fronleichnam:* the feast of Corpus Christi, the Solemnity of the most Holy Body and Blood of Jesus Christ. The Catholic Church traditionally celebrated this feast day the Thursday after Trinity Sunday, which is one week after Pentecost Sunday.

only see it once, and never again.

And there they stood, wedged into the buzzing swarm of the urban population near the new *Pestsäule*[2] on Graben Street. Wherever one looked, all one could see were people, people. Up and down the lane, row after row of onlookers stood waiting. All the way up to the roof hatches, heads pushed against heads in alarming abundance. A humming and buzzing noise rose from the crowd as if they were shouting, yet they only talked and whispered. Separate groups of Swabians had been brought from their lodging quarters by Viennese public officials and they greeted one another as old friends. Not all were at this procession; some had already had their papers cleared and were on their way to the Banat. The first Kehlheim flatboat had left two days ago and was already underway to Ofen (Buda). Soon it would be their turn. "It's about time," sighed Nikolaus Eimann, the man who had been so interested in Hungary at the *Schwarzen Adler* Inn years ago. Sure enough, he and all six of his sons, along with a few neighbors, had left Blautal in the Black Forest and had been in Vienna for over a week. They talked about who was assigned to which section of Hungary. Wörndle, the Blaubeuren school master's assistant, was sent to Temesvar to be a school principal there. Johann Schultheiss was sent to Werschetz where he was to start a vineyard. Peter Kremling was assigned to the border town of Weisskirchen and Kaspar Kraft to somewhere in the Batschka.

"What about those from the *Pfalz* who we met in Regensburg?" someone asked. "Staudt and Luckhaup?" Nobody knew about them. They had lost sight of them. However, some who were staying at the *Passauer Hof* Inn reported that Trauttmann, who was also from the *Pfalz*, had found lodging there as well.

Suddenly, the chatter stopped. Two battalions of grenadiers wearing tall bearskin hats marched down Kohlmarkt Street from the Hofburg, clearing the middle and forming a line to block the constant swell of onlookers spilling from the alleyways. The grenadiers stood side by side all the way to St. Stephen's Cathedral, and the city guard pulled back into the side streets.

The officials whispered to the Swabian farmers that these were the grenadiers who had stormed the Sultan's encampment at Belgrade. They were chosen for today's honor guard shortly after their arrival to the garrison in Vienna. Wherever they appeared, the audience enthusiastically cheered '*Vivat!*'

No sooner had the orders been completed to clear the way for the proces-

---

[2] A memorial that had been put up to commemorate those who died of the plague.

sion of the court, that the clock struck eight and from St. Stephen sounded forth the hollow, eerily beautiful tone of a bell. As it rang, the sound became more powerful and splendid, to the point that window panes rattled and the earth trembled. Never before had the people of Swabia or the Rhine[3] heard such a bell, and they all looked at one another. An official told them that the bell was called the "*Pummerin*" and had been cast from the one hundred and eighty Turkish cannons that had been left at the gates of Vienna in 1683. It had first tolled on the day that Kaiser Karl had returned from his coronation in Frankfurt. Since it was too heavy for the tower of St. Stephen, it was only rung on very special occasions.

Everyone held their breath and listened to the sound of this great bell. Trauttmann, who had been brought to *Petersplatz* with his family, also heard the explanation of the origin of this bell of St. Stephen. He was greatly moved by the idea that this bell, which was composed of the same metal that once spewed fire and disaster into the city, now was forced to call faithful Christians to prayer and devotion. He would have liked to express his feelings to his Eva but could not find the right words. She stood beside him, looking grim and dour as he had never seen her before. She would much rather have stayed at the inn.

When the ringing of the bell came to an end, the call went out: "The Kaiser is coming!" Like a wave these words were repeated over and over among the onlookers along the street.

Two horsemen of the Guard's Regiment led the parade, riding black horses with golden harnesses. They were followed by a long line of nobles and dignitaries wearing enormous wigs, the nobles' pages, and the high officers of the guard. Finally six horses came into sight, pulling a magnificent coach in which the Kaiser sat, looking very earnest and solemn. The last Habsburger! He did not look to the right or to the left as his subjects removed their hats to show respect; he passed by like a statue. Then came the Kaiserin: Empress Elisabeth Christine. Her glistening golden coach also was pulled by six white horses, and she radiated a dazzling beauty. Whenever she appeared in public, a thrill of joy went through the crowd, and they all paid homage to her. Even on this holy day, the people could barely contain themselves. The most beautiful woman in Europe, as Lady Montague of England had called her, felt that the cheers coming from behind the Grenadier Honor Guards were actually for her. She smiled and carefully nodded her head, her hair piled high and set with a hundred diamond pins that glistened in the morning

---

3 Recall that Swabian refers to any settlers who came from Germany

sun so that one could hardly take a closer look. Her eyes took in the entire crowd, even noticing the colorful *Trachten* of the emigrants, and many of them believed they saw a look of joyful surprise on her smiling face.

Perhaps among them she saw the *Trachten* of her countrymen from Braunschweig. After all, she was the daughter of the Duke of Braunschweig-Lüneburg-Wolfenbüttel. She had converted to Catholicism in order to become Queen of Spain just like her aunt, Amalie Wilhelmine von Hannover, who had become Catholic so that she could marry Kaiser Josef I. Josef I had died young, and now Elisabeth herself was Kaiserin, since her husband had risen to the throne after his brother's untimely death. Her proud aunt, the Kaiser's widow, only had daughters, and so had to stand aside and allow Karl to take the throne since she had not given her husband Josef an heir. Unfortunately, the beautiful Elisabeth Christine did not have a son either, her only son having died in infancy. The people still hoped for an heir to the throne, that God could still bestow this grace upon her. Whoever saw her in all her glory, a picture of good health, believed that this was still possible. Kaiser Karl, however, was taking measures in case this did not happen. In all his states, including Hungary, he had introduced a law called the Pragmatic Sanction which guaranteed that his little daughter Maria Theresia would inherit his throne. He was no longer holding out for a male heir.

Presently the four horse carriage of the Kaiser's daughter came in view, led by a group of squires. The princess, who was still a child, looked toward the public with big bright eyes, as the court mistress who sat across from her spoke to her. Suddenly Maria Theresa waved her hand, something that was not part of Spanish Court etiquette, to the group of farmers who stood there in the midst of her Viennese public. She appeared to ask questions and receive some answers from the court mistress, looked at them again and nodded and smiled.

The procession of the Court to St. Stephen's Cathedral continued. Next came the noblewomen in coaches drawn by two horses and many princely members of the court. Generalissimo Prince Eugene marched on foot, surrounded by Commanders and Generals, who were then followed by officers of all ranks. The public ministers formed their own group in the procession. The minister and presidents of the Imperial Court had precedence, after them came all the *Hofkammerräte* (Imperial Councillors). The officials who had brought the Swabians to the procession were sure to point *Hofkammerrat* Joseph von Stephany out to them, since he was especially concerned with their settlement. He, too, looked at the group with satisfaction.

A large group of titled chamberlains ended the procession. These were nobles who had in part purchased their titles with their wealth and who enjoyed the honor of serving food to the Imperial family at the large Court festivals.

The end of the procession was followed by four columns of guards, each ten by ten men of enormous size: a moving wall of fluttering helmet plumes.

All bells tolled to indicate that the Royal Court had entered St. Stephen's. Now the suspense eased and everyone gave their opinions, passed judgment, gossiped and praised. They found the Empress more beautiful than ever and little "Therese" adorable. The Spanish Maria Althan, the wife of the *Obersthofmeister*, supposedly had not come because she had demanded the honor of a four-horse coach, but this had not been granted to her. She thought it was her right. The Spanish were not loved in Vienna; it was thought that they overstepped their bounds at the Royal Court.

The farmers and their wives admired the richness and glamour of the court which had unfolded before them. But was there even one among the thousands who was thinking about the purpose of this religious holiday? Only thoughts of worldly things had been brought up by this parade. Of course, the religious portion of the celebration was just about to begin. The Kaiser's procession likely had just finished arriving at St. Stephen's. After a short break, the bells began to ring again when the next procession started coming out of the church.

Fronleichnam!

The Catholic Church knows no grander feast than this. The full glory of spring roars through it. The miracle of life which comes from the earth every year and is shown in its full splendor at springtime—this miracle dwells in the symbol of this feast, the body of the Lord. Christmas marks the turning point at which winter's cold days begin to get longer; Easter marks the beginning of spring; in it lies the promise of the resurrection; but *Fronleichnam* is the fulfillment of that promise, since by this time of year the great wonder of nature has occurred! This feast is the triumph over all hostile forces, a song in praise of God's great might. All the profoundness and mindfulness of the pagan Germanic traditions have been absorbed into the Roman Church. The barbarians converted from their belief in the God Wotan to a new faith in Jesus Christ, and they enriched and deepened the new faith with the traditions they brought to Christianity. Willingly and pliantly the church took on this spiritual heritage. And in the end, the church's strongest pillar is this ancient connection with nature. Other church feasts might wither or die away, but those which follow the rhythm of the seasons must remain, since they glorify and illuminate the miracle of nature, that which God created.

Chapter 10—*Fronleichnam* in Old Vienna

Today, all the streets were strewn with millions of flowers and the fresh new greenery of the meadows. Sprays of branches budding with new leaves leaned against the houses. It was as if the forest, fields and meadows had been brought into the city.

Amid the ringing of bells and waving of flags, accompanied by music and song, a second great procession came from St. Stephen's and wended its way through Kärntner Street. From altar to altar, the old Archbishop carried the Monstrance that held the Most Holy Consecrated Host, leading a three hour procession across Augustiner Street, past the Michaelertor at the Hofburg, along Kohlmarkt and Graben Streets, and back to the Cathedral. The clerics, the religious brethren and nuns walked in double rows at the front of the procession with the youth who had been entrusted to them. Next came the Brothers of the Schotten, the Augustinians, the Michaelers and the Dominicans, the Capuchins and Franciscans, Carmelites, Order of the Spaniards, the Minorites and Pozmanites, the Merciful, the Mechitarists and Piarists and Redemptorists, the Servists and many other orders. These were followed by the Jesuits with their noble seminarians and the notables of the University. The great magnitude of this veritable army of God's workers could barely be comprehended.

The Archbishop was preceded by his entire religious crew of cathedral lords and prelates. The Kaiser and Kaiserin followed with their massive Royal Court. Then came the Magistrate of Vienna, the nobility, the Guilds with their flags, and the multitude of faithful societies and brotherhoods.

Every time they arrived at a street altar, the whole procession stopped and the Archbishop led everyone in worship. Four young pages spread out a carpet before the Kaiser and Kaiserin, and the royal couple knelt down. A young canon, a Jesuit, read the gospel in Latin with a loud resounding voice, cymbals, drums and horns accompanied the Latin church choir, the vessels of incense emitted the intoxicating scent and everyone threw themselves to the dusty ground as the Bishop held up the symbol of the day, the Host, the Most Holy Body of Jesus Christ, in triumph for all to see. The miracle of nature became the miracle of the Eucharist.

The German farmers were full of amazement and untold emotion at the religious display they had just witnessed. In this procession, the entire social order had paraded before them, and they had seen its most powerful leaders in person, along with the strong brotherhood of the citizens and the guilds. But there was one element missing: the farmers had not been represented. Did any of those viewers feel that their class, too, should have been included in this procession?

The crowd was still in a daze. They were granted only a short pause before the Royal Court returned to the palace in the order in which they had come. After this, the honor guard dispersed. And like a sudden flood the throng streamed to the altars and took the flowers, tore down the little birch trees and took branches home as keepsakes. These were holy mementos of this religious feastday, keepsakes to bless their homes and protect them from need, illness and all kinds of evil that the year could bring.

The farmers, too, took what they could. For them it had been especially memorable. Many a farmer's wife took a few blessed green leaves to put in her prayer book which she would one day show her grandchildren as a memento of *Fronleichnam* in Vienna.

Eva Trauttmann looked at the goings-on without saying a word. She held her three boys back when they wanted to pick up flowers like the others. Only Ferdinand, the youngest, took one of the sprays which had been blessed and stuck it on his hat. But when she tried to grab it, Philipp Trautmann put his hand on his wife's arm.

"Give it a rest already!" he said. And she understood his threatening look. No matter how Lutheran she was, she decided it was not worth an argument, and so she let it go.

Chapter 11

Two Special Cases

Today there were two special cases for the Settlement Commission to decide. Twenty people from Baden-Baden demanded that Kaspar Melcher, who had no papers and had mixed in with their group, be denied further travel with them. They were disconcerted by the thought of him traveling to Hungary with them and refused to embark on any ship he was on. Even during the trip to Vienna, a few had threatened to throw him into the river, but nobody would say why.

Franz Hildebrandt spoke to each traveller individually. It turned out that they suspected he was a hangman, and they would not tolerate such a person in their midst. They were honest people, after all.

Kaspar denied this; he claimed to be a farmer's son. But then one of the men told him straight to his face that he had seen him in Karlsruhe, that he was really the son of the Karlsruhe executioner. Another of the men said he knew the boy's father, the hangman. They could not tolerate such a person to be settled in the new land with them. They would all rather go back home again before they accepted that.

Kasper, a wild young man with a large build and fiery eyes, fell on his knees before Hildebrandt and begged to be allowed to go to Hungary, for God's sake. He wanted to change! He wanted to earn an honest living like every other man! Would this not be possible anywhere in this world for him?

Actuary Hildebrandt raised his eyebrows and looked at the boy—he felt some sympathy for the young man. He liked him, but was also overcome by the gruesome thought that he was the spawn of someone who hung people for a living. As young as he was, he must have already skewered, drawn and quartered some poor sinners. It was understandable that people did not want to be settled in the same community or sleep in the same lodgings as him. Hildebrandt promised the settlers that they could go on without Kaspar. Another option would present itself for Kaspar.

"What other option?" screamed the young man. He shuddered at the thought of possibly having to become a hangman in Vienna.

He would be told of the decision tomorrow or the day after. He should come back to find out, replied the Chairman of the Commission.

Franz Hildebrandt was a deliberate, almost timid man. He was the Chairman of the Settlement Commission, which was temporarily located in the Viennese City Hall on Wippler Street where space had reluctantly been given for this purpose. He felt that he was only a representative of the *Hofkammerrat*. It reassured him that for controversial cases he had only to cross the street if he wanted to consult Stephany. Just don't make him personally responsible for official decisions! He needed someone to cover his back.

The German farmers came with their families in droves, to personally present themselves to the gentlemen of the Commission and to exchange the passes they had received in the German states. From here on, those passes were null and void. In Vienna, emigrants were given a new document for the Banat, either a certificate guaranteeing settlement or their final settlement pass, as well as the promised additional three guilders per person. But before the officials paid the money, they wanted to see each person for themselves. Also, all names had to be registered in a book. Those who belonged together would stay together. People who came from the same village or county would be settled in the same community, if possible. The officials in Vienna could not guarantee that, but the settlement passes which they issued included these requests. They saw to it that those who were from the same area were put on the same boat to Ofen (Buda) at the same time. At Ofen, some people were re-assigned, and those who were to settle in the interior of Hungary often had to finish their journey on foot.

The officials sorted the emigrants into categories. Farmers with legitimate passes were free from taxes for six years; skilled craftsmen for ten years, because there were not enough. Those without passes, some of whom had escaped from their overlords without having bought their freedom, received no travel money and had no assurance of settlement, according to the rules. That's the price they had to pay for their unlawful act. They were allowed to go to Hungary but were not officially processed in Vienna. After all, some German *Fürsten* were already complaining that Vienna was luring all their subjects away, and so Vienna did not officially make special allowances for those without passes.

Chapter 11—Two Special Cases

However, if a passless emigrant was in great need, the mild hand of the *Hofkammerat* always intervened. He took a lot upon himself. He even said that those who came without passes would be the most loyal among the new subjects. They would not turn around and go back! And he made sure the poorest among them received travel money.

The Commission was very adamant that everyone be truthful in their applications, especially when stating their occupations. Woe to the weaver who said he was a farmer in order to obtain a land grant! Count Mercy was likely to have him beaten and chased away. This was why the *Hofkammerrat* wanted truthful statements, and Franz Hildebrandt let no one through whom he suspected of falsification. Hildebrandt was also strict about religion. He was a member of the Order of St. Michael's Brotherhood and was thus bound always and everywhere to the protection and expansion of the one and only true Roman Catholic faith. He sent anyone that appeared suspect to him to the priest at *Maria am Gestade* to teach them catechism. If the person did not bring a certificate from the priest, he would not get a settlement pass. And in this way many were converted.

The second case which Franz Hildebrandt had to look into today was that of Philipp Trauttmann from Bobenheim in the *Rheinpfalz*. Had it not been clearly stated that only German Catholics need apply? Whoever came had to be ready to convert to Catholicism. But this man did not want to convert; he would not go see the priest at *Maria am Gestade*. Rather than convert, he would go to Poland or Schlesien to look for a new homeland. The officials told him, "*In Polen ist nichts zu holen!*" (There is nothing to be had in Poland.) But Trauttmann stood by his statement. He refused to convert.

Franz Hildebrandt took a good look at the seven people whom Trauttmann had brought before the Commission and hesitated to give the verdict that was on the tip of his tongue. He knew he could not send these people to the Banat. That region had to remain Catholic. But perhaps there was another area where they could settle, where their religion would not be held against them.

He asked Trauttmann to also come back in two days.

The *Hofkammerrat*, to whom Hildebrandt presented both cases, made the first decision very quickly: Kaspar Melcher could learn a trade which suited him, here in Vienna. He thought that Kaspar would be able to find a Guild which could give him his freedom within a year if nobody gave him away and he performed well. The young man could then go to Hungary as an apprentice, where he would find his good fortune like thousands of others.

Kaspar was pleased. He would be happy to become an apprentice if they could help him find a master craftsman who would take him. Hildebrandt told him to come back another day and he would take care of him.

In the case of Trauttmann, Councillor Stephany decided he wanted to see him in person. So the next morning Philipp Trauttmann put on his best suit and his Sunday hat and walked from the *Passauer Hof* over the *Fischerstiege* to the upper city. His wife gave him her blessing. She knew how important this meeting was. They had stayed in Vienna for eight days, and it could have been for nothing. They had rented a room at their own expense; only Matz had slept in the wagon, since it could not be left alone. They couldn't go on like this. The situation had to be resolved one way or another.

The night before, when complete darkness had fallen, Philipp had taken the Bible out from the deepest recesses of his wagon. It had been hidden in a feed bag full of oats. Back in the room, the family sat in a circle around him and listened to him. Trauttmann read to them the epistle of St. James from the New Testament and explained it in his simple manner. It is the epistle about patience and suffering. "Blessed is the man who perseveres under trial because, having stood the test, he will receive the crown of life that the Lord has promised to those who love him," Trauttmann read in a loud voice. "When tempted, no one should say, 'God is tempting me.' For God cannot be tempted by evil, nor does He tempt anyone; but each man is tempted when he is enticed by his own evil desire."

The boys, who had been overjoyed when they found out that the Holy Book had been saved, listened intently as their father read. They became very prayerful at his little sermon which followed, although they barely understood it. But when it was over, Matz insisted that no minister could give a better homily than Philipp. Eva agreed and gave her husband a kiss. She hid the Bible again after Philipp left the next morning and made the children and Matz swear never to say anything about the book, no matter what happened. They promised this and were proud to be let in on the secret.

When *Hofkammerrat* Joseph von Stephany was told that a farmer was waiting for him in the waiting room, he allowed Trauttmann to be let in. When he entered, Stephany stood up from his desk and went to shake his hand. The man had been described to him in a very positive way—and by Hildebrandt no less, who as a member of St. Michael's Brotherhood was Catholic to the core, but simply could not reject him. Even the pass that was laid before him was an obvious recommendation. Trauttmann must have pleased the Ambassador in Frankfurt as well.

Indeed, he did make a good impression with his vigor and the honesty of his speech. Stephany studied him in a friendly manner and let him talk for a

Chapter 11—Two Special Cases 117

while before he broke in, "I already know what this is about. Tell me, didn't you know that the Kaiser, himself a Roman Catholic, wanted only Catholics as new settlers?"

Yes, said Trauttmann, he had heard that.

"But then, why did you come anyway?"

He could not believe that in such a large realm, where there were already Protestants, there would be no place for him and his family, Trauttmann replied modestly. He had come at his own risk and had not asked for travel money. He did not want to be a burden to anyone. But no one could induce him to leave his German religion. He, his wife and his four children would have to be permitted to remain what they were. Also he was responsible before God for Matz, his farmhand and nephew.

The *Hofkammerrat* paced back and forth and seemed to be lost in deep thought. The words of this simple man who remained true to his religion touched his heart, which could be quite affected when the strife between Christian religions was discussed. He was so sensitive about this matter because he knew very well that his Viennese ancestors had also been Protestants. Back then, edicts had been issued one after the other. The first warned Protestants to return to the Roman Catholic Church. Next, they were threatened and given specific deadlines. Then all rights of citizenship were taken away. Viennese doctors were even forbidden to care for any sick Lutherans. Then came the final proclamation. Stephany's grandfather, who had told him all this, had been ten years old when the catastrophe broke out and all Protestants had to leave the city. Six thousand Viennese had to leave with wives and children because of their beliefs. The expellees were paid the appraised value of their homes, but they had to pay the state ten percent of that as a tax for leaving. In the end, many gave in and became Catholic. The Stephanys, too, remained in Vienna, and the children had from then on been sent to the Jesuit school. His ancestors had loved their homeland more than their religion. This farmer was willing to give the former up in order to save the latter. Who was right? Where was the truth? Couldn't God be served in every denomination? Did it matter so much which form the worship to Him should take, that people took part in bloody wars over this, and that hearts needed to be so burdened? Stephany felt himself to be Catholic, but he was saddened when he had to make an official decision based on his religion.

Trauttmann's eyes followed the Councillor as he paced back and forth. Was the *Hofkammerrat* trying to find a decision that would benefit him? The man must be having a hard time finding a suitable resolution.

Finally Stephany stopped in front of Trauttmann and looked at him in a friendly manner. "What you have said," began Stephany, "is not dishonorable in my eyes. Perhaps there will come a time when these sensitive questions will be judged less harshly, God willing. I do not want to close the way to Hungary for you. But I cannot send you to the Banat, where it is said that milk and honey flow. I have no authority for that. Stay on the right side of the Danube to go to Mohács and Fünfkirchen. From there the roads lead to Bellye, which belongs to Prince Eugene, to Högyész in Tolnau County, which is the property of Count Mercy, and then to Tevel and further on. That region is now called *die Schwäbische Türkei,* Swabian Turkey, because there are so many Germans where formerly many Turks lived. You should be able to find contacts there who will be able to connect you with one or another community. There is even a Protestant community there called Murgau. Don't ask too much and just go find a place. What happens there on private property is no concern of mine. The landowners there are looking for colonists. I am sorry that I cannot settle a capable and brave man like you on the Kaiser's public property."

Phllipp Trauttmann, who had listened carefully, was so surprised he did not know what to say. The Councillor gave him back the pass he had received in Frankfurt, saying, "Keep this and take care of it! It may be useful to you someday. Tomorrow, go to the Hungarian government offices in the Vordere Schenken-Strasse Nummer 49. On my recommendation, you will be given a pass to the Counties of Tolnau and Baranya in Hungary."

Trauttmann finally found himself able to speak. "Then not to the Banat, your High Born Eminence?"

"No."

"To Swabian Turkey instead?"

"Yes, my dear man."

"Past Mohács and Fünfkirchen, over to Tevel?"

"Yes. You seem to understand everything."

"Your Grace, I thank you with all my heart and soul. You have taken a heavy burden off of my heart."

"Good luck to you on your way," said Stephany and dismissed him.

Tears came to the eyes of the tanned man as the Councillor gave him these kind words of departure. He hardly found the door on his way out, his eyes were so watery. Had not the official at the border to Austria cursed at him, "Go to the devil"? But the kindness of the Councillor had made everything good again.

He could not get to the *Passauer Hof* quickly enough to tell his wife what he had experienced. She rejoiced with him over the news. However, her first and only question was, "Not to the Banat?" The boys, too, repeated: "Not to the Banat?"

The notion of the paradise in the Banat had settled in their minds, and it was hard to accept another region. Still, this new idea seemed like a good one. They were to go to Swabian Turkey. Trauttmann was certain that they would soon all be endeared to the concept of this new settlement, *die Schwäbische Türkei*.

Chapter 12

A Guest from the Banat

The *Hofkammerrat* had come to dinner exactly on time. To Tante Mathilde, he appeared quite cheerful as he encountered her in the hallway. For his part, he noticed that her face was flushed and that she was still busy in the pantry, so he teased her that perhaps he should not have been quite so punctual. He could see in her face that dinner was not ready.

She admitted that he was right. "But why, hmm? Can you guess?" she asked slyly and almost gleefully. No, he could not guess.

Because they'd had company, and she'd had to play the role of hostess. She had to be like Cerberus, the three headed watchdog instead of just cooking, she grumbled good-naturedly.

"Ah! So a male visitor!"

"Absolutely! Absolutely!" she said and hurried into the kitchen.

Lottel, who had heard her father's voice, burst from the living quarters. "Papa, Papa," she called, "Can you guess who was here?"

She flung herself against his chest, grabbed his hand and kissed it.[1]

"How can I guess that? How would I know what conquests you made in the Ballhaus Theater yesterday? By the way, you really performed well, very well!"

"Just think, Papa, Count Mercy is in Vienna!" she said, beaming.

"Impossible! My child, that is simply not possible!" said the Imperial Councillor. She hooked her arm into her father's and went into the dining room with him.

---

1 Hand-kissing was much more common in that era; it was a gesture indicating courtesy, respect, admiration or devotion by man towards a woman, by a vassal towards his master or a child towards his parent.

Chapter 12—A Guest from the Banat

"Why should it not be possible," she asked cheerfully. "Or are you perhaps thinking of the Governor?"

"Well yes, who else? Can there be another Count Mercy?"

"Ah so, you don't know. Oh Papa, I always believed that you knew everything!"

"What is it that I don't know?"

"Mercy's nephew has been adopted by him. And the Kaiser has awarded him the title of Count!" she responded merrily.

"You mean Captain von Mercy?"

"Not Captain, Major! He is now a Major," she laughed. "I guess you don't know everything about what is going on in the world, Papa!"

"You may be right. Whatever happens outside my official duties, I am always the last to know. Is the young man in Vienna in order to have an audience with the Kaiser?"

"Yes," she said importantly. "He wants to give his thanks to the Kaiser, and he has a mission at the Imperial War Council. And there was someone—well, someone he wanted to see again here in Vienna."

"Oh, it's you that he wanted to see?" The father looked into her shining eyes.

She did not lower her eyes, but simply replied, "Yes, Papa."

The Councillor shook his head. "He told you this straight out? He said this to you even though he has only seen you twice in his lifetime?"

"He at least let me notice it."

"Notice, eh? Be careful, my child, that you do not take the flirtations of a young Count as genuine. The fortune your aunt read in the cards may have higher demands on Madame Fortuna than she can fulfill."

"I know what I know," said Lottel stubbornly.

"Yes, yes, all right," grumbled her father. "Tante Mathilde has talked and talked for three years until you believed her fantasies. You know, Lottel, I always thought you were smarter than your old aunt. That's why I never seriously objected. But…"

Lottel set the table while her father spoke. She noticed that he spoke in the Viennese dialect, which he did when he had especially strong feelings about something.

"But Papa it is too late, much too late," she said serenely.

"It cannot be too late, Lottel, to remind you that you are just a young bourgeois girl."

"Oh Papa, oh, I have been part of the nobility for ten years, and he has only been a Count for two weeks."

"Crazy child! Our official nobility! That doesn't count for much in his circles! It's only paper!"[2]

"It seems that it does mean something, Papa. Why did he come to us first? Hmm? He arrived in Vienna at nine in the morning, and at half past eleven he asked, in French, if he could be permitted to speak to *Mademoiselle* Charlotte von Stephany. '*Oui, oui,*' I said."

The *Hofkammerrat* laughed.

Tante Mathilde came into the room, followed by the maid carrying the soup. The aunt now assumed the role of matron. She sat at the head of the table, made the sign of the cross and ladled out the soup. "I take it you've already told him everything?" she looked at Lottel and smiled.

"Not everything," said Lottel and quickly started to eat the soup. "I left something for my aunt to say."

"Oh really," she responded, tongue in cheek. "The warm regards to the Herr Imperial Councillor, or the respectful greetings from the Herr Governor?"

Stephany was annoyed. "All right, so a new Count was here. Do not make such a big deal of this courtesy visit. I can already see what is happening. The gentlemen in the Banat need me, and so they flatter you a bit so they can get what they want. I suggest to both of you that you not take this too seriously."

"How can you say that?" the quick tempered aunt asked. "Does the *Herr Hofkammerrat* not know that we have our own eyes and ears? Herr Major was not making fools of us. It is just as I prophesied back when he first saw Lottel. My cards never deceive me. Three days ago they told me: Good fortune will enter this house. And now it has arrived."

And when Stephany laughed heartily, she continued hotly, "At first I thought it would be His Excellency. But now it's the youngster. Well, one can be slightly mistaken."

The aunt signaled to Lottel to go and ring the bell on the *Glockenschelle*, which was connected to the kitchen.

The maid brought the meat and vegetables, and the aunt kept talking. She wasn't sure if everything was in order with the meal. The visitor had held her up too long. If this keeps happening, she would have to look for a Swabian cook, she joked.

The Imperial Councillor sighed, "Finally!"

---

[2] Nobility was an important social distinction between landed people of property and those who are noble on paper only. The *Hofkammerrat* has been given nobility as an official of the state; he was not born a noble.

Chapter 12—A Guest from the Banat

"What do you mean, finally, is that my thanks?"

"Dear Mathilde, for how long have I been trying to give you a cook?" said the *Hofkammerrat*. "Tomorrow she will be in the house."

"Why not today?" the aunt retorted.

"I asked you to be a mother to Lottel. That you are also a good cook, that was a bonus, and we are very grateful, but now I need you to spend more time with Lottel."

"All right, all right," answered the aunt huffily.

"The girl has to be out in the world more. She needs a worthy chaperone who can introduce her to society," the Councillor continued. "She has not been out much, so she hangs her heart on the first man she meets. From now on things will be different. But who is to accompany her to the comedy theater, the *Ballhaus*? Me? That won't do. I need someone to take care of Lottel. The cooking, anyone can do that."

"Excuse me, cooking is an art," said the Aunt.

"And a virtue!" answered the Councillor. "I know. However, I would prefer if the aunt is more concerned with Lottel, than with the *Kotelettel* she will make for dinner for the evening!"

The Aunt amiably replied, "All right, all right, I will take Lottel out more. But what about the cost of all the finery I will need? Who will pay for my stylish clothes," she asked the *Hofkammerrat*, "if I have to play the part of a society woman?"

Stephany laughed. "Now I've opened my big mouth, you're already giving me a bill for your services! "

Both women laughed. Lottel walked over to the *Glockenschelle* to call for the maid once more. "Dearest Papa," Lottel said "I have thought for a long time that we live too simply. When I see how extravagantly the families of other Councillors live…"

"Give it a rest, now, child," said Stephany. After the maid had left the room, he asked, "How long will the Major remain in Vienna?"

"Four weeks," said Lottel happily.

Tante Mathilde added, "He will give you the honor of calling on you at the *Hofkanzlei* tomorrow."

"Well, yes. They need me again. I will take this opportunity to take a close look at him, this nephew. A very close look. Will we have Turkish coffee today?" asked Stephany suddenly.

"But of course!" said the aunt and hurried into the kitchen to prepare the coffee herself.

When father and daughter were alone, the *Hofkammerrat* asked, "Were you over at mother's?"

Lottel lowered her eyes. In a whisper, she confessed, "I brought her a few of the flowers he gave me."

"You're a good daughter," said the Councillor.

It was a warm and sunny June morning in Vienna as Anton von Mercy drove out to the Belvedere to present himself to Generalissimo Prince Eugene as a representative of his uncle. The Prince was a morning person, and he held his audiences while others were still asleep. The Major was no exception; he was to arrive at seven in the morning. When he drove up to the palace of the lower Belvedere Palace, there were already several footmen standing in front of coaches and also a number of people of high rank driving away, apparently having already had their audience with the Generalissimo.

The Major checked in with a Colonel, the adjutant of the Generalissimo. Then a sleek French valet stepped forward and invited the Count to follow him. His Highness was waiting. The valet led him through a series of residences, rooms that were not ostentatious but furnished with the artistic taste of an aristocrat, and out into the open, into the park.

The change of scenery was startling. Even as one stepped out onto the narrow area covered with fine gravel, one saw a large park area in the style of *Le Nôtre*[3] which spread over a hill made up of terraces. At the top of the hill stood the fairy-like palace of the new summer castle, the upper Belvedere Palace.

"Ah!" an expression of wonder escaped from the lips of the young Count. He had heard that the Prince had worked on this project for twenty years and had poured much of his money into it, but he had not known that it was completed. The straight rows of neatly trimmed trees went up each side of the slope and blended into levels that went higher and higher until they reached the upper castle, making up a natural frame for it. Statues of Gods, demi-Gods and heroes peeked out from between the trees. On every terrace lurked two sphinxes of light grey sandstone. In the broad sunny center of the park, between the colorful flower beds, was the elaborate water works consisting of pools, grottos, bridges and dams enlivened with exquisite figurines created by master craftsmen.

---

3 André Le Nôtre was a French landscape architect and the principal gardener of King Louis XIV of France. Most notably, he was responsible for the design and construction of the park of the Palace of Versailles, and his work represents the height of the French formal garden style.

Chapter 12—A Guest from the Banat

"Marvelous, magnificent, wonderful!" cried Anton von Mercy, who had involuntarily stopped walking to marvel at the Prince's dream which had been made reality.

The servant smiled and gestured to the right, where a group of gentlemen stood in the morning sun, and in their midst stood Generalissimo Prince Eugene. He had gathered his artisans around him for a final review of their work and had been engaged in a lively discussion when the Major suddenly appeared. They broke off their conversation and observed with satisfaction the impression that their creation seemed to have made upon this officer, whoever he was. The Prince immediately realized who the officer was, since he had given the order that he was to be brought here. And the Count couldn't have made a better impression on him than he did by showing his delight in the Prince's masterpiece. The Prince smiled with satisfaction.

Anton von Mercy had never met Prince Eugene before; he stood before him for the first time. The Generalissimo took a few friendly steps toward him as he returned the Count's salute. Mercy told him his name.

"I know, *Conte*, I know! Ambassador of my dear Mercy! How is he doing? What's new in the Banat?" he asked in a distinctive accent.

The small man with the leathery brown face and great white wig created, at first glance, an impression of quite an ugly person. His nose was a little turned up, his upper lip was short so that his mouth was always open and his teeth were constantly visible. There was nothing to recommend his appearance except his bright soulful eyes. Otherwise, he was a living satirical figure for a Prince and warrior. Anton von Mercy involuntarily made himself smaller; he bent his shoulders a bit as if it was painful to let the great hero look up to him.

"The Herr Field Marshall Lieutenant is well, Your Excellency, and sends his respectful greetings," he answered. "There is much new in the Banat, and I have several requests which I will need to respectfully put to you as President of the Imperial War Council."

"I can imagine! Must have three day patience, *Herr Conte*. I have other business... How long is your leave?" the Prince said in broken German.

"I have a one month furlough, your highness."

"*E vero?*[4] That be good. Then we have plenty time. Would you like to

---

4 *E Vero?* (Italian) means "Is that true?" Although Prince Eugene of Savoy was born in Paris, his parents came from Italian families, which is why his speech was sprinkled with Italian phrases. His connection to Austria and the house of Habsburg came about because he had been refused a commission in the French army by King Louis XI, so he had secretly left Paris and joined Kaiser Leopold's army in 1683.

be my guest tomorrow?" he asked obligingly. "Many nobles come to see my Belvedere."

Mercy thanked the Prince for this consideration by bowing, and the Prince introduced his artisans: Master Lukas Hildebrandt, who had built the Belvedere for him, the artists, horticulturists and engineers who had designed the gardens, and the sculptors, all of whom were here for the final testing of their masterpiece. Lukas Hildebrandt knew Governor Mercy, who had ordered the plans for his castle in Högyész from him, and he greeted the adopted son in an especially friendly way. The Prince constantly looked at his watch and seemed to be expecting somebody. Finally he commanded, "*Avanti*! Let's begin!"

The Major was invited to stay and watch this show of the waterworks, which were now set into motion. The Prince's eyes lit up as the water's movement began in the upper area and then came into play nearer and nearer to the group of onlookers. Columns of water rose up to the sky and the sun formed a rainbow over the park, a glorious arch that framed the upper part of the castle. In a wide stream, the waterfall rushed into its basin, while beautiful marble nymphs rowed their boat made of stone mussels, so lifelike it seemed as if they were breathing. Next, the creations in the small pools directly in front of the onlookers began to perform. The Prince had tears running down his brown cheeks, he laughed so hard at the crazy antics of the statues of boys who were catching a sea monster and pressing its stomach so that it spit out water. The sculptor was happy to have delighted the Generalissimo so much by this show. "*Maestro, Maestro excellentissimo! Che allegro!*" the Prince called out over and over. He found these waterworks to be terribly entertaining.

Once everything was in motion the engineers asked the Prince to follow them. At this point, he bade the Major a hearty good-bye. "*A domani! A domani!*" he called after him. "Tomorrow afternoon!"

Then he walked to the upper area with the artisans, inspecting every portion of the great masterpiece, scrutinizing and appraising the choice of every rare plant, revitalized by every exotic flower he passed. He clapped his hands on the shoulders of one artist after another in his delight. Finally, finally, after so many years of worry and work, he was able to enjoy himself.

'How happy Lory will be,' was constantly on the Prince's mind. 'Where is she?' She had promised to arrive for the test. Admittedly, the Countess was usually not up so early. 'I should have waited to start,' he told himself.

As they walked up to the upper Belvedere, more of the aesthetics and artistry of the park unfolded before them. The beds of roses in full bloom

Chapter 12—A Guest from the Banat

at the upper castle gave off a bewitching fragance. The Prince took in this fragrance in a few deep breaths and enjoyed the feeling of accomplishment at the completion of the great work. He had not felt so well for a long time.

"The Countess," reported a lackey who had been following his master with a container of snuff and a bottle of seltzer water. He gestured into the depths of the park.

The Prince held his right hand over his eyes and looked down at a golden shimmering litter carried by two lackeys in red livery.

"*Scusati, scusati*," said the Prince, excusing himself to those accompanying him.

With a young impetuosity the Prince, whose sixty-one years did not slow him down, rushed down. When he reached the litter, a dainty, lively lady emerged. The prince delicately and chivalrously kissed her hand. She was Countess Lory, the Prince's friend and comrade, the widow of Count Batthyanyi. He already had known her when she was the young Countess Strattmann, the much sought after daughter of the Hungarian High Commissioner. But they had just discovered their love for each other at this older age. They defied the world and the gossip and saw each other every day. She had carried her girlish crush on the victor of Zenta over into her widowhood, and Prince Eugene, the confirmed bachelor, had never adored a woman as he adored her.

The artists knew the Countess well. She often interfered in everything which concerned them when the prince was away, a bit more than to their liking. She was the executor of his wishes and orders—she criticized but also awarded honors. And they showed her as much courtesy and reverence as if she were the spouse of the Prince.

Her face painted with costly make-up, the powdered Countess was pretty as a picture, and her age did not show. She was a bit taller than the Prince but as delicately built as he, and so they made a picturesque couple.

"*Bonjour, bonjour*, gentlemen," she called to the artisans. "Unfortunately, I arrived a bit late, but I saw everything on my way up here! I am enchanted! His Majesty will come tomorrow, and I am sure he will also be charmed by your work."

The Prince removed his hat when the Kaiser was mentioned, and the artists did the same and bowed low as if they stood in front of the Monarch himself. They were happy about this news from the Countess. The Kaiser was a great friend of the arts and architecture, and had done more building and supporting of the arts than any other Kaiser of Austria ever had. But the Prince looked at the Countess skeptically. The Countess returned his gaze with a look of triumph. "He will come," she said quietly. "Maria has promised me."

"Ah, then, it is true," replied the Prince. Now he, too, was convinced. The beautiful Maria Althan could make this promise. Now that the Kaiser's mistress was a widow, Eugene was in her good graces. His actual enemy at the court had been her husband, the *Herr Oberststallmeister,* who had been the Kaiser's childhood friend, his constant companion for twenty years. Her late husband had not been able to tolerate the idea that another was such close friends with the Kaiser, and so had resented the friendship between the Kaiser and the Prince.

Countess Lory and Maria Althan were neighbors on Schenken Strasse. Each had a palace there. Eugene's white horses could find their way to the one palace with their eyes closed, without a coachman to guide them; and the carriers of a black litter, who always wore masks over their faces, were similarly familiar with the other palace. The card game Piket was played in both palaces, and in between, quite a bit of promoting and scheming occurred.

The Prince gave Countess Lory a rose from his prettiest Dutch flower bed, and then he offered her his arm. They walked together to the Prince's newly completed upper Belvedere Castle, and Master Lukas gave them a tour of its interior.

When Anton von Mercy was walking back to his carriage, ready to go back to the city accompanied by his Hàjduks, Countess Lory was just stepping out of hers. The Major noted that she must be a lady of importance in the home of the Generalissimo, because her carriage was admitted to the inner courtyard. A group of lackeys and valets came running, bowing repeatedly, competing for the favor of the guest. She looked approvingly toward the departing decorated officer with his Hungarian Hàjduk Guard, and asked the chamber servant for the name of this officer. She said not a word when Baptiste told her his name, but looked once more in his direction.

"Mercy?" she asked herself. "A good family. If only the nephew of the uncle would carry on the name." Now she remembered—that must be the new Count, the adopted son. Perhaps he was the only one among this year's *Osterhasen* (Easter bunnies)—as those granted nobility at Easter were jokingly called—who had not risen through Maria's grace, the only one who had not bought his title from her. She wanted to know if he was among the guests invited for tomorrow's affair. Baptiste answered in the affirmative. The Prince had invited him personally, had even received him as a guest of

Chapter 12—A Guest from the Banat

distinction.

"Speaking of tomorrow, Baptiste," said the Countess, "please add the name of Baroness Helene Parkoczy, who was born Countess Erdödy, to the list." Then she walked over to her litter.

It seemed to Mercy that it was too early to drive to the Imperial Council. The *Hofkammerrat* would certainly not receive anyone at this hour. It was a beautiful morning and the scent of flowers was in the air, so the Major ordered his coachman to leisurely drive around the city. He had hardly seen much of this beautiful city of Vienna, this strong city which had resisted two Turkish attacks. He was trained and educated, was familiar with many fortifications and was learning much during the rebuilding of Temesvar. This system of fortress walls of Vienna, which had been put together so skillfully over the past five hundred years, was constantly being renewed, made stronger and beautified. The stronghold was hidden by a variety of beautiful parks, and the entire fortification was so well done that it could serve as a model and ideal example for other cities.

Mercy's interest as an engineer of building fortresses became aroused. His expert eyes took in the sight of the stronghold, which only left eight gates through which all the traffic could leave the inner city. And he marveled at the ingenuity of Prince Eugene, who had made the bold decision to also include the circle of suburbs into this fortification system. Twice these up and coming suburbs had been reduced to ashes, when the Turks had neared the city, but when Rakoczy's Hungarian Kurucs also threatened Vienna, Prince Eugene had put the army to work building a giant wall around the city's suburbs. The flourishing life surrounding the city should not be destroyed for a third time. How often had his uncle told him about this quickly executed construction of a new fortification with its nine new outer gates. A hundred thousand hands had built it, and it was finished in a few months. If this outer wall could be held, no cannonball would ever land in the inner city. And the Kurucs never did breach this wall and never set foot into Vienna.

Anton von Mercy was considered in Temesvar to be a sharp critic, but in Vienna his fault finding tendencies were silenced, and he did not ask himself how such a wide perimeter of wall could defend against a more formidable enemy, against an army. He only wondered how they could make a similar fortress out of Temesvar. He had to laugh at himself, that his thoughts kept returning to Temesvar. Had he no other thoughts today? His carriage was driven slowly encircling the city, as he had ordered, along the glacis, the slope that ran downward from the fortress walls. Mercy dreamed about his future as he took in the sights. On his right, he admired the beautiful memorials, to his left the splendid summer homes of the nobility, the villas and castles of the generals and ministers of the Kaiser, who were all enjoying the fruits of peace. He, too, would have enjoyed such idyllic conditions. Oh, if he could only live here! But, he could not even think about that. He could not leave his benefactor's side, his new father, whose life's work up to now was only half done. But must he leave him? Was it unthinkable that he could find a girl who would be ready to follow him to the swamps of the Banat? Since yesterday, he believed it could happen.

Halfway around the city he called out to his coachman, "Drive in through the Schotten Gate!" He could not overcome the desire to see the house on Renn Street where she lived. And he was in luck. Mademoiselle Charlotte and the aunt had just come out of the *Schotten Kirche* where they must have just attended mass. Market wagons were causing a traffic jam, and his coach was barely able to move. That suited him. He watched the beautiful slim girl beside her worthy aunt, striding along as modestly as if she were not the daughter of a very powerful man, looking more like a virtuous nun. When they arrived at the door of their house, Lottel took the prayer book from her aunt, smiled at the old lady and disappeared into the house. But her aunt went on to the market at *Hof*.

Do they do that every day, he asked himself. Then he would become a devout person again, as in his childhood, and go to mass every day. He was ready to burn all the letters he had in his pocket, letters which were to recommend him to noble society, if Mademoiselle Charlotte von Stephany would accept him and follow him to the Banat.

He drove to the Imperial Council offices.

"Welcome, Major." The *Hofkammerrat* greeted Anton von Mercy somewhat formally and coolly. He gave him a scrutinizing look and said, "And how is the Herr Governor?"

"I sincerely thank you, Herr Councillor, he is well. He sends many good wishes from the Banat and thanks you for the felicitous support and understanding which he has received from you." The *Hofkammerrat* nodded. He invited the Major to sit down. "We have only a few men in such important assignments as his. The Herr Generalissimo chose well to appoint him there."
"To hear that will make the Governor especially happy, Herr Councillor. He is totally committed to his task and has no other ambition. I love him like a father and he was gracious to adopt me as his son," said the Major.

"I have heard that and I congratulate you. You favored my house with a visit yesterday."

"It was the first place I went to, *Herr Hofkammerrat*. I wanted to pay my

Chapter 12—A Guest from the Banat

respects to the ladies."

Herr von Stephany smiled coolly. "And what brings you to Vienna?"

"Concerns with the fortress, *Herr Hofkammerrat*. And various disagreements with the Imperial War Council about the military border. This morning I had an audience with his Excellency, Herr Generalissimo."

"He met with you today?"

"I asked for this audience just yesterday, and he consented. He greeted me very graciously in the park, among his artisans. It was when his new waterworks were being demonstrated. He asked me to come back in three days. The President of the Imperial War Council was not available to speak to me yet," the Major said, tongue in cheek. The *Hofkammerrat* smiled at this joke. Prince Eugene, of course, was the President of the Imperial War Council, but he was not able to think about anything but his Belvedere castle at the moment. The easy manner of this young officer appealed to the *Hofkammerrat*, and the good impression which he had of him when they had first met a few years ago was reaffirmed.

"The Prince has been invisible to the whole world for days," said the Councillor. "Tomorrow there will be a feast for the dedication of his Belvedere."

"His Excellency honored me with an invitation to his dedication, Herr Councillor," said Mercy.

"That is indeed a great honor, Herr Count. I suggest you appeal to Countess Althan, who will most certainly attend the festival. And, don't forget Lory Strattmann-Batthyanyi! You will achieve much more in Vienna if you let these two ladies help you."

The Major was surprised. "Are these two ladies not enemies? The Governor warned me."

"They were once, but now they are intimate friends!" the Councillor said, laughing. "Sometimes they vie with each other to see who can give more favors. Sometimes they even combine their influence, which makes them even more dangerous. You are a bit behind the times, Herr Major."

Mercy smiled. "Thank you for your advice, *Herr Hofkammerrat*. I won't forget to use it."

There was a lull in the conversation. Stephany asked himself why the Count did not speak about his reason for coming. Had he only called on him out of courtesy? Did he have no wishes or requests? And Mercy wondered why Stephany did not ask anything. There must be a hundred things which would have interested him.

"You are staying in Vienna for a month, Herr Major?" asked Stephany after a slight pause.

"Yes, Herr Councillor, I had hoped to have the opportunity to talk to you about matters about the Banat."

Stephany smiled. "Aha! Requests? Complaints? Grievances? You are very diplomatic, Herr Major."

"No, Herr Councillor. On the contrary, I am here to listen to your wishes and complaints, and to give reports and clarify," Mercy said modestly.

"Then you, Herr Major, are well-informed about everything in Temesvar?"

"In everything. I am not only the adjutant but also the covert secretary of the Governor, his confidante and his son."

Stephany eyed the speaker in a friendly manner. "That is good to hear. Now tell me, what is the situation with the Serbs and their quarrel with the City of Temesvar?"

"That has been solved, Herr Councillor. The Governor named a Serbian Magistrate in addition to the German one. His seat is in the suburb, Palanka. The ban on Serbs living inside the fortress has been eased, and now there are twelve Serbian families living in the city."

"No more than that?"

"No, Herr Councillor. And there is peace now. Moreover, Temesvar is as much a German city as Augsburg."

Stephany nodded and thought for a bit.

"From what did the first mayor of the city actually die?" he asked the Major.

"Did gossip about his death travel all the way to here?" Mercy asked. "Herr Tobias Hold died of the Banat sickness, swamp fever, nothing else."

"So…? Does the administration of the city lie in honest hands?"

"*Herr Hofkammerrat*, in only the best! The merchant Peter Solderer is elected by the citizens year after year. He is a fine man."

"So, so ... He must have one enemy. We will speak more about that later. Now, please tell me what's all this talk about Saint Nepomuk? Why was this statue which had been so urgently requested not put up on a pedestal for two years? Rome even sent serious complaints to his highness, the Kaiser, and I never did find out what happened. I can tell you confidentially that the position of the Governor was in danger," said Stephany.

The Major thought back. "Herr Councillor, the conflict was three-fold. First of all, the statue was broken when it arrived, and for a long time we found no one who dared to repair it."

"I know," interjected Stephany.

Chapter 12—A Guest from the Banat

"Secondly, the archbishop led a complaint about assigning a new patron saint to a territory that, in his estimation, actually belongs to Hungary. We had to wait until the Holy Father had made a decision. And thirdly, there was a dispute between the Jesuits and the Piarists about where the statue would be mounted. Each order wanted the patron saint of the province to be mounted in front of its individual church."

"Oh, so that is why! The poor Governor!"

The Major laughed. "It was crazy. The Governor does not like to write, and does not usually report to you these minor things of little consequence. But he often openly cursed about these religious matters like a heathen."

"And how was this disagreement settled?" asked the Councillor.

"The Piarists were more clever than the Jesuits. They had named their church St. Nepomuk from the beginning, but that of the Jesuits was called St. Maria, so the Governor decided to erect the statue near St. Nepomuk. All processions lead to where the statue is now located, and the prestige of the Piarists has been raised."

"And now there is peace?"

"Oh no, the Jesuits will not rest until the statue is put up on neutral territory. They begrudge the Piarists this statue."

Stephany smiled to himself while he listened to this report. Now he said, "It must be quite difficult for the Herr Governor to stay calm and composed when dealing with such delicate matters."

"If he could only do that, *Herr Hofkammerrat*," answered the Major. "He has had outbreaks of anger which made me fear for his life."

"Oh, oh!" cried the Councillor with deep sympathy. Then he added buoyantly, "Herr Major, you will have to keep me better informed in the future. You must write often to avert any misunderstandings. We can prevent or diminish many problems from here. And during your stay in Vienna, would you honor us with your presence again?"

There. It had been said. Against his previous intentions, he had invited the Count to his house. In spite of himself, he liked the Major. He found an open mind and a good heart in his manner.

The Major stood up. He saw that the discussion had come to an end, but he felt gratified with the results. "I humbly thank you, *Herr Hofkammerrat*," he said and bowed. "I feel quite honored by your generous invitation."

Stephany shook hands with him. "We will see each other tomorrow afternoon in the Belvedere, Herr Count!"

Chapter 13

Baroness Helene

Baroness Helene had come home.

She had returned with her mind full of thoughts of the beautiful days in Vienna, feeling pleased with what she had achieved. Her mother's name had opened many doors in Vienna. Lory Strattmann-Batthyanyi had taken her under her wing. She was Prince Eugene's girlfriend, and so had arranged an invitation to the grand opening of Belvedere Castle and introduced the Baroness to Countess Maria Althan. Helene told all her troubles to the Countess and appealed to her for help, and like magic, it was as if all of Baron Parkoczy's past was erased.

The royal court in Vienna was predisposed to be forgiving in regards to Hungary. They were gracious and lenient. That the Baron had once fought with Tököly, oh, that was so long ago. He must have been just a youth at the time. The fact that he had also sided with Rakoczy was worse. But then again, so many others who had gone with him had all their rights restored to them. Some who were clever enough to have left him in time, such as Károlyi and others, were actually rewarded for changing sides. And the Hungarian Chancellor, whom the Baroness had visited accompanied by Lory Strattmann, found within his documents one which stated that Parkoczy, too, had long ago separated himself from the rebels. At any rate, he was not one of those who were considered to be outlaws. So he would certainly get his property back; he simply had to apply for it.

"Now then," Lory exclaimed. "He is not as much of a Kuruc as he thinks he is!"

The Chancellor smiled. "We will have to conduct further investigations as to his property," he said. That would take months. However, the Baroness

Chapter 13—Baroness Helene

refused to be satisfied with this answer. This issue with the property was the entire reason she had undertaken the trip. Now that Prince Eugene's girlfriend and the Kaiser's mistress were interested in her case, things were suddenly completely different. Instead of demanding the documentation that the Baron owned his properties, suddenly it was decided to search to see if another person had laid claims on "his" property. After some searching, it seemed that no one had come forward; the properties were not being contested. Only the Hungarian *Hofkammer* could seize the property. And what purpose would that serve? If the Baron was assigned to colonize, so that the income from the colonized portion of his property would be taxed, then one could say that he fulfilled his obligation, and so his family could be protected from having the property seized. And so they were able to come up with a generous solution for the daughter of the former protector of the crown, Christoph Erdödy. The tax for liberating Hungary had to be paid to the war fund. Two thirds of the property was to be settled in the next ten years with independent farmers who would pay these taxes. If these conditions were met, the Baron would remain the owner of all the land he currently occupied and would not have to pay taxes himself.

Helene gratefully accepted this decision. Even Imperial Councillor Stephany, though he was irritated, had not been able to withstand the force of the two powerful women, and the Hungarian Chancellor looked the other way.

Helene came home, ecstatic with the results of her visit. Pista rode out to Mohács to meet her and accompanied his happy mother to Dobok.

The first thing Helene did was go see her mother. She had to thank her and tell her what magic the name Erdödy could still work on the Viennese Court. The proud old lady was touched and gratified by the news Helene had brought her. She had secretly expected nothing else, and now her happiness was complete. She did not tire of asking questions and hearing stories about Vienna. She had known many of those who were now highly influential when they were children. She had seen the Kaiser himself when he had gone to Spain as a young Prince to fight for the crown there. She wanted to know more about the two beautiful women at the court, the Empress and Maria Althan. It made the old woman feel young again to remember all this. At the Court of Kaiser Leopold, she had once been the most beautiful.

However, the Baroness did not receive even the slightest thanks from her husband. He felt the decision of the court was shameful to his wife because she had demeaned herself to go and beg for pardon, and he would not accept their verdict. The sons grumbled about his stubbornness and took their mother's side.

"What? You inexperienced boys want to tell me what I should do? Don't antagonize me, that will not be good for you!" he shouted. "The war tax will not be paid, and I will shoot anyone who brings me German settlers, those beggars who want to be lords here and don't even have anything to eat at home. I am the Lord and Master here. If the Viennese usurpers want to have my property, let them come and get it!"

"Stephan, Stephan!" the Baroness cried. "You don't know what you are talking about. You don't know how well-disposed they were in Vienna toward us, how graciously this difficult matter was handled."

"I will not be tied down by their conditions. Everything will remain as it was!" he roared.

"That cannot be. I have made a commitment," said the Baroness. "This cannot be your last word. Pista will ride to Mohács with these papers and have old Martonffy explain them to him. If you will not comply, my dear husband, then we will have to take care of it. Just so you know: this property was promised to me. It was my mother's name which helped us to get this beneficial verdict."

"So? So?" the Baron said scornfully. "But I say, nothing happens without me! I am going to St. Marton until you come to your senses. *Isten hozott!*"[1]

The boys laughed out loud when their father left the room with these words.

The Baroness, who was close to tears over this unexpected departure, asked full of amazement, "How can you laugh? Tell me—why are you laughing?"

"Dearest Mama, it is far better that you do not find out." said Pista. "There were bad things, terrible things going on with Papa when you were away. It is better that he has gone to St. Marton for some time."

"He is leaving on the day of my arrival? Children, what has happened?"

"You know, Mama," Andor interjected, hoping to divert the conversation from this dangerous theme, "His drunkenness… We have much to tell you. The excessive drinking disgusted me so much, I left for three weeks, and Pista did something that Papa will never forgive."

"What did he do?"

"Oh, something funny. I almost died laughing about it. Papa almost beat Jancsi to death, but then Pista confessed that he did it."

---

1 *Isten hozott*: a Hungarian expression of greeting or departure, roughly meaning "May God be with you."

Chapter 13—Baroness Helene

The mother looked at Pista questioningly. "Are you going to tell me about it?"

"Oh, I was so unhappy about our daily drunkenness," said Pista. "Papa was always drunk while you were away. He did some crazy things, and I also drank too much. I wanted to keep the promise I gave to you, dear Mama, but the temptation was too great. Finally one evening I went down to the cellar and knocked the taps off of the wine barrels so that the poison ran out of them. The damage was great, but at least I had chased the devil out of the house."

Andor laughed. "Mama, you should have heard the screaming and shouting. It was as if the world had come to an end."

The Baroness looked at Pista. "And what did he do to you?"

"To me? He raised his fist toward me. I stepped back and yelled, 'Papa, I don't want to become a drunkard, and I don't want my father to be one either!' "

"And then?"

"That somehow made him a bit sober. Since that time we have not spoken a word to each other. But he bought more wine and had it brought to St. Marton. Let him get drunk there. Let him…" Pista broke off mid-sentence.

"Let him do what?" asked the dismayed mother. "Tell me!"

"Dear Mama, give him time," said Pista. "We will slowly win him over. I will ride to Martonffy as you suggested. We will make our plans without Papa. Andor can tell you a lot. He saw the Swabians at Bellye and Tevel. He lived like a bandit for three weeks and took a good look at everything."

"Yes, Mama, I know how to get Swabians to come and what we must give them. I know what they can do," Andor said, "I lived among them."

"Children, all this is not important to me," answered the Baroness. "First I need to have Papa here. I will go and drive after him. I will bring him home."

"Mama, please don't do that!" Pista begged.

"No, no, no. You are not telling me everything!" their mother cried.

"Andor, go and see if Papa has left yet," Pista said quickly, giving him a meaningful look. "Maybe Mama can still speak with him!"

Andor left and Pista stepped closer to his mother. "Dear Mama, I must confess that we did not tell you everything, but only because we were ashamed. Papa is not going to St. Marton alone."

"Not alone?"

"While you were gone, we had a lady housekeeper here. The beautiful woman Katicza, the wife of our main servant in St. Marton, Béres. It was high time that you came back."

The Baroness Helene paled and smiled bitterly. This was not the first time that she heard of something like this. But it was the first time she had heard it from one of her children. She felt ashamed for the absent husband. In order to prevent Pista from sharing more with her, she sent him away. "In that case, Andor should do nothing," she said, embarrassed. "He shouldn't go after Papa. I don't want to see him now…. Go, go tell him!"

"I am sorry, Mama."

"Go, go!" she said, her voice breaking.

And Pista left so that his mother could be alone.

Chapter 14

In The Meadows of Mohács

The heat of the early summer lay pressingly over the plains, and thunder and lightning rolled noisily over the fields. The scant crops, barely knee-high and choked with weeds, became more yellow every day. Philipp Trauttmann wondered at their sparseness as he traveled on his wagon through the plain. Wouldn't this soil produce more if it were properly tended? On his way he often stopped and examined the fields and shook his head. Did the people here sow the seeds so shallow? German plows go deeper, he said to himself.

Pista had finally ridden to Mohács to see the Notary Martonffy, and they both studied all documents which his mother had brought from Vienna. They looked especially closely at the terms and conditions which had to be met so that the *Hofkammer* would accept their land for settlement. They would receive German settlers only if they followed all the prerequisites. Martonffy knew what these terms were. But he also knew of barons and counts who had sought settlers for their properties, but did not give them what they were due. There were constant disputes in these situations, and sometimes the colonists left. Martonffy warned Pista not to tolerate such abuses on his property, and Pista assured him that this would not happen. In some way, his father must be won over. He did not yet know how, but he would convince the Baron to be fair to the settlers.

Towards evening, the old Notary led his guest out of town. He wanted to show him something, he said. They walked through the foot-high dust of the clay soil toward the banks of the Danube and came into the meadows. There they heard voices, saw smoke rising from behind the willows and rushes—and even heard singing.

"What is this?" asked Pista.

Martonffy smiled. "This is where the Viennese immigrant ships land. The Swabians who want to go to the Batschka and the Banat often stay overnight here," he said.

"And they sing?"

"Yes," Martonffy replied. "The Germans have a song for every situation in life. By the way, we're in luck. It seems that several ships docked here today."

During this conversation they had walked into a clearing where a colorful picture unfolded before them. German people wearing their traditional *Trachten* were camped there; some stood together chatting, a few women cooked dinner in copper kettles over an open fire and a group of young girls sang a hymn while a white-haired old man directed them. Down a ways, men and boys brought wood from felled willow trees and made shelters out of them, which they covered with reeds. A few women nursed their babies and watched as the men worked. These open shelters were most likely being prepared for them and their infants.

Martonffy asked a blond blue-eyed boy if they could speak to the shipmaster, and the boy called him over. The German farmers looked at the two gentlemen curiously, a few greeted them. The Notary asked the shipmaster about the final destination and origin of these people. "Everyone is going to the Banat," he answered. "A new ship comes every day, heading for that destination."

"Where are these people from?" Pista asked.

"I believe they are from Baden, *Herr*. I don't know any more about them. You must ask their priest, who is with them. My workers and I are from Vienna."

"They have a priest with them?"

"Yes, certainly. Two hundred families are here with their priest and schoolmaster. Those two were given cabins on the ship."

A few inquisitive young men had come closer to listen to this conversation, and Martonffy called them toward him. All had smooth beardless faces; not one was smoking a pipe. "Good evening, my good people. You certainly have been underway for a long time, is that not so?"

One of them answered, "Four weeks, sir."

"It will take you another two weeks to get to your destination," Martonffy continued. "Would you rather stay here? I know of plenty of nobles who have land for settlers where you will have it as good as in the Banat. Many Germans are already living in this area."

One of them, a big brown-haired man wearing a long white linen coat

Chapter 14—In The Meadows of Mohács

and a three-cornered hat made of rough felt, answered: "We are not looking for noblemen to control us. We're getting free land in the Banat. We will not do *Robotte*."[1]

"Free land? You can get that here on the right side of the Danube too. Haven't you heard of '*die Schwäbische Türkei*'?" asked Martonffy.

The men looked at each other. They had never heard that word. One of them suggested that this 'Swabian Turkey' might be worth looking at. The others laughed. "That name must be a joke," they commented.

The priest appeared, having been alerted by the shipmaster as to the presence of these two gentlemen. He was a strong, tall man with a steady gaze from dark eyes. "What would you two gentlemen like to know?" he asked, raising his hat. "I am Pastor Plenker from Baden-Baden and I am leading my community to the Banat. We have imperial passes."

"Oh please, your Reverence, we are not here to inquire about your passes, we are just curious passers by. I am Notary Martonffy from Mohács. My companion, the young Baron Parkoczy, is eager to colonize people. His father owns a large estate."

The priest measured Pista with a probing look. "You can look for people among the thousands who will come after us," he said. "Our community will not be split up."

"I find it unusual, your Reverence, that whole communities want to emigrate," said Pista. "Is there such poverty in Germany? These people don't look like beggars."

"Beggars? Gentlemen, since I will only see you today and never again, I will tell you the whole truth," said the priest. "Our community is affluent. There are no beggars among us. Only the overlords are responsible for the departure of their subjects. Their disputes and ambition always attract enemies into the German land; the people are being taxed first by this and then the other; and whoever happens to be master over the people also wants to be master of our souls. The great-grandparents of my community were all Catholic; the grandparents had to become Protestant. Their descendants were switched back to Catholicism thirty years ago, and now we are all to become Protestant again. Are we a herd of cattle, to be pushed back and forth this way? I gave a sermon and asked the question, to whom did Jesus Christ give the right to decide heavenly affairs here on earth. Did he give that right to Herod? No. Or to Tiberius? No. He gave it to his followers, the Apostles

---

1 *Robotte* is another word for *Frondienst*, the compulsory labor which had to be done for the *Fürst* or for the Lord of the Manor. Recall that a certain number of days per year was mandated for this work.

and especially to the highest among them, to Peter. Therefore in religious matters one must not follow secular leaders, but rather follow the religious leaders, those who come from Peter. After this sermon I read the Kaiser's Proclamation from the pulpit. He was looking for Catholic German colonists for the Banat and assured them all kinds of freedoms. People came to me and asked me to lead them into the promised land of the Banat in Hungary. Like the Jews who followed Moses out of Egypt, they said, they wanted to follow me, and so now I am leading them into their new homeland."

"Oh, so that is why your community left!" exclaimed Pista, who had been listening to the priest with fascination.

Martonffy asked. "So, is that how much the Lutheran religion is expanding its influence in Germany?"

"No, Herr Notary, no!" said the priest. "We just have too many sovereign masters. There is another principality where Protestants are leaving because they do not want to become Catholics. The masters have been ill-advised. I believe their careless treatment of the human soul is the strongest reason for German emigration. In addition, for many the emigration is a liberation from servitude. Thousands who possessed no property in their homeland want to acquire it here. They will be a blessing for this country."

A bell chimed in the nearby town. Martonffy looked toward the setting sun and thought of the long road back for him and his companion. So he was not unhappy when the priest excused himself upon hearing the church bell, to say an evening prayer with his community.

The religious leader of this small community stepped out into the open clearing, where the old schoolmaster who had kept time when the girls were singing was already waiting for him. He placed a slender cross in the middle of the clearing, and the hundreds who had followed their shepherd to the promised land of Hungary gathered around him. The priest then uncovered his head and folded his hands, and the community knelt down.

Their leader delivered the evening prayer in a loud deep voice: "Lord, God and Father, at the close of this day of travel we kneel once again before you to pray with thankful and humble hearts. It was through your goodness that we awoke today, healthy and happy. Your grace brought us safely through all dangers to this destination and your love will watch over us in the coming night. Most gracious Father in Heaven, be patient with our weaknesses and faults. If we have sinned against you or have broken one of your commandments, we ask that you forgive us in the name of Jesus, your son, who shed his precious blood for us. In this foreign land, we place ourselves under your protection from whatever dangers may be lurking for us. We

Chapter 14—In The Meadows of Mohács

know that you are everywhere. People in the nearby city are praying to you, too, their church bells proclaim it, and this strengthens our faith. Your love never sleeps and you watch over us even when we are sleeping. O Lord, protect us this night and defend us from all dangers that may harm our body and soul. Let us sleep tonight in peace and renew our strength for the coming day. O Lord, in your hands is life and death; only you will decide whether we will still breathe tomorrow. We place our souls into your hands. Amen."

Martonffy and Baron Pista, who had seen the German settlers for the first time, quietly stole away during this prayer. Soon after, the men with whom they had spoken, set up guards at each corner of the area in which the group was to spend the night.

Chapter 15

A New Homeland?

Philipp Trauttmann was detained in Dobok.

Baron Pista had ridden home from Mohács in the bright moonlight. He had been very impressed with the German colonists and thought over everything he had seen. These simple, honest, strong men moved into their new homeland with such confidence, bringing their religion and songs with them. They wanted to be free and not be beholden to any master. He had to admit that he liked them. Perhaps this country needed such farmers in order to flourish. The serfs who had to be beaten to work the fields did not put their heart and soul into their work. They were working on land which did not belong to them, and which was barely providing enough sustenance for them. Perhaps the gentlemen in Vienna were right, and this was the way of the future. These thoughts went through the young man's mind as he was riding home, and he spurred his horse to go faster. He would have liked to ride to his father in St. Marton to get him to change his mind, but first he wanted to tell his mother about what he had seen. He stood firmly at his mother's side; but could their land be settled without the father's blessing? He spent a sleepless night trying to think of options but found no way out; his father would have to be convinced, somehow.

The next morning in Mohács, Martonffy heard that there was a German farmer, traveling by horse and wagon with his family, who was looking for *die Schwäbische Türkei*. He wanted to speak to someone who knew the region and who could show him the way there. They directed him to the Notary's house. Philipp Trauttmann received a warm welcome from the old man, which did him some good. He showed Martonffy his pass and readily answered all of his questions. It was good to speak to someone who seemed

Chapter 15—A New Homeland?

to understand him; he had not experienced this since leaving Vienna. After half an hour they were good friends.

"Why do you need to drive all the way to Fünfkirchen or to Tevel?" asked Martonffy. "I have a better suggestion for you: settle in this vicinity."

Trauttmann declined. "No, no. I have to go to Swabian Turkey, I promised the man in Vienna that I would go there."

"My dear man, think about it. Why is that region called '*die Schwäbische Türkei'?*" asked Martonffy with a smile. "Is there anything so special about Tevel, that it can be the only area called Swabian Turkey? If we start a Swabian village here, where Turks used to live, then this too will be part of Swabian Turkey. We are going to enlarge its borders for you. Don't you want to be the first to live in this new village?"

Trauttmann seemed to like this idea, and Martonffy went on, "First of all, drive to Castle Dobok. There, ask for the young Baron Pista Parkoczy, and tell him that I send my humblest regards. Talk to him. Take a good look at the place. If you don't like it, in God's name, drive away and go wherever you want. It won't have hurt you any. But I don't believe that you will drive on."

And that was how Philipp Trauttmann came to Dobok. His brown horse had been limping on his front legs for a few days already. He could not have gone much farther as it was. Trauttmann wanted to give him a longer rest so his legs could heal. The friendly old man in Mohács had told him, 'Take a good look.' So this way he could have time to look into the place, at least until his horse was fit enough to go on.

This was the pretext he used to stay. This reason, too, placated his wife Eva and the children, who were now just as eager to head over to 'Swabian Turkey' as they had been to go to the Banat—'*die Schwäbische Türkei*' had become their new promised land.

Young Baron Andor was the first to see the peculiar wagon, flanked by the two armed young men. He walked up to the wagon to meet the newcomers. Trauttmann introduced himself and said he had spoken to Martonffy, who sent his regards to Baron Pista Parkoczy.

Upon hearing these words, Andor smiled broadly and said, "You are Swabians and are coming to us? And the Notary sent you here?"

"Of course we are Swabians, young man," Trauttmann said cautiously. "We were told to go to 'Swabian Turkey,' but my horse is hurt and I want to rest here if you allow it."

"Do rest with us, dear people," said Pista, who had come quickly after being called. "Put your tired horses in our stable. If Herr Martonffy sent you, you are our guests."

Upon receiving this warm welcome, Philipp Trauttmann stepped off the wagon. Matz and the two eldest boys stood at his side, all of whom already reached up to his shoulders. 'Four men!' thought Pista. Then Frau Eva got off the wagon with Ferdinand and little Trude, all of them happy to step out of their Noah's Ark, which was their nickname for the wagon.

"Seven is a sacred number," said Trauttmann and introduced his family with a smile. "If the Herr Baron will give us lodgings, I will gratefully accept. May God bless you for your hospitality."

And this was how Philipp Trauttmann came to Dobok, to rest his ailing horse. His black horse was also glad to sleep in a stable and eat oats again.

While they were there, Baron Pista showed them the intended place for a new settlement. Day after day, Trauttmann walked and took a close look at this area, sometimes with young Andor, sometimes by himself, sometimes with his sons. The boys carried their guns and Philipp his spade. He dug here and there and looked at the earth. It was brown near the top and black below. Was it hungry for good seeds? Would it be thankful for the sweat of hard workers? Only God knew that.

His brown horse had long recovered, but still Trauttmann wavered and hesitated. Should he stay? Should he go on? It seemed to him that the owner of the estate might not be serious about settling his land, since the Baroness and her oldest son enticed him and made promises, but he never saw the Baron. He asked, and they were evasive. Only if he was firmly resolved to stay would Pista take him to his father in St. Marton. Otherwise there was no point in going.

Trauttmann was undecided. He sent Matz, who was an intelligent young man, into the German communities of the *Schwäbische Türkei* to learn more about them. He was to find out what they had experienced in twenty years of settlement. And he looked at the rest of the Baron's land. Here he saw grains, corn, pumpkins, and peppers of a very low quality; even the cattle was of a lesser breed. He did not see any wheat. The locals did not even know what a potato was. Of the better field crops, not even a seed was to be found. No fruit trees far and wide! And no flowers. No song birds. Wild apples and pears flourished on the edge of the forest, but nobody thought to cultivate them. Blackthorn and rose hips thrived at the edges of the oak and acacia forests, in which wild bees had their hives. The people mainly ate dark bread, smoked meat, bacon and sheep cheese; no vegetables, fruit or honey. In winter they would also have sausages and game.

On this land which went as far as the eye could see, a few hundred serfs lived in wretched *Erdhütten* that barely protruded from the ground. They had

Chapter 15—A New Homeland?

nothing, just barely enough food and clothing for themselves. Each of these serfs was assigned a piece of land which he could cultivate for his own use, but when labor was required for his landlord, that had priority. The overlord's game could not be touched, even when they destroyed the serfs' crops. Possession of a firearm was a crime. One could not tell if these people belonged to any religion; no priest was to be seen among them. But the masters were devout Catholics and they drove to Mohács every Sunday morning to attend mass.

And here is where Philipp Trauttmann, from Bobenheim in the Palatinate, should settle with his family? His children should never even think of returning to their German fatherland but be firmly rooted here, to stay here forever? Trauttmann and his wife Eva spent sleepless nights thinking about it. They each worried about the other and did not admit to each other that they couldn't sleep. When the children were not looking, Eva shed many a bitter tear. But she could not burden her husband's heart, she must be stronger than anyone else in the family and remain courageous.

Baron Pista went to see his father. Since he arrived in the morning, he found him to be somewhat approachable. Caraffa, whom the Kuruc had taken along, barked joyfully upon seeing young Pista. Papa did not begin to rant when he heard that a German family was living at Dobok, and that they might want to settle there. Parkoczy listened quietly to his son and it seemed to Pista that his father was a bit ashamed of himself. He lived in this dilapidated mansion and drank with his main servant, Béres, and a few of his old Kuruc friends. The plump Cuman woman, Katicza, served them the wine and drank from everybody's pitcher as well.

"You want to test this idea with one family?" he asked crossly. "Then do it! But I must have my tenth. I will not give up a single acre entirely! A tenth of everything they produce belongs to me."

"That's from the third year, Papa, not before that! The State will give you six years free of taxation."

"From the third year. Hmm. What does Martonffy say about that?"

"He is for six years, Papa."

"He's an old ass," said Parkoczy. "Well, fine, then, from the third year."

"And how many *Joch* can I give the farmer to own?"

"Pah, give him as much as he can cultivate. He can have ownership with a tenth coming to me! Do you understand? That is not full ownership."

"Can Martonffy draw up the documents," asked Pista, "and you will sign them?"

"The farmer wants to have it in writing? Then we will never get rid of him, no, no!"

"The man has three sons, Papa. He cannot do this without written documents. He does not appear to be poor. He actually wants to go to Tevel and can hardly be restrained. Mama wants to try this. She promised it in Vienna."

"Then give that to him in writing," answered the Baron quickly.

This was far more than Pista had hoped for. Apparently, his mother still had some influence over his father when he was sober.

As he was leaving he asked innocently, "Mama would like to know when you will come home again, Papa."

"Me?" he asked, surprised. And somewhat emotionally, he asked: "Tell me honestly, Pista, is she very angry at me?"

"She is deeply hurt. I believe she cries very often."

"I'm sorry about that. Tell her the wine is to blame. I must be allowed to drink as much as I want. And you know, when I am sober, I get sickened by what is going on. Here I have my Kuruc friends; we drink and talk about the times when we deposed the House of Habsburg in Onod. But now your mother, too, has become black-yellow (true to the Kaiser) just like her mother. Oh, just leave me alone."

Trauttmann had asked for two days to think about it, after the young Baron had told him that his father had agreed to everything. But where was Matz? Philipp had told him that he could take a week to look over the area, no longer. The week had now passed. Had something happened to him? There were wandering gypsies and other such people around. And in the dense forest toward the south there appeared to be a savage at large, a hermit or some brutish creature. Trauttmann had recently thought he had seen him, but he had run away. The young Baron Andor said he had heard about him too. Trauttmann liked Andor because he told him many positive things about Swabian Turkey, which is where Trauttmann had actually sent Matz—but nobody knew about that. They had been told that he had gone to Mohács to buy some horseshoes.

Finally, on the evening before the decision had to be made, someone banged at the door of the stable where the family was staying. Ferdinand and Trudel were already asleep, but the others sat around a tallow light around the table. The father read from the Lutheran Bible, their beloved holy book, which they had happily saved from all peril thus far. Philipp Trauttmann sought advice and solace from this book in order to make his big decision, but he could not find it there.

Someone knocked again. It was Matz! Philipp went to the door to let him in. The blonde red-cheeked boy stood at the door, dust-covered and ex-

Chapter 15—A New Homeland?

hausted, a heavy club in his right hand and a full knapsack on his back. Eva had filled this knapsack with bread, bacon and cheese before he left. She was surprised that it was still full. Had he brought them something? She put the Bible safely away in its hiding place in her bed and got Matz something to eat. The boys were happy to see their good friend again.

Trauttmann said, "Well, Matz, sit down. You must be tired."

"I'm all right," he replied. "I got lost and almost didn't find my way back here."

He ate the baron's smoked meat and emptied a jug of water that Peter brought from the well. Philipp Trauttmann watched him contentedly. He was happy that Matz, his dead sister's son, had come back. Matz had come along as a hired man, because he truly had the wanderlust in his Swabian blood and the journey to foreign lands enticed him. He was an orphan and had to be in the service of a farm family to learn the trade, as was the custom. When he was of age he would receive his assets and would be on his own. His assets were kept in Bobenheim for him, collecting interest. In the meantime, Uncle Philipp gladly took him into his family and gave him a small salary. He was like a son to Trauttmann.

"Well now, Matz, where were you? Talk to us!"

"Ah, that was good, Aunt Eva," said Matz and wiped his mouth with his sleeve. "I didn't have anything to eat today."

He got up and placed the full knapsack on the table.

"Well, I have been by the Swabians in the *Schwäbische Türkei*. I went all the way to Tevel, and I was in Murgau which lies in a valley. The Protestants live there, almost as if they were in exile. The Catholics spread themselves out all over the place and own a lot of fields. The Protestants stay together in small groups and hire themselves out to the landlords who need help with their harvest."

Trauttmann and his wife looked at each other but said nothing.

"There are a lot of quarrels and conflicts with the counts, barons and bishops in Swabian Turkey, but the farmers there say that doesn't matter, the earth is good, and they won't let anyone take away their rights. They all plan on staying there."

Now he opened his knapsack and emptied it onto the table. "Take a look. Here is what they are growing in Swabian Turkey."

He showed them golden stalks of wheat, grains and barley and oats, beans and peas and all kinds of field crops which were unheard of here in Dobok. And these crops were flourishing, only one day's journey away! Philipp Trauttmann's heart lifted as he let the grains slip through his fingers. The worthy old gentleman in Mohács had been right. 'The borders of Swabian Turkey can be expanded.' Truly! What was possible there could also be done here. Eva held the grains in her hand and smiled at her husband. The boys, too, looked at the abundance in satisfaction. A happy, joyous mood came over them, such as they had not experienced in their long trip to this foreign land. Matz talked and talked and confirmed everything that Andor had said a hundred times over. Some days he had felt as if he were home on the Rhine again. And in the area which belonged to Prince Eugene, that's where everything was the nicest, he said. That's where people were the best off. That's where we should be. Compared to that, the land here looks like a desert.

"Matz," the farmer said cheerfully, "it only looks like that now. But just wait until you see Dobok ten years from now. Paradise is everywhere; you only have to till the land and work hard."

Matz looked at him, astonished, and Eva now saw that her husband's mind had been made up. From tomorrow on they would have a homeland again. She was pleased with this. If they could live so close to a German community as they worked to create a free and independent home, they did not have to be so anxious. Full of love and trust she looked toward her husband.

Matz went outside to bed and Hannes and Peter went with him. Suddenly Trauttmann ran after them, calling out, "Matz, you did not bring any potatoes."

"They didn't have any," said Matz. "In this whole country, there is not one potato."

Philipp went back into the stable, shaking his head. The boys, however, did not tire of asking Matz questions. He talked to them until his eyes could no longer stay open, telling them all about the hard working Swabians in Swabian Turkey. Then Peter and Hannes went to sleep, dreaming about their new homeland.

For the first time since they came here, Eva and Philipp went to bed very happy. It was as if their salvation had come. They did not need to talk about it; they simply knew that all uncertainty was gone. The couple tenderly embraced as if they had just married and slept with no worries until daylight.

Trauttmann chose to start his settlement an hour's walk from Castle Dobok. Fifty *Joch* would be his. Thirty-two *Joch* would be cultivated, ten would be pasture and eight were to be forest. In addition, a common pasture

Chapter 15—A New Homeland?

was to be fenced off for his cattle. He bought two more horses and a cow for his stable. He also bought two pigs and some sheep for a good price. And one of Caraffa's pups for his yard. He agreed to pay one-tenth of his crop after the third year, but required that he would be able to eventually buy his way free of this agreement. And the price for this was put in writing, a price no one would have paid even for the Baron's entire property. The Baron would not sign the agreement unless Trauttmann agreed to these terms, and he did agree.

New life came into the farmers, now that they knew that they were standing on their own land. They set to work building a house. Baron Pista wanted his serfs to make them one of the *Erdhütten* customary for this region, but they were going to build something different. The farmer and Matz got to work. They chopped down trees, sawed boards and carved small wooden molds. They kept bringing new and different tools out from their 'Noah's ark.'

After a few days Trauttmann, Matz and the two oldest sons went to the nearest pond. Trauttmann had already looked at the wet earth at the edge of this pond earlier. They set up a place to make bricks to be baked by the sun, laying boards on the shore and setting up the wooden molds on them. Standing in the warm water, they dug away at the mud at the pond's edge and prepared the first brick. They had procured a load of chaff from a nearby threshing site, which they mixed with the loam to make bricks. They needed the chaff to help make the material more firm, or they would not dry as proper bricks.

They were all thrilled and proud of themselves when they saw the bricks drying in the sun. The next day even Eva stood in the water. All of them helped. Even Ferdinand and little Trude had a job. Matz had tied a rope to the brick molds so that they could be dragged behind them. The children happily dragged the new bricks over to the area where Matz piled the dried bricks on top of one another. He put those that were only half-dried in loose layers, placing them so that the warm air could go through them.

They worked for two weeks on this brick project, which they considered more a happy time than a chore, until a few thousand bricks were drying in the sun.

The locals marveled at this achievement.

If only the bricks could be fired in a kiln, Trauttmann sighed. But that was impossible. There were brick kilns in Mohács and *Fünfkirchen*, the Baron's sons told him, but in the villages such a thing was unknown. So they had to build with mud bricks. Trauttmann had come up with the building plan for the house himself, but he sent Matz to the Notary in Mohács to find a professional bricklayer. There he found a German bricklayer, originally from the *Steiermark*, who would be able to come in two weeks.

That was good news. In the meantime, the bricks would dry more thoroughly and they could begin the work in the fields. From his 'Noah's Ark,' Trauttmann brought out two steel plowshares and other hardware, something unknown in Hungary at that time. There wasn't enough room to bring a whole plow, so they had brought only the metal parts. He had only seen wooden plows in this country. With those the people worked this dried out parched brown soil? A German plow went deeper. Philipp and Matz sawed and whittled for a week until they had finished two rough German plows complete with the iron plowshares, which would open the womb of Mother Earth so she could give her best for the future crops.

The first furrows were drawn. Four horses were harnessed, Philippp took the plow, which cut deeply, and Matz led the horses. The two oldest boys walked alongside, looked and learned. The neighboring serfs came out of their *Erdhütten* and looked at the iron plow. They had never seen such a thing. After a few days, the boys and Matz alternated leading the horses and guiding the plow. It was the end of summer and the pathetic crops belonging to the Baron and his serfs had already been harvested. 'Why would that fool plow now?' they asked one other. They wouldn't do that until October when it was time to sow the seeds. Trauttmann, however, took sixteen days to plow his thirty two *Joch* assigned for cultivation. He gathered and burned all the weeds, right down to their roots. His acreage now lay dark and alone in an infinite desert overgrown with thistles and weeds. Every drop of rain that God provided now went deep into the soil which he had worked.

The German bricklayer from Mohács finally arrived and now all their energy went into building the house. Trauttmann carefully watched every move of this worthy man and after three days he was also laying bricks. The house rose steadily from the earth.

Meanwhile, something seemed to be wrong with Matz. He was usually the most cheerful among them. After a hard day's work he often played his bagpipes in the evening and amused everybody. But now he was sick and could not say what ailed him. He would slip away from the group while they were having fun, and often cried in the middle of the night. One evening, Eva could not stand this any longer; she went to him and insisted that he tell her the truth. Had he done something wrong and had a guilty conscience? Or had he fallen in love in Swabian Turkey?

No, no, his heart was broken, but he did not know why. Sometimes he

Chapter 15—A New Homeland?

felt like he just had to go home, home, home.

"My boy, you don't have a mother or father there," said Eva. "You are like our own child to us. You don't want to leave us, do you? Now, when we have so much work?"

The nineteen year old whimpered like a sick animal. He could not help himself. He thought he was going to die of homesickness.

When Eva relayed this to her husband, who had also woken up, he was deeply concerned. That was a serious illness, he said. Many German youths died from this malady in foreign lands or with the military. The greatest sickness of all is homesickness. He had felt a bit of that on the trip from Vienna to here, only he had not wanted to tell her about it. He would have been ashamed to admit it to her and the children. But he told her to go to sleep and not worry about it. He knew of a cure and would speak to Matz in the morning.

The next morning, when the bricklayer began his work and Matz listlessly handed him a couple of bricks, Trauttmann spoke up.

"Well, Matz, I need you for a big job. Do you want to go to Bobenheim?" he asked suddenly.

"No, no, I don't want to go. I cannot. I will stay here," he said, ashamed.

"I would never have believed that you would be so ungrateful! I need a favor—I need you to go to Bobenheim."

"But, uncle, uncle," Matz stuttered, looking into Philipp's half angry, half smiling face.

"I want you to go home and tell my brother, Ferdinand, and all our friends that we have arrived safely in Hungary. But the main reason I want you to go is to bring us back some potatoes. What can we do without potatoes? We will supply all of Swabian Turkey with potatoes."

"Yes uncle, I can do that!" Matz answered eagerly. "I'll carry a whole bag of potatoes on my back, from Bobenheim to Dobok."

Trauttmann smiled at him with satisfaction. "It is now August," he said. "Tell me, Matz, that you will be back by October to plant the potatoes."

"A hundred times," said Matz. "I promise you a hundred times!" And he was a changed man.

That evening, everyone sat down together and prepared for his departure. Trauttmann wrote a number of letters to Bobenheim, to his brother and to his in-laws, who looked after his property, and to the orphanage who managed Matz's assets. Eva also had a hundred things to put into the letter for her parents. She wanted flower and vegetable seeds and copies of songs to teach to her children. Also some linen and blue cloth for a dress, and, and, and…

"And a donkey who can carry all that for over 200 miles," her husband put in. "Right, Eva?"

"Oh." She shamefacedly stopped her wishlist. The potatoes were of course more important than her wishes, and poor Matz had enough to carry.

Matz sat across from her, grateful for his good fortune. Oh, he would bring her everything she wanted. Nothing would be too heavy for him.

The next morning, Matz got up at the crack of dawn. "Don't hurry," said his uncle as he put a couple of *Taler* into Matz's full knapsack, "if you're too careless you won't even get to Vienna."

The hut in which they lived while their house was being built and the bricks dried seemed empty to Eva now that Matz was gone. She felt like her family was all alone in a foreign land; this was a feeling which she had not had while the lively Matz was with them. He had been a piece of their homeland which they had taken along. Now they had lost that and were all alone. It affected her greatly. Would she, too, be afflicted with homesickness? She resisted. Philipp had overcome it, she would overcome it too. She did not believe that Matz would return. She was surprised that her husband believed it and that he did not notice how alone they were now.

Chapter 16

At the *Sieben Kurfürsten* Inn

Things were going well at the *Sieben Kurfürsten* Inn in Temesvar. At first there was only a *Herrenstube*, a room for gentlemen who came to eat and drink, but a new *Bauernstube* had to be added for the German farmers coming in such large numbers. The name of the guest house drew these immigrants, and quite a few brought greetings for the host and hostess from Ulm and from Blaubeuren. Apprentice journeymen who were learning a trade sometimes came to the inn to visit the farmers, but they stayed overnight at the Trumpeter Inn. They were very proud and strutted about as if they were nobility, because their skills and craftsmanship were in high demand.

Johann Staudt and Michel Luckhaup, the ones who had spoken to the father of Jakob Pless in Regensburg before they left, had not been lost, as was believed in Vienna. On the contrary, they were the first to get to Temesvar and bring his greetings to the young couple. Luck had been with them. They had come from Ofen (Buda) with their *Gewährbüchlein*, the booklet which guaranteed them land, and were settled immediately. At that time things went much faster, one did not have to wait such a long time at the *Rentamt* or bribe the *Kontrollore* and *Kanzelisten*, like one did today. The surveyors who measured off the land being given away could not keep up with their work. No one had been prepared for such an influx of immigrants.

So the new arrivals often sat in the *Bauernstube* of the *Sieben Kurfürsten* Inn, where those who were already settled came by regularly, and where the newcomers got information and encouragement when they were ready to give up hope. Give up? Pah! There was room for everybody, one just had to be patient. Waiting was not so bad—the Governor looked after everyone's needs like a father. Naturally, life in the city was expensive. However, six

Kreuzer per day was given to every father, six to the mother and three to each child. If you had to wait in the country, you got two *Kreuzer* and half a measure of flour per person, for children one pint of flour and one *Kreuzer*. But in the country there was work for everyone. If an immigrant's house was still being built, he could help in the construction and get paid for it. Another six *Kreuzer* per day, in fact, to help build your own house! If the waiting settlers received lodging in one of the finished houses during the interim, the *Rentamt* paid for it, one *Kreuzer* per person per night to the owner of the house.

    The building of the houses was simple. The houses were all tamped out of the earth taken from the edge of the swamp. The mud was enriched with wheat chaff and turned into a mush. To make the walls, the mush would be tamped into wooden frames which had been reinforced by woven reeds or willows. The regulations for building houses were very strict, but there were inspectors who sometimes cheated the owners, in collusion with the carpenters. Hannes Staudt did not accept the house presented to him since it only had a main room, a kitchen and a stable. "Oho," he said, "where is the *Kammer*?" He was literate and could read the regulations. Every house had to be eleven *Klafter* (22 yards) long and three *Klafter* (6 yards) wide with walls that were eight *Schuh* (feet) high. There were to be four rooms under one roof: *Zimmer*, kitchen, *Kammer*, and stable.[1] That is what he had read. He insisted on a waterproof cane or straw roof, so the floor would be warm in winter and cool in summer. No corn husks, which would rot easily, oh no! Staudt told them this firmly and so got his four rooms. Two hundred Guilders was the cost of such a house when it was finished, and the well, which always had to be dug first, cost at least five Guilders. This sum was registered in the rental office against the owner of the house and it had to be paid off within six years. So it was good if you helped to build your house—the sum would be reduced, and you could make sure everything was done right.

    You could get hundreds of other things from the Kaiser, the people told the newcomers, who had not known this. Four horses, a cow, and two young

---

1 A typical house had the shorter side facing the street. The entrance was in the middle of the longer side. To go into the house, one entered the *Hof* (yard) and walked along the *Gang*, a walkway that went along one side of the house with the roof jutting out over it. One entered into the kitchen, which was in the middle of the house. On the left side was a room called the *Zimmer*, the biggest room, which was used as a bedroom and living room, and on the right was a room called the *Kammer*. The *Kammer* had various uses depending on who lived in the house, perhaps for grandparents to sleep, or for children if a family had a lot of children. The *Stall*, stable, was still under the same roof but had a separate entrance, so the stink from the animals did not get into the living quarters.

Chapter 16—At the *Sieben Kurfürsten* Inn

pigs could be purchased on credit, as well all kinds of farm equipment and household items. These were not gifts, oh no; nothing that was made from human hands was free, but it was inexpensive and could be repaid over time. Only the property was a gift. That didn't cost anyone anything, as it had been created by God.

The people listened. They had come from the Black Forest, from Baden and Württemberg, from Alsace and Lorraine, from Trier, Fulda and Bamberg, from Luxemburg, from the *Pfalz* and Breisgau, from Mainz and Fürstenberg, Nassau, Franconia and Baden-Baden, from Swabia and Switzerland, from Tyrol and the *Steiermark*, from Silesia and Bohemia. Susi from *Blautal* served them; they only saw faces from their homeland and heard only German words. The different German dialects, which were never heard together back home, were all mingled here, waging a merry war with each other in this foreign land which was to become the new homeland. Anyone with ears could hear that those from Swabia and the *Pfalz* were in the majority.

Leonhard Wörndle from Alsace, who had been a teacher's aide in Blaubeuren, was now the principal of the school in Temesvar. He came regularly to Frau Therese in the *Sieben Kurfürsten* Inn and never failed to go into the *Bauernstube*. He was very homesick, and every countryman from Alsace was like a brother to him. It was a true pleasure to him to eavesdrop on this Babylonian war of dialects from different areas. Sitting at the regulars' table, he predicted that a completely new dialect would evolve out of the many which were now being mixed together. In two hundred years, scholars would rack their brains over where this dialect came from, because it would not exist in the German states. "A Banat dictionary will have to be published to show this unusual dialect to those in Germany," he said.

The newcomers had complaints in many respects. They had to verify what possessions they had, and the officials wanted to know how much they had brought with them. A few informed the officials that they had brought two or three hundred Guilders and still expected to get more from home. Others thought, "To hell with them" and claimed to have nothing. They were afraid that every penny they claimed would be taken from them to pay for their property.

The *Bauernstube* in the *Sieben Kurfürsten* Inn was the right place to get information. "Go ahead and tell how much you have!" said Michel Luckhaup from Guttenbrunn. "It's better to have more, than less!" Neither the settlers nor the officials welcomed those who had nothing. Certainly, every farmer was entitled to thirty two *Joch* of land with house and yard. But it was given more gladly to those who brought money or possessions with them. One who comes with nothing usually gets less productive land and has to work twice as hard.

Luckhaup told the story of a swindler who came to his village, spent five free years on the property given to him and paid nothing to the *Rentamt*. A year before it was time to pay, this man up and left and went to the Batschka, settled there and thought he could do the same again. But Mercy caught up with him! He was sentenced to be an oarsman on a ship in the Danube, and his wife to had to get a job as a waitress.

Gretel, the head waitress, had just walked in and heard this. "Psst!" she warned. "You don't want to talk about a rope in the house of a hangman," she said, pointing with her thumb behind her. Susi was the unfortunate wife. Her husband was the rogue who had been sentenced to row ships on the Danube.

"Which one is Susi?" asked a few.

"You know, the one who always serves you! The pale, silent one who never laughs. She came here to Temesvar on the same boat that I did."

"Do you also know her husband?"

"Do I know him?" said Frau Margarete Anderl scornfully. Gretel had grown a bit hefty in the first few prosperous years working in the new inn and was very self assured. Her husband Josef, who still played the French horn, was now a gardener on the Governor's estate. But she had not given up her position, because she had to earn money for her children. She'd sent for her widowed mother to watch them. Also, she stayed out of loyalty to Frau Therese who did not have a mother and had to look after her boys herself, and so needed Gretel's help with the business.

The men urged her to tell more, but she resisted. What if Susi came in with Luckhaup's *Paprika Gulyasch* or Staudt's beer? Those two were big spenders today, they had sold their wheat for a good price at the weekly market.

And as predicted, Susi walked in. The silence which fell when she came in completely embarrassed her. They must have been talking about her. She didn't know where to look, and would have liked to disappear into a mouse hole. Gretel took pity on her and sent her upstairs to clean the *Generalszimmer*. A nobleman was staying there and had just gone to visit the Governor. Now she must hurry and tidy up the room. Susi fled.

Gretel could now speak freely to satisfy the men's curiosity. "Did Michel Luckhaup know the man's name?" she asked.

"Why would I not know that? His name was Anton Oberle and he came from Swabia," Michel replied and made a face; the paprika container must have slipped out of the cook's hand while making his *Gulyasch*.

Chapter 16—At the *Sieben Kurfürsten* Inn

"That's right," answered Gretel. "But you don't really know who he is."

"Isn't he just a farmer?" someone asked.

"Definitely not!" said Gretel. "He was a shipmaster for Ludwig Pless in Ulm. He was our captain when we came down the Danube to Peterwardein, on Therese's bridal ship."

"What!?" exclaimed Hannes Staudt and looked over at Luckhaup.

His friend laughed out loud. "Ah, ha! You could see right away that he was no farmer. We often laughed ourselves silly at how incompetent he was. He could not even hold the guide rope properly, and his plow tipped over several times at every furrow. But he had the best land in the village—he somehow managed to get that!"

"A shipmaster!?" the others chimed in.

"All the way to Vienna," Gretel continued, "he was after Therese. He wanted to steal her away from Pless. But in Vienna she told him to get off her ship and leave, she would not take him along. He begged her to let him continue, he would never get over the disgrace. Well, he was a good shipmaster, he knew his business, so Therese changed her mind and gave in. Once we had left Vienna, we had only gotten as far as Pressburg and he was already forcing himself on me, the rogue. I should leave the 'stupid gardener' Anderl and go with him. He wanted to be a ship builder down there by the Turks and needed a woman like me, full of courage and fire. Well, my Josef showed *him* some fire, and almost threw him into the water. After that he left me alone and looked for someone else. There were still two more girls on board.

"When we got to Neusatz and Peterwardein, Anton Oberle got a big surprise. The whole area was full of ships! Nicer than any he could ever make. These were the ships Prince Eugene had brought from Vienna. They were warships, and they were in good shape; they would not need to be replaced for a long time. Therese was stunned, too. Her bridal ship could not be sold for the expected amount. Jakob had to practically give the ship away.

"Anton Oberle decided, what the heck, I'll just be a farmer, and Susi went along with him. I had suspected her of wanting to be with him all along. She, a cabinet maker's daughter; he, a shipmaster—and they pretended to be farmers and swindled Mercy's officials. Now the former shipmaster is a convict and rows ships upriver from Pantschowa to Neusatz, and she is with us as a waitress."

"Serves him right!" a few men said.

"A cobbler should stick to his last," said others, meaning that one should stick to his original trade.

Michel Luckhaup, however, felt that Oberle could in time have become a farmer, if he had been industrious and patient. But he was a lazy good-for-nothing. He was always the last to get up in the morning and the first to quit in the afternoon. He visited the Wallachian (Romanian) women in the neighboring villages more often than his fields. Then, out of the blue, he sold his cow, his horses and everything else that he had not yet paid for. Suddenly he was gone, along with his wife. Two Wallachian women had children from him, but not Susi. Luckhaup laughed. "He just up and left his house, yard and fields and wandered off to some other place where he would get free land and a house again."

"*Zigeuner, Zigeuner!*" some shouted, calling Oberle a no-good gypsy.

Gretel said, "I feel sorry for him. He should have stayed with Ludwig Pless in Ulm. Now he has to row a boat with robbers and thieves. Frau Therese wants to go to the Governor and ask for a pardon for him."

"He doesn't deserve it!" said the German farmers.

Staudt and Luckhaup, who should have long been underway if they were to be home by evening, went to harness their horses. First they checked their guns, which were hidden in the straw on the wagon, to make sure everything was in order. As they drove through the *Wiener Tor*, they met a rider wearing a gold-collared military uniform and behind him, two civilian gentlemen on horseback. Luckhaup lifted his hat. "That was young Mercy!" he told Staudt.

"Oh? He doesn't look at all healthy," Staudt replied.

They urged their horses onward. As they drove, they talked about Anton Oberle. They were highly amused by what they had heard about their former fellow villager. When they had thought he was just a lazy farmer, it hadn't been so funny, but now they laughed as they remembered him, even a small thing like how he strutted around. They had thought that his unnatural way of walking was so pretentious! But it probably came from standing on the deck of a swaying ship. He did not belong on land. "We should have thrown him into the Marosch River!" they laughed.

Laughing, they drove through Jahrmarkt and Bruckenau, two beautiful new German communities immediately behind the forests of Temesvar. It was too bad that between these Swabian villages and their community lay two Wallachian villages, Staudt commented.

"Don't worry," said Luckhaup. "In time our children will buy them out!"

In the afternoon hours, when business was slow, Frau Therese went to the upstairs living room to be with her children and *Base* Gutwein. Her aunt had become quite old since they came to Hungary and constantly complained

Chapter 16—At the *Sieben Kurfürsten* Inn

about her woes. Yet she looked well and had become rather plump. It disturbed her that so many people were dying. She dreaded to hear the bells sound that announced someone's death. Unfortunately, they tolled quite often in the Fortress of Temesvar. She longed for a garden, a bit of earth, but that was not to be had.

For years Therese had been urging her husband to purchase a piece of land in Mehala, the suburb which had at one time been Turkish, and build a summer cottage for their sickly children, it would be good for their health. But he did not do it because he needed to put all his energy into the business, and besides he needed the help of his wife. Now he should send her away with the children? Or, the Aunt should care for the four children? Again and again he persuaded his wife to abstain from this wish, the children should just get used to the climate of their native city. He did this until their daughter died and the doctor ordered his other children to be moved to a better climate.

"For whom did you build the *Sieben Kurfürsten*?" the white-bearded doctor asked Jakob Pless. "Send your children away and call them back when they are grown. Whoever is born here will not grow old."

This greatly affected the father. Send them away completely? All the way to Ulm? No. But he could fulfill the longtime wish of his beloved wife. Jakob had recently been elected to the Temesvar city council, he was among the first citizens to settle here, and he wanted his family to flourish here, as it flourished on the Upper Danube where his older brothers had many descendants. He owed that to his children and to himself. So he went out to Mehala and purchased a cottage with some land. Leonard Wörndle went with him. The new principal was beside himself about the children who were entrusted to him. As a teacher, he'd had to watch how the children shook from the fever during his classes, but as a principal he wanted to do something about it. He, too, looked for some land, and he wanted to convince the *Stadtrichter* and the Governor to allow the children to leave the fortress and have class outside, in the open air. Better in the hot sun in the meadow, than in the damp classroom next to the fortress wall. Many laughed at this plan and thought Wörndle was a little crazy, but he was determined to do this. If Mayor Solderer did not agree, he was sure that Governor Mercy could be won over. The Governor supported anything that was good for his city.

Both came home satisfied. Therese was not only happy that Jakob planned to renovate the cottage he had purchased so that they could use it this fall, she also was excited about her friend Wörndle's plan. It was she who had enticed Wörndle to come here from Blaubeuren with letters she had her husband write for her. He was thankful that he had come. Even on his first day here, he had not felt like a foreigner in this country, and his social circle here was even greater than it had been in his beloved Alsace. Now he was the one who wrote letters for her to her homeland. Jakob preferred not to do the writing and he had not been that good at it. Wörndle, on the other hand, paid close attention and wrote exactly what she wanted to say in the letters.

Today, after a long, long time a letter had once again come from Ulm. A newly arrived immigrant brought it.

"Jakob, look at what I have!" Therese called to her husband. "A letter from your mother!"

His heart filled with a warm feeling just at hearing the word. Did all people have such a good feeling at the thought of their mother? In his mind she was the star to whom he looked for guidance in this foreign land, as a soldier and when in distress. He never would have thought that she would survive his strong father, he always believed she would be consumed in the thousands of self-created worries about them all. When Therese had told him about how, when the bridal ship left, his mother had called from the shore for Therese to be good and loving to him, it had touched him so much he wanted to cry. And every letter she wrote to him similarly affected him.

Therese knew this and left him alone with this latest letter. She served Wörndle, who came to sit with her and Tante Gutwein to talk to them excitedly about Mahala. There, Turkish sabers, coins and pitchers, bowls and pots were plowed up by farmers every day. He had picked some of these items up today and showed them to the women. "We should keep all these things," he said, "for our descendants. A museum should be built in the middle of the fortress to honor her past, before the surrounding swamp swallows everything up."

"We should build a proper church instead!" exclaimed *Base* Gutwein. "What we have here is a disgrace, especially when I think about the beautiful churches at home in Ulm and Regensburg."

Now Wörndle had his hands full, explaining to the old woman how much would be involved in building a cathedral as beautiful as Mercy wanted it to be, and how it was not yet feasible in this land which at this time was only producing bread.

"But you want to build a museum for that old junk?" she asked derisively. "God comes first."

He put the items away, seeing that he would not receive any understanding for his ideas here.

Jakob Pless came out of his room with his face flushed. He wordlessly handed the letter to Therese and went out again.

"Should Herr Wörndle read it to us?" she called after him. He nodded and disappeared.

'It must be something heartbreaking,' she said to herself, 'since he does not want to be here when we read it.'

Wörndle read: *"My dear beloved son and daughter! At my feeble age of 78 years I feel that it is my duty as a tender mother to think of you and to write to you. I hope, in my old age, that these few lines will find you in good health, if God wills it. As your loyal mother, who is still your mother even from so far away, I pray daily that the good Lord of everlasting love may hold you in good health and give you his eternal blessing."*

Wörndle took a breath. Then he continued: *"There is not much to tell about me, old and weak as I am. Old age itself is an illness that is hard to bear, and I am also constantly sick. This will probably be the last time I can write to you. Dear children, I could write for a long time about everything that is going on here. However, Jakob Müller, the Master Wagon Builder, should show you the letter from his brother. Jakob lives in a German community close to where you are, and his brother who lives here wrote him a nice long letter about happenings here.*

"Your brother from the Schwarzen Adler in Blaubeuren visited me and said that money was tight and you should give him at least until St. Martin's day to get your money. No need to worry, your money is invested in his business. There was much wheat this year but it was hard to sell since nothing could be sold down the Danube anymore. It seems that you are now growing your own down there. Heretofore our blessed Kaiser had to send ships laden with wheat to Hungary for the army. My dear Jakob, you were eating bread made from German wheat in Peterwardein and Belgrade, without knowing it. For a long time, German regiments, German bread and German money have traveled down the Danube to Hungary, but nothing and no one ever comes back. Where are you all? Dearly beloved children, I am forever comforted by the thought that you are in a German country and that your children and grandchildren will remain loyal Germans. With many tears, I give you my best and loyal wishes, since my grave is near and I will never see you again. Live well and piously. The time will come when you, too, will be old like me. I kiss you and my grandchildren with motherly gentleness, and I remain, until my death, your loving mother, Maria Elisabeth Pless.

"P.S. Therese's brother and all my children, grandchildren and great grandchildren send you all their love and kisses. We think of you with every day that God gives us. Do the same and do not forget us, who love you with

all our hearts. Live good Christian lives, so that you may die in peace and see your relatives once again in Heaven."

They were silent when Wörndle had finished. The letter had touched them to the core. This motherly heart—such an everlasting source of love and goodness and wisdom!

Base Gutwein blew her nose, and Therese took her youngest on her lap and hugged him. Pless did not come back into the room. These letters were his torment and his joy. And he thanked the Lord, quite often, that his children, too, had a loving mother, just as he had.

Chapter 17

Father and Son at their Great Work

Young Anton Mercy did not look entirely healthy. Years of intense hard work had left the older Mercy unscathed, but it was hard on the nephew. The climate greatly affected him, and the vigor of his youth seemed to have faded prematurely.

How happy he had been when he came home from Vienna, a man engaged to be married. He had spent several blessed weeks with Lottel. The *Hofkammerrat* had given his blessing to their engagement, and also his adoptive father, the Governor, had sent his approval while the Major was still in Vienna. And now they both waited longingly for their ardent desires to be fulfilled. He, in this nest of malaria, surrounded by a hundred dangers; she, blossoming to radiant womanhood in the shadow of the Viennese court, constantly swarmed by admirers.

Oh, this often tortured him more than his recurrent fever which simply would not go away.

He had promised the *Hofkammerrat* he would wait a couple of years, loyally remaining at the side of his tempestuous, adventurous uncle and be the mediator between him and Vienna so that this great project would succeed. He owed his uncle that much, even without this pledge. But it was taking too long! And the two older men did not seem to realize this. They worked their influence, negotiated and had a lifelong purpose to fulfill, but never realized what they were denying the young couple: precious time that could never be replaced.

The Major's dissatisfaction grew day by day. He wanted to break these family chains and escape the tyranny of his uncle, his adoptive father, in whose shadow he would never come into his own. The older man's will subjugated everyone else's, his obstinacy never allowed the validity of others' opinions. Count Anton yearned for his bride and his own ambitions. But when swamp fever came over him, and he shivered so much that his teeth chattered, he despaired and did not dare wish his Lottel to such a place. He suffered much mental anguish in this house and could not bear it much longer.

Here was a never ending stream of people who came and went, of negotiation and consultation, review and dismissal, straining all intellectual and physical energy, by day and by night. It was as if the governor's house was the focal point for the creation of a new world. The construction of the formidable Fortress of Temesvar, that everyone praised and everyone could see, was just a secondary concern for the man who kept all the threads together in his head, since it was a long term project and at this point was in the capable hands of skilled experts. The land beyond, this country without a population, was his greatest worry. Over a hundred new villages had already been measured off or laid out; existing villages enlarged; and the colonization proceeded step by step. Future cities like Weisskirchen and Werschetz had already begun to be established. Others were being planned or were being rebuilt from heaps of rubble. Marshes needed drying, miles of swamps needed draining, and the streams which spread out lazily over the plains like hundreds of tributaries needed diverting to regulate the course of the water.

The Fortress of Peterwardein was to be a Gibraltar on the Danube, standing over the river as the entrance to the Banat. The Military Frontier, the idea which had come from Prince Eugene, had to be set up and settled with soldierly people, so they would protect this new civilization. A Banat Militia had to be created to fight against the constant Tatar invasions and to combat bands of robbers which had formed ever since there were people to rob. If the thousands of settlers were to be able to farm in peace, to sow and reap and as taxpaying citizens strengthen this imperial province, they would need the powerful shield and protection of a leader in this wild country. Yet, with agriculture, the work was only half done. Business needed to flourish, industries transplanted from the West, because the abundance of raw materials in this new territory were worthless if they could not be converted into refined products. Numerous factories and workshops arose in the southeast section of Temesvar's fortress: chimneys smoked, windmills clattered, saws cut, hammers pounded, and this section was almost its own little city with all of the workshops, the Dutch oil presses, the textile factories and the paper mills. And the water pump system that supplied drinking water for the city was its crowning jewel.

Chapter 17—Father and Son at their Great Work

The hundred thousand mulberry trees that Governor Mercy had brought from Sicily now bordered the streets, feeding the silk worms whose golden cocoons supplied the material for the first silk factory of this land. He would apply the death penalty to anyone that destroyed these trees. The death penalty! Those who ruined his idealistic plans would be hung. Mercy thirsted for everything useful and beautiful which he had seen during his military campaigns in Alsace, France, Italy and Sicily, and he brought it all here, to the paradise he was creating. He enticed colonists from all European countries to settle in the Banat in the name of the Kaiser, whom he used as a medium to bring people to this new land. He told potential immigrants they needed to bring nothing with them but their will to work and their health. Naturally these qualities were essential.

Count Mercy was surrounded by talented, industrious, hardworking men who wanted to earn glory and honor and a new homeland. The only thing he still needed was to finally reach his goal. No one of his lineage had achieved the full height of his potential. Will he obtain it? Will it be granted him, this promised Land, that his mind's eye sees so close at hand? He believes in his vision, feels the power of a thousand hands working towards that vision, and neither resistance nor failure discourage him. Whatever obstructs, he casts down, and whatever fails, would be repeated ten times, if necessary. Luck does not just come about, it must be forced.

He said this to his pale nephew every day, and he said it today to the *Obristkapitän*, the Colonel in charge of the border guards, who reported to him about the revolt of the Illyrians and asked that the Germans be removed from the border area around Weisskirchen. "The Croatians and Serbs, too, are jealous of the foreigners; they don't want to put up with them."

At this, Mercy exploded. "Who here are foreigners? And who is putting up with whom!?" the Governor shouted at the Colonel. "The Illyrians came earlier—but as refugees. They fled to this land to be saved from death and destruction in Turkey, and they should serve as border guards against their mortal enemies. But the Germans were **called** here by the Kaiser. He took them from one end of his empire and transferred them to another. They are not foreigners. And there will be no talk of tolerance, Herr Colonel. Someday, next to the Illyrian regiments, there will be just as many Banat German border regiments, and just as strong. If someone touches one hair of a German, the Major should lay the leader of that community, their *Knes*, over the whipping bench. Twenty five lashes!"

The Colonel ventured to make a different suggestion: "Perhaps it would help keep the peace if Germans were required to do *Robotarbeiten*, compulsory labor, or if even a few German companies of border guards were created now."

"No, no," Mercy barked, "the first generation of Germans are completely free! Do you want to prune the grapevine before it has taken root? There is no debate about that. You must give me some other suggestions, Herr Colonel. Where I put the Swabians, there they stay." Seeing that he was dealing with an iron will in this matter, the *Obristkapitän* recalled his other complaints.

"What, your men have not been paid? For three years? That cannot be, that should not be!" Mercy cried and went to his desk. "It is better that God should wait rather than hungry soldiers' families." He wrote a payment order from the War Treasury. 'Our cathedral has time,' he said to himself, resigning himself once again to delay one of his dearest plans for another few years as he gave the *Obristkapitän* the payment for the border soldiers.

As rough as he was with his military commanders and lower ranks, he was just as forceful with his son, his engineers, factory owners and builders, and especially with all the doctors whom he had summoned to stop the many deaths. Alas, these had not waned; the deaths never stopped. He had already built more hospitals than churches across the countryside. And in the city? May God have mercy! Was he alone the only one who could tolerate this climate? Everyone had their turn; no one came out of here healthy. Even Anton could not shake his fever and it often gave the Governor grave concern. Must he do without him in the end?

After the Colonel left, Anton von Mercy came to the Governor. He stood in front of his uncle with his yellow complexion and weary eyes. Yes, his youth had withered during these years of work dedicated to the building of the fortress and the personal service to his adoptive father. He was dead tired again today, and his appearance shocked the older Mercy.

"My boy, what's wrong with you?" he asked. "Should I excuse you from your duties?"

"Oh no. Today is not my fever day," the younger Mercy said calmly. "The engineers of the Bega Canal wish to speak to you. They want to divide the canal into four rather than three parts in order to solve our problem. I was with them and informed them what we want to accomplish."

"You did? The canal will only be half its worth if it does not completely drain and cleanse the groundwater underneath the fortress. It has to be dug much deeper, and create a slope as it winds its way around the fortress. That will be good for the health of the city. But why a fourth arm?"

"Herr Freimaut, the engineer from Holland, will explain it to you," Count

Chapter 17—Father and Son at their Great Work

Anton replied. "He thinks the plan for the canal is brilliant. It will drain one hundred thousand *Joch* (about 220 square miles) of swampland. We will be able to float the timbers to build the factories and businesses, and the canal will be like a traffic lane to New-Barcelona[1] and give us a connection to the Theiss and Danube Rivers. If this canal system can fulfill the fourth function, to bring health to the city, Freimaut thinks it would be an accomplishment worthy of ancient Rome."

The Governor beamed with pleasure. "Really? The Dutchman says that? That makes me happy! We had to give him the idea, hmm? Hopefully he will be able to make it happen." He broke off. "But Anton, you can barely stand up! My boy, what is wrong? Sit down! Sit down!"

The Major grabbed the armrest of a chair. "It seems that it will come today after all... I just have to take my quinine…" he stammered as a sudden attack of the chills left him shivering and trembling. He sat down.

"You're worrying me…I can't stand this anymore. You must get a change of air, Anton."

"Oh, it will go away," Anton said and stood up again. "I'm going to send the engineers in to you and go lie down for a bit."

"Do that! Do that! We will talk about it later. You will have to leave this place!"

With a weak smile on his feverish lips, Count Anton von Mercy left the room. He would have to leave! These words from his uncle were so liberating! And it was good that his uncle had been the one to say them.

The Governor had a strenuous day. The construction of the Bega Canal was one of his major undertakings. It was to go in a straight line from Facset to Temesvar, would be divided into three tributaries here, and after fulfilling its purpose, including powering a few mills, would flow back into its old river bed through a detour of sixteen German miles. Mercy placed all his passion in this project. He was not easily persuaded that a fourth tributary was necessary in order for all his hopes to be realized. The costs were piling up and the Vienna City Bank was becoming increasingly difficult. It was the sole lender for the Banat, whose taxing capacity could only be referred to as negligible. But Mercy did not want to do anything halfway. If the fourth tributary was necessary, then it must be built. If the City Bank balked, he would personally give his own money, so that the Banat could become a civilized and prosperous land. In thirty years, the Banat would no longer owe a single *Heller*. Mercy was no financial expert, but when it came to the big

---

[1] Neu-Barcelona later became Gross-Becskerek.

picture, his gut instincts always turned out to be correct. He detested anyone who doubted in the future of his province and would not tolerate his presence; he needed everyone to believe in his vision.

And so, after brief deliberation, he authorized the construction of the fourth arm of the canal on this day. He was convinced that this would save the lives of future generations.

After his discussions with the engineers, the governor had even more meetings. His designs for the country's progress were without end and involved hundreds of people. However, there were also pleasant encounters that did not involve predicaments and sacrifices. The Italians from nearby Mercydorf brought the first silkworm cocoons and a few delicious melons for the Governor's table. The Spaniards from New-Barcelona sent a delegation with rice, figs and olives. These plants all thrived here, they said, but eating the fruit was not good for the health of the populace. They also wanted to try to grow sugar cane. All this kept the Governor exceptionally busy. He found it difficult to tear himself away from the various envoys who brought him messages, and was late coming to the dinner table. He was happy that his nephew, having overcome his latest bout of fever, was already at the table. He needed somebody whom he could talk to.

And they finally had a long discussion. Initially, Governor Mercy talked about the events of the day, ate the melon from the Mercydorfers with such gusto that it alarmed his nephew, and also tasted the figs and olives from the Spaniards. Then as they sat with their Turkish coffee, of which Anton took two cups today, and smoked their *chibuks*, the conversation became more personal. The Governor spoke in a fatherly tone. "Anton, I now realize that you must go away from here. It will be hard for me. Who can replace you? But we should not dwell on things we cannot change."

"Then I am going to Vienna, Herr Papa?" asked Anton.

"No, no, my Herr Major. First of all, you should recuperate," smiled the Governor. "You'll scare your bride with the way you look. Also, you should wait until you are a Colonel, you have almost achieved that rank…."

"Oh, Charlotte would take me even if I only wore a Lieutenant's uniform. And I will get well on the way," said Anton.

"That's questionable. However, I know exactly where you can recover your health: on the other side of the Danube in 'Swabian Turkey'. There is much for you to do in that area. The work there is only half-done. Go to my retirement home in Högyész; stay at my empty castle for a short while, visit my Lorrainers and send them greetings from their Count. Tell them Lorraine has a trump card in Austria. The young *Herzog von Lothringen* (Duke

Chapter 17—Father and Son at their Great Work

of Lorraine) is courting Maria Theresia and may one day be Kaiser. And when you are healthy, my son, go and bring your bride home. You have my blessings."

"Home, Papa, but where to?"

The Governor looked up in surprise. "Ha, if she fears Temesvar like you, then go to Högyész with her. I will not be going there for a long time. My work here is not done. You're thirty now? Actually, it is high time for a Mercy to get married, we do not live to be too old."

Count Anton smiled. "You will live for a long time, you are not susceptible to this climate at all."

"Who knows when, where or how one might die? You are now going away from me. Who knows if we will see each other again?"

"Papa, I'm going to bring my wife to see you. We cannot leave you here alone with these morbid feelings," Count Anton said earnestly.

"I have always had these feelings, my son. But just now I was thinking more of the possibility of another war. I would be happy if Charlotte had the courage to come, since I will not be able to come to the wedding. Incidentally, I have a bone to pick with her father. Actually, several," Mercy said with a smile. "You can tell him that. But as a relative I have to be easy on him. Why doesn't he work toward making this region a self-governing principality? I wonder! This is a missed opportunity! And he should put pressure on the Vienna City Bank because we need money, a lot of money. You can also reply verbally to some questions which he recently asked again. He wanted to know if any noble families resided in the Banat. No, not even one. It must have been idle speculation that Hungarian nobles ever held estates here, since not one noble family has made a claim. And then—remember how you and I laughed about this—he wanted to know how many Hungarians there are in Temesvar. I have looked into it and found the exact number: Three! A small merchant, a coachman and a servant."

Count Anton smiled. "How is it that there are so few?"

"They never liked the climate here. They'll wait until we've drained the land of St. Nepomuk dry of its swamps and fumigated it of disease-carrying insects." He laughed. "By the way, their *Primas*[2] repeatedly asks Rome that Nepomuk be dropped as saint of this region because he was a Bohemian and not a Hungarian."

With this kind of cheerful conversation, the Governor prevented the

---

2 *Primas*: Primate—a title or rank bestowed on some bishops. In Hungary the Primate was an Archbishop and also, after 1715, a ruling Prince (*Fürst*) of the Holy Roman Empire.

tone from becoming too melancholy on this eve of his nephew's departure. The next morning, Count Anton embarked on his journey even though his fever was intense that day. He had often heard that one could escape this fever by leaving. And so he left. However, his coach did not pass through the Peterwardein Gate, but instead rumbled through the gate that led to Vienna.

Chapter 18

The Governor's Excursion

The Governor felt very alone in the Palace of Mehemed Aga. He missed his son, his coworker and partner. Exasperating reports kept coming in from all over the countryside. In one area, there was flooding every year and the settlers had to be taken care of to prevent them from leaving; in another, epidemics took the lives of settlers and animals; at the Banat's borders along the Danube and Theiss Rivers, people lived in constant fear that their belongings would be stolen even in broad daylight. It was said that a Tatar bandit named Haram-Pasha led a band of thieves, who rode through the countryside wreaking havoc and drove off with their loot by wagon. As a rule, the Banat Militia, which was spread out over the vast country in twenty two posts and villages, usually came too late to prevent these robberies. Even the ships that brought Swabian immigrants along the Danube and Theiss Rivers were held up and robbed.

On this day, *Stadtrichter* Solderer, the mayor and municipal judge, came to see the Governor personally. Peter Solderer was a popular mayor; he had been elected by his fellow citizens at a very young age and had been reelected eighteen times. Today he had much to report. First he told the Governor that a group of newly arrived immigrants had been robbed of everything they had by the armed bandits.

"And I have something much more serious to report, so tragic that I hesitate to tell you about it. People are saying that a ship with German immigrants was forced to dock near Mohács and did not continue on its way. The fifty families on board have disappeared."

"What!? Am I to believe that this could happen? And I have not heard anything about it?"

The *Stadtrichter* was better informed, since he was in charge of getting extra horses to the various towns for people who were traveling and needed to change horses. The military was responsible for conveying letters and money through their field posts protected by armed guards, but he himself arranged for goods to be transported by teams and wagons and for extra horses to be transported throughout the region. And so his people reported to him from everywhere in Hungary.

Besides this, the mayor was a board member of the Municipal Authorities, which kept a list of farming immigrants and directed them to their final destination. "Your Excellency, I can introduce you to immigrants who can tell you about this," said Solderer. "Some had a brother, a father or a friend among those who disappeared. One young lady even lost her bridegroom."

"Not lost forever, they will be found! They must be found! I will find them!"

Count Mercy seethed with rage. Had he not worked for many years with his whole being for the cultivation of this land? It wasn't enough, that he could not overcome the acts of God and the high incidence of death, now the robber bands were gaining the upper hand? Now entire boatfuls of people were taken? His settlers were kidnapped while traveling to their destination, perhaps dragged into slave labor. What would his good friends in Vienna think of him? However, since the legendary Haram-Pasha had been pursued for so long in vain, he doubted that the man even existed.

The mayor continued to talk about the incident and also endeavored to inform the Governor about other events, telling him about the imminent completion of Temesvar's City Hall and requesting the courtesy of His Excellency's presence at the opening ceremony. As the worthy mayor went on and on, the Governor's mind was otherwise occupied; he was forming his own plans. He had to recover these kidnapped people.

"Well and good, *Herr Stadtrichter*. I thank you for everything," he interjected as Solderer paused, "but I need something else from you."

"Your Excellency, I am entirely at your service."

"Could you organize a trip for me through all of the Banat and Batschka with a number of good horses? I have wanted to undertake such a trip for a long time, but not as Governor, only as a simple traveler. No one should know who I am. Only that way can I find out about the actual conditions in each area."

"Your Excellency, that can be done. I am flattered that you assign this task to me. My only worry is your safety. I will not be able to safeguard you from all eventualities. Please do not hold me responsible!"

Chapter 18—The Governor's Excursion

"Let me worry about that. I need two strong Hàjduks, to come along, and nobody else. The country is not unknown to me. Where do we start?"

"In the East and the North, Your Excellency." Solderer walked over to the large map on the wall of the Governor's office. "While I work on planning your visit to the South, which will be more difficult, I suggest you take a look at the area around Lugosch." He pointed with his finger to the East. "Then up to Lippa, then west along the Marosch River to Arad, then zigzag across the heath to the Theiss River. Here you cross the river to Zenta and are in the Batschka. Then you go straight across to the Danube, to the point where the German settlers were kidnapped. Next, go in a southerly direction to Neusatz and Peterwardein. When you cross the Theiss again you will be in the Banat, where you can visit New Barcelona and then Pantschowa. There you cross the Military Border to go to Weisskirchen, and maybe even to Orsova. On the way back, through the old roman mining area, through Oravicza to Werschetz. It will be very difficult. The roads are unfinished, the plain is endless and hot, the marshes are populated with billions of insects, the border counties near Transylvania are mountainous and have no roads. Six weeks are not enough for the whole trip, and I must hold two hundred horses in preparedness."

The Governor stood behind the mayor, looking thoughtfully at the map. "It is a large region. It has gone through many trials and yet is still unexplored. Only God knows what treasures are in its earth; that is for coming generations to find out. Our generation, my dear *Stadtrichter*, will not uncover the full potential of this land; we simply stand at the threshold to the future. But we must establish law and order to make this land liveable for honest hardworking people."

He turned away from the map. "You're right," he said. "The round trip would take six weeks. I cannot take that much time off, and cannot travel incognito for that long. I will take a shorter trip and will let you know which areas I would like to visit. The regions which have the most problems will be my priority."

At this point the mayor asked to take leave.

"One more thing: My adjutant will go to City Hall without delay to take care of those newly arrived immigrants who lost everything. He will make a list of all stolen items. We must deal with that matter very quickly. Where did the new immigrants come from?"

"From the Black Forest, Your Excellency."

"And what was their destination?"

"Guttenbrunn, Your Excellency."

"Bravo! A splendid community, well situated on a high plain sloping toward the Marosch River. Very suitable for expansion. Good-bye, *Herr Stadtrichter.*"

Soon after this conversation with the mayor, the Governor began his trip. He dressed as a man of higher standing and was accompanied by two armed guards. He wanted to appear as if he was looking to buy some property in a good area and settle down. This way he could ask questions and do research without raising suspicion.

The trip was a success. He experienced how different things appeared from ground level, so to speak. As soon as he came to the eastern area of the Banat, the air seemed fresher. One could almost feel the powerful wind of the Carpathian mountains. Here he found the solution for which he had been looking so long. He could send the sick regiments here, to the fresh air of Lugosch, to recover from swamp fever in the summer. They would get rid of it very soon in this climate. He was surprised that none of the doctors had discovered this region.

The ride to the northern border of the land, which led into the Marosch Valley, revitalized him even more. Here the fortress of Lippa had once guarded the border. Mercy did not look at the ruins of the fortress, rather focused on the village, which was flourishing. A temporary bridge supported by floating structures was built across the Marosch River and led to the other side, to a shrine called Maria Radna which had survived the Turkish occupation and was still intact.

Mercy withstood the temptation to visit the Hungarian side of the river. He stayed on the Banat side, and drove from Lippa straight towards Neu Arad.[1] The river was bordered by pitiful Wallachian villages. Villages? Twenty *Erdhütten*, half of them uninhabited, were called a village. In the midst of them, proud and clean, lay the German village with the good well. The villagers were so proud of this well that they named their town Gutenbrunn.[2] He was quite familiar with the town; it was one of the first settlements. And now, in addition to those from *Franken*, the *Pfalz* and Württemberg, new settlers from the Black Forest had been added to the mix. However, not all of the settlers from the Black Forest had reached this

---

1 Neu-Arad was a new town settled by German settlers from *Franken* (Franconia) in 1724. It was built across the Marosch River from the town Arad, which at the time was inhabited by mostly Romanians and Serbs, as well as some Hungarians.
2 Guttenbrunn literally means "good well" (*guten Brunnen*).

destination. Mercy's adjutant had given him the names of the families whose members had not all arrived: the Zengraf, Müller, Lulay and Krämer families were all separated from their kin due to the mysterious incident.

They received fresh horses at the *Wirtshaus* but the Governor did not want to stop at the inn, as there were no problems to be resolved there. Then along came Michel Luckhaup, who looked at the stranger curiously. 'Heavens, where have I seen him before?' he thought to himself.

"Pardon me, sir, are you not from Temesvar?" he boldly asked, lifting his hat a bit.

The Governor looked at the farmer in a friendly manner and replied, "It could be that you have seen me there."

"At the *Sieben Kurfürsten* Inn, right?" Luckhaup surmised in his broad dialect.

"Could be, could be."

"Yes, that must be it!" Luckhaup exclaimed. "I am the new *Dorfrichter* here, the village mayor and judge. Michel Luckhaup is my name."

"So, so. I am pleased to meet you. Now, tell me, what problems does your community have? I can let them know in Temesvar."

"Well, we would like to have a church, but we don't have enough money. Mercy should send some our way."

"I'll tell that to Mercy. But I heard the bell ringing before, don't you have a church?"

"We had a bell brought to us from Vienna, but our masses are held in the big *Wirtshaus*. *Herr*, where we dance is not a good place to say our prayers."

"Hmm. Otherwise are you satisfied? Your community is no longer free from taxes, correct?"

"Yes, yes. We are not unhappy. We've worked like dogs, but we're getting by. And, you know, since we are paying taxes more work is being done. Before that, many discouraged people just wanted to give up and let the plowing go. Now they're all plowing, since they know they have to pay."

The Governor laughed. "It is very good to know that," he said as he walked toward his wagon, where the horses had been changed. "Mayor, I heard that you wanted to plant plum trees. You will receive a thousand plants next March. You can also have grape vines. Just ask Mercy for them."

"*Herr!*" exclaimed Michel Luckhaup, who began to have an inkling of who this gentleman might be. "Thank you, a thousand thanks! But we still have one big problem."

"And what would that be?"

"There are too many robbers here. We have to keep our guns loaded all the time. When you are driving, take a good look at the road from Lippova to Arad. Wouldn't it be nicer if only Germans were settled along the Marosch River?"

Astonished, Mercy looked into the intelligent eyes of the farmer. Then he shook hands with him. "Goodbye, mayor, I see that the community is well taken care of by you. I will tell them everything you said when I get home."

Mercy nodded to him once more from his coach and proceeded to drive through the village. The very end of the main street was being extended with additional homes, and before he turned off the road to Arad, he did stop a bit to see that. Here houses were being built, wells were dug and the new residents, strong men, brown-haired hearty women and girls in Black Forest *Trachten,* helped with the construction. Would they ever see their kidnapped relatives again? Over there an official was already handing over a few straw-thatched houses to their new owners. The system seemed to be working very efficiently.

The Governor found the sight of all this highly gratifying. And he thought about the wise mayor's suggestion throughout his whole trip. Yes, why should there not be a whole chain of German villages. The few primitive Wallachian families could be resettled and moved together into a bigger community. The Wallachians still lived a nomadic lifestyle and needed only grazing for their animals.

The Governor anonymously visited all the colonies on the great plains. Before, no plow had ever scratched the surface of the large steppe; now, this Garden of Eden supplied the daily bread for thousands. Every region had brought in a good harvest of grains. In many areas, new settlers had joined the communities. They impatiently awaited the completion of their simple, carefully built houses and for their fields to be measured off and assigned to them. The universal complaint, however, was the shortage of craftsmen. Any community that had its own wagoner, bricklayer or carpenter idolized these skilled workers. The craftsmen were so well-regarded that many were elected to be mayors of their towns. "Send us blacksmiths, cabinet makers, tailors and shoemakers," one rural mayor told Mercy. "We'd give a bushel of corn for just one well-made horseshoe!"

'We should be able to meet this need,' the Governor said to himself, 'if we can give the craftsmen some land, a house and a yard, just like the farmers get.'

The next place that he visited had one more gripe: there were no potatoes in this country. The settlers in Neudorf, originally from Baden-Baden, missed these very much. If they had known that these were unknown here, they

Chapter 18—The Governor's Excursion

would have brought a sackful with them. After giving it some thought, the Governor realized that he had never been served potatoes anyplace outside of the table of *Hofkammerrat* Stephany in Vienna. He remembered that Tante Mathilde had served them. But it had never occurred to him that this would be an important staple for the people. He had never thought to bring them here, and his advisors had never mentioned potatoes to him. Now it seemed to him a curious omission, to have introduced tobacco, melons, olives, figs, mulberry trees, almonds, apricots and walnuts, but not the celebrated potato. He would remember that. He would write to Holland to obtain some.

The Governor was amazed by these residents of Neudorf. They had already built a church—on their own, with their own funds! A scant six years after its residents had arrived, a church steeple already towered over the town. Tomorrow it would be blessed and the *Dorfrichter*, the village's municipal judge and mayor, invited the visiting gentleman to take part in the dedication.

Consequently, the gentleman stayed overnight. His coach needed a minor repair and Father Plenktner offered him lodgings in the rectory. There was something about this property owner, Florimund, that made the pastor think that he must be a person of great consequence. So even though he already had a guest, a visiting priest from his order who was here to assist in tomorrow's dedication, the pastor made room for the stranger. And he was already gratified by his decision during the evening dinner. Such a worldly gentleman! He had been a soldier, he had seen death and brutality, he was well acquainted with great men. The man even knew who was to marry the Princess Maria Theresia, the heir to the throne. And he spoke so enthusiastically about this new land, praised everything about it, and could not be more impressed by the vitality of this new community.

"Well, it should be no surprise to you, *Herr!* When two hundred families from Baden-Baden put themselves into working for a cause, we soon get results," the priest said merrily in his peasant's dialect. "The builder of the church could not make the steeple high enough to suit the farmers. They felt that the whole country should be able to see the church steeple of Neudorf!"

What the Governor saw the next day confirmed the pastor's statement, a hundred times over. The town was completely energized about its *Kirchweih*, the consecration of their church. Finally, this beloved festival from their homeland, the *Kirchweihfest*, could be transferred here; at last their customs and traditions would take root in this foreign soil.

Already in the early morning the young men of the community were presented their *Kirchweih* hats, which had been decorated with flowers and gold-colored ribbons by the girls. Their festive procession to the church was watched by young and old alike. No bishop was present to consecrate the first village church, since there was none in this region, so the pastor performed this sacred duty. Then he walked up to the raised pulpit and gave the first homily from this august platform. The stranger sat beside the mayor as the only guest of the community, and he was eager to hear what the pastor had to say on this important day. The man immediately touched his heart with his first sentence: "Dear brothers in Christ," he began, "Rejoice, you no longer stand alone in a foreign land; God now has his own home in your midst, and this once foreign land has become your homeland." He built his entire sermon on this pleasing thought. God's hand was now visible in this promised land: the new homeland had been found.

At noon, the young men jubilantly wound their way through town as was the custom at *Kirchweih*. The *Kirchweihbuben* were welcomed everywhere as they stopped at each house to receive its hospitality. After the evening worship, the traditional dance around the barrel began. As the musicians played lovely traditional songs, the girls sang and danced, encircling a barrel of wine. Yes, this was the baptism which converted the foreign land into their *Heimat*, their homeland.

The Governor left the happy community before sundown and drove over the endless plains. His dream, which had been formed the day after the conquest of the Banat, was beginning to take shape. The seed, which by some fortunate destiny had been given into his care, was beginning to sprout. He only hoped there would be no frost to stop the progress which had been made.

Mercy crossed the Theiss River and came into the Batschka. This was new territory. Here, between the Theiss and Danube Rivers, lay perhaps the most promising area of the Kaiser's new province. His heart was filled with joy when he saw the abundant blessings that came from the settlers' first efforts. When he had lain bleeding on a battlefield near Zenta as a cadet, he would never have thought that such crops would eventually thrive here! Yet this was also a region with widespread flooding; at least three canals ought to be built to drain the area, and the one near Temesvar hadn't even been finished. A great deal of work needed to be done. And this area was near the main territory of the robber bands: the Serbian-Turkish borders were not far away. Haram Pasha was a terror for young and old.

The Governor visited Militia posts in the area. Much had been accomplished here: Many a good-for-nothing had become a productive gardener; robbers and thieves had been pardoned and put into the imperial service.

Chapter 18—The Governor's Excursion

They did their duty and defended the land against Tatar bandits as well as they could, and yet they protected their own former friends and accomplices.

The traveling Governor did not spare *baksheesh*, bribes for these men. He kept company with these dangerous fellows, ate and drank with them, and bought himself his security in dangerous areas and even accompaniment through the wild settlements along the Theiss River and the shores of the Danube. A venturesome young Serbian, a non commissioned military officer, went with him as his guide.

Mercy's ears were sharp, his eyes everywhere. How did these *Betyaren* make a living? They did not cultivate any land, they had pitiful livestock and seemed to live from fishing and making baskets from reeds. Perhaps some of them were millers, since here and there a ragged watermill clattered on the Danube River. The Governor came to his conclusion based on hundreds of small details: these were robber villages. Just as on the Marosch River, so on the Theiss and on the Danube. Here, people paraded around in their stolen clothing which were originally from the Neckar region; there, he saw household items which would never be owned by people who lived in the same room as cattle. A woman offered to sell him a German song book, and he purchased it. Printed by Ploß in Heidelberg!

The bandits looked at him with daggers in their eyes. Mercy felt their stare on his back as he walked amongst them, and he even felt that his guide, the Serbian Corporal, was of their mind. He was certain that this young man had once been one of the *Betyaren*. So the Governor asked his guide point-blank: "Are these the kidnappers who held up the ships?"

The Corporal shrugged his shoulders. "Those poor people," he said, and nothing else. Mercy took that as an admission that the *Betyaren* were behind this. He urged his guide to help him find those who kidnapped the people four weeks ago. The Kaiser would give him fifty Ducats if he would point to where these people could be found.

The young man was stunned. "F-fifty Ducats…?" he stuttered.

"Yes!"

"*Herr*, robbers did not do that," the guide said in his broken German, smiling ambiguously. "And the *Schwabski* were not harmed."

"Will you speak more clearly?" asked Mercy, whose patience was nearing its end.

"Give me money, then I will tell you something," the Corporal said.

Mercy pressed a couple of gold pieces into his hand and the Corporal crossed himself, as if the gold had come from the devil. Then he said: "They were great lords, people of wealth and power, who did that. It is said that this has happened three times on the Danube."

"What?"

The young man lowered his voice but spoke very spiritedly. "They held up *Schwabski* ships and took the people away. They were told to come to their property. They would be better off with them than with Count Mercy. Even if they didn't want to go, they must. The men cursed, the women cried, but it did no good; they were marched away by Pandurs[3] with guns and swords."

"Where to?" Mercy wanted to know. He was beside himself because of this discovery.

"Don't know, that's all I heard." The guide summoned one of the many men loitering on the banks of the Danube. They had a discussion in a foreign language that the Governor did not understand. The man pointed to the other side of the Danube.

"*Herr*," translated Mercy's guide, "those you are looking for are not here. They were not captured here. That happened on the other side near Mohács. The people here only watched."

"Over there?" Mercy asked suspiciously. He was silent and thoughtful. He really wanted to cross the Danube into Swabian Turkey and follow the trail to the kidnapped people. For now, he had to be satisfied with what he had learned here. It seemed there were Hungarian nobles who wanted to colonize their estates in this manner! Well, Anton would get the full details over there. He would find those who were kidnapped. But did not the young man say this had already happened three times? How could that be possible? Upon further reflection, he realized that it certainly was possible. After all, usually there was no one to inquire about these people. Those from the Black Forest had been split up with their group, so that is how it was discovered they were missing. However, many groups which Vienna had reported to be on their way had not arrived in the Banat. That had been confirmed, but no one had ever followed up on these disappearances. Whoever did not arrive at his destination was simply considered a non-arrival. No one had ever been concerned about it.

This discovery of what had happened to the missing people compensated for all of the hardships he had to endure on this excursion. He had to find a way to prevent this from happening again; this could not be tolerated. These robber villages would have to be moved. The shores of the waterways, these future transportation routes, should be in German hands. The *Betyaren* who

---

3 Pandurs: armed and liveried servants of Hungarian noblemen

Chapter 18—The Governor's Excursion

were petty thieves must be transferred inland, and the big-time bandits must be stopped completely. He would make sure that all this happened!

The Governor continued his arduous trip, driving toward Neusatz. Mercy marveled at the proud Fortress of Peterwardein, which looked completely different from the last time he had seen it. It had been resurrected from the ruins. Austrian soldiers had rebuilt it. Also, the people who lived on the borders had been required to do *Robotarbeit*, compulsory work, here. They had almost worked themselves to death on this job, but it had to be. The Danube River needed her Gibraltar. Whoever wanted to be in control of this land had to be able to secure the Danube at this bend in the river.

Mercy did not visit the border town of Weisskirchen this time, since he had just spoken about that area with the *Obristkapitän* who was in charge of the border guards. Then, too, the Governor was well enough known there that he would risk being recognized. In this southern stretch of the new border, which stretched from Croatia and Slavonia to Transylvania, a new generation was growing up who would be protectors of the Kaiser's realm. The people who set roots in this area, be they Croats, Serbs, Wallachians (Romanians) or Germans, had been raised with a hatred of the Turks and were to become soldiers of the Kaiser. So the towns along this border were to be like a living protective barrier against the Turks. The Hungarian Diet made a formal statement protesting against this arrangement. It felt less threatened by the Turks than by the Kaiser's guards at their back door. The Kaiser's generals laughed at their protest. After all, they said, the Hungarian Diet always protests everything!

The Governor also did not visit the mining areas which still bore evidence of their ancient Roman heritage. Instead he drove to Werschetz. When he had last seen this town, it had been a desolate Turkish nest, with a paltry remnant of Serbs who were worn and battered after years of Turkish rule. That was how it had appeared when Mercy had set forth to clear the land of all Turks up to Orsova at Prince Eugene's command, after Temesvar had been taken. And today? The seed of Mercy's vision had sprouted here, as well. The Swabians and Bavarians who had been sent here were already at the forefront of the community. The Governor, still unrecognized, walked up and down the wide new streets. The emblems of authority still hung at the door of the *Knes*, the head of the Serbs: a whipping cane, shackles and handcuffs. However, the Germans were a separate municipality. At their mayor's house, Balthasar Schmidt, there were no such external signs of power; they had no meaning there. The people here had brought grape vines from the Rhine and seedlings of fruit trees from Tirol. Mercy marveled at the young plants. He hoped that they would send a bottle of Werschetz *Liebfraumilch* wine to his home in Temesvar. He also stopped to see the construction of the church which the German settlers were paying for and building themselves. The pastor was quite jovial as he spoke to the Governor. He came from the Archdiocese of Mainz and had never thought of working at this last outpost of Christianity. But the people here had called him, and he came gladly—under the condition that a church would be built. He had written to them: no church, no priest. So they went to work and were building one. Yet it now seemed to him that the first Werschetzer burgundy grapes would be ready to press before the first mass was said in the church. He felt like progress had come to a standstill.

Mercy, on the other hand, felt that everything was progressing along very nicely. He introduced himself as a landowner named Florimund and asked how things were going in the community.

"Hmm!" said the portly blonde priest, "Hmm! Serbians and Germans, that's all right. But Serbians, Spaniards, and Germans—that isn't going too well. I wish these quarrelsome Catelonians would leave. I really would rather not have to officiate at all of their funerals. In this climate they are dying like flies."

"What kind of work are they doing here?"

"They are supposed to grow rice and develop the production of silk. I ask you: who needs rice here? Bavarian steamed noodles are more nutritious! Not only that, but by the time the leaves of the mulberry trees are ready for the silkworms to feed on, the Spaniards will all be dead. Our water is no good for them. It is no good for us either, but we don't drink it!"

When the Governor left, he asked the talkative and lively priest for his name, which he had not understood when he had first been introduced.

"My name is Johann Peter Arzfeld, Monsieur Florimund. Arzfeld," he repeated.

The Governor went to Neu-Barcelona, which had been given this new name by the Spaniards who were the majority here. *Becskerek*, the old name of the almost uninhabited Turkish-Serbian town, was unpronounceable for them. They had held high hopes when they migrated into the realm of their former king, King Carlos who was now Kaiser Karl VI. Unfortunately, these poor people could not tolerate the local climate. The canal, which flowed to them from Temesvar, went through nasty swamps. Its lethargic water wound its way around town but did not have a place to drain properly. Thousands of fish, which had been flushed onto the land whenever it flooded, were rotting in the sun here. Pestilence was in the air.

Mercy was unsatisfied as he began to head home; he felt as if he had just

Chapter 18—The Governor's Excursion

seen a declining community, and the kidnapped settlers whom he sought had not been found. But this mood disappeared during his homeward journey as he reflected on everything he had seen. He intended to write an account of his trip, for himself and his eventual successor because he thought that he could not correct all these problems during his term of office. His adopted son and co-worker had failed him; who knew whether he would return. This climate had been his deadly enemy. He hoped to have some news from Anton when he got home.

Fortuitously, he heard from him even sooner. Some letters, which had originally come from Vienna, were sent to him when he was underway. And look—a letter from Anton! Oho! So he had not gone to Swabian Turkey, but directly to Vienna instead? That lovestruck young man! He had done this as if it were self-evident, didn't even try to justify this decision. Oh, just wait, his adoptive father would give him a talking-to! But Anton was so happy, truly ecstatic. The Governor couldn't begrudge him that.

Now he looked at the other letters. What news did he read here? Once again war clouds were forming in the West. The Kaiser had intervened in Polish affairs. He had campaigned against the King of France's father-in-law becoming King of Poland.[4] Very bad. France would take its revenge and seize more German territory. Where? From the Rhine area? They had already acquired Alsace—and who took Alsace will also want Lorraine. Would young Maria Theresia marry the Duke of Lorraine if he was a man without a country? Mercy, as a Lorrainer, was born a German citizen, but he was not sure whether he would die as German or French. War? He was ready, always ready to be called to war. But who would finish his great work, this peaceful work in Hungary? This was more important to him than any victory on the battlefield.

Shortly after Count Mercy came home, Temesvar held a festival. The new City Hall, built by a Viennese architect, stood completed on the Parade Square opposite the Palace of the Governor. On its gable was the new coat-of-arms and seal, which had been created by the founders of the new German city. This crest depicted a fortified Turkish wall, with an open entrance gate flanked by two towers. This was what Temesvar had looked like when Prince Eugene had marched upon the fortress for the first time. And to celebrate what

---

4 In 1733, the King of Poland, August II, died and the King of France, Louis XV, supported his father-in-law, Stanislaw Leszczyński's claim to the throne. The Habsburg dynasty (the Kaiser) supported the Elector of Saxony as their candidate for the throne. Despite many protests, Stanislaw was elected King of Poland in late 1733. This led to the War of the Polish Succession.

Temesvar had become, the Latin inscription on both sides of the city's crest paid homage to County Mercy and praised the "Noble House of Austria," to which the city was forever indebted as it pledged its loyalty and gratitude.

The military troops, the mayor, the citizens, Wörndle's pale young students, and the clergy led by the Jesuits were all gathered together here for the first time to honor their city. Mercy stood with the generals to watch this festival. He was quite serious and reserved on this occasion.

Peter Solderer, Temesvar's mayor, gave a festive speech to entrust the new City Hall to the governor's protection.

"No one values the diligence, capability and loyalty of the citizens more than our esteemed Governor. Furthermore, let it be known that for all posterity, I had one of the cornerstones of this City Hall inscribed in Arabic, stating that until 1715 a Turkish bathhouse was located here. But, only three years later, this area was ruled by German authorities. In the future, the citizens of Temesvar can look at the inscription on the cornerstone and compare it with the inscription on the gable of the courthouse, to see how far we have come. Let us now shout '*Vivat!*' three times—the first hurrah for Kaiser Karl, the second for Prince Eugene, and the third to Count Klaus Florimund Mercy, the benefactor and father of the Banat."

"*Vivat! Vivat! Vivat!*" resounded over the square. "*Vivat* Mercy! Mercy! Mercy!" cried out the city council members and waved their hats. "*Vivat!*" the youth and officers called out. The women waved from the surrounding windows and applauded thunderously. Then suddenly, without knowing who started it, the heartfelt tune of "Prince Eugene, the Noble Knight" began and everyone sang along. The festive chorus resonated up to the gable of the newly dedicated City Hall.

Count Mercy gave a simple military salute to thank them for the homage paid to him; now he listened to the song which sounded nearly prayerful to him, almost like a hymn. He was deeply touched whenever he heard it.

His thoughts wandered as he contemplated the future … When would the army call him again?

Chapter 19

An Unusual Wedding Feast

The traditional prescription to get rid of the fever—to get out of the region where it persists—worked wonders for Count Anton. He left and the *Wechselfieber* stayed behind. As he travelled, he feared a relapse, but by the time he reached Ofen (Buda), the Count felt that he was finally free of the disease.

A messenger had already ridden ahead. The Hàjduk whom he sent out rode continuously, wearing out three horses until the the bride received the message that the happy day was imminent. Lottel drove out on the highway to meet Anton. She and Tante Mathilde took their carriage on the road to Hungary almost as far as Schwechat, to *Schloss* Neugebäude. Behind the castle, at a special cross called the *Kugelkreuz*, the aunt wanted to ask God for His blessing upon Lottel's upcoming marriage. Lottel did not want to pray at this time. She had already taken care of that in the Schotten Church that morning. Her soul was not with God but flew along the road toward her beloved. As she looked into the distance she thought that the approaching cloud of dust might be him.

"Say another prayer here, my child. This is a fitting place to ask for God's blessings on your union, especially for the two of you," the aunt said as they stepped out of the coach.

"Why especially for us?" asked Lottel.

"Don't you know? This is the place where Kaiser Leopold and King Jan Sobieskie met after the liberation of Vienna. This cross, which is called the *Kugelkreuz* because it is set on three Turkish cannon balls, represents the victory of the Christians over the Turks. So this is a good place to pray, because in a short time you will go down to Turkish country."

"But, Tante, the Turks are not there anymore," Lottel said laughingly, as she looked again toward the fast approaching cloud of dust.

The aunt knelt at the cross and let her rosary glide through her fingers. But she did not even have enough time to pray one Our Father. A happy cry put an end to the prayer ritual—it was him, and Lottel fell into his arms. Right in front of the coachmen and Hàjduks they embraced each other fervently as if intoxicated.

"Finally! At last…"

"Please, *Tante*, say another prayer for us," Lottel said serenely to her shocked aunt. "And then follow us back to Vienna!"

She climbed into Anton's coach, completely unconcerned by the look of consternation on her aunt's face, and drove ahead with him. Only Anton's parting gesture, a respectful kiss on the old woman's hand, stopped the aunt from making an outcry about their scandalous behavior. What was left for her to do? She had to accept it. However, instead of completing her prayer, she left the cross to stand alone with its three Turkish cannon balls and asked her coachman to quickly follow the other vehicle. The wedding was to take place in three days, but who knows what can happen in the meantime?

The couple had been separated for so long and had so yearned for each other that they were now intoxicated with joy. In three days! Just three days! The bridegroom appeared pale to Charlotte and she exhorted him to tell her about it. "Fever? *Wechselfieber*? Does it hurt?" And she drowned out his protests that she might catch it from him with a passionate kiss. What did that matter to her? Nothing could come between them!

And nothing did come between the happy pair. They were married in the *Schotten Kirche* as planned. On the way to the church they passed the grave of her beloved mother. Her father had decorated the grave with flowers, so that the deceased should also know that a marriage was taking place in the family she had so loved and which she'd had to leave too soon. Her only daughter was now happy, and would gladly follow her husband anywhere, wherever fortune would take him.

Count Anton kept his word. Even now he did not go to Swabian Turkey, but brought his bride to his adoptive father in Temesvar. He introduced her as Charlotte, since the governor did not like the nickname Lottel for a married woman. Radiant in her feminine beauty, she approached the elderly governor and courteously kissed his hand, whereupon he joked that he didn't have it as good as his nephew, who got to have a kiss on the lips. The day was one to be celebrated. And since his soldierly bachelor quarters would not do in this case, he ordered a "wedding feast" for the young couple at the *Sieben*

Chapter 19—An Unusual Wedding Feast

Kurfürsten Inn. Frau Therese should show off what her house had to offer. He invited the *Stadtrichter* and Generals with their wives, as well as the engineers who had built the fortress, Count Anton's friends and colleagues.

On the way to the inn, the Countess walked through the city for the first time. The new buildings were reminiscent of Vienna, and the quaint narrow shady streets made her feel at home. But she was shocked at the way the people looked. Everyone seemed to be sick: pale, gaunt, yellow-colored faces were everywhere. They were like walking corpses. Women and girls who came out of the neat houses were strangely bloated as if they suffered from dropsy, excess fluid in the body. They all looked at Charlotte with wide eyes as if she were a wonder from heaven. To her husband, she looked like a blooming flower in the desert. He understood her questioning glances only too well. She didn't say anything, but her lapse into silence spoke volumes.

Frau Therese Pless and her husband warmly welcomed their esteemed guests. They offered the Viennese Countess only the best of what was available in this part of the world: carp from the Bega Canal, roasted venison from the local forests, roast chicken and vegetables from their own backyard. Everything was exquisitely prepared in the Swabian style. Locally grown tropical fruits completed the menu; delicious-looking melons were passed around. And the young couple was toasted and welcomed to the community with wine from Werschetz.

But how strange. Anton repeatedly told his young bride quietly not to eat from this or to only try a taste of that. Despite all the respect and honor given to her, she could not help but notice a strange restlessness and moving around at this feast. Guests would stand up and pace back and forth. One guest's teeth chattered with the chills; another was overheated and drank an enormous amount as if to douse the fire within. And the yellow faces! Lottel silently asked her husband with her eyes and he understood her. "Some have fever," he said quietly. "Don't eat the melons!"

She did not eat any of the tempting fruits which had been grown in a swampland. And her eyes looked carefully, sharpened by an increasing fear, and seemed to see a shadow of death on their faces. The men were gaunt and haggard, and the women were bloated here, too, just as she had seen in the streets.

"How long can one survive here?" she asked the Governor. "Oh, some have been rattling like this for ten years," he laughed, "but it has never bothered me. Don't worry about it, my child."

After dinner, the women drifted from the room, and the men drank Turkish coffee and smoked their Chibuks loaded with local tobacco. The men needed these antidotes to fight the poison of the fever within them, but for women they were strictly forbidden. Frau Therese had prepared a fine café au lait for them in the Viennese style, as she had seen it at the Regensburger Hof in Vienna. She served it herself and the young Countess accepted it gratefully. She was accustomed to drinking this type of coffee with Tante Mathilde.

The discussion which followed weighed heavily on the bride. "Oh how beautiful you look, Countess!" said a General's wife admiringly. "After half a year of living here, your good looks will be gone."

"Don't have any children, my dear," whispered another woman. "Four of my little ones died here."

The memory of these conversations haunted young Charlotte in the next few weeks. Her husband did everything to comfort her, but he already felt a specter of the fever stretching its arms out to his beloved and his comforting words did not come from the heart. Charlotte was now expecting a child. She was in quiet despair. Why had they told her such things at that awful wedding feast? It seemed to be certain that her child would die. She cried as she confessed to her husband her distress, her fears for the future.

The Governor saw all this and he exhorted the young couple to leave, comforted by the thought that at least he'd had a few weeks of sunshine in the house.

"Don't worry about me, I am fine. The rumors of war have died down and I will stay here for awhile. You should go to *Schwäbische Türkei*, in God's name, to my castle in Högyész, where I would have liked Anton to go before the wedding. I am now in my seventies, but I will not be joining you for awhile. I am busy with matters here; I will be able to visit you by the time I am eighty years old to see my grandchild."

And so they left. The older Mercy gave his adopted son a hundred tasks to do in *Schwabische Türkei*, since Anton was to work there in his place: he should look for the kidnapped Black Foresters, he should seek to colonize all the way down to Slavonia—the *Hofkammerat* in Vienna would gladly support him. The Governor dismissed them with his fatherly blessing, convinced that all would go well; but despite this, the old soldier felt a pang that a Mercy had left his assignment.

Chapter 20

The Missing Settlers

Frau Eva Trauttmann sat with her needlework on the steps of her stately white-washed house, which was built in the Franconian style. Its gable was adorned with the forms of two crisscrossing horses' heads. The lucky horseshoe they had found in Vienna was secretly buried under its threshold. It was an old custom of his ancestors to bury such a sign of good fortune, Philipp had explained to her.

Their two youngest boys, who had been born in this new homeland, played at her feet. Her husband jokingly referred to them as their "Hungarian boys". They were already toddlers now and they tussled and fought with each other. Every once in a while, Eva good-naturedly complained, "This house has too many men in it!" If she didn't have Trudel, she would have never been able to keep up with the housework.

Suddenly, there was a bright clacking sound in the distance. It sounded as if somebody was hammering on a board. The farmer's wife looked up in surprise. What was that? Just then Trudel came along the porch and called, "Mother, do you hear that? That's the Black Foresters' call to vespers!"

"No, really? That is supposed to be a church bell?" Eva Trauttmann was incredulous.

The girl laughed. "Well, it doesn't sound like the bells in Vienna and Regensburg. Do you remember the great bell in Vienna?"

"Of course I still remember, child. Since when do our neighbors have this?"

"Since today! Wagners Joseph rigged it up."

Her mother just shook her head.

"Look, look!" said the girl and pointed toward the row of houses which had been built in the last year. People came out of their homes dressed in their Sunday *Trachten*. The men wore long cloth coats and knee-length white stockings with wide brimmed hats on their heads. The women were dressed in short colorful skirts with dark petticoats and wore little caps over their brown hair. They seemed to be giving each other their opinions about the sound of the bell, then they all headed in the same direction. The bell had called them to Sunday church service.

"Schneider Franz[1] will be leading the service," the girl said derisively.

The mother reprimanded her daughter. "That is nothing to make fun of," she said. "Isn't it nice that these poor Catholic people, whom the devil has driven here, have already built a church? Whether it's Schneider Franz or Wagners Josef, it doesn't matter. If Schneider Franz is good at leading the prayers, let him! Then they can praise God even if they don't have a priest!"

"Well, that's true," said Trudel, a bit ashamed. "After all, our father is not a pastor, either."

"After all," her mother smiled, "he's just a farmer. And yet he still preaches God's word to us so nicely!"

Trudel sat down outside of the house with her mother and began to knit. The thin needles, which Ferdinand had fashioned out of acacia wood, moved nimbly and busily. She used self-spun sheep's wool to make stockings for the whole family. Even though it was Sunday her lively fingers did not rest. Her quick blue eyes were everywhere; she did not need to look down while doing this work. Trudel was well acquainted with all those who went to the church and knew what was going on with each of them. While Eva was bent over the bonnet she was working on and the boys chased after some geese which had been sunning themselves on the meadow, the daughter chatted and told her mother all sorts of things she had learned about the people from the Black Forest.

My God, how those poor people had suffered. The Trauttmann family in comparison had such an easy time when they had driven here from their German homeland; why had it been so difficult for those others? Because of a life-threatening storm and high winds on the Danube, they had taken refuge on an island near Ofen to wait until the storm was over. Three children died by the time they got to Mohács. During the storm they had lost the second ship that had been traveling with them, and to this day no one knew what had happened to their friends.

---

1 It was common to refer to a person with the last name first. Thus, Franz Schneider would in conversation be referred to as Schneider Franz or Schneiders Franz.

Chapter 20—The Missing Settlers

Frau Eva had already heard this story many times but she always learned something new from Trudel's repetition. Trudel had befriended a couple of girls from the Black Forest and was always full of new stories when she came home from visiting them. Her mother encouraged this companionship. The child had such a lonely upbringing without girlfriends her own age. So now she let Trudel prattle away. Trudel's father and older brothers were out in the fields looking at and appraising the upcoming harvest. This was their great Sunday pleasure. Perhaps they would even bring home some game. At any rate, they wouldn't be back before sundown.

How things had changed since they had come to Dobok! She often regretted that there was nobody to write down their experiences, from the first hour of their trip to Hungary to this day. Her husband had no interest in doing this. He felt that one should look forward, not backward. For that, his grandchildren would have time, once they were well established and settled in with a good piece of land to call their own. "How can they look back," his wife asked, "if there is no one left who can tell them where they came from, and what their ancestors experienced?"

"There will be enough schoolmasters who can write that down," Philipp replied. "Stop bothering me about it! My fingers are too stiff for that business."

So Frau Eva tried to commit every one of her experiences to memory so she could share them with her grandchildren.

She thought back to their first year in Dobok. They had been so isolated back then, especially after Matz had left them. And after the house had been built, Philipp had gone away too. One morning he harnessed the horses and drove off, taking only little Ferdinand with him. He had to go buy seed for the fall planting; the local seeds were not good enough for him. He told her he would be back in two days. But his sons, who always kept their loaded guns by their beds, knew better. In the evenings they held target practice and made a lot of noise. They acted as if they were fierce and violent men, and the serfs from the neighboring property stayed away from them. Not until the third day, when Eva was beside herself with worry, did she learn that it would probably take another three days before he came home. He had driven to the Swabians but hadn't told her because he didn't want to cause her alarm. He was driving all the way to Murgau, to the Protestants. If he had told her of his plans, and that it could likely take him a week, she would have raised objections—so he had told his sons not to tell her until after three days. Now that the week was almost half over, they finally told her. They were so proud to have been put in charge of protecting their mother, sister and the house.

Although she wasn't happy that the men of the house had planned this without her consent, there was nothing she could do about it now. She was well aware that a good sowing was the most important thing; she knew this better than her sons did. In the evenings she went to bed later than when her husband was home, and let the tallow light burn all night. Only one of these fall evenings had been disconcerting. Eva was half asleep when she heard howling, as if of many dogs. Their dog, Packan, the son of Caraffa, cowered under the windows outside. She listened to every sound and understood the animal's fear. She had never heard this kind of howling but she knew from the stories Baron Andor had told that wolves howled like that when they were among the sheep in the *Puszta*. And where were her sons, the protectors of the house, on this night? In their beds, each of them sleeping like a log—but their mother kept watch for them too.

Finally, Philipp came back. With an impish smile, he drove into the yard with sacks full of grain, and all was right with the world. Eva would have liked to scold him, but she could not. She felt it was a shame to have even one day where they did not get along.

And Matz came back in October. Yes, he did indeed come back! Heavily laden with greetings and letters, with all kinds of items from back home, happy and healthy, he entered the room. He had taken the same route back to the Rhine that they had taken to Hungary, had spent one week at home with Eva's mother and brother-in-law Ferdinand, had told the family in Bobenheim all about the trip to Hungary and made them wish they had come too. When it was time to leave, he got everything together that he would bring back to Hungary, including a bag of potatoes. That was the most important thing!

"The whole town laughed at me about those potatoes," Matz said. "Ferdinand told me, 'There is no way you will carry those potatoes all the way to Hungary! Write and tell us how many you brought there!' he teased me."

Ferdinand was almost right in his doubts. Matz hadn't even made it to Frankfurt with the entire sack. And by the time he got to Regensburg, only half of them were left. He had noticed that he was carrying too heavy a load on the first day already, and he still had three months to travel before he got to Dobok. What to leave behind? The beautiful things for Bas' Eva? Oh no! The potatoes? Oh no! It was a difficult choice. Then he had a brilliant idea. He decided to live from the potatoes while underway to lighten the load he was carrying. If he could bring half a sack to Dobok that would be a good

Chapter 20—The Missing Settlers

beginning. They could not ask more of him. But, God knows, however many potatoes he roasted along the way, it seemed the load still did not lighten by much. He became addicted to them and could no longer travel without feasting on the odd potato.

At Ofen, he discovered that he only had ten potatoes left in the sack! He was terribly ashamed of himself. He wandered throughout the city and its surroundings, where there were already many Germans, asking where he could get more potatoes. He would have given his last *Taler* for them, but the answer was the same everywhere: "We wish that we had potatoes for ourselves! There are none to be found in Hungary!" Distressed, he thought about returning to Vienna. He would be able to find some there, he thought. But he decided against this. Didn't he need to be in Dobok by planting time? He no longer reached into the sack, but headed home, a bit mortified. Yet for the feeling that he was bringing the first ten potatoes into the promised land of Hungary, and that from these ten there would eventually be millions, for that he would not have given an entire kingdom.

To this day, Frau Eva had to laugh when she thought about how cleverly Matz spread everything that he had brought out on the table, how he immediately gave Philipp the letters from his brother and her mother so that he would read them right away, and how he kept talking and telling stories without pause, so that no one had a chance to ask him about the potatoes. Then when they finally did ask, what a pitiful face poor Matz made! She would never forget it for the rest of her life. Completely embarrassed, he reached into the bag and brought out the ten potatoes. As gently as if they were gold nuggets, he placed them on the table.

"Matz! Matz!" the farmer taunted him, "for that you went all the way to Bobenheim and back? Ha ha ha!"

"*Vetter*,[2] it was a bad year for potatoes in the *Pfalz*," Matz answered saucily. He was a bit hurt when they kept making fun of him. "Is that my thanks?" he exclaimed and spoke not another word about it. Finally, after three days, when they were all sitting at the table talking about their homeland, Matz told them the story about the heavy sack of potatoes and his large appetite. The children laughed and Frau Eva cried a bit over this story. *Vetter* Philipp, however, did not poke fun at him. He took the potatoes to the cellar and buried them in straw so that they would remain in good condition for spring planting. No one spoke about them again.

Oh, how long they were consumed with 'Potato Matz's' journey home.

---

2 *Vetter*: in this case means uncle. It was also used as a term of respect for an older man.

Hannes, who liked to tease, gave him this nickname. Matz didn't let it get to him; he laughed about it with the rest of them and said that the name would one day be an honorary title.

The grain crops were planted in October. The family worked cheerfully despite strong winds and storms. Philipp Trauttmann cleared his field of overgrown weeds once more, then sowed the plowed fields with their first crop. He paid close attention to when the leaves fell off the trees. Since they fell early, that was a sign that there would be a good harvest next year. He hoped for no rain on St. Gallus Day in October, and no snowfall yet by St. Andreas Day in November. And all of these wishes came true.

The first winter was spent peacefully. Philipp had seen to it that they were well fed. There was plenty of game and they slaughtered some pigs; they wanted for nothing. Since there were no craftsmen for miles and miles, the four men in the household had to do everything themselves. Philipp was the smith and shod the horses. 'Potato Matz' was the shoemaker for all of them. Peter and Hannes were the carpenters. They whittled, sawed and hammered, making fodder cribs for the stable; and, chairs and benches for the house. With their father they built a fence around the yard and garden, as the neighboring serfs watched in amazement.

Frau Eva spun sheep's wool and little Trude rolled it into balls. Ferdinand was the scholar. He was determined to retain the education he had received in Bobenheim and read, wrote and did arithmetic on his own. His father often gave him problems to solve, and his mother encouraged him in this learning. Never forget anything you have learned! And add to your knowledge every day. She even knew a Swabian saying about it.

Alle Tag' e Stückle weiter	Every day a little further
Alle Tag' e bißle g'scheiter:	Every day a little wiser
Büble, merk's, es ist gar gut,	Boy, remember what you have learned
Wenn man's nit vergessen tut.	It does you no good if you forget it.

Frau Eva had been so lost in quiet reflection, she had completely tuned out Trudel's chatter. But now a different voice pulled her out of her reverie.

"Good evening, *Bas*'[3] Eva," croaked an old man's voice. He had just come from the vespers with his countrymen and hobbled up to the house to talk to the farmer's wife. He liked to visit her because she reminded him of

---

[3] *Bas*' was dialect for Base. In this case it is being used as a term of respect to refer to an older woman.

Chapter 20—The Missing Settlers

his daughter Kathl, whom he had lost during the trip. *Bas'* Eva offered him a seat on the porch, and sent Trudel to get Jörge and Lippl, who had wandered off a bit too far.

Others from the Black Forest walked by and wished them a good evening. They no longer looked as disheartened as when they had first come. They awaited a good harvest and had found good fortune. Many walked toward the fields to take another look at their bounty before the sun went down.

The old man, Jost Zengraf, however, was among those who could not be reconciled to the way they had been forced to settle in this area, against their will. He often asked himself, 'Did the Danube bring us to the savages? What happened to us would not even happen in America. We had official passes from Vienna to go to the Banat and were herded over here like cattle! We were kidnapped at the Danube and cannot find out where our children and friends went. And no one concerns himself with our fate—not the German Kaiser or the Hungarian King!' He could not understand this and would not stop lamenting and complaining about it.

Bas' Eva would console him as best she could, telling him that he would someday get news about his daughter. Kathl must have arrived in the Banat with her relatives. He should try to be happy here. "Look at what happened to our family. We were supposed to be sent to the Banat, but were not allowed to go there. We have it pretty good here, and are happy with our lot."

"Yes, you can be, you are all together," he had replied. "What does the accursed old Baron want with me here? I only want to go to where my children are, or back home into German territory, so that I can die there."

Eva had once quietly told him that she believed the Baron would release him if he were convinced that the others would stay. First he must allow some time to go by, so that these events are more in the past. He must have patience. Next year she would speak to the young baron, or to the Baroness Helene, that good and noble woman.

This was another story which she would like to see written down for her grandchildren. Otherwise, who would know about this twenty years from now?

Like a lynx, old Baron Parkoczy had prowled around their fields during the first harvest season and was beside himself with jealousy over their bountiful grains. The tenth he received had been honestly measured, but he still wanted more. Finally one of his spies discovered the house garden where the ten potatoes had been planted. The farmer had made a test strip there. He planted eight of the potatoes whole, and two of the potatoes were cut up into many pieces, each piece with at least one or two "eyes", for these "eyes" were the new shoots. Frau Eva tended the plot as if it were a great treasure. They all sprouted, and the harvest brought two hundred beautiful big potatoes. Although the Baron's people did not know what kind of vegetable this was, they felt their overlord should have his share, but the farmer refused to give them any. His home and garden must be free from the ten percent rule. The next day, the Baron and his two sons rode over on their horses and demanded to see what had been harvested.

"How dare you, cheeky farmer?" he cried. "I must have ten percent of everything that grows on my soil."

Philipp Trauttmann showed the gentlemen the small harvest and gave each one a potato to hold.

"What are these?" they asked after they sniffed them.

The farmer shrugged his shoulders. "In all of Hungary, only I have these," said Trauttmann. "I grew them in my home garden. Next year they will grow out in the fields, and your Grace will get your tenth. Now, I have two hundred. Next year, I will have two thousand. Then I will tell you what it is and how you eat it, but not before."

"You can eat this? *Az ebadta*, you cursed farmer, I want to eat my twenty pieces of them," said the Baron.

Trauttmann flushed angrily. He almost shot back, "So, bite into it, maybe you'll like it!" but thought better of it. "Herr Baron," he said, "I too would like to eat some, but it's better if I save it. It is my seed for next year. However, if you would like to eat with us, Herr Baron, then my wife will cook the twenty for you."

"How presumptuous of you! You dare to invite me for dinner?" Parkoscy ranted.

Trauttmann shrugged his shoulders. "In all of Hungary only my wife knows how to prepare and cook potatoes."

"Potatoes? So that's what they are called?"

Baron Pista urged his father to go along with this "joke", and Andor did the same. He confirmed that he had never seen a potato when visiting the Swabians.

So the Baron deigned to eat at the Trauttmanns. Frau Eva was called and was asked to prepare the potatoes. She told the gentlemen that she would have the honor of serving them in about an hour.

Ah, what a delight! The Baron would have liked to have all two hundred of the potatoes. He had never eaten anything better. Then Trauttmann told them how he had gotten the seed potatoes. They laughed at Matz, but still praised him for bringing such a good thing into the country. The other one hundred and eighty potatoes were stored in the cellar to plant the next year.

The Baron thoroughly enjoyed this potato feast, and the following two grain harvests were so bountiful that the tenth which the Baron received was practically more than his own harvest. As a result, the Baron developed a great desire to acquire more German colonists. From now on he wanted Swabians on his land, only Swabians! He heard that Counts Batthyanyi, Csaky and Karolyi were colonizing their property, but no one was ever sent to him. He waited year after year to no avail. Then he helped himself to a boatload on the Danube. He brought his Kuruc friends from St. Marton with him and they forced the thoroughly drenched, tired and distraught Black Foresters, who had almost been shipwrecked in a bad storm, to come with them.

They were told that it would be like paradise, that many Swabians already lived in the vicinity, and they would be given double everything that was promised them in the Banat. There was no going against these armed men. So that no one would disclose what had happened, the men did not allow anyone to remain behind. In Dobok, a row of new houses was built across from the *Erdhütten* of the Magyar serfs, who were supposed to keep their eyes on the newcomers. They were given the same amount of property as Trauttmann had received, as much as they could cultivate! And so, many of them reconciled themselves to the idea. The few who were still against it and still wanted to leave were monitored. Young Mathes Zengraf, whose bride had been in the second ship, ran away from Dobok one day. Halfway to Mohács he was caught and brought back. In St. Marton he was given the *Bastonade*—thirty lashes on the soles of each foot. That's how the Turks had punished slaves who ran away.

Those who were still discontented were told that they were fools; nowhere in the world would they have it better. And now the first harvest was ready: over a thousand acres of former wasteland had been turned into cultivated acreage in the first year. When he was sober, Baron Parkoczy felt himself to be a God. His surprise attack had succeeded and would bring abundant blessings. At first, Baroness Helene was distraught by her husband's actions. But when the people stayed and worked the fields, she too, dared to hope that everything might end well.

The Baroness sometimes came to the Black Forest colony; she looked after the sick and listened to those who were unhappy. She said that she would report this to the Baron, and would make inquiries about what happened to those from the second ship, find out if they were in the Banat or where they were. One should not give up hope for a reunion. With these words she comforted them, but she never brought them new information.

Baron Pista promised the poorest and most dissatisfied, in his father's name, that they would only pay half of the tenth of this first harvest. The great boon that was still in the fields made him especially generous.

Jost Zengraf, the old man, brought this news to Eva today. This was devastating to him. He felt that there was no more hope—now all would be content and no longer want to find the others. But Frau Trauttmann wisely told *Vetter* Jost that this would be quite favorable for him. She would talk to the Baroness about his situation, perhaps even this year already, right after the harvest. The old man understood. If all the others would remain, they could let him, the useless one, go. That seemed plausible.

Finally, the four Trauttmann men came in, along with Matz. All big, sturdy men! Hannes had killed a roe buck in the forest. Trauttmann said the roasted buck would be served at the harvest dinner. He was very excited about the upcoming harvest. He was itching to bring his sickle to the fields and start already! It was mid-June. The harvest was quickly approaching. Vetter Philipp quoted the saying *"Zu Peter und Paul werden die Kornwurzeln faul!*—By the feastday of St. Peter and Paul (June 29), the grain will be ready to harvest."

"Eva," he exclaimed, "this will be a great year!" Then he turned to the old man. "*Vetter*, just be content, stay here with us. Nowhere else is better than here!"

"Naa, naa," croaked *Vetter* Jost tearfully. "I want to go to my children, I must go to my children." He left without even bidding them good night. Even if all of them wanted to stay, he did not. His grandson Mathes did not either, even if he had been punished with the *Bastonade* once.

In the meantime, Trudel had brought the two runaway boys back. All nine members of the family stood in front of the house they had built themselves, in the happiness that they themselves had forged. 'How much longer will our family be together like this?' Frau Eva asked herself. 'Matz has long been ready to get married, and the two oldest boys should also be thinking about a wife.' Three new farmers would soon leave the house and start their own homes in this small colony. And another three future farmers would be left at home.

But where would the older boys find her future daughters-in-law? Matz already seemed to have an understanding with a girl from the Black Forest. For her sons, Swabian Turkey was not too far away. The people from Tevel had come over for seed potatoes twice already, and the boys had been to a dance there. They had come home with wonderful news of a town full of

Chapter 20—The Missing Settlers

girls where one could easily find a Swabian girl to marry. Their eyes shone when they told her about it.

Let it be as God wills it, she thought. There would still be four children in the house if her two oldest sons became farmers on their own. And their father would not be thinking about retiring for a long time yet. He was the youngest of them all!

These were the thoughts going through *Bas'* Eva's mind at the end of that Sunday before the big harvest, while her husband worriedly looked to the west at a dark cloud bank that thundered and flashed with lightning.

Chapter 21

Delibáb

The castle was now much more prosperous. This made it possible for the Baroness Helene and her elderly mother to achieve their dream of sending Pista to the Imperial Court in Vienna. There, the fine young man, who had been taught next to nothing, might improve himself and be elevated beyond his rural, agricultural nobility. Perhaps he could be become one of the Hungarian Imperial Guards, have the opportunity to travel, and would come home as a man of the world. If the Countess Lory asked for this on his behalf, it would definitely happen.

Pista was happy to go. Unfortunately, this made the rift between his parents permanent… For a time, Pista and Andor had hoped for a reconciliation between their parents. They had cleverly arranged that their parents at least got together at the ancient harvest festival, ever since the Germans had brought new life to this celebration. The festival was traditionally a big day for the serfs. The harvesters brought their masters a wreath made of wheat and flowers from the fields. The oldest harvester made a speech to the landlord, who served them all wine. The Baroness personally prepared her specialty for the harvesters, lamb stew with potatoes, which they had never eaten, and served it to them herself. The first dance, with the oldest harvester, belonged to her.

The cymbals were played, accompanied by a shepherd's flute. The Baron's sons danced with the young harvest girls out in the open in front of the castle. They were still dancing long after their mother had retired and their father was inebriated.

After the second harvest, the settlers from the Black Forest brought their wreath to the castle and chose a speaker who was to pledge that they would

Chapter 21—Delibáb

now remain voluntarily. This was the moment of encounter, perhaps of reconciliation, for the parents.

But it was an illusion, it only lasted one night. As soon as Pista was ready to fulfill his mother's wish, Parkoszy was beset by an uncontrollable fury. "My son will not become a soldier of Vienna! I forbid it!" But Baroness Helene defied him and Pista went to Vienna. Since his father refused to pay for it, his grandmother, the Countess Erdödy, gave him the means to go.

Andor felt very alone, stuck in the middle between his estranged parents. He often wished that he could have gone with Pista. At night he secretly rode over the *Puszta* to the *csárda*, the inn where his girlfriend lived. She did not know who he was and took him for a young *csikos* (a mountain horse herdsman). Had any of the horse thieves who frequented the inn known what was going on, he would never have come home alive. But Margit was clever and skilled in the art of deception. She pretended to go to sleep while her mother attended to the *Betyaren*. Then she and Andor met at the old windmill out in the *Puszta* after he had left the inn.

There was nothing else for him to do other than hunting. He also was gradually becoming interested in agriculture. It was a pleasure to see how Trauttmann and the Black Foresters tended their crops. The serfs, who were good-natured, decent people, sometimes watched the Germans in amazement. Trauttmann told Baron Andor, "Young man, give your serfs their freedom once you are in charge, and they will work as hard as we do. They are learning already! They are watching everything we do. When you take over, there will be much to change. You still have a pastoral economy in Hungary, where your land is mainly used for grazing. Which is nice, too! It's great to sit back and take it easy, but that is not the way we work. We are farmers, where your serfs are shepherds, so we can get twenty times more from one *Joch* of land than you do." The young Baron understood. It was the difference between using the land for grazing or for agriculture. He had already noticed this difference back when he had lived among the Swabians in *Schwäbische Türkei*.

Trauttmann now owned eight horses and two colts. On Sundays his sons often rode to far away pastures. For at least one day of the week, Hannes and Peter wanted to have it as good as the shepherds had it throughout the year. One day, Andor accompanied them, even though he was a Baron and they were mere farmers. He wanted to show them an especially rich pasture. They rode far out into the plain, going south. They brought a lunch of potatoes, bacon and young corn with them. Packan, Caraffa's pup, ran beside them. He was now a full grown dog and no longer feared the wolves' howling.

In a peaceful hollow they found a lush pasture and a gurgling creek for their horses to graze and drink. The young men loafed around there the whole day. They ate, talked, slept, and shot at vultures who were circling over a dead animal. Actually, they were useful, these vultures, but since they also attacked living animals when they had nothing else to eat, they were loathed and feared.

In the sweltering noon hour, the two Swabians had an amazing experience.

They lay in the burning sun; the ground was scorching hot, and a veil of rising heat waves enveloped the distant horizon. Andor suddenly interrupted the conversation about horses, vultures and calves and waved at both to be quiet. As if transfigured he gazed up at the sky. A sea, a completely calm ocean with not a single wave, spread out over the heavens. The image approached, it grew nearer and nearer, soon the old windmill would be in the water; but no, it stopped advancing. In the distance, dark objects glided through the sky. Were they birds? Were they ships?

"Yes, yes, yes," Andor murmured, "Delibáb is coming over the *Puszta*, the fairy Delibáb."

Hannes and Peter looked at him in bewilderment.

"It is *Fata Morgana*," Andor tried to explain again. But they also did not understand that and were speechless.

Suddenly the sea was gone. The haze shifted. The air waves shimmered in the heat. And in the same place in the sky, towers rose out of the mist, church steeples and palaces; a city was created before their eyes. A magnificent high spire towered over this city.

"Delibáb, Delibáb," whispered Andor and folded his hands, enchanted. "Look, look!"

The boys looked. It seemed to them as if many, many soldiers rode through the gates of this beautiful city…

A strong breeze blew over the steppe. In the distance, to the west, snow-white clouds rose into the sky and quickly accumulated. In an instant, the midday spell was broken. The magical city dissolved into nothingness.

Andor jumped up and exclaimed, "You have not seen this before? You never even heard of it?"

The boys, who were made speechless by this display in the sky, looked at each other questioningly. Neither had seen or heard of such a thing before this.

"Well, you are always bending down too much working the fields. You are looking at the earth instead of up to the heavens. Every Magyar knows the sorceress of the *Puszta*, the fairy Delibáb."

Hannes scratched his blond head. "I don't know, I don't know. This must be witchcraft. The first was like the ocean, where you can sail to America. The other—that was Vienna."

"Oh yes, that was Vienna!" Peter agreed.

"What?" Andor exclaimed. "Vienna!?"

"Vienna! Vienna!" the boys insisted. "Vienna, with St. Stephen's Cathedral!"

"Well, I'll have to ask Father Franziskus, my old teacher in Mohács, about that," said Andor. "He says that the sky is God's mirror, and that the fairy sometimes shows us distant, beautiful lands, images of Asia and Africa, maybe even China."

But the boys stood by their claim that what they had seen was Vienna.

Chapter 22

All Kinds of Conflicts

Hofkammerrat von Stephany was having a bad morning. He was in a bad mood because his gout was flaring up. The weather was going to change, Aunt Mathilde had already told him the day before.

Yes, a change in the weather was coming, and it seemed his orderly world was shattering. Cries of "War! War!" resounded through the narrow streets of Vienna. Army recruiters had once again set up their tables in every available public space. They rattled their sabers and jangled gold and silver coins under every young man's nose. Beer flowed out of a barrel to the right of the recruiters, wine from a barrel to their left, and their enthusiasm was flowing as well. "War with France, war with Italy, war with Spain!" they called out, as if one enemy was not enough. They enticed the recruits even further with talk of the spoils of war. Finally, good times were here again for the military. Prince Eugene, the old lion, was already on his way to the Rhine. New regiments were to follow. "Come and join them, if you're not a coward!" Training and military exercises took place everywhere. The recruits marched out of Vienna in small groups. Weeping girls ran alongside, accompanying their loved ones to the city gates. Half-drunk troops cheered and sang:

Nun, mein Gredel	Now, my Gretel
Setz' auf den Schädel	Put a wide-brimmed hat
Ein' randigen Hut;	on your head
Nimm mein Ranzen	Take my knapsack
Wir müssen tanzen	We have to dance
Auf Leben und Blut.	For life and blood.

Chapter 22—All Kinds of Conflicts

The *Hofkammerrat* went to his office despite his gouty foot, since these were grave times, and the walk across the *Marktplatz Am Hof* to the *Judenplatz* was not too far. He went past the military hustle and bustle and saw that the mood for this useless war was positive. This pleased him because he had feared that it would be otherwise. Prince Eugene, the Generalissimo, was now old and in poor health and had never thought he would lead troops in war again. But when he received the order, he did not hesitate for a moment and headed for the Rhine where he was to form an army. Prince Eugene had been called to checkmate the French aggression, and Count Mercy, who was already in South Tirol, was to be the *Oberkommandant* in charge of the fighting in Italy. Mercy had been chosen for this because the area was very familiar to him. He reluctantly tore himself away from his peaceful work in the Banat, and his removal also caused the *Hofkammerrat* much distress. It annoyed him and disturbed his plans, since he had hoped that Anton would be the Governor's successor, but the adopted son was still too young. Then, too, Anton could not tolerate the climate, and Lottel did not want to live in Temesvar either. So the *Hofkammerrat* would have to work with a temporary replacement or even a new Governor. The whole thing was annoying. Stephany hated this stupid war, in which the choice of a Polish King was now to be fought over in the West. Again and again, the German border lands along the Rhine had to bleed whenever diplomacy failed. This time the German States did not want to become involved. The *Fürsten* who ruled the various provinces of the German Realm claimed that this war did not concern them. Lorraine was already flooded with French troops. Would Franz Stephan, the Duke of Lorraine, forfeit his dukedom? Now? The French were again occupying the *Rheinpfalz!* The emigrants had told him this alarming news. And their numbers had doubled despite the late season. They fled their homeland in droves and brought along satirical songs like this one:

"Ja, was nur Händ und Füße regt,	Any creature that can move hands and feet
Was geht, was schwimmt, was Eier legt,	Anything that walks, swims or lays eggs
Hat seine Feinde gern vom Leibe.	Keeps its enemies at bay.
In Teutschland ist es umgewandt	In Germany, this is reversed
Wir öffnen unserm Feind das Land	We open our land to our enemy
Und leiden, daß er bleibe."	And suffer, for him to remain.

This bitter verse was the latest. It was passed from one person to the other among those who disembarked the Ulm and Regensburg emigration ships in Vienna and sought passes to Hungary. Leaving their homeland had been made easier for them.

As the *Hofkammerrat* slowly made his way across the square through the throng of people, there was a big commotion. A noble cavalry troop came from Bogner Street and rode toward the Schotten Gate. "That's *Herzog* Stefan von *Lothringen*," a few people cried.

"Jesus, it's the handsome Frenchman," exclaimed a buxom young market-woman. The cry was also taken up by her co-workers and the women who had come to the market: "The handsome Frenchman!" It was indeed the young Duke of Lorraine, Franz Stefan, who had been chosen by the Kaiser himself as the bridegroom for his daughter Maria Theresia, his heiress.

The recruiters stood up, and their willing victims, those who were being enlisted, were awestruck as they watched the magnificent procession. Franz Stefan had come from the Imperial Palace for a farewell audience with the Kaiser, since he was to rush to Generalissimo Prince Eugene's side. After all, his dukedom, Lorraine, was at stake.

"*Vivat, vivat!*" cried the recruiters. "*Vivat!*" cried the recruits. "My God, what a beautiful couple they will make!" exclaimed the portly market-woman, who could not keep quiet. She kept watching until the duke was almost out of sight. "We have never seen anything like it in Austria."

The *Hofkammerrat* had to agree with this observation made by the common people. Two of the most beautiful creations of God had willingly come together in this match.

When Stephany finally arrived at his office he found several letters, from the Banat and also from his son-in-law and daughter in Swabian Turkey. The Commander of the Fortress of Temesvar had written a letter introducing himself as temporary deputy Governor. He would now be in charge of the colonization. The people in the cities and rural areas were heartbroken that the Governor had been called away. To replace him was a difficult responsibility, and he asked for the *Hofkammerrat's* support.

On the other hand, the letter from his son-in-law was full of good news. Count Anton reported that he had been promoted to Colonel and that the region he was in charge of had expanded beyond Swabian Turkey. His territory now extended down to Esseg, and the Generalissimo had even put him in charge of Bellye. In addition, he believed that the criminal who had kidnapped those Black Forest emigrants three years ago could be found. And Lottel? Ah, she had recovered her good humored Viennese temperament in Swabian Turkey. She invited '*Grosspapa*' to the baptism of her first child around Christmas.

Chapter 22—All Kinds of Conflicts

At this wonderful news, the pain from the old gentleman's gout suddenly disappeared from his leg. And the fall sun outside shone twice as brightly as before.

Trauttmann's grace period was over. On top of the one tenth of his crop that he had to give to the landowner, now he had to pay taxes to the state. They were not high, but this double burden brought it home to him that he was not an independent citizen. Was he a free farmer like those in the Banat? No! Until he freed himself of this tithe he could not consider himself to be so. If he did not buy his freedom, how should his children do it? Who knows, maybe their inheritance could be taken away from them. Now that his two eldest sons would soon become farmers on their own, and 'Potato Matz' even before them, it would be a good idea to act prudently and calculate whether he could buy his freedom.

All of his possessions from back home in Bobenheim had finally been sold. He had been receiving the money gradually, including Matz's inheritance. The family was going to stay here; here was their home and they could do as they pleased. But he had to free himself of this tithe, first for his property, then for the land which Matz was going to own. His sons, however, could still work with him for a few years. For them, he was willing to wait and see.

One Sunday morning, Trauttmann harnessed his horse and drove to the Baron in St. Marton. He had heard that only in the morning could one have a rational conversation with him. The Baron was in a good mood today.

"What do you want, farmer? How many sacks of potatoes did you cheat me out of this year, hm?" was the Baron's lighthearted response to Trauttmann's morning greeting.

Philipp had dealt with so many landowners of various types that this talk did not bother him. He kept his thoughts to himself and quietly explained to the Baron what he wanted. Wherever the German Kaiser settled German colonists on public land, they were free and did not have to pay ten percent of their crop to private landowners. They only had to pay the state taxes. Trauttmann was not as well off because he had settled on land owned by the nobility and had to pay a tithe every year.

"What?" the Baron shouted. "You don't want to give me my tenth anymore?"

"That's right, your Lordship," the farmer responded as he reached into his pocket and withdrew a document which he had received years ago. "I want to be released from the tithe, as it is written here."

"Written? Are you saying that I signed something?" The Baron laughed scornfully. But then he looked at the paper and it gradually came back to him. He cursed Martonffy, the old goat. How could the Notary have put something like this together? The Baron made a movement to tear up the document but Trauttmann grabbed it from him and put it back in his pocket.

"This is not valid!" Parkoczy shouted. "I was duped."

"Herr Baron, it is a valid document. If a Notary puts a document together and a landowner signs it, it is legally binding," Trauttmann stated firmly. "I have brought you the payment for fifty *Joch* land, to absolve me of my duty to pay the tenth of every crop."

"In seven years you have already earned that much, you scoundrel, and now I should give up my tenth forever? Never! Never!" stormed Parkoczy.

"*Herr*," said Trauttmann, "I would recommend that you do not call me a scoundrel again. I tell you my money is inherited from my father. It came from the *Rheinpfalz*. If you will not take my money today, I will be better off if I just set my house on fire and leave this area."

At these words, the Baron was speechless. He stared open-mouthed at this German farmer who dared to make such a statement. The farmer was a head taller than him. And he looked rather fierce at this moment. But was not he, the Baron, the one in charge? 'Where is the *Fokosch*?[1] Where is the whip?' he thought to himself. His blood was boiling. But he composed himself, he wanted to be prudent. Who knows what could come of this? All the people from the Black Forest were settled without any written agreement, and this man could turn them against him. That thought quickly went through the Baron's head.

"You want to burn down your house and go away?" he snarled at the farmer.

"If you don't give me what is lawfully due to me, that would be the best thing to do."

"You want to take me to court?"

"Why not? My rights are clear and plain."

"Ha, ha. Do you know how long such litigation would take in Hungary. One hundred years!"

Philipp Trauttmann had a better opinion of his new homeland. "I don't believe that," he said. "But I can drive over to Tevel, where Count Mercy is said to be residing now. Perhaps I can find another piece of land in Swabian Turkey. Something for me and for my sons, who will be getting married

---

1 *Fokosch*: Shepherd's axe, also used for punishment beatings.

soon. Under no circumstances will my sons settle here after what I've experienced with you. I would forbid it. And I would also advise Matz against it."

Trauttmann did not even notice what an impact the name of Count Mercy had made on Parkoszy. The Baron sat as if paralyzed and let the farmer talk. Mercy was that close? That 'Crazy Mercy', from whom he had snatched the people from the Black Forest? Trauttmann must be prevented from going to Mercy at all costs. "I'll be damned, you farmer, I do not want to go to court with you. Give me your money, you are free of the tithe. But there is one condition: you must not speak to those from the Black Forest about this, you will not go to Tevel, and your sons will stay here."

Trauttmann considered this. "Herr Baron, there is nothing about that in our written agreement. But I am not a gossip. What I do is of no concern to any of those from the Black Forest, and it is better for me if I don't have to go to Tevel. As for my boys, they are free men and can do what they want. They likely will not want to be farmers here, and Matz won't either, if they do not get the same rights as I have."

"They will have to wait that out," said the Baron derisively. "Today we are only concerned with your case. Pay up, farmer, keep your mouth shut, and go. I've talked long enough with you today."

Trauttmann did not say another word. He gave the Baron two thousand five hundred guilders, fifty guilders for every *Joch* of land, to release him of his tithe. The Baron certified this on the document with his signature. "Paid off, Sept. 15, Anno 1733. Parkoczy."

Trauttmann quickly bade the Baron farewell, walked to his wagon, which Ferdinand had been watching, and drove home.

'Just let one of that old devil's servants come within a stone's throw of my house again, they'll get it!' he thought to himself. 'Now I am free—completely independent!'

That evening, when the family was gathered together, Matz finally told them something which had been on his mind for a long time. He wanted to marry Imhof's Bärbl, one of the settlers from the Black Forest. He asked *Vetter* Philipp to speak with her parents to make the arrangements. "I think they will approve. Maybe I can even get my own fields this fall and then get married around *Fasching*."[2]

"I will be happy to negotiate the marriage. It would be an honor," said Trauttmann. "But we will see about the fields. We'll talk about that later."

Bas' Eva was thrilled that 'Potato Matz' had finally opened his mouth.

---

2 *Fasching*: Carnival or Mardi Gras, a festive season which occurs immediately before Lent.

She had known for a long time that he was going with Bärbl, who was a well-behaved, industrious and strong girl. "She's a good worker and will run a household well," said the aunt. She also let her oldest sons know that they, too, should think about getting married. "It would be great to have more women in this house full of men. I could use the help."

Hannes interjected that this was news to him; it was fine and good for the mother to be talking about this, since he and Peter had been wanting to look for brides for awhile already. If they were allowed to, they would be happy to go right away, even before the fall planting. Perhaps there could be three weddings by *Fasching*.

"For heaven's sake!" their mother exclaimed, "how will we manage that?"

But their father asked, "Where will you look for brides?"

Peter told him with a grin, "When we were in Tevel, we heard from Niklas Wekerle that there is a *Mädeldorf*, a town full of girls, in the Batschka. A widow is in charge of the whole town. Once, *Markgraf* von Baden provided dowries for one hundred and fifty girls from the Black Forest and sent them to this *Mädeldorf*, but all of them have already been married off. But now this widow has brought fifty more girls over. We would love to go take a look."

Their father shrugged his shoulders but said nothing. That showed that he was not against the idea. Then he started to talk with Matz about the Imhofs. He wanted to know how they stood financially, and what kind of dowry Bärbl would get when she got married. Matz told him that the family was one of the Black Forest families who had been split up. The grandfather, who had emigrated with his two sons' families, had brought five hundred *Taler* with him. One son's family was here, the other son's family was with the grandfather, God knows where. Therefore, Bärbl could be considered to be poor.

"The Baron will have to face a judge one day for what he has done," the farmer declared.

And before they all turned in for the night, he told his sons, "We will plant the seeds in the second week of October."

They took this to mean that they were free to go. The next day, their mother and Trudel washed and ironed, cooked and baked, and prepared the boys' finest outfits for them to go find their future wives. The boys got the family's best wagon ready for a trip and groomed the two youngest and fastest horses. Eckerts Adam, the smith from the Black Forest, put fresh horse shoes on for them. Once the clothes were packed into the trunk which served as a seat for the wagon, and their knapsacks were loaded with good food, the

Chapter 22—All Kinds of Conflicts

boys cheerfully departed.

Their father waved from the window and said, "Take good care of the horses, and don't do anything crazy."

But their mother stood at the gate as they drove off, drying her eyes with her apron. She stood there until she could not see them anymore. As she watched them disappear into the distance, her only thought was, "Go with God!"

With great pleasure, Parkoczy re-counted the money a few times after Trauttmann left. He had never had so much cold cash in his hands. It would be wonderful if the Swabian's two sons and nephew would each pay him the same amount, he thought. Then he would have enough money for a long, long time. He almost regretted his gruffness. Well, he wouldn't go running after them now; they would certainly come to him by themselves. His mind was racing. He would have to keep a close eye on his colony, day and night. The devil take Mercy! Why did he have to have a castle so nearby, in Högyész? What if one of those from the Black Forest went to him and told him about what had happened? ... No, no, that must be prevented at all costs.

Two days later Parkoczy was informed that there was something going on at the Trauttmanns. On the third day, he heard that the boys had left to go settle somewhere else.

What!? They had the audacity to do this? Well, yes, hadn't the farmer threatened him with this? And Matz would probably leave as well. Three potential farmers, each of whom could cultivate fifty *Joch* of land, were now lost to him? He flew into a wild rage when he heard about this. He asked Katicza to call his Kuruc friends and their sons together.

Should we capture a ship again, they asked. They were ready.

"No, I need you to catch two runaways. Go after them with your fastest horses. Force them to turn around. If they resist, give them the *Bastonade* and throw them in the back of their wagon. The horses will find their way back and bring them home."

Like an unleashed pack of hounds the serfs dashed off across the plain in pursuit of the Swabians. Such a hunt was exciting for them. Oh, how they wanted to catch them. "Hoi, hoi, hoi!"

As was customary, Philipp Trauttmann negotiated the marriage for Matz with the relatives of Bärbl Imhof. He made the arrangements as if Matz were his own son. And the family accepted. She would convert to Protestantism if Matz wished it. Her parents did not try to hide the fact that she had no money at this time. That may change in time, but they couldn't promise anything.

After Philipp told Matz all about his visit, he also discussed the financial situation with him. A young couple without farmhands or grown children to help them cannot undertake too much in the first years. He should at first take over a small acreage, but should have an option on fifty *Joch* of land. This would have to be in writing. They should accept the tenth rule but work for its removal, so they could pay it off in due time just as he himself had. Before that, he should not pay one *Kreuzer* to the Baron. It would be better to move elsewhere than continue with the ten percent option, because with this encumbrance, every descendant of the Baron could drive the Swabians from his property. You cannot stay somewhere with such a fragile hold on your land, you must build somewhere where you are completely independent. The Baron could not be trusted. Ever since his oldest son was gone, he could no longer be counted on to treat them with decency.

Trudel called them all to the table. Mother had cooked a special meal for Philipp, the marriage negotiator, and Matz, the bridegroom. Ferdinand came in from the stable, where he had just fed the horses. Just after they had all taken their places at the table, a horse neighed at the front gate. They all listened. It neighed again.

"Isn't that our horse?" asked Matz.

"What are you talking about?" asked Eva. "The boys must be past Mohács already."

A jumble of loud voices was heard outside, and Ferdinand ran to the window. "Father, father!" he cried in confusion. "Our wagon is here!" The color drained from his face and he ran out to open the gate.

Philipp had a dark feeling of foreboding. He threw his tin spoon on the table and followed Ferdinand.

"Stay there, Eva!" he ordered as he left.

The driverless wagon came through the gate, and behind it came a number of settlers from the Black Forest: men, women and children, with old Zengraf in the front. He clenched his fists. "Oh, *Vetter* Philipp! *Vetter* Philipp!" he cried out as the women wept.

Trauttmann ran over to the wagon. His face contorted, he looked inside unable to say a word. His sons lay on the floor of the wagon, spattered with blood. They seemed to be unconscious. He touched their faces and their hands—they were warm. They were alive. Their mother rushed forward, screaming, but her husband held her back.

"They're alive. Maybe they were attacked by gypsies," he said to her.

"Oh no, oh no," Jost Zengraf interjected. "Gypsies did not do this!" and

Chapter 22—All Kinds of Conflicts

he balled his fists. In the meantime, Ferdinand opened the tailgate of the wagon and Matz pulled Peter out. The father was the first to see that the boy did not have his boots on and his feet were swollen and covered with blood. It was the same with Hannes. The clothes had been ripped from their backs, and their heads had been beaten and were bleeding.

"What happened here?!" the farmer cried out. He felt as if a knife had gone through his heart.

Eva sank onto her knees upon seeing her battered sons and cried her heart out. "They went out to look for brides and this is how they came back," she wailed. "O my God!"

Reluctantly, old Zengraf approached the farmer. "Don't you realize who is responsible for this foul deed? The old devil over there, the Baron. That's what he had done to my son, Mathes!"

Yes, there was no doubt about that. The Baron must have caused this to happen. Wild-eyed, Trauttmann looked around and asked all the people to leave the courtyard. He did not need their sympathy, he would take his revenge. They all left, and Matz closed the gate behind them. Only Bärbl Imhof stayed. She had already fetched water from the well, and the boys' mother washed the head wounds. Trudel and Bärbl tended to the horribly beaten feet, dressing them with wet cloths.

The boys began to move a little. The cool water did them some good and they slowly regained consciousness. Their father and Matz carried them into the house and carefully put them in their beds.

In this situation, Bärbl knew what to do. Two years ago, young Zengraf from the Black Forest had tried to escape, and when caught, he'd gotten the same treatment as the boys. One of the serfs, an old man, had brought him an herbal salve for his feet. Should she try to find him? It had helped young Zengraf. This salve was left over from when the Turks ruled the area. Eva thanked Bärbl a thousand times for her help and sent her to go look for the man with the salve.

There followed days of misery and quiet rage. The boys had to tell their mother about the attack, over and over. They had been assaulted by a horde of twenty serfs. They believed that these people had come from old Parkoczy. They could not be one hundred percent certain of this, but they would recognize every one of their attackers if they saw them again. The father walked about the house in silence, consumed by an inner fury. He asked his sons a few times if they could stand up properly. No, not yet.

The father sent Matz to Mohács, telling him to travel in secrecy. He rode away in the middle of the night under cover of a heavy fog. Unless something happened to him, he should be on his way back by now. He was to tell Martonffy about what had happened here and ask for his counsel to see what could be done about the Baron in accordance with the law. Philipp also told his nephew to buy three good guns and bring them home with plenty of ammunition.

The farmer did not get any sleep that night. Even though the Baron had apparently completely taken leave of his senses, he was the overlord of all of these German settlers, and none of them could leave the area without his knowledge. He definitely must have spies. Trauttmann was worried that Matz could easily get the same treatment as his sons had, despite their caution and secrecy. But he had felt it necessary to send him. He needed to find out—if there was a legal recourse to counter this shameless act, then he would go that route. He was responsible for everybody in his family, could not immediately act in anger and perhaps lose his home which they had all worked so hard for. But if the law would not help him and he had to resort to other options, he would. He was determined that, somehow, justice would be served.

Matz had followed his instructions well. He came back with the three guns and information from Martonffy. "The Notary sends his best regards. He told me that the country is ruled by martial law. The farmer who acts against his master will be hanged. Every proprietor possesses the *jus gladiis*, the right to use the whip. The Hungarian law does not deal with independent farmers and their rights; any law regarding such farmers does not exist yet. A farmer could file a suit with the sitting judge in Mohács, but maybe he would only laugh at the farmer's complaint.

"Laugh?" Trauttmann gritted his teeth in anger. "He'd better not laugh at me! If there is no justice through the courts, I will administer it myself!"

The settlers from the Black Forest met in front of their prayer house on the first Sunday in October. The older people believed that they should finally form a municipality. They had already been here three years. The majority of them would probably stay here, and the time had come to bring some order into their community. Not only was a priest needed so he could say mass, they also needed a leader. Then maybe such awful things as just happened might not be repeated. Whom should we elect as leader? Who should be in charge?

"Trauttmann!" many of them answered. "Only Trauttmann!"

The three oldest were asked to go to Trauttmann's house and ask him whether he will accept the honor..

Chapter 22—All Kinds of Conflicts

That afternoon, when the men came to the house, Peter and Hannes were just making their first attempts at walking. It was almost time for the fall planting, but they were still useless for the work. But they could walk! They could not wear boots yet, but with their feet tightly wrapped and wearing good *Opanken*, sandals like the Slovaks wore, they were able to move around. The Turkish salve had done wonders.

Philipp Trauttmann was not insensitive to the honor offered to him. It was a great tribute to be asked to create a new town and be its first mayor! But he declined; he could not even think of accepting that office until he had resolved the situation with the Baron, not until everything was set right. He invited all from the Black Forest who wanted to leave, but were being kept here against their will, to come to his house that evening. "Let any who would like to have a word with Herr Parkoczy meet with me tonight."

Ten men came. Old Jost Zengraf, Niklas Lulay, Michel Hames, Kaspar Jäger, Adam Eckert the smith, and others. Young Mathes Zengraf, Jost's grandson who had been beaten, was the first one in Trauttmann's yard. Ferdinand and Trudel set up benches and chairs in a semicircle. The visitors, as well as Trauttmann's three grown sons, all took their seats. Only Trauttmann was standing. He told them all what he intended to do. His opinion was that this man, who seemed to believe that he could get away with anything, had to be taught a lesson.

"This man kidnapped human beings and the arm of justice has never reached him. He ostensibly freed those that he kidnapped, but the first one who tried to go his own way was almost beaten to death in the Turkish manner. You others are constantly being watched by his spies. In reality he still regards everyone as his serfs. Even me! Although I purchased my independence from him, he denied my sons their freedom! He didn't ask why my sons were leaving, he just had them beaten. That's because of his guilty conscience. He is afraid of every man who dares to leave Dobok, and if he isn't stopped, he will give everyone the same treatment that he gave my sons and Zengrafs Mathes. How can we punish this reckless tyrant?"

"Beat him to death!" cried old Zengraf and a few agreed with him.

"Is there no one in this big beautiful country who will give us protection?" asked another old man.

"No one," answered Trauttmann. "Matz secretly went to the Notary in Mohács and asked for legal advice. There is no justice for us. We have no rights. The landowners have the right to have the farmers beaten, and they have the right to hang anyone who defends himself."

"What!? That can't be?!" The people were outraged.

"Hung until dead," said Trauttmann.

All remained silent.

Trauttmann continued, "Men, I want to get all of you your freedom. Sharpen your scythes, load your guns, bring a club or a pitchfork. It doesn't matter what you bring as long as you can defend yourself. We are going to gather in front of the Baron's rundown manor and demand our rights. He must give them to us, he must recognize that we are free men and can leave if we like. Even if blood has to be shed, he will have to do this!"

"Yes, he must give us our rights!" The decision was unanimous.

Next morning fifteen of them marched toward St. Marton. Peter and Hannes were on horseback because the trip was too long for them to walk. Every man from the Trauttmann house had a gun. Only two of the others had guns. Everyone else carried a variety of weapons. Young Zengraf brought two sturdy hazel clubs which he had soaked overnight in salt water, since this would make them heavier. The others laughed at him when he showed up with them. But he clenched his fists and remained silent. Only Trauttmann exchanged a long look with the youngster. They understood each other.

"We have to go in the morning while he is still sober," Trauttmann had said the day before. So everyone met at his house early the next morning.

It caused quite a sensation among the serfs when they saw armed men walk past and stop at the residence of their Lord and Master. Eckert, the blacksmith, hit the rotten gate three times with his hatchet, creating a big hole and causing the door to fall off its hinges.

"Good morning," he called out brightly.

Katicza stuck her head out of a second story window. A few serfs boisterously yelled, "Hoi, hoi!"

"The Baron should come down to us," Trauttmann called up to Katicza. Soon Parkoczy appeared at the window. When he saw the armed men, he stood as if rooted to the floor. His lips moved soundlessly and his eyes went blank.

"Come down, come down here," all shouted to him. Parkoczy disappeared but came back to the window with two loaded pistols. He laid one in front of him and held the other in his right hand.

"Who brought you here, you rebels?" he yelled. But seven rifles were aimed at him and it was suddenly very quiet.

All rifles were cocked.

"We ask that you come down, we have to talk to you," said Trauttmann.

"We just want to talk! Nothing will happen to you," the others called out.

Parkoczy now turned to his serfs. "Go and get Berés, Janczi, Antal and

Chapter 22—All Kinds of Conflicts

Farkas," he ordered.

"Watch out!" Trauttmann said to Hannes and to Peter. They turned their horses and pointed their guns at the serfs who wanted to leave. "Anyone who leaves here will get shot in the back!" Hannes called out. And none tried to leave.

"Get him down here!" Trauttmann said to his men. Eckerts Adam, the blacksmith, and young Mathes Zengraf did not have to be told twice. Parkoczy didn't shoot, he didn't curse, he pulled himself together and went with the two boys, walking tall and defiant. The Baron left his pistols behind, but brought with him his feeling of superiority, which he had recovered.

"What do you want from me, you insurgents?! Do you know that I can have all of you hanged?" he asked in a lordly and domineering manner.

"You just try it!" the farmers laughed.

"Herr Baron," Trauttmann began. "You kidnapped these people and are holding them here as if they were serfs."

"I have told these indigents that they are free farmers. What else do you want?"

"They should be able to go wherever they want."

"I won't allow that!"

"With what right did you capture Mathes Zengraf and give him the *Bastonade*?"

"With the right of the landlord, you stupid farmer. Don't you know my rights?"

"With what right did you stop my two sons who went looking for brides, stop them and had them beaten half to death?"

"They were looking for brides?" said Parkoczy, and his voice faltered.

"I am a free farmer and sit on my property which I have paid for. Why did you do this to me?" Trauttmann cried out, shaking with anger.

"That was a mistake," the Baron admitted.

"So, that was a mistake. We will make sure these mistakes do not happen again! We'll beat you to death if you ever touch a German man again. Do you understand that, Baron? Do you?" and he shook his fists in front of the Baron's face.

"For that kind of talk you have earned the gallows!" Parkoczy yelled and took a step back.

"What?!" Trauttmann shouted, enraged. "You had my boys half beaten to death and I deserve the gallows?! Are you drunk?'

Parkoczy clenched his teeth and balled his fists, but said nothing and did not move.

Trauttmann composed himself. "I ask you, in the name of these people who have chosen me to represent them and asked me to be the *Richter* of their town: Will you give all of them their right to go wherever they want?"

"No!" yelled the Baron. "Whoever has settled here must stay here!"

"Hoho, hoho! We want to leave!" some called out.

"We want to know where our children are. We want to go look for them!" old Zengraf shouted.

"Maybe later, but not now," said Parkoczy, somewhat bewildered. "Not now! Nobody can leave!"

A wild tumult arose. They realized that the Baron feared his crime would be found out, and shouted epithets and insults of all kinds at him. Mathes Zengraf jumped up in front of the Baron and yelled, "If I leave tomorrow to go to the Banat to see my bride, what will happen? Tell me!"

"You'll get the *Bastonade* again!" answered the obstinate Baron.

The big young man grabbed the older man by the neck and threw him to the ground. Then he began to tug at his boots. Eckert, the smith, understood what he wanted and immediately helped him. In no time, the Baron was barefoot.

"On the bench with him! On the bench!" a few called out. They laid the gasping, struggling Baron on a bench next to the door of the house. Mathes got ready, waving his hazel club in the air. The thought that he could now take his revenge gave him fiendish satisfaction. Philipp Trauttmann made no attempt to prevent this, since he felt that he had gotten nowhere with the obstinate Baron. If they now quit and went home, everything would remain as it was. God knows, they might even be taken to court for the disturbance they had already caused, so they might as well finish what they had started. At any rate, the Baron richly deserved the *Bastonade*.

At that fateful moment, a trumpet suddenly sounded in the distance. Soldiers, the Kaisers' soldiers, must be nearby. They had never been here before, nobody knew what this could mean. They all looked at each other, somewhat frightened and yet relieved at the same time.

"Halt, halt!" called Trauttmann, feeling that he was relieved of his self-imposed duty. The Baron, however, took advantage of the moment. He nimbly tore himself away from his tormentors and ran into his home, leaving his boots behind.

The humor of this situation was lost to those present. All stood in awe of the sudden appearance of ten men on horseback, senior officers, Hàjduks and a trumpeter. At their head was a dignified Colonel. Beside him, a bit intimidated, pale and sad, rode the young Baron Andor.

Chapter 22—All Kinds of Conflicts

"We are at the right place, Herr Colonel, my father lives here," Andor said. He was greatly concerned to see this gathering of armed Swabians and so many serfs. A servant ran to Andor and told him in breathless haste what was going on here. This alarmed Andor greatly. The Colonel and his men had come to the castle in Dobok looking for his father, and he had brought them here, taking detours to make sure that they did not pass the settlers' houses. He suspected why the Colonel wanted to see his father, and did not want him to see the colony in Dobok. And now the Swabians were here and were causing a disturbance!

"What's going on here?" asked Count Anton von Mercy. "Why are you all here, armed?"

Everyone looked toward Trauttmann, their spokesman. "Sir," he said, "we were trying to bring justice to this evil landlord for his transgressions. Maybe you can take care of this instead."

"Who are all of you?" asked Mercy.

"These are some of the people from the Black Forest, whom the man inside this house kidnapped from the Danube River. They were supposed to go to Count Mercy in the Banat, but he brought them here."

The Colonel's face lit up when he heard this and he exchanged a satisfied look with his companions. "I have been looking for you," said the Colonel. "Where do you live?"

"An hour from here, over in Dobok," Trauttmann replied.

Now they quickly told Mercy how the Baron acted toward them, what he had done to them and why they had gotten together today in desperation. In the meantime, Andor had dismounted and rushed into the mansion to his father.

"Calm yourselves," said Count Mercy. "Go home and leave the Baron to me. I will come to you when I'm finished here."

This satisfied everyone except old Zengraf. "Herr Officer, are we going to have to stay here as serfs of this landlord, or are we free?"

"You are free," said the Colonel. "Any of you who want to go to the Banat are free to do so. Your friends are all there."

"Hurray!" the old man crowed. "Hurray!"

Then they all went home. The matter had turned out much better than they had expected. Only Mathes was dissatisfied. Scowling, he broke up the hazel clubs which he had so carefully prepared.

Chapter 23

A Solemn Conclusion

What was this terrible news which spread like wildfire through the streets of Vienna?! Field Marshall Mercy had been killed in action! As soon as the Imperial War Council was notified, all of Vienna knew it. The *Oberkommandant* of the troops in Italy had fallen, Count Mercy was dead! And rumors of a massive defeat of the Kaiser's soldiers filled the air.

Hofkammerrat von Stephany, too, received a letter from Italy from Mercy's headquarters. He was badly shaken up by this sorrowful news about his friend and colleague. Dead? Dead? Mercy had just written to the *Hofkammerrat* a week ago, telling him that he'd had another heart attack while he was preparing for battle. Again he'd had to give up command of the troops just before he was to make an important decision for which he could have been immortalized.

'I seem to have no luck,' he wrote to his friend. 'It is the lot of the Mercys to do the work and have their successors get the credit.' But he quickly added that his health had greatly improved. Although his eyesight had been affected, his vision seemed to be coming back and he was regaining his strength. Soon he would be reinstated. The now-memorable letter concluded with the words: 'Do not forget my Banat! Only if the Banat becomes a sovereign dukedom or principality will this valuable land be a part of the Kaiser's Empire forever. Do not forget my paradise!'

And now this man who had been so full of fire and passion was dead. But he did not die from his illness; he fell in battle as a hero. As he had hoped, he had recovered quickly and had once again taken over the supreme command of the troops in Italy. With the fierce intensity that he brought to everything he did, Count Mercy had prepared the attack on the enemy which had been

Chapter 23—A Solemn Conclusion

postponed because of his illness. In his thirst to act, he had overturned all of the battle plans of the man who had temporarily replaced him, and rejected the view that came from headquarters that the timing was not right for an attack. Mercy pushed forward to fight at Parma and rode at the head of his troops to his death. As *Oberkommandant,* he had dared to ride too far ahead. Two musket bullets shattered his forehead, and he had soundlessly dropped from his horse. His death paralyzed the whole army. Mercy was interred at the church in Reggio and a dignified funeral was held there.

This information was written to the *Hofkammerat*, and the letter also divulged what was being said about the dead man: that Mercy was a warrior, a daredevil, but he was no general, no *Oberkommandant*. This slander also reached Prince Eugene, who in spite of his poor health and an inadequate army was holding his own against the French. The Prince wrote to the Kaiser and defended Mercy's memory. He had always valued Mercy as a friend, and regarded him as one of the bravest and most honorable of the Kaiser's Generals. Some may judge him based on his last undertaking and complain about his stormy temperament, but: 'Your Majesty, with the death of Mercy you have lost a great man.'

That is what the Prince wrote, and the Kaiser publicized his tribute to Mercy. A public memorial service was also held in Vienna to honor the fallen general. Stephany sent an express messenger to Swabian Turkey with an invitation to the service. He wanted his daughter and son-in-law to witness the honor given to the great man. But the messenger reached Count Anton too late; he had been away, applying the same fervor which his adoptive father had for the good of their cause. A true-born Mercy had departed, but his replacement was not unworthy of the name.

When Stephany received the reply from his son-in-law, who had been shocked and greatly saddened by the news, the memorial service was already over. Ah, but the old Governor would have been so happy to hear the news that Anton sent! He had not only found the missing people from the Black Forest, whom so many had presumed dead, he also exposed many other Hungarian landowners as kidnappers of German colonists and ordered that they be taken to court, like Parkoczy. He wrote that the Viennese were not well-informed about everything that the colonists in Hungary had gone through. There was much to rectify and many lost human rights to restore.

How proud Klaus Florimund Mercy would have been of his nephew, his adopted son and pupil!

Now he was dead. But Stephany was determined to watch over Mercy's great legacy. As for his last request: 'Do not forget my Banat!'—the

Hofkammerat took the entire contents of Mercy's appeal to heart.

There was a great deal of excitement in the *Bauernstube* of the *Sieben Kurfürsten* Inn of Temesvar on St. Martin's Day. Swabians had come from everywhere to attend the great Fall Market, and among these were the Black Foresters from Dobok. Those who had been missing for so long, whom some had given up for dead—they were here! At the market, old Jost Zengraf had found his daughter, Kathl Jäger. She almost fainted at the shock of seeing him. Every year on his names day[1] she had a memorial mass said in remembrance of him—and now here he was, standing in front of her butter basket and the plucked geese she had bought for St. Martin's day with a big smile on his face! She made the sign of the cross and was about to utter a saying used to ward off ghosts that appeared in the light of day. But then Mathes, her brother's lost son, walked up right behind her father, and he could not be a ghost since he immediately asked after his fiancé, Margaret. Now she had to believe it, it was really them.

And oh, the stories they all had to tell as they sat in the *Bauernstube* of the inn, amazing stories of everything they had experienced. It turned out that the Baron who had them kidnapped and settled on 'his land' on the other side of the Danube was not the rightful owner of the property on which he had committed his terrible deeds. He had been removed. Young Count Mercy caught him and banished him to a small castle which was supposed to have belonged to his family a long time ago. He was waiting there until his court case.

Everyone wanted to know if all those from the Black Forest were going to come to the Banat now. "Oh no," said Eckert, the smith. "Only ten families want to come here, the others send you their regards. They are established in Dobok and don't want to start anew. The land which they settled will soon become crown land of the Kaiser and then they will be independent, just like you farmers in the Banat. They just send you greetings and ask that you don't forget about them."

In the *Bauernstube* young Zengrafs Mathes seemed to be putting everyone on with his stories, which could not possibly all be true. First he told all about their capture by armed Kurucs. Then about his attempted escape, for which he had received the *Bastonade*. And then they were supposed to be-

---

1 Names day: the feast day of the saint after whom one is named. This day was usually celebrated yearly instead of a birthday.

Chapter 23—A Solemn Conclusion

lieve that fifteen Swabians with sharpened scythes, pitchforks, clubs and guns assembled in front of the Baron's residence in order to capture the Baron in the presence of his serfs. They wanted to give him the *Bastonade*, in the manner that he had punished those who did not follow his orders. Their leader, Philipp Trauttmann from the *Pfalz*, had told them that they could be sent to the gallows for this uprising. But that didn't matter to them, they wanted to finally be free of this demon, and so they did it. And now they were free of him.

The listeners did not quite believe these stories. Some were only half-listening, others not at all. All of them had other things on their minds, and most wanted to go home already, since nighttime came early in November. At last, only the Black Foresters were still sitting and talking to one another; they had to stay at the inn because their settlement papers were not yet in order.

In the 'Black Forest' Inn on the upper main street in Guttenbrunn, everyone rejoiced upon hearing that the missing settlers had been found and that some of them would come to their community. Jägers Kathl brought her ailing father along as proof. She sent her older son to Margret's house to let her know that "Mathes is coming, you can order the musicians, we'll have the wedding by St. Catherine's Day!"[2]

After old Jost Zengraf had been shown his room, he called Kathl and her husband to his room and pressed a wallet into his daughter's hand. It contained his life savings, which he had brought from Germany. He was so happy that he had been able to bring this to her after all. Now his heart was light... And he fell into a peaceful sleep from which he never woke.

A new Governor ruled from the Palace of Mehemed Aga on Temesvar's *Paradeplatz*, a brave General of high rank. He continued the work that Count Mercy had begun. It was he who laid the cornerstone for the cathedral which Count Mercy had wished for. It was his name signed on the record that was sealed into the cornerstone and sunk into the ground for all posterity, not that of the great man who had dedicated two decades of his passionate life to this city and country. That was the lot of the Mercys.

And that greater dream, which the Governor had pursued until his last hour, appeared to also be nearing its fulfillment. It was not in vain that he had confessed this innermost desire to the *Hofkammerat*...

---

2 St. Catherine's Day is on November 25. St Catherine is the patron saint of unmarried women.

A noble gentleman travelled incognito through the Banat. He stayed at the *Sieben Kurfürsten*, anonymous and unrecognized, as well. He was a proud young man, a picture of handsomeness and knightly charm. He was thankful for everything and gave a gracious smile to one and all. The name of the inn charmed him and the attractive hostess even more so. In addition to his younger companions, who seemed to be soldiers, a tall gray-haired man with bright intelligent eyes stood out. The innkeeper soon learned that he was the Viennese Imperial Councillor, *Hofkammerrat* von Stephany. The gentleman's servants were allowed to tell him that. But who was the main person in the party, the one everything seemed to revolve around? His visit caused quite a stir among the regulars at the *Sieben Kurfürsten*. They guessed and surmised but could not come to any satisfactory conclusion. Even Wörndle, the school principal, could not solve the mystery.

Frau Therese served her specialty for the Viennese visitors. The young Count, or whoever he was, thanked her graciously for the dinner. He had not had such a splendid meal since leaving Vienna, everything had been delicious. He extended his hand to the hostess and graciously shook her hand. It was the smoothest man's hand she had ever seen. She almost kissed it. When she shared this with the workers in the kitchen, Gretel, the plump waitress, clicked her tongue and mischievously declared, "If I were younger, I would gladly dance a Ländler with him."

That afternoon, the gentleman had a long meeting behind locked doors with the new Governor. Herr von Stephany chaired the meeting.

The next day, the distinguished little party began their trip accompanied by heavily armed mounted Hàjduks. Young Colonel Mercy had come from the other side of the Danube to meet the gentlemen at Peterwardein and be their guide. Nobody knew the Banat and the Batschka better than he. At the *Sieben Kurfürsten*, senior officers said that the Viennese gentlemen had a special mission. What was it? All kinds of rumors were flying.

After four weeks, the mysterious traveling party returned, and set forth for Vienna with extraordinary haste at the onset of winter. It was said that the gentlemen had encountered a terribly dreadful disease in the south. None wanted to be responsible for losing even an hour before they went back. And then, in the last moment, the secret was given away. One of the gentleman's servants had fallen for a girl who served drinks at the inn, and told her that the gallant handsome man was none other than the Duke of Lorraine, the bridegroom of Archduchess Maria Theresia!

This revelation took everyone by surprise. No one knew what to make of it, and the regulars at the *Sieben Kurfürsten* racked their brains all winter

Chapter 23—A Solemn Conclusion

long. Even the city councilors, who usually knew everything, were mystified. The mayor, school principal Wörndle, and the proprietor of the inn argued frequently about the possible consequences of this noble visit. Slowly rumors circulated which were never confirmed and yet seemed plausible. The young duke was here looking for a Dukedom, the Commander of the fortress told the mayor. But he never elaborated on this, he only smiled. "What need does he have of a Dukedom?" asked Wörndle when the mayor told everyone about this conversation. "Is he not the Duke of Lorraine?" They did not understand and thought perhaps it was a joke.

When Franz Stephan married Maria Theresia during the next *Fasching* season, and soon after gave up the Dukedom of Lorraine to become Grand Duke of Tuscany, the reason for his trip to Temesvar became clear. This news hit the Councillors' table in the *Sieben Kurfürsten* like a bombshell. So the Banat was a scorned bride!

Leonhard Wörndle, who passionately loved to talk politics, was beside himself. He could not understand it and did not want to believe what had come of it. "Lorraine too, Lorraine?" he cried out when he heard the news from Vienna. "Alsace is gone and now Lorraine?! German territory has been ceded to Stanislaus of Poland, father-in-law of King Louis XIV of France?! And after his death France swallows it up?" He was greatly distressed; there was no holding him back. "And the young Prince, who one day should be German Kaiser, was forced to do this?"[3] No, he could not understand it. Full of scorn he hummed the satirical poem which had been brought from the Rhine in the previous year.

"Ja, was nur Händ und Füße regt,	Any creature that can move hands and feet
Was geht, was schwimmt, was Eier legt,	Anything that walks, swims or lays eggs
Hat seine Feinde gern vom Leibe.	Keeps its enemies at bay.
In Teutschland ist es umgewandt	In Germany, this is reversed
Wir öffnen unserm Feind das Land	We open our land to our enemy
Und leiden, daß er bleibe."	And suffer, for him to remain.

Nobody contradicted principal Wörndle, they didn't want to aggravate him even more, but he could not stop talking about this topic.

"And even if the Duke of Lorraine had to renounce his homeland be-

---

[3] Recall that Mercy had been called to fight the War of Polish succession, where the French supported Stanislaw's claim to the Polish throne and the Habsburgs wanted someone else. Eventually, in 1736, Stanislaw abdicated the throne, but received in compensation the Duchy of Lorraine from the Duke of Lorraine, Francis Stephen, who married Maria Therese that year. The Duchy of Lorraine was to revert to France upon Stanislaw's death.

cause the cursed diplomats messed things up again," he continued, "Why, oh why did he not choose the Banat and Batschka, which have such a great future ahead of them, as his Dukedom? If I were him I would have transplanted all Lorrainers to Banat and created a large German Empire here in the East. Why would a Duke from Lorraine, who is married to the German Kaiser's daughter, make himself an Italian Grand Duke? Hm?"

Wörndle held forth on this topic the whole evening in the crowded dining room, so much that he made some of the regulars in the *Herrenstube* uncomfortable with his ravings. Jakob Pless, the owner, wondered to himself, 'if I only knew why he feels the need to yell so much?'

"Alsace is gone! Lorraine is gone! What's next? The *Rheinpfalz*?"

The host fled into the *Bauernstube*. There the talk was about the excellent fields, rich pastures, the price of grain and the first ten years' freedom from taxation. And some talked about the inheritances they still had coming from their former homeland. If they received everything from back home and the first crop was bountiful, then they would not want for anything. This kind of talk pleased the host of the *Sieben Kurfürsten* much better. 'Who needs to listen Wörndle's speeches?' he thought to himself. 'These farmers will create their own Dukedom here for themselves!' Those in the *Bauernstube* intermittently heard Wörndle's rantings whenever Susi, the waitress, opened the door in between the rooms. "Lorraine gone… Alsace gone… *Rheinpfalz*?" The farmers perked up their ears, but they then went on talking about the new homeland instead of the old. Most did not like to be reminded of the old country, because they would be overcome with homesickness.

Spring came and with it came the terrible disease from the south, which had been kept secret.

"The plague! The plague!"

This frightful cry resounded from all sides, and the accounts were gruesome. In the midst of these, word of Prince Eugene's death came from Vienna. This news would have been earth-shattering at any other time, but no one had any emotion left to feel anything. Only the Turks seemed to appreciate the significance of this information; they grew more and more aggressive at the borders which the Prince had once established, and seemed about to cross them to break the peace. Mercy dead, Prince Eugene dead, the plague ravaging the land—it was too much at once.

The capital city was still free of the plague. The *Stadtrichter* enforced a strict quarantine, since he did not believe that the malaria-scourged city could withstand an outbreak. Then a battalion of Green-Infantry came from *Siebenbürgen* (Transylvania) to relieve the feverish troops. These healthy

Chapter 23—A Solemn Conclusion

troops were joyfully welcomed when they arrived.

Three days later, the battalion was chased out of the city. The civilian population revolted against the military authorities, they went to the palace shouting, threatening, pleading. The incoming troops had brought ten cases of the plague with them! They fled to nearby Palanka, where barracks were built for them and they were fenced in to shut them off from the world. There the entire battalion perished from the plague.

The epidemic hit, devastating both city and countryside. All work stopped, commerce came to a halt, the crops rotted in the fields, no one brought in the harvest. All that could be done was to pray, hold funeral processions, and beseech their patron, Saint Nepomuk, for help. People avoided each other on the street and stayed holed up in their homes; nobody buried the dead. Soldiers were sent out to burn them on funeral pyres. Gruesome, barbaric methods were used to defend against this disease. Where the plague broke out anew, the community was surrounded by palisades and nobody was allowed to leave. Anyone who tried was shot dead by the guards.

Vienna sent good advice, elaborate regulations, and a dozen doctors. The native Serbs and Wallachians took the doctors as sorcerers and beat most of them to death. Entire villages died out; whole streets in Temesvar were deserted; food was distributed with poles through the windows; no one knew which of their relatives or friends were still alive. The church bell could no longer be tolled because its message drove people crazy.

Aunt Gutwein died very soon, followed by Jakob Pless, who had always been vigorous and never sick. No one came to the *Gaststube* of the *Sieben Kurfürsten* Inn anymore. Horrified, Frau Therese locked the doors and fled with her children to Mehala. She wanted to take Wörndle along since he was still single and had no one to care for him, but he had already been stricken by the illness. He resisted death and did not surrender easily. 'What? This is to be the end for me? For this I lived and worked and ventured to a foreign land to get a better future?' He rebelled against this thought; he did not want to die here. "Take me away," he stammered. "I want to go to Germany, back to the beautiful German Realm." Those were his last words.

Nothing was harvested or planted, the cattle died in the barns and people died in their beds, alone and abandoned.

It took almost two years until the epidemic passed. A whole army of German pioneers had died. Tens of thousands of Germans had paid for the conquest of this country with their lives. The once highly-acclaimed Banat was now called the graveyard of the settlers. No colonists came anymore. Only hunger came. It crept through the land and put a stranglehold on life.

In Vienna, old *Hofkammerat* Joseph von Stephany still sat at the loom upon which the threads of fate for the Banat and Batschka were to be woven into a prosperous whole.

Everything had ground to a halt; the influx of immigrants had abruptly stopped. Instead of new colonists, German ships brought wheat and flour to Hungary. Plows in Hungary stood still and the surviving colonists would have perished if the Kaiser and the German states had not helped.

When the plague had been considered to be over, the *Hofkammerrat* sent his capable secretary, Gottmann, down to the Banat. He should assess what could be done after this collapse. Was it time to give up? He received a hundred letters saying that all was lost, yet he did not believe it. The plague had also been in Vienna at one time. His young wife had died of it, but Vienna had recovered and was flourishing, and he himself had endured what had to be endured. He saw his secretary as his future successor and wanted to put him to the test on this trip. He hoped that Gottmann's heart would be won over by this unfortunate country during his trip.

After three months Gottmann returned, full of sorrow and yet full of enthusiasm. The Germans were harvesting again! They alone, with their firm trust in God, had proved themselves to be resilient. The Spaniards, the Italians and the French had disappeared without a trace; the ones that survived had run away; their villages were empty. But none of the German settlements had died out completely. They had defended themselves against the epidemic, had quickly buried their dead and had lived prudently. Everywhere in German communities, renewed courage was awakened. All wanted to stay where they were. They plowed new furrows around the graves of their departed.

Count Anton reported the same from Swabian Turkey. They must begin their great work anew and not despair. No, one could not despair. Joseph von Stephany would be the last to give up on his and Mercy's life's work. As long as his old bones held up, he would stay at his post.

New messengers were sent to the German states. New Settlement Proclamations by young Empress Maria Theresia, who ascended the throne in difficult times, were read from every pulpit, and the great Swabian migration to the East began anew.

Those who now arrived came forth into a German heritage.

The dead had sanctified this earth for future generations.

Epilogue

The colonization of the ethnic Germans into Hungary, which came to be known as *der Grosse Schwabenzug* or the "Great Swabian Migration," chiefly took place in three phases.

The Swabians' experiences have been summarized in the following poem:

Die Ersten fanden den Tod,	The first encountered death,
Die Zweiten litten die Not,	the second encountered hardship,
Erst die Dritten hatten Brot.	only the third had bread.

The setting for the Great Swabian Migration was this first wave, which encountered death. Many of approximately 15,000 German settlers from the first colonization were killed in Turkish raids, or died from bubonic plague. This first wave was called the Karolinische Ansiedlung, or Karolinian colonization, which occurred from 1718 to 1737 under Emperor Karl VI.

So what happened in the other phases of colonization?

The second phase took place under Karl's daughter, and so is referred to as the Maria Theresianische Ansiedlung, or Maria Theresian colonization. The approximately 75,000 German Colonists who settled from 1744-1772 had to rebuild many of the settlements. They were successful in re establishing the towns, but their life was filled with hard work. Hence, *"Die Zweiten litten die Not*—the second wave encountered hardship."

The third wave consisted of approximately 60,000 new German settlers who were able to increase the economic prosperity of the Hungarian farm land. This third phase is called the Josephinische Ansiedlung, or Josephinian colonization, which took place under Habsburg Emperor Joseph II from 1782 to 1787. The Banat region later came to be known as the "breadbasket of Europe." Thus: *"Erst die Dritten hatten Brot*–only the third had bread."

The colonization covered the regions of the Banat, the Batschka, *Schwäbische Türkei, Ungarisches Mittelgebirge* (Central Hungarian Highlands), *Syrmien-Slawonien*, and the Sathmar region south of the Theiss River. (See map, p. v.) Volkmar Senz calculates that a total of 200,000 Germans settled in these areas by the end of the colonization period.

After 1789, the government sponsored colonization was discontinued, but some settlers continued to arrive in Hungary until 1829, after which only those with 500 Guilders cash were allowed to migrate. During the colonization period, people of other nationalities also settled in the region. Among them were Serbs, Croatians, Bulgarians and Romanians, and to a lesser extent, Slovaks, Ruthenians, Czechs and a few French and Italians.

Hungary's population became truly multi-national, consisting of 12% Germans (around half of which were Danube-Swabians), 28% Slavs, 43% Magyars and 15% Romanians, along with other nationalities, by 1890. At that time, there were around 1 million Danube-Swabians in the settlement areas. In the Banat, Batschka, and *Schwäbische Türkei*, Germans constituted 27, 26 and 34% of the population respectively; they lived side-by-side with their Serbian, Croatian, Hungarian and Romanian neighbors.

During the settlement period, more than 1,000 German villages were established in Southern Hungary. Plans for the villages were laid out in Vienna. The towns were generally built in a square checkerboard pattern, with the Catholic church and its surrounding square in the center of the town. The style of the buildings was a modified Baroque, and came to be called "settler's Baroque." Each village, however, had slightly different designs for the decorative finishes on the buildings, and the differences are still visible today.

The houses were built perpendicularly to the street, and consisted of a series of adjoining rooms, with the parlor on the end which faced the street, and sheds for domestic animals on the opposite end. Long covered porch ways extended the full length of the house. The Swabians were known for keeping their houses and gardens clean and carefully maintained. Each houseplot was surrounded by a fence, and the courtyard within the fence contained grape vines, fruit trees and the household garden. The streets in the villages were wide and were used as pathways for community activities, such as baptism, wedding and funeral processions. Cattle were also led down the street to the common pasture in the surrounding area of the village.

Crops were grown in the fields surrounding the village. The specialty crops grown in this area were sugar beets and hemp. Other crops were wheat, corn and alfalfa. The farmers also kept horses, cattle, pigs, chickens and geese. The home gardens included grapes for eating and for wine production, vegetables, and fruits such as peaches, apricots, melons and tomatoes.

Schools were built in close proximity to the church in each village. Teaching was done in German. Whether or not the people were pious, the social customs of the village centered around church activities. Sunday dress for the women consisted of the *Tracht*, or village costume, which included a distinctive dress plus decorative shawls, scarves and aprons. Each village had its own type of dress and hair style. Baptisms and weddings were festive events for family and neighbors, and included a street procession and special dinner. The major feast of the year was *Kirchweih*, the church consecration day, and was held in autumn.

In the larger cities, where people were craftsmen and shopkeepers, a German middle class and cultural life developed. Here, schools in German areas of the cities also had instruction in German. There were also German language newspapers and magazines. Concerts, plays and balls were held, and Temesvar was known for its fine German theater events and other cultural activities.

Eventually, the ethnic German settlers came to be called Danube-Swabians. Danube – because most had come down to Hungary via the Danube River, and Swabian because Ulm, Swabia was a common point of departure for the original settlers.

Adapted from the "History of German Settlements in Southern Hungary" by Susan Clarkson, with permission of the author.

Additional Sources:

Kann, Robert A. A History of the Habsburg Empire, 1526-1918. Berkeley: University of California Press, 1974, p. 607.

Senz, Ingomar. Donauschwäbische Geschichte: Wirtschaftliche Autarkie und politische Entfremdung 1806-1918. München: Universitas Verlag, 1997, p. 328-329

Senz, Josef Volkmar. Geschichte der Donauschwaben: Von den Anfängen bis zur Gegenwart. München: Donauschwäbische Kulturstiftung, 1987, p. 58, 59.

Appendix

The Habsburgs and Hungarians had a contentious relationship from the beginning. The following is a summary of the history behind the rebellions of John Zapolya, Imre Tököly and Ferenc Rakoczy.

The Ottoman Turks invade Hungary, 1526
Zapolya battles the Habsburgs over the Hungarian Throne

The Habsburgs had claimed Kingship of Hungary in 1526, when Hungarian King Louis II died in battle during the Turkish invasion of Hungary. Louis left no heirs and there were two claimants to the throne: Austrian Archduke Ferdinand I of the Habsburgs and John Zapolya (Szapolyai), prince of Transylvania.

Ferdinand claimed a hereditary right to the throne, since he was married to Louis' sister, Anna. The Habsburgs and Louis' father (King Ulászló) had arranged the marriage in 1506, before Louis was even born, in order to assure that the Habsburgs would inherit the Hungarian Kingship. The Habsburgs had a habit of using marriages to gain power; they also had a vested interest in Hungary, as it was the only country between Austria and Ottoman Turkey.

Zapolya claimed the right to the throne because of a 1505 declaration requiring the election of a 'national (not foreign) king'. The Hungarian estates had wanted to assure that their next king was Hungarian, and actually had Zapolya in mind when creating the 1505 resolution requiring a national king.

After Louis' death, both claimants were legitimatized by different factions. In November 1526, diets in Tokay and Székesfehérvár elected Zapolya as king. In December 1526, a diet in Pressburg (Bratislava) elected Ferdinand as king.

This led to a civil war being fought during the war with the Ottomans. Habsburg forces fought Zapolya's forces. As Ferdinand's forces drove most of Zapolya's men out of central Hungary, many Hungarians who previously supported Zapolya resigned themselves to side with Ferdinand. Eventually, Ferdinand was elected the sole monarch of the part of Hungary that was not occupied by the Turks. Zapolya allied himself with the Ottomans and ruled Transylvania as a vassal of the Turks.

So in the 16th and 17th centuries, Hungary was divided into three sections: Royal Hungary, Ottoman-occupied Hungary, and Transylvania. The Habsburgs ruled Royal Hungary in the north and west; the Turks occupied

Appendix

middle Hungary, and Transylvania in the East was ruled by a Hungarian prince who was a vassal of the Turks, although Transylvania maintained its independence in domestic affairs. The borders of these regions changed as the Ottomans tried to take over more of Hungary, but this division of Hungary into three sections remained virtually unchanged for some hundred and fifty years.

The time under the Turks was absolutely disastrous for Hungary. Turkish armies demolished entire villages and ravaged anything that stood in their way, not only in the major wars but also during constant skirmishes in times of relative peace. The population of almost exclusively Magyar-inhabited regions – the Great Plains and hilly country of Transdanubia – was pretty much wiped out already in the mid-sixteenth century. By the mid-seventeenth century the damage extended over 90 percent of the plains and two thirds of the arable lands in the Turkish occupied areas.[1]

Towards the end of the seventeenth century, some one hundred and fifty years after the Turks invaded Hungary, the second major clash between Hungarians and the Habsburgs occurred. This kuruc rebellion occurred during the reign of Leopold I, who was both Holy Roman Emperor and King of Royal Hungary beginning in 1655.

---

1 Lendvai, The Hungarians, p. 101

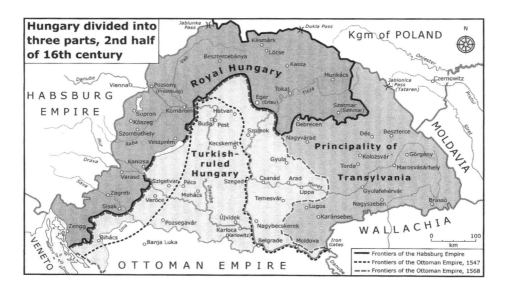

Tököly's Kuruc Rebellion, 1678-1683

From 1678 to 1683, the kurucs fought against Leopold I, under the leadership of Hungarian Count Imre Tököly (Thököly). They rebelled against Leopold because he restricted their freedoms. During the 1670s his empire persecuted Protestants in the small section of Hungary that he ruled. Leopold suspended the nation's constitution in 1673. As Leopold's government demanded more and more taxes and required other sacrifices from the Hungarian people, Tököly's army (also known as the kurucs) began to fight against the Imperial army. Leopold finally restored the constitution and the ancient rights of the Kingdom of Hungary, and included freedom of religion for Protestants, at a Diet in Sopron in 1681. But Tököly refused to recognize the decrees of this Diet, which had been agreed upon by the Hungarian estates.

Tököly wanted to continue fighting. He joined with the Turks. In 1682 and 1683, when Tököly's troops flooded Habsburg Hungary, most of the Catholic nobility decided to side with the kurucs. However, the Catholic Hungarian nobility reverted back to the Habsburgs after the Habsburgs began to defeat the Turks.

Tököly and Turkish Pasha Kara Mustapha laid siege on Vienna in 1683, but the Habsburg troops defeated them in a crushing blow. Tököly's fortresses were captured and his kuruc rebellion was squelched.

The Siege of Vienna served as a wake up call to Leopold. He wanted to assure that the Turks did not attack Vienna again, and decided to drive them out of Hungary once and for all.

Habsburg and Hungarian relations between the rebellions, 1683-1703

In 1686, the Habsburg army took over Buda and kept going farther into Hungary to fight the Ottoman Turks.

In 1687, at the Diet of Pressburg (Bratislava), Leopold sought accommodation with the Hungarian estates, while trying to further establish his absolutist monarchy. Leopold agreed to respect protestant rights and uphold the Hungarian constitution which he had previously suspended, and granted amnesty to the rebels. The Hungarian leadership, noting that the Habsburgs were fighting the Turks to free Hungary from the Ottoman empire, agreed to modify the constitution, and voted to abolish royal elections, instead recognizing the Habsburgs' hereditary right to the throne. They also sacrificed the right to resist the King, which had been granted to them in the Golden Bull of 1222.

As Leopold conquered more and more of Hungary from the Turks, he began to institute a plan to keep the Turks out and deal with the problems in Hungary. Turk and Tatar incursions had caused much damage and reduced the country to extreme poverty. In 1689, Leopold set up a commission to re-settle the depopulated areas of Hungary. The commission, chaired by Cardinal Kollonich, encouraged Germans to settle in the regions freed from the Turks. An additional goal of the resettlement was to bring in subjects who were loyal to the Kaiser. In 1690, Leopold also commanded that 200,000 Serbs fleeing a Turkish counter-offensive had to be taken in by Hungary.[2] Leopold supported the Serbs partly because he knew they would be motivated to fight against the Turks.

Kollonich's commission required the holders of estates in the recovered areas to produce legal documents of ownership. To keep ownership, they then had to pay a tax for the damages of war. The time allotted to prove ownership was short (6 months), and the tax was high. The nobility did not take kindly to this, as they had always had the privilege of being exempt from taxes. (Taxes were for peasants!) The way the Hungarians saw it, Cardinal Kollonich favored the pro-Habsburg nobility and used the proof of ownership requirement to discriminate against the less loyal nobility.

Another change was that the army was no longer to live off of the population. This was significant because during the war to free Hungary from the Turks, the officers and impoverished soldiers of the Kaiser's army had extorted ransom and plunder from the population, as was commonplace for armies in 17th century Europe, and had caused much suffering for the Hungarian people.

In 1690, Leopold recognized the traditional constitution of Transylvania; and in December 1691, he issued a constitution that guaranteed religious and national rights of the traditional groups in the Diet.

By 1699, at the Peace of Karlowitz, most of the Kingdom of Hungary including Transylvania had been won, but the Banat was not to be captured for another twenty years.

Leopold's re-population plan was helping the area to recover from the devastation caused by over one hundred and fifty years of Turkish rule. Yet, some Hungarians still found Leopold's policies to be oppressive. The peasants found the heavy taxes exacted to pay for the war to be especially burden-

---

2 Lendvai, The Hungarians, p. 99

some. In addition, many Germans and Serbs who settled were granted civil and ecclesiastical autonomy, at a time when this was denied to Hungarian Protestants.

Rakoczy's Rebellion, 1703-1711

Ferenc Rakoczy II (Rákóczi) was the grandson of George II, Prince of Transylvania, and Tököly's stepson. At first, he was not interested when the kurucs asked him to lead a rebellion. However, he changed his mind when he observed the economic, constitutional and religious restrictions imposed by the Habsburgs, and noted that only a small number of Hungarian noblemen were allowed to hold government office. Rakoczy led the peasants in a war for independence (a second kuruc rebellion), promising any who joined his army that they would be exempt from taxes and obligations to their overlords. The nobility soon joined the rebellion as well. In 1704, Rakoczy was elected prince of Transylvania. He governed his kuruc state with a senate consisting of the nobility and the clergy. Ironically, Rakoczy needed to impose higher taxes than the Habsburgs had, in order to pay for his army, and economic conditions worsened under him. He also had problems with the peasants and nobility resenting each other. The peasants objected that the nobility had joined the rebellion after them and yet were given all the government positions; the nobility was not happy at the prospect of emancipation of their serfs, which was the reason the peasants began to fight for Rakoczy to begin with.

At the Diet of Onod (1707) the Hungarian nobles deposed the Habsburg dynasty in Hungary and set up an aristocratic republic. By 1708, most of Hungary was under Rakoczy's control.

The kurucs were very violent, especially toward the later stages of the war. They often tortured and killed innocent civilians, including women and children. Throughout the war against the Habsburgs, the kurucs resorted to intimidation, threatening the population with death or expulsion if they did not join the kuruc side. At the Diet of Ónod two of Rakoczy's men drew their swords and, in cold blood and in full view of the assembly, murdered a nobleman who was speaking out against some of Rakoczy's practices.[3]

Eventually, the Habsburgs won the conflict against the kurucs. Peace was finally negotiated between the Hungarian Estates and the Habsburgs dur-

---

3 Frey, Societies in Upheaval: Insurrections in France, Hungary, and Spain in the Early Eighteenth Century, p.2

ing the reign of Charles VI, (Leopold's son and also Kaiser Karl VI in this novel), at the Peace of Szatmar in 1711. This Peace reverted the division of power between the Habsburgs and the Hungarian estates to the constitution before 1670. Charles granted amnesty to the kurucs and restored religious and constitutional freedoms. He recognized the political, social and economic privileges of the Estates, including the right not to be arrested without valid legal title, to be subject only to him, and total exemption from taxes. The Hungarian peasants were not helped by this peace because the nobility was given unlimited power over the serfs. The Estates approved the treaty and voted to crown Holy Roman Emperor Charles VI as King Charles III of Hungary. Rakoczy refused to accept the treaty and fled the country.

This ended the kuruc rebellions.

Sources:

Findling, John E. and Thackeray, Frank (editors) Events That Changed America in the Seventeenth Century, Greenwood Press, 1998.

Frey, Linda and Frey, Marsha. Societies in Upheaval: Insurrections in France, Hungary, and Spain in the Early Eighteenth Century, Greenwood Press, 1987.

Kann, Robert A. A History of the Habsburg Empire, 1526-1918. Berkeley: University of California Press, 1974.

Kontler, László. A History of Hungary: Millennium in Central Europe. New York: Palgrave Macmillan, 2002.

Lendvai, Paul. The Hungarians: A Thousand Years of Victory in Defeat. Princeton University Press, 2003.

Tapié, Victor L. The Rise and Fall of the Habsburg Monarchy. New York: Praeger, 1971.

Wheatcroft, Andrew. The Enemy at the Gate: Habsburgs, Ottomans and the Battle for Europe. New York: Basic Books, 2009.

Glossary and Pronunciation Guide

Read the pronunciations as if they are English words, except for these special rules:

a - like a in ha
ah - like ah in ah-ha!
ç - like ch in the scottish word loch or the h in huge.
ou - like ow in now

Base or Bas'	Bah-zĕ, Bahs	aunt or cousin; could also be used to refer to any older woman
Bastonade	Bah-stŭn-ah-dĕ	a whipping across the soles of the feet, a punishment used by the Turks
Bauernstube	Bou-ern-shtoo-bĕ	farmer's room—room at the *Wirtshaus* where farmers congregated to eat and drink
Betyaren	Bet-yar-en	1. outlaws or highwaymen 2. scoundrels, rogues, rascals
Chibuk		Turkish pipe
Cuman		a Turkic people who occupied parts of southern Russia and the Moldavian and Wallachian steppes during the 9th, 10th and 11th centuries and were driven out by the Tatar and Mongol invasions, some of whom passed into Hungary where they were absorbed
Danube Swabian		called Swabians in this novel
Diet		see Imperial Diet or Hungarian Diet
Dorfrichter	Dorf-reeçt-er	the mayor and municipal judge of a town
Erdhütte	Aird-hitt-ĕ	a house that was mostly underground with very short stamped earth walls protruding, and a roof atop. South Slavic peoples lived in these types of houses during the Ottoman occupation. The houses were inexpensive and adapted to their lifestyle, which was often nomadic since they mostly raised animals (instead of growing crops) in uncertain times.
Fasching	Fah-shing	Carnival, a festive season which occurs immediately before Lent.
Frau	Frou	woman; if used before a name, means Mrs.
Frondienste	Frone-deenst-ĕ	mandated work that the common people had to do for their overlord, either working on his land or his house or working to keep up the infrastructure, for example repairing or building roads. A certain number of days of *Frondienste*, also called *Robotarbeiten*, was required every year.

Glossary and Pronunciation Guide

Fronleichnam	Frone-<u>liec</u>-nahm	The feast of Corpus Christi, the Solemnity of the most Holy Body and Blood of Jesus Christ.
Fünfkirchen	<u>Finf</u>-keerç-en	The German name for Pécs, a city in Hungary west of the Danube River.
Generalissimo		A military rank of the highest degree, superior to a Field Marshall or Grand Admiral. Prince Eugene was a Generalissimo.
Fürst	Feerst	can be used in a general sense to refer to any ruling monarch
Hàjduk	<u>Hie</u>-duke	a mercenary foot soldier in Hungary
Herr	Hare	sir or can be used before a title to denote respect, e.g. *Herr Stadtrichter*. If used before a last name, e.g. Herr Trauttmann, means Mister Trauttmann.
Hofkammer	<u>Hohf</u>-kam-er	Imperial Council
Hofkammerat	<u>Hohf</u>-kam-er-aht	Imperial Councillor
Hofkanzlei	<u>Hohf</u>-khants-lye	Council Office or Chancellery
Hungarian Diet		assembly of the Hungarian Estates
Imperial Diet		assembly of the various principalities of the Holy Roman Empire of the German Nation
Kaiser	<u>Kye</u>-ser	Emperor. In this book, the Holy Roman Emperor of the German Nation.
Kantor	<u>Khan</u>-tor	church organist and choir master
Konstabler	Cūn-<u>stah</u>-bler	artillery officer
Kurfürst	<u>Kūr</u>-feerst	English: Prince Elector. Ruling monarchs who had the power to elect the Kaiser.
Kurucs		Hungarians who fought with the Turks against the Habsburgs
Magyar		means Hungarian
Ofen	Oh-fen	The German name for the city of Buda, which later was combined with Pest to become Budapest.
Ordinari-schiff	Or-din-<u>ahr</u>-y shiff	name of the type of ship that took passengers from Ulm to Vienna on a weekly basis
Pasha		a titled official in the Ottoman empire
Pfalz	Pfalts	the Palatinate. A region on the western border of the Holy Roman Empire of the German Nation. Also called the *Rheinpfalz* (Rhenish Palatinate). Not the same as the present-day German State Rheinland-Pfalz (Rhineland-Palatinate).
Puszta	<u>Poos</u>-ta	(Hungarian) a treeless plain in Hungary
Rheinpfalz	<u>Rhine</u>-pfahlts	Rhenish Palatinate (see *Pfalz*)
Robotte	Row-<u>boat</u>-ĕ	another word for *Frondienste*

Saint Stephen		(975–1038) the first king of Hungary, who Christianized the majority of Hungarians and is the spiritual patron of Hungary.
Stadtkommandant	Shtat-kum-an-dahnt	military ruler; city commander
Stadtrichter	Shtat-reeç-tr	the mayor and municipal judge of a city
Schwäbische Türkei	Shvay-bish-ĕ Trk-eye	English: Swabian Turkey. An area mostly in southern Hungary and also in Croatia, bounded by the Danube and Drava Rivers and the Plattensee.
Swabian		Any German who settled Hungary is referred to as Swabian, whether he came from Swabia, (which is in southern Germany) or a different region.
Tatar (Tartar)		A member of any of the Mongolian peoples of central Asia who invaded eastern Europe in the 13th century.
Trachten	Traç-ten	the clothing people wore. Every area in Germany had a different local costume which had developed over the years, and so the Trachten they wore could identify from which area they came.
Ulmer Schachtel	Ool-mer Shahç-tel	wooden boat that was typically taken on the Danube from Ulm to Vienna and then to Hungary
Vetter	Fett-r	can be used to refer to an older man. Also means uncle or cousin.
Wallachia		a region in present-day Romania; most Swabians referred to all Romanians as Wallachians
Wirtshaus	Veerts-house	an inn where food and drink are available
Vivat	Vi-vaht	(Latin) Long live!

About the Author

Adam Müller-Guttenbrunn was born Adam Müller, on October 22, 1852 in Guttenbrunn, which was in the Banat region of the Austrian empire (today Zăbrani, Romania). He was born amidst a community of Banat Swabians, a son of peasants. He went to school in Temesvar, but dropped out and tried his hand as a barber's apprentice. In 1870, he moved to Vienna, and went to business school. After working in Linz as a telegrapher while he furthered his studies and writing, Müller-Guttenbrunn came back to Vienna in 1879. There, he became a theater critic and theater director.

It is for his work as a writer of Danube-Swabian *Heimatbücher* that Müller-Guttenbrunn is best known. In the last fifteen years of his life, Müller-Guttenbrunn turned to fiction writing as a result of a trip back to the Banat in 1907. It is because of these novels, which promoted the culture of Danube-Swabians at a time when they were being encouraged to assimilate to Hungarian culture, that he is referred to as *der Erzschwabe* (arch-Swabian or true Swabian). His works celebrated the Danube-Swabians from the Banat, his native land, and its German cultural world. He exalts Banat village beauty, customs and traditions.

Die Glocken der Heimat, his 1911 novel about settlement in the German community of Rudolfsgnad, was awarded the *Bauernfeld-Preis*. His most famous literary work was *Der Grosse Schwabenzug* (The Great Swabian Migration), published in 1913. It was followed by *Barmherziger Kaiser* (1916) and *Joseph der Deutsche* (1918), to form a trilogy of novels, each of which covered one of the three waves of colonization by Danube-Swabians. Müller-Guttenbrunn was a prolific writer and created many other literary works about his homeland before his death in Vienna in 1923.